PERCEPTIONS *of* MORALITY

PERCEPTIONS *of* MORALITY

JOHN K. ONDA

iUniverse, Inc.
New York Bloomington

PERCEPTIONS OF MORALITY

iUniverse books may be ordered through booksellers or by contacting:
iUniverse
1663 Liberty Drive
Bloomington, IN 47403
www.iuniverse.com
1-800-Authors (1-800-288-4677)

ISBN: 978-1-4502-4240-0 (pbk)
ISBN: 978-1-4502-4238-7 (ebk)
ISBN: 978-1-4502-4239-4 (hbk)

Library of Congress Control Number: 2010912782

Printed in the United States of America

iUniverse rev. date: 8/14/10

For Mary:

In loving memory of Mary I. Onda (1929-2008)

My beloved Mother.

A beautiful, wonderful lady.

A hard-working woman.

A woman with a heart of gold.

I was blessed to arrive into this world and have Mary as my mother for 52 years. I treasure all the many fond memories that will always remain with me. She always stood by me, as I did her.

I will never forget her face, the sound of her voice, the gentleness of her touch. For whenever I was with her, I always knew I was loved.

I will never stray from the values she taught me, the uncompromising morals she always emphasized to me. They are her gift and my legacy. A legacy I will forever be proud of.

I do all I can to honor and cherish her memory. She remains my inspiration. She will always be the light of my life.

I will miss her until my dying day.

Mary, 1950

Also to acknowledge those individuals, living or deceased, who were forced to suffer from any type of pain, physical or emotional distress, along with the many other circumstances that catapulted their lives into total disarray–all due to some form of inadequate, inappropriate, or possibly even malicious medical care. They were victims. Truly undeserving victims.

The error may have been the result of a surgical miscue, an incorrect diagnosis, or just a simple case of poor judgment on the part of the doctor at some point of their patient's treatment. And even if this physician's mistake caused death to befall, while it would most certainly be a tragedy, it could not be classified as a crime by our legal standards. Society willingly accepts even our most intelligent, most gifted professionals are susceptible to a rare mistake. Doctors, alike all of us, are not infallible.

However, it is an appalling crime against humanity whenever a doctor of medicine arrives at the conclusion that their patient has incurred some type of difficulty while undergoing treatment, then proceeds to do little or nothing to help right their health. While this kind of situation certainly isn't typical, *it can and does occur.* In most cases, it is brought about due to the fact that the doctor was fearful of any potential damage the oversight may inflict upon their unsullied reputations, along with the ramifications that could eventually follow if the patient were to learn the entire truth of the matter, and then chose to pursue civil litigation against them.

For all the innocent souls who endured such dire events and weren't able to obtain any form of justice. Be it monetary compensation for what may have been a lifetime of overwhelming anguish, proper medical treatment in an attempt to reverse the oversight, or even a simple apology from their doctor who rendered such a monumental disservice upon them–a disservice that very well may have either physically or mentally overwhelmed their lives forever.

The famous statue of Lady Justice seen at courthouses throughout this great country of ours is undoubtedly synonymous to those individuals whose lives were shattered due to their receiving substandard medical care, consequentially resulting in their filing a claim of medical malpractice. For the blindfold Lady Justice wears may be interpreted by the general populous as a form of arcane symbolism. However, for the large majority that has sought civil retribution against the medical community, her blindfold is viewed in an entirely different light. To them, it represents an alarming travesty of our society. It stands for a complete lack of morality, coupled with justice that went unserved.

Prologue

"Damn, I hate these places," Vernon Park Chief of Police William Gill thought to himself, while pulling his Hyundai Sonata in front of Cicero's Funeral Home. The engine off, he tilted the windshield mirror to observe his necktie. Content with his appearance, he opened the door and stepped onto Broad Avenue. As he walked around his Sonata, Gill scanned the street, recognizing only three other cars parked nearby. While beginning to climb the awning-covered stairway that led to the entrance of the funeral home, he saw Gene Polachek standing at the top of the stairs.

"I was getting worried about you, Butch," Gene said.

"We just got home a little while ago," he said. "And I sure wasn't about to come here in full uniform."

Gene waited until Butch drew near. "Should I ask how it went?"

"Okay, I hope," replied Butch, though in reserved tone of voice. "The Allegheny County DA put me through the ringer while all those other bigshots kept staring me down, but Frank Dague kept vouching for me. On the ride home, Frank kept telling me that I had done my job." Butch let out a sigh of concern. "I don't know. We'll just have to see what happens."

"Frank Dague. He's our county's DA?"

"Yeah. Nice guy."

Together they stood under the black awning facing the street. "John leave already?" Butch asked of him.

"No. He's still inside."

"Where's his car?"

"He didn't bring it," said Gene. "Me, him and Mary were here for the afternoon viewing. John came with Mary, and I followed in my car. When we left, Mary went home and I drove John to the bar for what was supposed to be a few drinks and a sandwich."

Gene rubbed the side of his head as if it ached. "Damn, when we got outta Mike's, we were both ripped. John was pounding Grey Goose like water, and he wants to go back when we leave."

"I've never seen John drink vodka before."

"Tell me about it," said Gene. "That's why he had his mom bring her car. John was planning on drinking today."

"How's he now?"

"Sober as a judge. He switched to Mountain Dew and had a hamburger before we came back up here." Polachek looked down to the stairs, then said, "Butch, he's really taking this hard."

"Yeah, they were pretty close. A lot closer than we were to him. Just make sure you take it easy going home." Chief Gill paused while removing a piece of lint from the arm of Gene's sports coat. "I'd hate getting a call from the nightshift that they're holding a well-dressed little guy named Polachek for DUI."

Gene eyed his friend who towered some eleven inches over him. "You makin' fun of my jacket, ya big prick?"

"Not at all," said Butch, casting a wry smile. "Gene, you look sharp. It's just been a long time since I've seen you in a sport coat. Last time I remember was high school graduation."

"Probably was, not unless you count that monkey-suit I wore at your wedding," said Gene, grinning in return. "But you know John and his fancy suits. I wasn't about to sit next to him lookin' like some bum."

Butch nodded in understanding. "How was the afternoon turnout? Looking at the street, there can't be many people inside now."

"Just the family and John are in there, although it was crowded this afternoon," said Gene. "A lot of his old gang showed. His mother's and son's friends. And all our guys came."

"Good."

With the evening darkness falling, Butch held his wristwatch close to his face and said, "Well, I'd better get in there. Gene, don't worry about John. I'll take him home."

"Nah, I promised I'd go back to the bar with him."

"No more drinking tonight, Gene," said Butch, the change in his tone discernable. "I have to talk with John, and you know about what. Gene, do me a favor. Go home. I'll drive John."

"Why didn't you just say so in the first place," he grumbled, feeling for his keys. "Tell John I'll see him in the morning."

Soon inside the funeral home, Gill signed the guestbook then moved into the viewing room. All of the empty wooden folding chairs only heightened the forlorn the room cast. Somberly he stepped towards the casket and knelt in prayer. After making the Sign of the Cross, Butch arose to his feet. He turned to the dead man's family members seated alongside John Valone. His condolences offered to the family, Butch took the chair next to John.

"I thought I'd be here earlier, but the meeting kept dragging," Butch whispered.

"I know, Amy sent me a text." Valone turned slightly, gesturing towards the rear entranceway. "Go in the back. I'll tell the family we don't want to disturb them."

Shortly thereafter, they were situated in a smaller room on the opposite end of the funeral parlor, seated in comfortable Victorian chairs angled toward each other so the armrests touched, both positioned to have an unobstructed view of the door. They had been best friends since grade school some twenty years ago, yet both felt the tension of the moment. For these two men in the prime of life realized the horrible secrets they shared–both understanding how the consequences would forever ruin their lives if ever uncovered. The small-talk about Gene, their afternoon spent at the bar, and their being permitted to use the room completed, it was John who broke a momentary silence. "So we've both had long days, huh?"

"Too long," said Butch. "Bernie Ferguson, the District Attorney of Allegheny County and some of his top assistants were there the whole time with me and Frank Dague. A few state police, and a bunch of detectives and criminologists were in-and-out all day. I never thought the meeting would end."

On John's right side hung a set of black drapes that were drawn shut to cover the sheer white curtains underneath. He pushed the end-panel to view Broad Avenue. "No cop cars out there," he said, allowing the drapes to fall back into place. "That's a good sign."

"For now," replied the cautious Butch Gill, clearly on edge. "I stuck to the story we agreed on. I think—I hope they believed me."

"Ah, I'm sure they did," said John. Playfully he slapped Butch's knee. "You got an honest face. Besides, they have any reason not to believe you?"

"None that I know of. Ferguson must have asked me ten times about that night, and if I was absolutely positive that I was with you and your mom at the exact time it happened. From what Dague told me, they don't have any witnesses or any other kind of proof that even suggests I was lying."

"Sounds like more good news to me."

"Most of the news is good, but there is some bad," said Butch. "John, we've got lots to talk about. Although to be honest, I'd rather wait for another time."

"Stop worrying about the room. Mr. Cicero told me and the family we could use it anytime we wanted."

"I'm not worried about the room."

"Then what's your problem?"

Butch leaned closer, his face a study of determination. "Okay, the truth is we got way too much serious shit to talk about. I'm afraid you'll want to get drunk later, then you'll mess-up and shoot your mouth off." He gave Valone a penetrating glare. "Get my point?"

"Relax, you big troll," as John always called him. "I'm only drinking pop. The mass starts at nine in the morning, and I don't plan on being in church with a hangover."

"You promise me you'll keep quiet about what I tell you?"

“My word of honor,” said John with a smile, holding up his right hand.

William Gill nudged his chair closer, yet his facial expression remained hesitant. “Alright, John, you know I trust you. But this ain’t kid stuff. This is serious. And you’d better understand I sure as hell don’t want to do a twenty-to-life stretch in jail because of you.”

CHAPTER ONE

Vernon Park, Pennsylvania, a small, yet somewhat affluent town located some fifteen miles southeast of Pittsburgh, was one of the few locales in the rustbelt of Western Pennsylvania that survived the decline of the steel mills that had begun circa 1980. All of the surrounding towns that were booming during the heyday of the mills now lay steep in decay, desperately in need of being bulldozed into the Monongahela River. Unemployment was off the charts, houses were in shambles, most of the communities' youth long having gone elsewhere seeking opportunities. What remained of their aging population now going through the motions of living out their lives.

This was not the culture of Vernon Park. During the steel-mill era, the town was a hamlet with few businesses and small frame homes built about Broad Avenue. But nearly all of the land that was located to the north and west of town was farmland owned by three families, all whom remained intent on keeping it that way. The elder people who still called Vernon Park home would always tell those asking why the farmers were so insistent on holding onto their property were twofold: they preferred working their own land as opposed to laboring for an industry they had the foresight to realize was bound to fall by the wayside. Yet of greater significance, they had observed the suburbs of Pittsburgh beginning to sprawl towards them.

By the mid-1980's, the old-timer's were gone, and their heirs began selling parcels of land for new housing developments. Vernon Park soon became an upper-middle class community. Professional men and women flocked to the area during Pittsburgh's renaissance period. Certainly there were many pricey neighborhoods closer to Pittsburgh such as Mt. Lebanon or Upper St. Clair, though they mostly offered stately, yet older houses with outrageous prices. Those who decided to relocate to the rolling hills of Vernon Park gave them the opportunity to have their own house built at a sensible cost. Another reason that led to people deciding Vernon Park would be an opportune place to live was that only a few years prior, Route 55 had been widened to six lanes, making it a much easier drive into Pittsburgh, as opposed to the traffic that congested the parkways circling the city, the never-ending construction of the bridges leading into downtown Pittsburgh, the meandering roads and side-streets–all they had grown accustomed to coping with on their daily commute.

Naturally those from the immediate area looking for a fresh start while being able to stay close to their roots also sought residence in Vernon Park. Two industrial parks, shopping malls, and numerous small businesses sprung-up seemingly overnight. Shopkeepers who were hanging on by the skin of their teeth in the surrounding areas also flocked to town. To them, it was a chance to earn a respectable living while remaining close to home–something that was unrealistic less than a half-generation ago.

*****

Michael Perella was born in Vernon Park, his father had been employed in the steel industry until his passing. His older brother Dennis was married, and Mike lived with his mother Elaine. Upon graduating from Vernon Park High School in 1996, Mike went to work toiling at several menial jobs, saving every dollar he could. His ultimate goal was to open a bar and restaurant. The kind of establishment where not only could the townspeople frequent and be welcomed, but where his boyhood friends were certain to be his best customers, and would be given the run of the place.

It took six years before Mike could afford to put a sizable down-payment on the building; almost another year of remodeling the bar and his upstairs apartment; furnishing the bar exactly to his and his friends' liking; listening to their suggestions; following through every detail. His dream finally materialized when in the summer of 2003, he'd opened Mike's Pub.

It was December, 2007, the Friday before Christmas weekend, and Mike's Pub was jumping. Even with two bartenders, they struggled to keep up. There weren't any seats to be had at the large rectangular bar while others stood behind those seated, talking with drinks in hand. Between the bar and the elevated booths that were filled to capacity were trays of food Mike had put out for his customers.

Situated along both sides of the far corner of the bar, the section all the regular customers knew was reserved for them, sat four of Mike's closest friends. Gary Rowland, handsome with wavy-blonde hair, trim, angular of build. Next was Dave Bodette, his body-type similar to Gary's, but with a full-beard and his jet-black hair pulled into a ponytail. Around the bend from Bodette sat Gene Polachek, his baby-face made him appear slightly younger than the others, his shaggy-brown hair badly in need of a comb. Despite being smaller and stockier than his friends, Gene was a sturdy young man, having toiled in a coal mine since high school. On Gene's left sat Bob Cook, tall, ruggedly handsome, dark brown hair, noted for his baritone voice. He looked more like a linebacker than an attorney. While they enjoyed each other's company, they all awaited another friend who'd promised he would be there.

"It's almost five," said Dave. "He ain't gonna show."

"John told me he'd be here," insisted Gene.

"How about Butch?" asked Bob Cook.

"He was on dayshift today," said Gene.

David Bodette shrugged his shoulders as he gulped what remained of his beer. As he pushed a chip that signified he had a drink coming next to his glass, he called to the bartender Dale Lambert, "When you get time, kid."

Bodette looked to Gene. "Let me ask you something. You've lived next door to him since we were kids. With all the money John's got, whys he's work? Hell, if I had half of what he must have, I'd give my share of our construction company to Rol. I'd be drinking on some beach somewhere in the South Pacific where the women don't wear nothin'."

"Bo, you should go to Samoa," said Gary, tugging at Dave's ponytail. "You'd fit right in with them wild-looking natives. They probably put a bone through your nose and make you their chief."

"Probably make him stew," Gene laughed.

"Nah, too skinny for stew," Rol chuckled. "They'd barbeque him on a spit with an apple in his mouth."

"Ah, bite this apple," Dave remarked, gesturing below his belt-buckle. "Seriously, why younse guys think he still works?"

"John likes the kind of work he does," said Bob.

"Yeah, but after what happened to his dad, you'd think he wouldn't want to be traveling all the time," Dave said.

"He seldom goes beyond metropolitan Pittsburgh anymore," Gene said. "Sure when he worked for that company in Pittsburgh he had to fly all over the country. But ever since John started his own consulting business, he stays within driving distance of home."

Their conversation soon shifted to The Pittsburgh Steelers, who were in the midst of a season that had everyone talking Super Bowl. Gene was in the middle of insisting the Steelers' defense was the reason why the team was winning, when Gary Rowland stood and pointed towards the door. He called out, "There he is!"

They all watched, each man with their own sense of friendship, along with perhaps just a slight touch of envy, as John Valone slowly made his way towards them, while being stopped by many of the patrons who sat along the bar leading to their corner. He had a captivating magnetism about him that caused people to gravitate into the circle of his charm. His devilish good looks and boyish appeal; the polite and soft-spoken demeanor he accorded everyone; even the way he carried himself. Valone had the world on a string–although he never flaunted it.

"Gentlemen," he greeted them, first shaking Bob's outstretched hand. He then good-naturedly nudged Gene while moving behind

Dave and Gary, wrapping his arms around them. "You guys getting our little buddy drunk?"

"Ah, Gene's okay," said Rol.

"How come you didn't go home and change?" Dave asked of him, as he brushed the sleeve of John's cashmere topcoat.

"I can't stay too long," he said, stepping into the space created by Dave and Gene. "I promised Mary I'd be home for dinner. But tomorrow, I'll be here when they open."

Bodette continued smoothing John's topcoat. "How much this thing cost?"

"I don't know, it was a present from my mother," said John, as he waved to the bartender who was on his way. "Dale, how's it going?"

"Good, John," he said. "Even though I don't have time to take a leak."

Dale motioned across the bar to a cute brunette. "Allison's okay in the kitchen, but she's too slow out here. All she's doing is bullshitin' and showing off her new sweater."

"And her tits," said Gene, breaking into a wide grin.

Their laughter from Gene's wisecrack still going on, John asked, "Where's Mike?"

"Upstairs taking a nap," said Dale. "He and his mom were here early this morning getting the food ready, and he's working to close tonight."

"Make you a deal," said John. "Get me a Miller Lite and give the bar a drink, and I'll go drag his lazy butt down here."

"You got it," Dale said.

John shed his topcoat and placed it around the backrest of Gene's chair. "Make sure Bo doesn't grab this while I'm gone."

With Bodette in a playful headlock, John saw Dale approach. He reached for his wallet. "What's the damage, kid?"

"Seventy-eight and a quarter," said Dale.

A hundred was tossed onto the bar. "Keep it, pal."

"Thanks, John."

Valone smiled at him. From the day he'd met Dale, John liked the young man. He was always courteous–a trait many of his age-group lacked. "Gimme a couple minutes," he said, lifting his beer. "You guys hold down the fort until I get back."

After knocking twice, John opened the door of Michael Perella's apartment to see him lounging on his recliner. "Wake up, you loafer."

"I'm up," said Mike with a yawn. "What time's it?"

"A little past five. C'mon, get up. It's packed down there, and Dale needs help."

John sat on the sofa, sipping his beer as Mike changed his shirt. As he checked his cell phone for messages, he heard Mike say, "My brother downstairs?"

"I didn't see him, but the bar's jammed."

"Then he's not here yet," said Mike, while opening a stick of gum. "If he'd seen you, for sure he woulda come talk to you."

"How's Denny been? I haven't seen him lately."

"Not so hot," said Mike.

"What's up with Denny?"

"Well, for one thing his wife left him last month," he said, somewhat insensitive. "Just packed her stuff and took off one night when Denny was at work. Then about a week ago he found out that the auto plant where he works is closing at the end of the year."

John sighed heavily. "Oh, jeez, I didn't know."

"It'll probably be in the paper about—"

"How come you didn't tell me sooner?" he cut in. "At least I coulda called him."

"You know how he treats me."

"Get off it, Mike. So you're Denny's kid brother. Ain't no big deal."

"John, I was a change-of-life baby," he declared. "Denny treats me more like a kid than a brother. And you know how he gets when he's pissed. Mad at the world. Our mother's been trying call him for days to get him to come over the house for Christmas, but he hasn't called her back. So Elaine asked me to get hold of him. Yesterday he finally called. He said he'd be here either today or tomorrow."

"Okay, so talk with him when you see him."

Mike took a moment, then said, "To be honest, I really don't look forward to seeing him whenever he's pissed."

"He's still your brother, Mike," said John. "You gotta stand by him. Denny will be okay."

Michael chewed hard on his gum. "Hope you're right."

John lifted from his seat. "I won't say anything to the guys about Denny, but just in case I don't get a chance to talk with him here, tell him I'll be giving him a call."

"Yeah, sure."

As Mike bounded down the stairs, John pulled the apartment door shut. *"Pretty damn callous about his own brother,"* he thought, as he began the descent.

John arrived back in the corner to find his friends had been joined by William Gill, an officer with the Vernon Park Police Department. Though his sheer presence commanded respect, Butch was just one of the guys when he came into the bar. Out of uniform, he desired no preferential treatment from anyone.

"Butch, you big troll!" John greeted him, reaching for his hand. He leaned against the wall next to Butch. "They do it to you again this Christmas?"

"Three twelve-hour shifts starting noon tomorrow," he said. "Of course the chief won't work a shift, and the other two put in for off-time. It's me and Luzanski for the next three days."

"Awl, so you can sleep at the station," Dave said.

'Yeah, our tax dollars hard at work," Gene added. "Besides, what happens around here? Somebody runs a stop sign?"

"Just make damn sure you're not runnin' any stop signs this weekend," Butch said, though poking at Gene. "Or else I'll write your ass up."

"Butch, tell John about Chief Martin," said Bob Cook.

"What's with him?" said John.

"He's retiring next year," Butch said. "He already sent for the paperwork."

"Great," said John. "You'll move up in the ladder."

Butch smiled, showing his straight, white teeth. He reached for the bottles of Miller Lite Gene had slid towards them and said, "If things go like I'm hoping, maybe way up the ladder. They may make me chief."

"How they gonna make you chief with those other guys having more seniority than you?" John asked.

"The chief has to be available twenty-four-seven," said Butch. "The other two guys are getting up in age, and they already told Luzanski and me they don't want it. I've got eight more months on the job than Luzansk does, so it'd be my choice if the older guys say no when the time comes."

"So they're gonna make you the Chief of Police!" said John.

"Settle down, nothing's for sure yet," Gill replied. "We'll see what happens when Chief Martin does officially retire."

"Don't you guys just love it," Bob Cook's booming voice required their attention. "We may have two future chiefs with us at this very moment. Butch in Vernon Park, and Dave in Samoa."

"Ah, go chase a fuckin' ambulance," Dave fired in return.

"—the hell's he talkin' about?" said John. "Samoa?"

"Never mind," Butch grinned, pulling at John's shirt-sleeve, while their friends continued exchanging barbs. "You going home soon?"

"Last one," he said. "Dinner with Mary."

Butch nodded as he eyed an open booth. "I need to talk with you a sec."

"What?"

Again Butch tugged at his shirt. "C'mon, it won't take long."

With both men now seated across from each other in the booth, John looked down to see the guys at the bar pretending not to notice. They were a close-knit bunch, the kind that never kept secrets from each other. John turned to face Butch. "Okay, what's so important that you had to bring me up here?"

"Vicky's moving back to the area," he said in pensive voice. "She quit her job in Harrisburg. She's planning on selling real estate at an office just outside of town."

"Yeah, good for her."

"She's staying with me and Amy until her apartment's ready, and she wants to know if you'll meet with her this weekend."

"Why's she want to see me?" he asked in tone measured not to offend. "I haven't talked with your sister since that night in here."

"John, I'm sorry, but I'm just the messenger. Vicky wants me to ask you over to my house. Or if you'd prefer seeing her elsewhere, okay."

Valone looked to the ceiling, seemingly searching for the proper words. "Butch, there's no way I'd ever want you mad at me. Never. But I'm going to tell you like it is."

"Say whatever you want, John."

He drew a deep breath. "Alright, your sister can be a terrific girl, but she can turn into a real ballbuster in a heartbeat. Still, I was in love with her and I hoped we'd get married. Just before I was ready to give her an engagement ring, she began issuing ultimatums that I refused to accept. So I was a fucking bum. You heard her say it yourself that night."

"John, I understand," said Butch. "Hey, it's your business, not mine. But knowing my sister, she'll bust my balls until I find out what you want to do. Just please tell me what to say to her."

"Tell Vicky I'm still the exact same guy I was," he said. "Tell her I still have my same friends."

His emotions churning, John took a passing glance at the bar as he drained his Miller Lite. "Mary's going shopping tomorrow morning around ten, ten-thirty, so tell Vicky if she wants to see me, she can come to the house at eleven. That'll give me an hour with her before I come in here, although she'll end up telling me to go to hell way before then."

"Tomorrow at eleven at your house," said Butch. "Okay, I'll tell her."

"And make sure you tell her what I said about my being the exact same guy I was. Then tell her I'm definitely coming up here at noon to spend the afternoon with the guys. If she doesn't like it, tell her I said don't bother coming tomorrow."

Once they'd rejoined the group, John observed Gene sitting with his head propped-up, his eyes closed.

"Put your jacket on, Gene mean," said John, lifting his own coat from Polachek's seat. "Time to go home."

"Ah, I ain't drunk," he mumbled. "I finished-up midnight last night and I didn't get enough sleep."

"How many times have we heard that line before," said John, looking to his friends.

"He isn't too bad," Bob Cook said. "Don't worry, I'm leaving pretty soon. I'll take him home."

"He'll get home safe," said Butch. "I'll make sure."

"Alright," said John, reaching for his wallet. "Just remember he's already totaled three cars from falling asleep." Out came a fifty for Dale. "Guys, I gotta go. See ya tomorrow."

CHAPTER TWO

The automatic garage door was barely lifted high enough before John pulled his Ford Taurus into the garage. Out of the car, he walked between his Cadillac and his mother's Mercury Sable. Ever since his teens, he'd prided himself on keeping their cars clean and waxed. The garaged Cadillac was spotless. Mary's Sable, though somewhat soiled about the mud-flaps, remained clean. As John began taking his shoes off, he looked to see Mary opening the door that led into the kitchen.

"Son, you're home on time," said Mary Valone.

"Hey, when it comes to having dinner with my favorite girl, I'm always on time," he said, reaching to embrace Mary. He gave her a kiss on her cheek. "I'm hungry. What's for dinner?"

"Janet sent us some of her home-made ravioli," she said. "And on the way home, I stopped at the bakery. I bought fresh bread and some goodies for Christmas."

"What about all those stuffed peppers and that lasagna you were making last night?"

"They're for Christmas."

"Don't get me wrong, I like Janet's ravioli, but can't I sneak a couple peppers, too."

"They're not cooked yet," she said. "And neither is the lasagna. I'll heat them on Christmas morning. We'll have them, a salad, baked potatoes, and succotash. Janet's bringing more ravioli and meatballs, and I bought your favorite peanut butter cheesecake for dessert."

John could only grin at his beautiful, petite mother. An old movie buff, in spite of Mary's auburn hair worn just below shoulder-length, she'd always reminded him of Rita Hayworth. And she still did, for the years had been exceedingly kind to Mary Valone's retaining her youthful appearance. He knew how she'd always looked forward to the holidays–despite his penchant for not enjoying them. Yet he happily went along with all of her many holiday traditions when it came to Christmas Day dinner: the custom-made pad that would be placed on the mahogany oak dining room table; the lace tablecloth used to cover it; the gold place-settings; the gold-trimmed dishes used only for special occasions; the gold flatware would come out of hiding and be lined next to the plates on red serviettes; the salad fork; the dessert fork; the extra plate nobody ever used. John didn't mind–he would be content to eat from paper plates and a plastic fork. The holiday frills made Mary happy was all that mattered to him. He placed his thumbs inside his pants at the waistline and smiled. "I'd better go easy on the cheesecake."

"It's Christmas," she said. "You can overeat a little."

Minutes later they were having dinner, seated next to each other at their dining room table built for eight. John lifted the serviette from his lap to wipe his mouth and said, "Anyone else besides Janet coming over for Christmas dinner?"

"No, Janet's daughter and her husband can't make it home this year. Did you ask Gene and his dad?"

"They go to Gene's sister's house for Christmas."

"I asked Nancy Schriver and the Huber's if they wanted to have dinner. They said thanks, but they have other plans." Mary frowned, her lovely face exhibiting an almost apologetic expression. "It's sad, John. You and I are the only family we have."

"I know, Ma," he replied, not having any desire to comment further. "That's why we should have gone to The Bahamas like I wanted."

"I couldn't take off from work."

"Sure you could have. Heck, you haven't used any vacation-time for years now. And I can't remember the last time you called-off sick. You've got to have plenty of time coming."

"Close to forty weeks," said Mary. "John, I would've loved going to The Bahamas, but this is one of my busiest times of the year at the hospital. I have a pile of work that must be finished before the end of the year."

"So someone else coulda did it."

Mary shook her head. "Nobody else is allowed to do my job."

"Huh?" he said, crossing his forearms onto the table. "What, you still don't have an assistant? You've been there almost twenty years now."

"Counting the old hospital, twenty-one years next April. John, as you know, I'm the Medical Staff Secretary. I'm responsible for keeping all the information as it pertains to all the doctors who have privileges to practice at the hospital. That kind of information must be kept confidential. Mr. DeTorrio picked me for the job because I assured him that I wouldn't be a blabbermouth about anything that dealt with the medical staff."

"He picked you because you could type a hundred-twenty words a minute, you knew how to use a computer better than any other secretary there, and you agreed to go to those meetings they used to have at night."

"John, at the time I accepted the promotion, your father and I were separated. Oh, I wasn't thrilled at the prospect of working overtime every week and handling all the workload by myself, but we needed the money back then."

"I realize that, Ma," he said. "Still, what would happen if, God forbid, you got sick and couldn't work for an extended time?"

"I'm not sure." Mary paused to sip her lemon-water. "I'd guess Janet would have to cover for me at the departmental meetings. As for the rest of my job, I really don't know."

"Helluva way to run a hospital," he said, sarcastically. "Sounds like that DeTorrio guy doesn't know what he's doing, not having employees trained for jobs they might be needed on."

"Oh, he knows what he's doing, John. Trust me, he knows."

John let out a huff as he shifted back in his chair. He'd heard many stories about Anthony DeTorrio, the Executive Director, along with his various other titles at Valleyview General Hospital. Some were shocking; most were appalling; all of them at the very least made him restive that his mother worked for the man. Reaching for a slice of bread, he decided upon a different tactic. "Ma, you're fifty-four now. Why don't you just retire? Money isn't a problem for us anymore. Just retire and enjoy life."

"I've considered it," she said in a low-keyed tone. "Although the cost of health insurance is becoming outrageous and I wouldn't be eligible for Medicare for eleven years."

"So what. I'll pay for your health insurance."

"I couldn't let you do that."

"Ma, I'd really like for you to get out of that crummy hospital. Okay, how about if you work for me as my secretary? I'd pay you what you're making now, plus I'll add you on to my insurance plan."

Mary grinned, envisioning herself employed by her son. "What would you have me do, dust your desk and PC's all day?"

"No, no, I'd find lots of stuff to keep you busy."

Her bright hazel-green eyes sparkled at his white lie. "Thank you, John, but for the time being I think it best I keep my job." Another sip of water after her last bite of ravioli. "However I am thinking about taking an early retirement."

"The sooner, the better," he said. "I've heard too many horror stories about that hospital from you and Janet."

Mary arose from her seat to say, "And I'd be willing to bet they all have some basis in fact."

Her candid commentary tweaked a nerve, although as John pondered asking her to explain, he saw Mary clutching at the small of her back. "Ma, what's the matter?"

"It's nothing," she said, though continuing to rub at the small of her back. "Probably just the beginning of mild arthritis."

"You want me to call Dr. Mancini?"

"For what, a little back pain? John, at my age, many people begin experiencing some sort of back pain. It's simply a function of getting older."

"You sure you're okay?"

"I'll be fine."

Without giving him a chance to contest her reply, Mary said, "Are you going into town tonight?"

"No. Tomorrow afternoon."

"Would you please take care of the dishes?" she said, appearing considerably more at ease. "Just rinse the plates and put everything into the dishwasher. I'll empty it in the morning."

"No problem. Are you going over Janet's tonight?"

"No. I'll be with her all day tomorrow."

"What are you doing tonight?"

"Resting," she said. "It's been a long week. I'll be in my bedroom watching TV until I fall asleep."

John stood to kiss her cheek. "Okay, Ma, get some rest."

As Mary walked past the kitchen telephone, she stopped to say, "Oh, I almost forgot, your Aunt Linda called."

His facial expression turned surly. "What'd she want?"

"She called to say hello and—"

"Ma, if you're planning on asking me to go to their house this weekend, forget it, I won't go. You want to go by yourself, be my guest."

"Linda didn't invite us to her house," said Mary. "She just called to say hello, and asked how everything is with us."

"Wonderful. If you ever talk with her again, tell her and that idiot son of hers that I said hello, don't bother me, and goodbye."

She sighed. "John, sometimes it's better to put the past behind you."

"Not when it comes to either of them."

"Yes, your cousin Paul made a mistake—"

"He made a big mistake calling you an f'ing bitch," he again interrupted, throwing his serviette hard onto the table. Mary remained quiet as he moved closer. "That's why he got his ass kicked."

"Paul didn't mean to swear at me. He was frustrated."

"Frustrated, my ass. He's a lazy idiot with a big mouth and no respect for anybody."

"John, put yourself in his position," she urged of him. "Your dad didn't leave him anything."

"Apparently that's the way he wanted it. Despite the fact that you two were divorced when he was killed, he still thought enough of you to leave you five hundred grand. So why didn't he include his sister and her bastard son in his will?"

"Linda told the executor that she had spoken with Jim only weeks before the accident, and he'd mentioned that he would be making provisions for Paul and her in his will, but he never got around to it."

"Ah, baloney," he said. "Look, Mother, I don't want to argue with you. Let's just stick to the facts, please. My father, your ex-husband, left you five hundred thousand dollars and the rest of his estate to me, period. His attorney out in Los Angeles drew up the will. Everything was perfectly legal. There weren't any last-minute provisions, any hidden codicils, or any other legal mumbo-jumbo tying-up his estate in Probate Court. But regardless of what was stipulated in the will, the day after I was certain our money was secure in the bank, out of respect for you, I did as you asked and wrote a check for two hundred thousand dollars payable to Linda and Paul Valone. Now, remember what I told him when I handed Paul the check?"

"You told him to invest it wisely," said Mary, her tone signifying she knew what course their discussion was taking.

"And what happened?"

"Paul lost it all on a stock."

"That's right. The ninny gets an email from somebody involved in a pump-and-dump stock swindle telling him to buy whatever the stock was, that the price was gonna skyrocket within a matter of days, so in that miniscule sliver of a brain he has, he thinks, 'Gee whiz, isn't this guy just peachy for letting me in on this. All I gotta do is buy this stock and I'll be a gazillionaire.' Idiot. Just like P. T. Barnum used to say, 'There's a sucker born every minute.'"

"Paul's not as intelligent as you are, John."

John cast his brown eyes upward while shaking his head. "Mary dear, Paul's not as intelligent as Ms. Schriver's dog. Thinking he is would be an insult to the dog."

"Nancy really likes you," said Mary, trying to lighten his mood. "She always tells me how polite you are to her."

"Nancy's a very nice lady, plus nearly every time I see her outside walking her dog, I stop to pat the little furry mutt."

"His name's Bigi, and he's a pure-bred Bichon Frise," she insisted. "Don't ever let Nancy hear you say that cute little dog's a mutt."

"Oh, I know better than that," he smiled. "Nancy might call me a you-know-what like she does the guy down the street. Getting back to Paul, so he blew the money we gave him and Linda. Guy bounces from one minimum wage job to another, yet he pisses away two hundred grand like it grows on trees. Never asked for any advice how to invest all that money. Money if it had been invested properly would have provided them with a security blanket for years to come. Now be honest, was I upset when Linda told you what Paul had done?"

"No."

"Did I get mad when the walking wizard himself came over here crying that all his stock was worthless?"

"Not really. You called him an idiot again. But no, you weren't actually mad."

"Ma, you've got a darn good memory," he said. "I wasn't mad. It was our gift to him and Linda. Paul's the one who fell for the internet stock scam. It was his stupidity that cost them. That's on him, not us. And when he begged me to give him more and I refused, and he swore at me, what did I do?"

"You called him an idiot again."

"That's because he is an idiot. And when he pleaded with you to give him some of your inheritance, what did you tell him?"

"I told him absolutely not, and I'm positive I called him an idiot!" said Mary, displaying a grin to match her son's. "That money's my nest-egg. I sure as hell wasn't about to give that idiot any of it."

John couldn't help but cough while biting his tongue to avoid laughing. His emotions were twisted by the humorous nature their conversation had taken on, along with the resentment he felt. He pointed to the front door of their split-level house and said, "What did Paul say when he was standing over there?"

"That's when he cursed at me," she replied. "Then you jumped down the stairs and pushed him out. I'll never forget Linda yelling at us that she intended on calling a lawyer to sue you."

"That's why I called Bob Cook and told him what happened," he said. "Bob assured me that if there were witnesses who saw him try to punch me first, Paul was at fault, regardless of how badly he was hurt."

"Both eyes were swollen shut. His nose was broken."

"Ma, I don't care. He deserved everything he got for swearing at you."

John stepped closer. Placing both hands atop her shoulders, he gazed into her deep green eyes and said, "Mary, you're a wonderful mother and I love you dearly. I know you had it rough when I was growing up. It was even harder on you when I was in college, and I realize all you gave up for me just to make sure I had everything I needed. I appreciate all you've done for me. So as I've said to you before, now it's my turn to do all I can for you. And there wasn't any way I'd ever let Paul or anyone else insult you and get away with it. I don't care who they are, how big and strong they are, whoever they are, I just don't care. Because if anybody, and I mean anybody, gets even the slightest bit out of line with you, I promise you they'll have to deal with me."

"I love you, John," she said, her voice cracking as she kissed his forehead.

"I love you, too, Ma, and I always will. Now go ahead and get some rest. I'll take care of the dishes. You need anything, let me know."

Mary Valone walked towards her bedroom, tears streaming down her cheeks.

CHAPTER THREE

Tired of channel-surfing, Mary pressed the power-button on the television remote. After setting it on the nightstand next to her bed, she shifted onto her side hoping to fall asleep. Despite her being entirely content with her Christmas preparations as well as her talk with John, she remained restless. Thoughts forever crystallized in her mind were flashing back–not of Paul or Linda Valone–she couldn't stop thinking about the hospital.

Mary knew the complete saga of Valleyview General Hospital, along with the evolution of Anthony DeTorrio's career. His rise to power had been swift and sure, leaving countless bitter enemies in his wake.

She had started working at Carbondale-Mercer Hospital, located near the geographical centerpoint between the two small towns bordering Vernon Park that the facility derived its name from. Across the river was the town of Mt. Scottdale, the former home of St. Anne's Hospital.

Carbondale-Mercer opened in 1955, a far-superior facility to the smaller Catholic hospital. Regardless of the sociological differences between the two organizations, community planners had hoped that their administrations would attempt to work in unison to some extent. Yet as Mary had learned, those hopes never came to be. She knew that an acrimonious rivalry had been born, and battle lines were formed. Due to the sentiments then existing as a result of the warring hospitals strife, their administrators were reluctant to extend any olive branches.

As the second part of the 20th Century passed, the tensions between the two hospitals remained. The opposing medical staffs despised each other–any opportunity one faction had to berate their counterparts was seized with vigor. Their attacks were notoriously spiteful when it came to legal proceedings. For whenever a claim of malpractice was brought against a doctor on either staff, a plaintiff's attorney needn't search for a physician to testify on behalf of their client. All that was required was to cross the bridge to the other hospital in order to secure a doctor who would be more than happy to oblige. Although tensions eventually began to slacken as new doctors replaced the old, matters remained status quo until 1988.

It was in the summer of 1988 when a major confrontation broke out at Carbondale-Mercer Hospital. Although just another typist at the time, Mary recollected when the doctors' who staffed the hospital rebelled against their long-time administrator, Kent Flynn. Since his appointment in the mid-1960's, Flynn had made every effort to quell the petty animosities that existed between the feuding medical staffs. Of even greater importance to him, Kent Flynn had attempted anything within his scope of influence to improve the overall quality of Carbondale-Mercer.

Flynn made a fateful error that summer when he'd threatened to go public with documented proof that Carbondale-Mercer surgeons were performing unnecessary operations upon patients in order to increase their own incomes, as well as to generate additional revenues for the hospital. A peacemaker at heart, Flynn had first summoned many of the surgeons to a private meeting, desiring to convince them to put a stop to their unethical ways.

Much to his chagrin, nearly the entire medical staff of Carbondale-Mercer rose up in arms against him at the quarterly Board of Directors' meeting. Ironically only two months prior, Flynn had hired a man who'd worked in a hospital in New Jersey to serve as an administrative assistant. The new employee was at that meeting. His name was Anthony DeTorrio.

DeTorrio was a clever, manipulative and extremely devious man. Mary could still visualize the first time she'd ever laid eyes on him. For a thin, somewhat frail-looking individual, his presence emitted power; power that was easily usurped from those superior to him; power he enjoyed brandishing; power he was perfectly eager to use to crush or humiliate anyone who dared challenge him.

Despite his short tenure, DeTorrio made a bold play in the midst of the clash. He'd begun seeking-out doctors and board members without Flynn's approval. He'd preached to them that Kent Flynn was completely out of contact with the economic realities of the times, in addition to making other detrimental observations to slur Flynn's character and leadership abilities.

His backstabbing tactics proved successful. At the December Board of Directors' meeting, Kent Flynn was ordered to resign. Soon thereafter, Anthony DeTorrio was named Administrator of Carbondale-Mercer Hospital, overstepping those with far-more experience.

DeTorrio did not disappoint their confidence. Within the next few months, all of the facilities concerns disappeared. The issue that had caused such a furor between the doctors and Flynn was a non-starter to him. When the union that represented all of the hospital's employees except for Administration and Nursing was set to go out on strike unless they received an appropriate increase in pay, DeTorrio had instructed his bargaining team to extend only a four percent hike–spread over the a five year contract. The enraged union leadership had stormed from the negotiations with plans of a picket-line. After picketing for a week, another collective bargaining session was called. Upon the union team's entry, they found DeTorrio the only person seated across the table. The union leadership opted to accept the meager contract proposal. They'd told the rank-and-file there wasn't any other viable option, since DeTorrio vowed that anyone who refused to report to their job would be terminated–themselves included–and scab workers were waiting to replace them.

Though publically discrete, the C-M Board of Directors' applauded his tactics. To them, Anthony DeTorrio's efforts were generating much needed capital. Revenues had risen during his brief incumbency, and short-term projections indicated they would continue to accrue at moderate rates. Equally significant, the medical staff in general was elated with their dynamic new leader, a man who did not back down when put to task–a man who wasn't afraid to thumb his nose at morality.

Years later, DeTorrio had stunned everyone by granting some of St. Anne's doctors' admission privileges to his hospital. And while many of the doctors at Carbondale-Mercer weren't pleased, DeTorrio prevailed upon them it was the proper stratagem. He was proven correct, as their incomes increased due to the high volume of consultation fees with their once-rival colleague's patients. DeTorrio knew every loophole in the insurance regulations. Any patient admitted–regardless of their ailment–was probed from head-to-toe by the time they were discharged. Yet his physicians' boosted earnings wasn't the only reasoning behind Anthony DeTorrio's controversial change of policy.

Nearing the turn of the century, DeTorrio's mastery had only continued to grow stronger. His board members were getting long-in-the-tooth and did as told for the most part, although some of them had begun displaying an annoying character trait: they were listening to their consciences instead of him. Something that inflamed him–something DeTorrio was determined to remedy once and for all when a self-serving proposal he'd submitted was voted down.

From that point forward, whenever a board member resigned or had passed away, they were replaced by one hand-picked by DeTorrio. His only real criteria were they be a wealthy bastion of the community, along with being in favor of his totalitarian style of leadership. By January of 1997, the last of the old stalwarts were gone. Finally Anthony DeTorrio's Board of Directors' were comprised entirely of his personally-anointed cronies, all rich puppets who voted on issues as instructed.

Despite his confidence, DeTorrio still took a huge gamble later that spring. He had approached each of his board members one at a time. A new, larger hospital was his ultimate objective. It shocked the local community when word got out a meeting of both hospital boards' had been assembled. It was at that meeting when DeTorrio inquired if St. Anne Hospital would be interested in merging with Carbondale-Mercer. At first, there weren't any takers, the old pride of St. Anne's board blocking their even considering the proposal. However, they were wise to take the pragmatic overview. The vacated steel mills stood along the Monongahela River as rusted monuments of the past, and they faced an aging infrastructure. Outdated medical equipment was still being used. Most importantly, revenues had been in decline. It took some arm-twisting, but the St. Anne's Board of Directors' eventually relented. And when the county offered to donate ninety acres of prime land zoned commercial along the Vernon Park and Mercer border, Anthony DeTorrio's dream hospital would soon come to fruition.

As the new Valleyview General Hospital neared completion, there were many meetings between the two organizations. It was resolved that the Valleyview Board of Directors would be comprised of all current members from both boards if they chose to stay on. And due to the fact that C-M had a greater number of seated board members than St. Anne's, they were ensured controlling vote–thus maintaining DeTorrio's stranglehold of power.

With great fanfare, Valleyview General Hospital opened in June of 2000. To celebrate the occasion, a huge stage was erected in the center courtyard. Local politicians, board members, doctors, staff workers from the varied departments, along with the general populous were welcomed to attend the gala ceremonies. Several important dignitaries, including a state senator of Pennsylvania came to commemorate the grand opening. Alike the growth of Vernon Park, a new, ultra-modern, technologically-advanced hospital in this relatively small residential area outside of Pittsburgh was indeed noteworthy.

Many of the leading personalities in attendance gave long-winded speeches praising the magnitude of what had been accomplished through the diligence of the great man. DeTorrio, humble as could be, spoke only briefly to thank everyone for their many superb efforts. After his speech was concluded, the crowd had cheered wildly in thanks. And while the audience continued to bestow him with laurels, some of those in attendance, Mary Valone included, had contemplated otherwise. Among her thoughts, she'd wondered exactly where the digits 6-6-6 were concealed on the Executive Director's balding scalp.

CHAPTER FOUR

The next morning, Mary found John sitting in front of his computer. Knowing his tendency to keep odd-hours for whatever the reason, she asked, "Have you been up all night?"

"Nah, I fell asleep down here," he said, keeping his eyes trained on the computer.

Mary moved to stand behind him. "Good morning, Son."

"Good morning, Ma," he said, turning his head to accept her kiss. "Sleep okay?"

"Pretty well."

"How's your back feeling?"

"My back's fine."

"Great. Glad to hear it."

Mary inched closer to see a spreadsheet displayed on the screen. "Are those numbers from the job you're working on now?"

John swiveled around to face her. "No, I finished all that stuff." He observed her squinting to view the PC screen. "Where are your readers?"

"At my office." She edged nearer. "What are those numbers?"

"Here, Ma, please sit," he said, standing to offer Mary his chair. Once she was seated, he knelt on one knee while scrolling the spreadsheet downwards. "See better now?"

"Yes."

With the touch-pad, he positioned the arrow on the screen to keep circling a figure at the bottom of a column. "That, Mother, is the sum total of all your money."

Mary gawked in amazement. "My Lord, that's over six hundred thousand dollars!"

"The total will be close to six hundred and ten thousand when they tack on the interest at the end of the month," he said proudly. "That's what happens when money's invested wisely. It keeps growing."

Mary continued staring at the screen in awe. "Where's yours?"

He scrolled to the left, snickering as Mary's nose neared the flat-screen. Though viewing her in profile, he could see the disbelief on her face. John clicked on a block to highlight a column total. "There, short-eyes."

"That's over ten million dollars!" she blurted out, reaching to hug him. "How did you manage that? The amount I recall Jim's executor estimated was somewhere around four million after taxes and his fee."

"That's right, but you're forgetting all the preferred stock he had in LMG. Remember Mr. Gimble, the principal owner of LMG?"

"Not really."

"You met him at the funeral service," said John. "Mr. Gimble told me that he'd be taking LMG public in the near-future, and advised me to hold onto the stock. Don't you remember when the executor asked me if I wanted to liquidate the stock?"

"Vaguely." She paused while studying the column of numbers. "I was probably still in the state of shock when I heard you would be inheriting four million dollars, not to mention the five hundred thousand Jim left me."

"He owed it to you," declared John in a resonant tone. "My dad wasn't a bad guy, but I remember when you two were separated. He was making at least three hundred grand, and he'd send you peanuts while he was living a life of luxury in Los Angeles. And when you started—"

Mary held up her hand as to stop his narrative that was assured to continue. "John, I know," she said. "That's how your father was. Just be glad he never remarried and left us his estate. Now please, I have to start getting ready. Let's get back to the stock."

"Yeah, alright," he grumbled. "So that's why I held onto the stock, knowing that Mr. Gimble intended to take LMG public."

Mary lounged backwards. "Now I remember, the company went on NASDEQ."

"Yep, and my dad had sixty thousand shares of preferred stock in LMG that were worth five dollars per share. But once common stock was made available to the public, the value kept going up." He moved the arrow onto the calculator icon. "Let's see, sixty thousand shares at five dollars per—"

"Three hundred thousand," said Mary.

"My mother, the math professor," he said. "Okay, three hundred thousand dollars. But when word got out that LMG was about to go onto NASDEQ, the value of the preferred stock nearly quadrupled. Then whenever it was official and common stock was issued, the preferred stock price kept going up. So I began selling small lots. When the bid hit a hundred, I sold them all. Okay, what do I need to multiply the sixty thousand shared by?"

"The average selling price per share that you received."

"You're sharp, Ma. Forget a math professor, you shoulda been a stockbroker." He stood, taking a moment to rub the morning stubble on his chin. "Darn, I seem to have forgotten the average price. Do me a favor, click on—"

"Don't give me that bull," she said, backhanding his thigh. "With that memory you've got, you know exactly what it is. Come on, tell me."

"Minus brokerage fees, a little over eighty-eighth-point-two."

Quickly Mary keyed the figure into the calculator. "Oh, Lord! Five million, two hundred and ninety two thousand dollars! When you inherited the stock, it was only worth three hundred thousand."

"That's the way it's been done for years with big corporations, Ma, especially the successful ones. The fat-cats always figure out ways to get rich. Sure they want the corporation to succeed, but if the company starts tanking, in all actually they don't care. They've already made their millions. They've already got their Swiss bank accounts and giant yachts. It's called, 'take the money and run.' Heck, remember what happened after LMG went public?"

"No, not really."

"LMG started going downhill fast," he said. "Mr. Gimble placed some new guy in charge who wanted to expand the company too quickly. Every time I look, their stock keeps going down in value."

"I didn't know," she said. "Jim always used to say the stock market was risky unless you really knew what you're doing."

"It is. Just ask Paul the idiot. That's why I only invest our money in safe financial instruments. I'd rather we yield a little less profit than chase some pie-in-the-sky stock and lose a big chuck of cash."

"That's why I let you handle all my investments," Mary said, lifting from her seat. "You're the one who should have been the stockbroker."

"Nah, too much stress. That's the last thing I'd need, some guy up my butt all day screaming at me to sell, sell, sell. I'd end up smacking him before my first coffee break."

Mary grinned. "Son, knowing you, that's probably what you would do. Well, I'd better get moving. Janet's coming at ten o'clock."

"Where are you two going today?"

"She has our whole day planned. She wants to stop for breakfast. Shopping at the mall. Dinner at the Olive Garden. Then back to her house for a snack and some wine. How about you? Are you still going into town?"

"Yeah, for a couple hours. There's a football game on TV."

"Just please don't drink too much," she urged of him. "There are too many drunks out there this time of year."

"Don't worry, I'm only having my three or four beers."

A half-hour later, feeling refreshed after a shower and shave, John was dressed in Lee blue jeans and a plum-shaded Polo shirt. As he ate what remained from last night's ravioli, he heard a horn tooting in the driveway. "Ma, Janet's here," he called.

"Tell her I'll be another minute," she yelled from the bathroom.

With the garage door opening, John slid into his sneakers and walked towards the powder-blue Lexus with the vivacious Janet Silva behind the wheel.

The power window opened. "Get in here, cutie," she beckoned.

"Hi there, pretty lady," he said. "My, my, don't you look nice today."

"Sweetheart, flattery will get you everywhere with me," said Janet. "If I were only ten years younger, I'd kidnap you, lock us in a bedroom, and throw away the key."

"Hummmmm, not a bad idea," he replied in jest. Although Janet had teased him in such ways before, John still felt himself blushing. "So, you're kidnapping my sweet little mother today instead of me, huh?"

"Your sweet little mother needs kidnapped. Mary needs to get out of that hellhole of a hospital and live it up for a change."

"I couldn't agree more," he said. Able to hear the door leading into the kitchen close, he saw Mary putting her shoes on. "Hey, Jan, do me a favor."

"For you, anything."

"Mary told me that you two are going to your house later on for some wine. Do me a favor, instead of Mary's usual one glass, try getting her half-kicked. I don't want her running around the house all day tomorrow cleaning everything in sight. Hell, the place is spotless now."

"Sure thing," she smiled.

"Thanks, Jan," he said, while opening the door for Mary. "See you on Christmas. And by the way, the rav's were great."

With Mary now inside the car, John said, "You girls have fun today."

"We will," they said together, waving to him.

Soon back inside, he went to the basement to await Vicky's arrival. John was most at ease there as opposed to their plush, formal living room that Mary kept in pristine condition. When it came to their home, Mary enjoyed an elegant décor–John favored the practicalities of comfort. He'd speak with Vicky here in his own domain.

The finished basement had been given a total makeover. Dark wood paneling on the walls; a white suspended ceiling; the entire floor and stairway overlaid in a deep-pile mauve carpet; two sliding-glass doors shielded by vertical blinds that led to the backyard.

Along the wall adjacent to the stairs hung a 56-inch plasma television. On either side of the television were identical cherry-wood hutches that contained John's movie collection on DVD's and VHS videotapes. Centered is a wooden coffee table, with the entire area surrounded by a black leather couch and three matching leather recliners. Above the couch, a framed poster of his favorite movie star, Robert DeNiro, is illuminated by a built-in spotlight. The poster depicted DeNiro, Ray Liotta, and Joe Pesci in *Goodfellas.*

Positioned along the back wall stood an unsparing oak desk that once was his father's. Atop the desk were two laptop computers and a speaker-telephone.

Across the room as the base of the stairs is a ten-station home gym; next to it a Stair-Master exercise unit. Fanatical about his physical conditioning, John religiously exerted himself at least an hour per day–and it showed. While most of his friends remained in relatively good shape for men approaching their thirties, John's athletic 6' 1", 190 pound sculpted physique made him appear even more youthful than his twenty-eight years of life should have portrayed.

Yet what always caught John's attention was the 9' antique pool table centered under a stained-glass lighting fixture. A custom-made pool table with its hand-carved wooden legs, green felt covering the thick slate surface, and leather pockets. Pool tables of its exceptional quality were a thing of the past. It had belonged to the Vernon Park Italian Club. When Dennis Perella, the Italian Club's head steward had informed him it was for sale, John arrived the next morning with a U-Haul and three friends to help him.

Between the sliding doors was a small bar with four black stools in front. Only glasses and other assorted sports memorabilia decorated the mounted shelves behind the bar. The bar hid a mini-refrigerator that contained soft drinks and protein milkshakes, for John never had taken to drinking at home. It was his personal retreat–a sanctuary where he could work, exercise, shoot pool, lose himself in the movies or simply relax. As did the upstairs, the basement smelled of money.

John sprawled on a leather chair. Running his fingers through his dark brown hair, his thoughts remained transfixed on Vicky, the many images of her forever captured in his mind's eye. Her sultry appearance;

her long, satiny golden hair; her luscious body. All of the endless nights of sexual pleasures they had given each other. Deep in his heart, John knew he wanted her back. The infatuation he felt for her still burned strong. Nevertheless his manful pride, as well as the hurt endured more than two years after their last encounter.

Victoria Gill is Butch's older sister by one year. She'd know John ever since grade school. After her graduation Vicky had moved closer to Pittsburgh and didn't see John again until Butch's wedding years later. It was only due to her brother's persistence that they went out on a casual date the following weekend.

Their ensuing relationship during the next two years was filled with as many wonderful moments as there were heated and bitter quarrels. They had made love on their third date. Vicky had been like a goddess to him, a fascination of his erotic dreams that had turned into reality. With her, it was an incredibly passionate occurrence. For when they were together, it wasn't just a young couple craving the lusts of lovemaking. There was always an erotic energy between them.

He'd been with other girls before and after Vicky, though none of them even remotely generated the yearnings that she was able to instill deep within. She had blossomed into a ravishing and amorous woman, yet intelligent and cultured. Despite their constant feuding, John wanted her for his wife. Mary loved her as the daughter she never had, relentlessly pleading with her son to ask his beautiful girlfriend to marry him.

Vicky shared all of the same loving emotions for John–except for when it came to, as she claimed was, the 'bad side' of his character. She openly despised that her lover frequented the area taverns, regardless that her brother was usually with him. John would justify his behavior by saying he was only in the company of friends, wasn't looking to cheat on her, and that he'd never missed work due to his being out too late. "I like hanging out with my friends," he'd told her on countless occasions.

Their tumultuous relationship came to a screeching halt in October of 2005. Having grown tired of their incessant bickering, John hadn't telephoned her, disregarding her messages that were accumulating on his cell phone. He'd arrived at the conclusion that it was time to take a stand, neglecting her plans to attend a social event on Saturday evening. Enraged from being slighted, Vicky Gill charged into Mike's Pub later that night to find John sitting at the bar with Gene Polachek, Bob Cook, Dave Bodette, and her brother.

Sparks were flying from Vicky's cobalt-blue eyes as she confronted him. "You lousy prick!" she'd screamed to the top of her lungs. "You ignored me all week so you could go boozing! John, I've had it! It's either them or me! You can't have both! Choose! Right now!"

John always had the knack of being able to pacify her whenever she would vent her anger. But that time, he'd opted against it, his pride stung by her embarrassing flurry of insults in front of his friends. The dispirited expression he wore had then evolved into a cold smirk. "Gee Vick, that's a tough choice. Gimme some time to think it over. I'll give you a call when I've made up my mind," was his response.

His snide repartee along with his friends' chirping doused fuel onto the fire. Their boy's club mentality had pushed her over the edge. "You fucking bum, don't ever call me again!" she'd blared in retaliation.

A week later, James Valone was killed when his corporate jet crashed in Texas. All of John's friends, including William Gill and his family attended the funeral services–Vicky Gill did not. Her absence cut deep to his core. In the weeks and months subsequent, Butch had asked John if he should intercede on his behalf. The answer was always no.

John remained trapped in the prism of time when he heard the doorbell chiming. He glanced at his Seiko. "She always was punctual," he said aloud, then started up the steps to see his former lover, remaining uncertain what to expect.

Her stunning beauty intact, Vicky appeared more attractive than ever. John greeted her cautiously, pretending not to notice her indicating she wished to hug him.

"Let's go downstairs," he said, extending his arm as to suggest she walk in front.

"John," she began, seeming tense as she took her coat off, "I want to say one thing first. I am so sorry about your dad. Even though I was angry at you, I still should have called to express my sympathy."

"It was a bad time for both of us," he said, softly. "Would you like something to drink? There's pop in the refrigerator, and I think Mary made coffee this morning."

"Whatever you're having," she said.

While he poured their Pepsi's, she scanned the room. John only filled the glasses halfway, as he couldn't stop himself from using his peripheral vision to steal views of Vicky in her red blouse and tight-fitting designer jeans. Though she'd situated herself on the end of the sofa, Vicky never blinked when he took the chair across the way.

"This is unbelievable," she said. "The carpet and the furniture are fabulous. The pool table. Your desk. The *Goodfellas* picture. Everything's really nice."

"Yeah, I like it down here. Mary and I have an understanding. She can do whatever she wants with the rest of the house, but the basement's mine."

"Is Mary home?"

"No, she went out."

"How's she been?"

"Good."

"I always liked your mom. Does she still work at the hospital?"

"Uh-uh."

"Please tell her I said hello." Vicky paused while looking at the home-gym. "Where are the washer and dryer?"

"They're upstairs now. Mary and I decided the house needed some remodeling."

"May I ask what was all done?"

"Not that much," he said. "We added three rooms and an extra bathroom to the back of the house. They built a bigger deck that extends the length of the house, and I wanted a third garage for the Cadillac my dad left me."

"The remodeler did a good job," she said, bypassing any additional dialog about his late father–and the undisclosed sums of money Butch could only guess John had inherited. "The bricks match perfectly. Did somebody from Vernon Park do the work?"

"No, some construction outfit near to Pittsburgh," he said, unwilling to disclose that Gary and Dave had done the remodeling. "I'll give you a tour of the upstairs if you want."

"Maybe later," she said. Despite John's outward calm, she sensed the apprehensive side of his personality that was his nature to shield. "Umm, may I ask something about your job?"

John liked how she was phrasing her questions–Vicky didn't sound like the same inflexible girl who was accustomed to having everything her own way. He decided to open-up a little. Following a drink of Pepsi, he said, "Sure."

"Butch tells me that you're in business for yourself now."

"Yeah. Now I'm my own boss."

"Why'd you quit working for that consulting firm in Pittsburgh?"

"AAF Business Solutions," he said. "Vicky, it was a combination of reasons why I quit. When I started there out of college, they wanted me flying to their corporate headquarters in Miami maybe once a month. Then they wanted me flying directly to whatever city in the U.S. they needed me in. You remember when I used to be out of town for an entire week."

"Yes, and I also remember your saying they were considering transferring you to the corporate headquarters in Miami."

"They were going to transfer me to Miami, although I still would have been required to do some traveling to their other offices." He paused for a sip of pop. "After my dad, I wasn't ready to tempt fate again. Plus there's the lifestyle down there. It's too fast for me. Too many wacko's on skateboards with their I-Pod's. Then I had to consider Mary. I didn't want to leave her here by herself."

Adept at reading faces, John saw his answer seemed to disappoint.

"So what type of work are you doing now?" she asked.

"I'm still a business consultant, Vicky. I do whatever the company who hires me asks. Obviously that varies from job to job."

"Trying to downsize companies, I suppose."

"If I know that's what they intend to do anyway," he said. "Although I actually try to encourage them not to eliminate as many jobs as they want. I have all kinds of business models that illustrate that if a company downsizes too much, the loss of productivity will outweigh the salaries they're saving by eliminating jobs. So I figure I'm trying to save as many people their jobs as I can."

"It's terrible how many people are losing their jobs anymore."

"I agree, but that's the economy today. That's why I'm more selective about what offers I do accept. If I know up-front that a company's intent on massive job-cuts or outsourcing entire divisions, I won't take their offer. Basically I try to stay with software upgrading, feasibility studies, cost and market analysis, stuff like that." John reached for his Pepsi. "Hey, enough about me. I hear you're into real estate now. You like it?"

"So far. It sure beats working at that horrible state job I had in Harrisburg. Most of my co-workers were just plain ignorant."

As their conversation carried on, both were mindful not to offend the other by avoiding possible topics that could stir friction. All throughout their chat, Vicky remained congenial, while John grew more relaxed. The bickering he was primed wasn't to be. He also kept hearing the line William Hurt had tried on Kathleen Turner in the film *Body Heat–"You shouldn't wear that body,"* the voice continued to repeat.

It was eleven-fifty when Vicky stood to put her brown suede coat on. "John, I'm glad we had a chance to spend some time with each other. I'd like to stay longer, but Butchie let it slip about your plans. You're almost late now, so I'd better be leaving."

Vicky pulled a piece of paper from her purse. "Here's my new cell phone number. Call me if you'd like to go out sometime." She handed him the paper, then bent to kiss him flush on the lips. While it wasn't the impassioned kind he had savored before, it was a far-cry from the peck on the cheek he'd expected.

"Sit down a sec," he managed to say.

She couldn't help notice his confused facial expression. "What's wrong?"

"Vicky, I really enjoyed seeing you again. We talked about all the proper subjects, and we didn't get on each other's nerves. And while I'm happy that you want to start dating again, I admit that I'm a little surprised. I might regret this, but I'm gonna take a chance anyway. Exactly what did Butch tell you about my plans today?"

"Just that you and the guys are going to the bar to watch football."

"And that doesn't upset you anymore?"

"No, not at all," she said, smiling. "Ever since we broke-up, I've come to realize that your being around your friends isn't so bad. It seems like every single man out there is either unemployed, on drugs, or just out for a one-night-stand. Butch and I've talked about you many times. He respects you very much. He keeps telling me what a responsible guy you really are, and what a big mistake I made in leaving you." She batted her eyelashes at him. "And we were pretty good together. Weren't we?"

"I thought so," he replied in bashful tone.

While inwardly enamored with her seemingly new perspective, John felt it wise not to demonstrate any further emotion. As they climbed the steps to the landing he lagged behind her while adjusting himself, trying to conceal the bulge in his jeans.

"I'll give you a call sometime after Christmas," he said, not wanting to sound overly anxious.

"My girlfriend's having a party at her apartment on New Year's Eve. We could go there if you'd like."

"Umm—I'm not sure yet," he said, still playing hard-to-get. "Maybe."

"Just please try to let me know soon," she said, as she draped her scarf around her neck. Now the peck on the cheek. "Have fun today. Bye."

John viewed her as she walked towards her Kia Sportage. While Vicky had accepted his apprehensiveness gracefully, he sensed her more discontented than she'd let on. "Ah, you're being an idiot now," he said, reaching into the closet for his jacket. "She's changed."

CHAPTER FIVE

Mike's Pub wasn't nearly as crowded as John expected when he arrived to find Gene Polachek and Bob Cook in their reserved corner. The large, flat-panel LCD television mounted onto a support beam that had been installed exclusively for them was set on ESPN's college pre-game show. Mike and Dale Lambert were behind the bar waiting on the sparse crowd, pacing themselves for what promised to be another busy day.

"About time you got here," Mike called to him.

Dale placed a Miller Lite in front of John and said, "That's on me."

"Thank you, kind sir," said John, tipping the bottle as to make a toast. He nudged Gene. "Pick us a winner yet?"

"I kinda like Cal State," Gene said.

"I thought I heard on *Sportscenter* their quarterback has a bad knee."

"Nah, he's startin'. Don't matter anyway, Cal will run all over them. I could gain five yards a clip behind their offensive line."

"I don't know about that, but okay, I'm in," he said. "Bet a hundred for me."

John noticed Bob Cook's sly grin. "What's with you, Counselor?"

"I hear you had a visitor this morning," Bob said.

Feigning to be annoyed, John eyed Gene. "Buddy, you don't miss a trick, do you, ya little schmo?"

"Ah, I wasn't nebshittin'," Gene said. "I was making breakfast when she pulled into your driveway. I couldn't help but see her."

"Yeah, yeah," said John, while squeezing the back of Gene's neck. "Robert, next time you need a snoop, here's your man. Anything that goes on where we live, he always knows about it."

"How'd it go with her? The snoop here says she looked pretty sexy. You get any?"

"Who's the fuckin' snoop now!" Gene quipped at Bob.

John offered a smile and said, "Guys, what can I tell you. Yeah, she looks great, and she didn't act like the pampered princess she's been her whole life. But she burned me once and I won't go through that again. Please, let it go at that."

Moments later, Gary Rowland joined them. "Hey, Mike," he yelled across the bar. "Does your brother still have that old pickup truck?"

"I think so," Mike said, pacing towards them. "You see him, Rol?"

"He was a couple cars in front of me when I was driving into town. He's parked at the auto parts store down the street."

Instantly they observed the distress written across Mike's face as he said, "I'll be right back."

With Michael out of sight, Dale approached. "He told me his brother's coming in today," he said, caution in his tone.

"Just be your normal polite self to him," said John.

"That's for damn sure," replied Dale. "I've heard too many stories about him."

The four men sitting across the bar from Dale also knew the many stories told them about Dennis Perella. Despite being some forty years removed from his high school days, Denny's exploits as a middle linebacker remained legendary in Vernon Park. He was notorious for tackling the opposition with such ferocity that the other team's ball-carrier would dive to the ground whenever they saw the human freight train charging their way. Both Butch Gill and Bob had played high school football–many a night they'd talk about viewing grainy footage shown them by their coach prior to a game.

From time spent at The Italian Club, they'd listened to the accounts told by Jack Risso, Denny's best friend. One drunken night, Bob had asked why Denny didn't go to college to play football–Jack explained why. After high school, Dennis Perella immediately enlisted in the Marine Corps, spurning several football scholarships extended him. His reasoning: another of their gang had been drafted a few years prior and was killed. Denny simply wanted to even the score.

After basic training, Denny had been shipped to a location near the Cambodian border where the fighting was fierce. Out in the bush with his comrades on his first patrol, Denny had volunteered to be the 'point man,' an easy target for enemy fire.

Dennis Perella took a bullet in the leg during his second week in the jungle. A month later, his platoon was ambushed by a contingent of North Vietnamese when he was shot in the chest. Denny continued to shoot, a fearless warrior unafraid of death. Another bullet struck him, puncturing a kidney. Bleeding profusely, he'd kept shooting until his wounds rendered him unconscious. When the medics arrived, Denny was helicoptered to a MASH unit. His injuries were such that the medic who'd treated him didn't believe he'd survive the flight. With the exception of Private Perella, his entire platoon of forty-three men died that day.

It was during his convalesce at an army hospital in Saigon when Denny's new lieutenant came to visit. After he'd presented Denny with his Purple Heart, the lieutenant informed him that since his kidney had been removed, he wasn't considered fit for combat. Yet he'd implored upon the officer to let him stay in country and finish his tour of duty, even if it meant his being assigned to a non-combat division. So impressed with his grit, the lieutenant saw to it that Denny's request was approved.

Upon his release, Dennis was attached to an explosives unit that specialized in landmines and other heavy munitions. Understanding he would not see any further combat with the infantry soon caused Denny to grow discontented with his new duties–working with equipment that might kill the enemy wasn't nearly as gratifying to him as putting a bullet between their eyes. When then President Nixon began scaling-down the war in the early 1970's, Denny was soon on his way stateside, not having sustained any additional injuries. Yet all of the exigent pressures Vietnam offered had taken their toll.

Now on their third beer, the football game underway, the bar beginning to fill, nearly everyone took notice when Dennis Perella strutted in. For if ever a mere mortal could grab Satan's tail and heave him over the gates of Hell, it was Dennis Perella. A barrel-chested, thickly-muscled terror of a man with a deep crease running across his forehead. His imposing glare alone caused alarms to ring of impending danger. He had a Roman nose and savagely-piercing dark eyes; his hair still cropped in marine fashion; from an earlobe dangled a silver skull-and-crossbones trinket. People in his path hurriedly moved aside as Denny stalked towards the corner of the bar.

John stood to greet him. "Mr. Perella. Great seeing you again."

"Same here, pal," he countered, sporting a broad grin as they shook hands for an extended time. "How the fuck've you been?"

"I'm doing okay, Den. I just wish you'd come around more often."

"Ah, I've been spending more time with my boy ever since his mother ran off. When I do get out, I still go up the club."

"I was sorry to hear about your wife," John said in earnest.

With the speed of a light being switched on, Denny's expression turned vile. "Fuck her."

John frowned in acknowledgment. "How's your boy?"

"Real good," said Denny, the corners of his mouth uplifted enough to pass for a smile. "Senior year in school. Damn kid gets nothin' but A's."

"Good for him. Your son always was a smart kid." John turned to signal Dale. "What are you drinking, Den?"

"Gimme a Coors," said Denny, as they moved to sit. He gazed about the bar. "Where the fuck's my brother."

"He's been gone about ten minutes now. Probably takin' a dump." John elbowed Denny's ribs. "Den, remember these guys?"

"I remember your pals," Dennis said, a nod of his head serving as his recognition to the other three men. He grinned at Bob. "Especially him. I remember him from the Hershey trip. And whenever you guys shot partner's out the club, younse guys never lost."

"Ah, we just got lucky, Denny," said Bob Cook.

"Lucky my dego ass," was Denny's response, albeit good-natured. "You two won every game. We tried getting you guys drunk. We'd play dirty-pool and still none of us could come close to winning a game."

Dale stood patiently waiting. He looked to John and said, "You ready."

"Absolutely. Give this man a Coors and get the rest of us."

Once he'd opened their beers, Dale moved away, relieved the keg of dynamite clad in an army jacket had ignored him. Bob, Gene, and Rol also appeared calm as they, John, and Denny viewed the football game.

"Hit that motherfucker!" the entire bar heard Denny shout at the TV.

With his friends focused on the game, John turned to Denny and said, "Den, I hope you don't mind my asking, but I just heard about the auto plant. You gonna be alright?"

"Hell, yeah," he said. "I'll collect my pension, and I'll get unemployment for at least six months. My pension alone will more than enough to cover the bills."

"So you just planning to retire?"

"Nope." Denny almost smiled. "Remember that barn behind my house?"

"I think so. I haven't been out to your house for too long now."

"I made it into a garage. I'm gonna have my own auto repair shop." Denny chugged his beer, then said, "The tax-free kind, so you won't be seeing any advertising."

"That sounds great, Den," said John–though frowning. "Except for the advertising part."

"Why's that?"

"Oh, I can just imagine your smiling face on a billboard," he said, chuckling. "Under your picture, the sign should read, 'Denny's Auto Repair. Bring me you wrecked car or else I'll beat you up.'"

"Fuckin' wiseguy!" Denny bellowed, then punched John's arm. "You always were a fuckin' wiseguy."

Able to hear their commotion from the kitchen, Michael Perella appeared. As he moved behind the bar, he stepped towards them tentatively. "How've you been, Den?" he braved to speak.

"Just how in the fuck do you think I've been," Denny growled. He turned to John. "You know, even though this place ain't too bad, you should come up the club more often. Me and the same bunch are there most weekends. Stop by one of these nights."

"Promise I will," John said.

"You still got my pool table?"

"Sure do. You ever want to shoot a few racks, you're always welcome."

Dennis nodded, then turned to his sibling. His foreboding facial expression, along with his slamming his empty bottle on the bar indicated the return of Mr. Hyde. "You keep leavin' messages on my machine that you want to talk. Well, here I am. What the fuck you want?"

Ashamed by his brother's crude behavior, Michael hung his head. "If it's okay with you, let's talk in my apartment," he said in passive tone.

Shortly thereafter Dale made his way back to the corner. The younger man with the face of a choirboy said, "You ask me, that guy belongs in a zoo."

"Nah, he isn't as bad as he acts," John said. "Denny's really a nice guy once you get to know him."

Dale wasn't buying John's rationale–Denny's crass temperament, along with the few stares he'd received from those dark eyes had convinced him otherwise. "I don't want to get to know him," he said. "I'm telling you, he belongs in a nuthouse."

"You shouldn't be so quick to criticize him just because he blew-off a little steam at Mike," John countered. "That man went through hell in Vietnam."

"Damn, John, when was Vietnam? Forty, forty-five years ago?"

"Doesn't matter, Dale," Bob Cook put forth. "I've dealt with plenty of veterans. It's a fact that war can leave permanent psychological scars."

"I understand that—"

"No, Dale, you don't understand," John broke in. "None of us can appreciate what it must be like to go into battle. We can't even begin to understand what it must have been like spending every minute of every day with the threat of death all around. We can't comprehend what went through Denny's mind when he saw one of his buddies lying on the ground dead. Think about it, those guys woke up every day knowing they might be the next one tucked into a body-bag. Like Bob said, that had to be psychological torture at its worst. Sure Denny flips-out once in a while, but remember that man fought for our country in some political war that America had no business even being involved in, and he damn near died because of it."

"All the psyche classes at Penn State paid off, huh, John?" said Bob.

"Miss Trombino being our professor didn't hurt us any."

"Yeah, she was a honey," Bob grinned.

With Dale remaining quiet, Bob said, "John, remember those pictures Denny showed us that night at his house?"

"Oh, jeez, how could I ever forget."

"I saw them," Gene followed, turning to Rol. "You were there."

Gary Rowland offered a grimace in response.

"What pictures?" Dale asked.

"Tell him, Cookie," said John.

"No way," Bob said. "You tell him," he mumbled to Gene.

Gene shrugged while taking a swig of Miller Lite. "Okay, kid, you asked for it. One night a bunch of us went to Denny's house. Some guy you don't know asked Denny something about Vietnam, so Denny told us about when he and some other marines were sent out on a scouting mission. One marine took a sniper's bullet. Poor guy died on the spot. They were pinned-down a long time before one of Denny's buddies finally got the sniper."

"Did the shot kill him?" said Dale.

"No, but for sure he wished it had," Gene said. "Because they pummeled the shit outta the slanty-eyed gook."

"Then they killed him."

"Hey, bartender, how 'bout a drink over here," called a man from across the way.

"Go ahead, Dale," said Bob. "And get the whole bar a drink on me. I want you to hear this. Maybe you'll learn something."

When Dale returned moments later, he said to Gene, "Then what happened?"

"After they got done pounding him, Denny had one of his pals take some pictures. Those were the same one's we saw."

"Keep your voice down," said Bob.

Gene nodded. "The first picture shows the sniper on his knees with Denny standing behind him grabbing his hair. In the next photo, Denny's holding a machete to the gook's throat. The third photo is almost identical, except when it was taken, Denny was slitting the gook's throat. The next one shows Denny holding the gook's head up, as the blood flowed from his throat. Denny was grinning from ear-to-ear. In the last picture, Denny's still holding the gook's head. Just his head. He'd just chopped it off."

Dale Lambert stood silent, his mouth opened. "That's unreal," he managed to say.

"No, Dale, that was justice," John insisted to him. "Justice in the true biblical sense. An eye for an eye. A life for a life."

"Well, what do you think, Dale?" asked Bob. "Was it justice or not?"

"Yeah—I guess it was."

Something still irked Dale as he fronted John. "Let me ask you a question. Mike's always told me that he and his brother aren't very close. You know why?"

"Not really."

"Alright, try this one. I watched him practically the whole time he was down here. From what I saw, he barely talked to these guys, but he treated you great. Why's he like you so much?"

"Ah, it ain't no big deal," said John. "I helped him out of a jam a few years ago."

*****

"Ain't that the truth," Robert Cook thought, his mind whisking him through the winds of the past. From his seat between them, Bob viewed Gene and Rol with their forearms resting atop the padded railing along the edge of the bar, seemingly content enjoying the game. In spite of their not adding any additional commentary to John's last words, the

vibes he sensed apprised him as to what they were thinking–both felt extremely fortunate they weren't there.

In the summer of 2000, they'd begun to frequent The Italian Club. As they remained today, Dennis Perella and his group of friends were the dominating faction of the membership, his volatility even worse in those days. Denny and his gang where all some twenty to thirty years older than Bob and company. And while most of the members took to the younger crowd, Denny at best tolerated them.

The topic that prevailed among the older men one evening was their annual trip to Hershey, Pennsylvania, where a high school all-star football game would take place. Jack Risso was complaining that he'd already mailed a check to ensure their poolside suites, yet there were only six men in total who remained committed to the trip.

Later that night, Butch Gill and Bob had asked Jack Risso if they could tag along on their trip. Jack had welcomed them, as did the other men who were going–all except for Dennis Perella, who'd ridiculed the idea. Yet as the evening pasted, Denny finally agreed to allow them to join in their weekend excursion. Michael Perella had quickly declined the offer; Gene and Gary had also opted-out; David Bodette was gung-ho; only after much coaxing did John Valone finally give in.

Bob Cook's acute reminiscence took him to the parking lot of The Italian Club as he observed Denny loading cases of beer and other assorted liquors into Jack's van; he could still envision Denny staggering in the parking lot at their hotel in Hershey, heaving an empty bottle of bourbon at a concrete post, sending slivers of glass spraying about. "Another dead solder," Denny had slurred, before toppling onto Bob's car. He could still hear Jack's forewarning, "Guys, he's in a crabby mood. Just let him do whatever he wants."

They had been told they'd be sharing one suite with The Italian Club gang having two suites. The fourth was dubbed, 'the drinking, poker, and sex room.' Jack Risso had laughed when Butch inquired about the football game–there weren't ever any intentions of attending. The Italian Club crew used that gag to discourage their wives from coming with them. For all intents, the weekend was their opportunity to be together, drink like fools, play poker, clown around in the swimming and whirlpools while being free to 'look for something strange' without their wives ever finding out.

Friday evening remained a drunken blur to Bob. He'd been in the process of regaining his sobriety early Saturday morning when Denny had barged into their room, yelling at them to get out of bed–he and the guys were in need of poker players. The festivities had resumed.

The sun having set, the younger men were sluggish after another grueling day of non-stop drinking when Denny entered their room. "Buncha sissies," he'd called them. "C'mon, we're in the whirlpool. Maybe that'll wake you girls up."

His forearms goose-bumped, Robert Cook could still feel the hot waters of the whirlpool while Denny and friends continued to drink and carry-on. No one noticed the hotel manager heading their way.

"Fellas, would you please hold it down a little. People are complaining about the noise," he'd said affably.

Like a rocket, Denny had sprung from the whirlpool. "The sign says open all night, mack, so fuckoff," he had snarled.

The manager was left speechless. He'd wanted no parts of the man with the crazed visage about him. A hasty exit followed.

A few beers later, Denny had looked to John and said, "Hey, kid, go into my room. Inside my duffel bag there's three joints in tinfoil. Get them. Yeah, bring matches and an ashtray."

John had returned and placed everything behind Denny. He'd lit the first. Following a prolonged drag, Denny passed it to Jack. Lighting another, Denny kept it for himself. Bob Cook could still hear the shoe leather of the Pennsylvania state trooper tapping the pavement.

As the trooper and the hotel manager stood above Denny, all had grown quiet as Denny and Jack extinguished the marijuana in the whirlpool. The manager had pointed to Denny and said, "Him, Sergeant."

The state trooper, his name Belczyk engraved into a bronze tag worn above his shirt pocket, had squatted between Denny and Jack. He'd then lifted the towel that covered the ashtray. "You forgot to drown this one," he'd remarked, staring directly at Denny. "Guys, I'll go easy on you, but I want to know who supplied it. And I'd better not hear that you guys found it here, or else I'll book every last one of you for possession."

"I brought it, Sir," immediately had called the voice of John Valone.

They'd all listened as Sergeant Belczyk read John his rights. Having identified himself as a law student, Bob suggested John not say anything further until he could consult with an attorney. Belczyk had then permitted John to get dressed and had advised Bob he would permit him inside the Pennsylvania State Police barracks a mile east on the turnpike if he so elected, where John would be spending the night. Everyone watched in silent disbelief as John was led to the patrol car, with Bob preparing to follow behind in his own car–their only consolation being Belczyk had felt it a waste of time bringing charges against Denny for harassing the hotel manager.

At the barracks, Bob was instructed to remain outside of a barrier that surrounded the interior offices where Sergeant Belczyk had taken John for processing. Seated on a wooden bench, Bob had sorted through his contacts contained in his cell phone. With it being after 2 A.M. he'd decided against calling his parents or Mary Valone–instead calling a company he held a credit card with, hoping he had enough to obtain a cash-advance to use as bail.

Robert Cook envisioned John and Sergeant Belczyk emerging from his office, a bottle of Mountain Dew in John's hand. "Thanks again for the pop, Sarge," he'd heard John say to his complete amazement, as they walked at arms-length towards the gate.

"You can mail me the buck," Belczyk had responded.

He'd then looked to Bob and said, "Mr. Cook, I understand that you and John have just graduated from Penn State."

"Yes, Sir," Bob had said.

"Are you fellow Penn Stater's going to behave yourselves until tomorrow?"

"Yes, Sir," they'd answered in synch.

"Good enough for me," Belczyk had said. "Mr. Cook, take John back to the hotel. He's free to go."

"Any charges against him, Sir?"

"No, I ran both your names through the state's database. Neither of you have any criminal record whatsoever. If neither of you were involved with marijuana in college, I find it hard to believe John turned into a dope-pusher just like that. I know the marijuana probably belonged to that gorilla who got nasty with the manager, so why should I put John through the hassle. Get back to your room and go to sleep. Both of you look like you can use it."

"Thanks again, Sarge, I appreciate your understanding," John had said.

Bob Cook drove below the speed limit on the stretch of the Pennsylvania Turnpike back to the hotel, all the while asking John why Sergeant Belczyk hadn't pressed charges against him. John had offered that Belczyk was a Penn State graduate himself, and that he was a regular guy. Nevertheless, Bob recalled his fears as he'd contemplated the next obstacle awaiting them–what would Dennis Perella's reaction be?

"At least the morons were smart enough to get out of the whirlpool," Bob had said, as they walked towards their room through the outer courtyard. The sliding door leading to spare room had then opened.

Once inside they'd found the entire group, all astonished at their return. John had fielded one question after another–except from Denny, who was sitting at the poker table glaring at him.

Bob remembered Denny saying, "Alright, kid, start at the beginning. I wanna hear everything again."

After John had finished summarizing every detail for him, the unmistakable scowl Dennis Perella exhibited had only grown in ferocity prior to his saying, "Hey, kid, while I can respect what you did for me, don't stand there lying that you didn't tell that cop the truth. Because if you hadn't, you'd still be at the station."

"Denny, I'm being honest with you," John had said, remaining unintimidated by the ex-marine. "I kept telling the Sergeant it was mine, but he wouldn't buy it. So I ended-up telling him that I'd gotten into the whirlpool with you guys just before he came, so I really didn't know who it belonged to. That he believed. I guess he decided to cut me some slack."

With that assumption, Denny had dug into the cooler and grabbed a beer. "Just like that, huh? No report. No fine. No nothin'. You're a fucking liar!" he'd shouted, before throwing the can at John.

"Denny, take it easy," Jack Risso had pleaded to him. "The kid just saved you from jail. What he's saying makes perfect sense to me."

His other friends taking the same stance had only added to Dennis' fury. "You guys better knock it off!" he'd thundered. "This is between me and him." Denny's ire had been quickly heeded, as the only sound in the room came from the spinning can on the tiled section of floor.

As he reached for the can, all eyes were focused upon John Valone. Though retaining his composure, he glared boldly at Denny.

"Mr. Perella, I'm going to repeat myself one more time," John had said. "I told the cop the marijuana was mine because your brother's mentioned some of your legal problems to me—"

"None of that matters—"

"Shut the fuck up!" John had roared. "You can babble whatever you want when I'm finished. I'm talking now, so shut your fucking mouth!"

Bob Cook could still recall the collective gasp heard about the room–all dumbfounded by John's foolish bravado. Anticipating Denny's charge, Jack Risso and his other friends had positioned themselves to cut him off as best they could. Bob, Butch and Dave readied to sheppard John Valone out of harm's way.

"What'd you say, punk!" Denny had shouted.

"What are you, stupid and deaf?! Fuck you, I'm tired of your shit. You wanna try beating my ass, come on, big man, I'm right here," John had then challenged.

Much to their surprise, Denny had only laughed before saying, "Keep talking, boy."

"Fuck you, boy!" John had blared, his tone turned even more vicious. "Ever since I met you, all you've been is a pushy, loud-mouthed bully. You expect everybody to bow down and kiss your ass, even these guys you've known your entire life. Then I try to help you out of trouble and you thank me by calling me a liar! Look around, dickhead, see any cops! No, that's because I didn't give you up. So here, big man, here's what I really think of you!"

At that moment, John had elbowed Bob and Butch aside. With a snap of his wrist, he'd flung the can at Denny, striking his forehead. The eruption still hadn't occurred as the short-fused dynamo remained hushed while wiping blood from his brow. Bob and friends had begun attempting to forcefully drag John out of the room.

"Get your fuckin' hands off me!" he'd screamed, shoving at each of them. "I'm waiting for big mouth to do something about it."

"Denny, please don't," Risso had urged of him.

"Relax, Jack," Denny had said. "He wouldn't have stood-up to me unless he really is telling the truth."

"Bob, I'm getting out of this loony-bin," John had said.

Sipping his beer, Bob recalled John's eyes remaining fixated on Dennis Perella–a brutal rage about him. He'd gone on to say, "You guys stay if you want, but I'm leaving right now. I'll fuckin' thumb a ride home."

"Kid, you don't have to go," Denny had said. "I believe you didn't rat me out—"

"Fuck you," John had again interrupted. "I'm leaving because I can't stand the sight of you. Fuck you and fuck your Italian Club. You ever wanna try kicking my ass, I live at 102 Pinewood Lane. Stop by some day and show me how tough you really are."

Butch, Dave, John, and Bob drove home that night. The other men stayed until check-out time on Sunday. The police never came.

As Robert Cook had learned weeks later, John had stopped for a beer at another bar in Vernon Park. Somebody there recognized him and telephoned Dennis Perella, who'd arrived shortly thereafter. When John had seen him enter, he'd knocked his stool down and stood with his fists clenched. Instead, Denny approached in peace to apologize for his behavior. He'd repeatedly thanked John for not revealing the truth to the police. It was fact Denny had legal issues–he was already on criminal probation for several other offenses. Had he even been arrested in Hershey, the terms of his probation stated he would be sentenced to five years in jail.

They ended up at The Italian Club and drank into the wee-hours of the morning. Denny no longer treated John like an outsider. His respect and gratitude displayed for John Valone was overwhelming. In the parking lot when the club had closed, the brawler had said," John, if you ever need a favor, no matter what it is, you let me know. I owe you."

*****

They all heard the pounding on the steps as the two brothers made their way back downstairs. Denny seemed in a better mood–Mike appeared relieved. They spoke for a moment under the archway leading into the kitchen, then Denny bid his brother goodbye.

"I'll be seeing you guys," said Denny, waving to them across the bar. "I'd stay longer, but my son's home waiting for me. Have a good holiday."

Michael soon came to their corner balancing five shot glasses with one hand, a bottle of Crown Royal in the other. With a gulp, the shot he'd poured himself was gone. "Whatever you guys want, I'm buying," he said, beginning to pour himself another.

"Crown Royal's okay with me," Gene said.

"Why certainly," Dave said.

"I'll have one," said Gary.

"What the hell, Diane's gonna bitch at me anyway," followed Bob.

John Valone turned his glass upside-down before saying, "You know I never drink that stuff, Mike. But since you're buying, I'll have another Lite."

CHAPTER SIX

The dark of an early December night had fallen on Pinewood Lane when Mary Valone and Janet Silva arrived home. The wind whistled through the trees as they entered Janet's ranch-style house.

"Give me a minute to change, Mar," said Janet. "Make yourself comfortable. There's a cheese and cold-cut try in the frig."

They'd lived on Pinewood for years, though had become fast-friends while employed at Carbondale-Mercer Hospital where they'd worked in the Medical Records Department. When Valleyview General Hospital opened, Mary was promoted to Medical Staff Secretary, and Janet was selected by Anthony DeTorrio to be his Executive Secretary. While there were others equally qualified, Janet was chosen due to her marital status as well as her alluring appearance. Janet Silva remained an attractive woman despite being in her mid-fifties. Alike Mary Valone, the ravages of time hadn't even begun to fade her beauty. The shapely, buxom-chested blonde divorcee' had been pursued by many men at the hospital–DeTorrio at the head of the line.

While Mary did have a few last-minute Christmas items to buy, it was her friend who was in her thoughts when they'd departed that morning–Janet needed some cheering-up.

"This is for you, Jan, from John and I," said Mary as she handed her a small, gift-wrapped box that contained a twenty-four karat gold necklace and matching bracelet.

Elated with her present she hugged Mary, then reached under the tree for Mary's gift before heading into the kitchen. He returned with two long-stemmed glasses and a bottle of red wine. Mary had unwrapped her gift to find an exquisite crystal vase.

"Thank you, Janet," she said. "It's beautiful. I have just the right spot for it in the living room."

"I bought John some Polo shirts," said Janet, while using a corkscrew to open the wine. "I'll bring them over on Christmas."

"I'm sure he'll like them."

Janet smiled. "Come on, Mary, you can have a few more," she said, already pouring.

"Maybe just one. I had enough at the Olive Garden."

"I like wine. It makes me feel good—and it helps me forget."

After an awkward pause between them, the topic that she and Mary had avoided their entire day finally surfaced when Janet said, "I still can't believe that son of a bitch suspended me because of Dr. Burke. Like it's my fault he can't keep his dick in his pants."

"I'm sorry, Jan," said Mary. "Dr. Mancini told me what happened. He's never harassed me in the past, although I'm still worried about Burke when he starts his term as president next month."

"He won't bother you sexually, Mary. Burke only goes for the young stuff anymore. You and I are too old for his tastes."

"His wife Barbara is such a wonderful woman."

"Yes, she is," said Janet. "Though Barbara made the mistake of getting old. Burke's been running around on her for years now. How old is he?"

"Seventy-three or seventy-four."

"Whatever he is, I suppose Dr. Burke thinks he's entitled to screw whomever and wherever he wants. Did you ever meet Robin, the woman who used to work at his office?"

"No, I've spoken with her on the phone, although I never met her."

"Burke fired her last month," Janet informed. "He got rid of Robin so he could have his new girlfriend, Lisa Graham, work for him. She's the reason all this started."

"Lisa Graham. Isn't she the girl Burke was—fooling around with?"

While drinking her wine, Janet nodded slightly. "She's some whore he met in New Orleans. Now Lisa's his office worker and his mistress. Didn't Dr. Mancini tell you about a Mark Nelson?"

"—No," said Mary, failing to see the connection. "Sam just told me about Dr. Burke and Lisa in the doctors' lounge. He never mentioned any Mark Nelson to me."

"Sam probably doesn't know all the facts. Tony made damn sure Burke kept it quiet. And you wouldn't know about Nelson since he didn't die at the hospital."

"I don't understand, Janet. If the man didn't die at the hospital, how do you know so much about him?"

"Because that was the same day I overheard Tony swearing at Burke," she replied a bit crossly, then gulped what remained of her wine. "Here's what really happened. Mark Nelson, who was younger than us, had been to Burke's office complaining of chest pains. Now you're certainly aware that Burke's been passing himself off as a cardiologist?"

"Oh, yes, I know his medical credentials inside-out. Dr. Burke's a general practitioner whose expertise in cardiology consists of a one week seminar. Tony started letting Burke evaluate some of the hospitals' cardiograms because they're friends from the old hospital, and Burke comes cheaper than any board-certified cardiologist would. That's why Dr. Harvey's gone. Tony refused to renew his contract."

"Exactly. So now Burke's acting like a cardiologist at his own office, although mostly to his younger patients without any history of heart disease. To get his license to practice cardiology, Burke would need at least three years training. He has one damn week. Did you know he actually had the balls to put an electro-cardiogram into his office a few months ago?"

"Sam told me. He said Tony was steaming, since he thought Burke would be decreasing hospital revenues." Mary took a drink and said, "Although it really won't matter, since Burke assured Tony he would always order as many cardiograms for his patients if they're admitted so the hospital can make their money."

Janet poured herself another, then topped-off Mary's glass. Her cheeks were flush from the wine and her livid disposition. "So Mr. Nelson went to Burke's office complaining of chest pains. Burke took a cardiogram and read it as normal. He assured Nelson there wasn't anything wrong with his heart, and suggested he stop smoking. Later that same night, Mrs. Nelson phoned Burke's office. His service picked-up, and the wife begged for Burke to return her call because her husband was in a cold sweat and had severe angina. But instead of Burke calling Mrs. Nelson, Lisa returned the call and told her that Dr. Burke advised she give her husband some aspirin and bring him to the hospital in the morning. If the bitch wanted to play doctor, she should have told the wife to call an ambulance and take him to the hospital immediately." A swallow of wine. "Well, the next morning Mrs. Nelson woke up with a dead husband in bed."

Mary sat tight-lipped, her head bowed.

"I heard Burke tell Tony that Mr. Nelson probably died from a massive myocardial infarction," Janet went on to say. "You know better than I do a heart condition like that doesn't occur overnight."

"No," said Mary. "Burke misinterpreted his cardiogram."

"What's really a damn shame is since Burke was Mr. Nelson's PCP, the funeral director called to ask if he wanted the body sent over for a postmortem. Of course Burke said it wasn't necessary and instructed the mortician to list congestive heart failure on the death certificate. Mary, you can add another death Burke and Tony swept under the rug in order to protect the hospital."

"Jan, whenever it comes to Tony, I wouldn't put anything past him," said Mary, her tone now just as ambivalent. "He never fails to find a way to conceal the truth."

"Don't I know it," she said with a huff. "Anyhow, it was next afternoon when the little twerp called me in. He told me he'd paged Burke without his responding, nor was he answering his cell phone. So he insisted I go find him. When I asked if he had any idea where Burke could be, guess what he shouted at me."

"—I'm—"

"His exact words were, 'How in the fuck would I know where he is, you dumb Jew bitch!'" Janet finished her drink. "That little bastard. I just pray for the day when somebody who isn't on the payroll overhears him insulting me. It actually makes me physically sick when I hear different people I speak with say how congenial he is to them."

"He's a hypocrite, Janet. He's always been a hypocrite."

"Then you've got all those flunkies on the Board of Directors voting to keep increasing his salary, which is over a half-million now. I've heard Tony brag he makes more money than any doctor on staff."

Janet stood, her knees pressed together. "Mary, the wine's running straight threw me. Drink another glass, and eat something."

While Janet was relieving herself, Mary Valone recollected some of the many vicious remarks that had been leveled at her by Anthony DeTorrio. She'd become so upset after one of his tantrums, she was crying at home after work. Though when John found her weeping, she wouldn't admit the reason.

Anthony DeTorrio remained on Janet's mind when she returned. Seeing Mary's empty glass, she poured. "I hate that little bastard," Janet said.

"Janet, I honestly don't know how you can tolerate working for that man. He's insulted me before, but he's never called me anything as vulgar as what he called you."

"Oh, I've heard worse that Jew bitch. He really gets his rocks off insulting me."

"Ignorant little son of a bitch."

Janet vigorously nodded. "Getting back to Burke, when I went to look for him, the receptionist told me she had just seen Burke pass by and he was going in the direction of the doctors' lounge. So I went there and knocked on the door. Nobody answered, so I knocked again and called his name. I heard what sounded like 'come in.' So I opened the door, and there he was screwing Lisa. He looked over his shoulder at me, then turned away and kept on going. I didn't say anything, but the mistake I made was I left the door opened."

Janet paused for another long swallow of wine before saying, "I didn't know what to do, so I stopped by your office, but you weren't there. After about twenty minutes I went back to the Administration

Building. When I came into the front office, there was Tony sitting in my chair with his feet propped on my desk. I was so nervous when I tried to explain. He just sat there with that smirk on his face. When I'd finished, he screamed something like, 'You stupid bitch, you should have closed the goddamned door! You're suspended for two weeks without pay. Maybe next time you keep your nose out of places it doesn't belong!'"

Janet Silva took a piece of cheese, and washed it down with another gulp of wine. "That's the kind of administrator we work for, Mary. He has no regard whatsoever about the quality of healthcare we provide. All he's concerned about is himself, keeping revenues up and the medical staff, in that order. He's a despicable little man."

"I feel so bad for you," said Mary.

"The fact he made us resign from the union still burns my ass. If he wanted to, that schmuck could invent a reason to fire either of us. So help me, the day I quit I'm going to slug him in the mouth."

Janet lurched forward, her face a deep shade of crimson. "How about some more wine?"

"No, I've had plenty," said Mary, using her hand to cover her glass.

At last Janet managed a grin. "John asked me to get you a little tipsy."

"I figured as much."

"Honey, you are so lucky to still have him at home with you. He is such a sweetheart."

Mary beamed at Janet's complementing her son, then said, "Jan, I've been thinking of quitting the hospital. I keep telling John to get married so I can help take care of his grandchildren."

"You should quit, regardless of what John does. You don't need all the bullshit anymore."

"I just might after the Joint Commissions' inspection this summer."

"The hell on the JC, Mary!" she said. "You're too damn dedicated as it is now. Let the little piss-ant worry about them. The day you quit, Tony will pull out what's left of his hair since no one else knows your job. You and I are the only two confidential secretaries there because

Tony's convinced the less people who really know the truth about what goes on at the hospital, the better he is."

"He was the same way at the old hospital."

"I remember all too well," said Janet, shaking her head in disgust. "Although from what I keep hearing, don't be surprised if that changes real soon."

"Why, Janet? What have you heard?"

"I was talking with Pam Kramer from Medical Records. Do you know her?"

"I say hi when I see her, although I don't know her that well. Did you hear she's going to be promoted?"

"No, not her. All Pam kept talking about was this other girl who'd started work the same day as she did. Her name's Debbie Nichols. Do you know who she is?"

"I think. Thirtyish, on the heavy side, long black hair."

"That's her! Janet exclaimed, as she downed yet another glass of wine. "Pam introduced us one day. Real snotty bitch. I couldn't believe the shirt that girl was wearing. When she walked, I could almost see her fat ass. And her hair was so greasy, she looked like she hadn't washed for a month. Anyway, Pam told me that Mrs. O'Donnell from Personnel called her in and told her to start wearing more professional clothing to work. Yet she still wears the short skirts. Lord, if I were that overweight, I'd wear baggy dresses that dragged the floor."

The two ladies cackled at Janet's latest remark. The wine was making Mary giddy. "Maybe she thinks she'll catch a man dressing like a bimbo," Mary said.

"As usual, you're absolutely right," said Janet. "And according to Pam, she has her eye on Tony for the time being. Pam told me that every time he walks into the department, Nichols flirts outrageously with him. She mentioned one day in particular when Tony came in. Nichols actually put her arm around him. They were whispering, and the supervisor just stayed at her desk, afraid to move. Then they took off together. Now here's the best part. When Debbie came back into the department, she had holes in her nylons on both kneecaps. Don't you just wonder what they were doing?"

Mary only offered a shrug before saying, “It doesn’t surprise me one bit. I’ve heard all kinds of stories what a pervert he is.”

“Repulsive pervert is more like it,” said Janet. “Ever since that day, Pam told me that every time she speaks with Nichols, all she talks about is how she’s going to be promoted out of Medical Records. She keeps telling Pam that she’d like working in either of our offices. She actually has delusions about marrying Tony or a doctor, that’s how stupid she is. Still, don’t be surprised if that fat slut gets transferred into one of our offices.”

As their conversation continued, Janet struggled to stay awake. Eventually Mary saw Janet’s eyes were closed.

“Jan, I’d better be leaving,” she said in a whisper.

“Okay, Mary,” replied Janet, wavering to lift herself up. “Let me find my keys.”

“That’s alright, I can walk home.”

“Forget it, I’m driving you. I think I’ll kidnap your son.”

*****

Mary awoke on Sunday with a thumping headache. She made her way into the bathroom, fumbling about the medicine cabinet for Advil. Not only was her head ringing, she also felt a mild pain in her lower back. It astounded her that she’d slept so long, recalling she gotten home shortly after ten o’clock, and had passed-out the moment her head hit the pillow–that was twelve hours ago.

After a hot bath, Mary was covered by a pink flannel bathrobe as she made her way into the kitchen. The clanging of the weights repeatedly hitting the metallic base of John’s home-gym only enhanced her headache. With the coffee pot readied to brew, Mary began the descent to the basement. Able to hear her in the kitchen, John had stopped exercising and was toweling his bare-chest and abdomen when she arrived at the bottom of the stairs.

“Hey, look who’s awake,” he said, keeping a straight face as she strolled towards him.

“Good morning, John.”

“Morning, Ma.”

As Mary kept rubbing her forehead, he said, "Oh my, don't we look a little rugged this morning."

"Janet and I had a few drinks."

"I can see that. I'd say you had a few too many."

"You're right about that. My limit is two. I had about eight."

"You'll feel better after some coffee," he said, gently massaging her shoulders. "There I was home alone last night watching *The Deer Hunter* and *Taxi Driver*, while my pretty little mother is out getting herself all liquored-up. What's the world coming to?"

"Oh, be quiet," she said.

Together they walked the steps. Once at the kitchen table, John pulled the chair back for her, then poured Mary's coffee.

"Head hurts, huh?" he said.

"Yes."

"Bad?"

"Yes."

"Well then, I may have some news that'll perk you up, but I'm only going to tell you if you promise me you'll take it easy today. I promise that I'll run the sweeper, and help you with all the cooking on Christmas morning before Janet gets here."

"John, the way I feel, all I want to do today is rest. You win. No Sunday cleaning. Just tell me something, anything that will make this damn headache go away."

"Guess who was here yesterday?"

"I give up, who?" was her reply, prior to sipping her coffee.

"Vicky Gill."

Mary's hazel-green eyes lit-up. "Why didn't you tell me Vicky was coming here? I would have loved to see her."

"You already had other plans. Besides—ah, you know."

"I want you to invite Vicky over for dinner on Christmas."

"Not on Christmas."

"Why not on Christmas?"

"It's too soon."

"Invite her on Christmas."

"She's having dinner with Butch and his family."

"Invite her in the evening."

"I didn't buy her anything."

"Then get off your butt, take a shower, and drive to the mall. Go buy Vicky a nice piece of jewelry."

"Ma, the next piece of jewelry I'm hoping to give her is the diamond ring I got stashed in my bedroom."

Mary Valone's radiant smile exhibited her joy. "Vicky's a beautiful girl."

"Yeah, we're going to give it another shot. Vicky doesn't seem as uncompromising as she was before."

"I want you to invite her here for dinner some night soon."

"We'll see. I'm going to ask her to Bob Cook's New Year's Eve party. If she doesn't scream at me for being with my friends before the end of the night, then we'll have her over."

Mary slapped his arm. "Be serious, John. You'd better learn how to compromise, too. Neither of you are getting any younger. It's time for you to settle down and have a family. Vicky always was the perfect girl for you, so hurry up and marry her. Then I can retire and babysit my grandchildren."

"Whoa, Ma," he said, throwing his arms up in the air. "Slow down. I'm not going to marry her just like that. That's too spontaneous for me. I'm the planning type."

"I know why you and Vicky broke-up," she continued to press. "I'm not telling you to give up your friends entirely, but you have to make some concessions yourself. Wives don't like it when their husbands are out gallivanting in bars every night. Just ask Janet. That's why she and her ex-husband are divorced."

"Ma, I understand what you're saying. All I can promise you is that I'll do my best to make things better between Vicky and me this time around."

"Isn't it funny how life is?" she smiled. "I was just telling Janet last night that I'd like to see you get married. Maybe my dream will finally come true."

"Janet like the stuff we got her?" he said–searching for another topic.

"She loved them. I just hope the holidays help Janet of her depression."

"Janet didn't seem depressed to me yesterday. What's bothering her?"

"She's upset because she was suspended at work."

"What'd she do wrong?"

"Nothing, John. Not a damn thing."

"Then why did she get suspended?"

"Because Mr. Anthony DeTorrio wanted it that way."

CHAPTER SEVEN

"Vicky!" Diane Cook exclaimed, upon their arrival to her and Bob's home on New Year's Eve. "I'm so happy that you and John could make it tonight."

"It's wonderful seeing you again, Diane," said Vicky Gill. "Your house is so beautiful. Every house in this development looks beautiful."

Once inside, Vicky moved towards some of the other women she knew. Diane clasped John's arm and said, "You're lucky to be getting a second chance, so try being a little more considerate this time."

"Yes, dear," said John, to the charming brunette he'd known since grade school. "And a Happy New Year to you, too."

Bob Cook neared, directing John's attention at Butch Gill and Dave Bodette, seated on a brown sectional couch watching a football game as their wives and other guests mingled about the trays of hors d'oeuvres.

While observing Vicky seemingly cheerful speaking with Amy Gill, Sharon Bodette, and Diane, John said, "Bob, I gotta hand it to you and Diane. This really is a nice house."

"Costs enough to live out here with all these rich pricks," said Bob. "Although when Rol told us the land was about to go on sale, Diane had her heart set on building our own house. When you gonna start on yours?"

"Whenever," said John.

Comprehending the foundation behind John's answer, Bob offered only a shrug. Together they gazed at Vicky. "Damn, she looks great in white," said Bob, viewing the sleek dress Vicky was wearing. While Diane and the other wives of his friends and neighbors all cast attractive appearances, the sultry Vicky Gill easily stood-out.

"I told her the party was casual," John said, clad in a mint-green Polo shirt and light Lee blue jeans. "She still had to get all dressed-up like she always has to be the belle-of-the-ball."

"Ah, so she wants to make a good impression," Bob said. "I'm just glad you brought her here. Butch told me that you and Vicky might be going someplace else tonight."

"Yeah, well, she called me every day this week because she wanted to go to her girlfriend's party. I almost gave in, but I decided to test her. I told her this morning it was either here or at Mike's."

"That's the way you gotta do it," Bob assured him. "Buddy, the secret to handling women is to always let them have their way whenever you don't care what they want to do. Then whenever you really want to do something, she won't have any choice but to give in. That's the way I play it with Diane."

"I'll keep that in mind, Counselor," said John. "C'mon, swanky joint like this, you can afford to buy me a cold one."

Instead of their heading towards the gathering of people, Bob led John through the dining room–that Diane had insisted was off-limits for the evening. They entered the kitchen with a built-in breakfast counter, a cooler of beer on top. From their seats they could see all of Bob's guests, yet remain relatively inconspicuous to the crowd–arrangements they were accustomed to.

"These are our beers," said Bob. "I got Heineken and some other imported junk in the refrigerator for those snobs out there if you want to try any."

"Nah, grab me a Lite," John said, while perusing the crowd. "I don't see Gene or Rol."

"Gene's here somewhere," said Bob, handing John his beer. "Rol and Karen went to Wheeling to play the slots and dog races."

"At least they got a chance of winning on a dog race," John said. "Forget them slot machines. They're computers programmed to bleed you dry."

"I shoulda had you tell Diane that ten grand ago," Bob replied. "Maybe she would have listened to you." While gesturing to his side, Bob said, "Get a load of these goofs."

John turned to see Dave and Gene entering the kitchen.

"Hi, guys," he said. "Mean Gene, where you been hiding?"

"I was downstairs shootin' pool with some fish," said Gene with a grin. "Easiest fifty bucks I ever made."

"Where's Allison? I don't see her out there."

"Stood me up. Says she has the flu."

"Don't worry, Gene," Dave said, a wide smile across his face. "The circus is coming to town next week. Maybe the bearded lady will go out with you."

"Here's your bearded lady right here, ya hairy fuck!" Gene yelled, while cupping his crotch with his hand.

Their impulsive roar at Gene's spur-of-the-moment comeback caused some of Bob's guests to take notice. With the women remaining near the living room, they saw Butch walking towards them.

"Let's give Butch the bank story," John whispered to them.

As Butch entered the kitchen, he said, "What are you bunch of trolls yakking about?"

"We were just talking about you, Officer Gill," replied John. He eyed the others. "Guys, I suppose it's time we tell him. We need him in on the heist."

"Might as well," Bob said.

"What heist?"

"Relax, Butch, everything's all set," said John, sounding confident. "All we need to know is what shift you'll be on this week."

"I'm dayshift for the next three weeks."

Looking downward, John sighed. "Oh well, guess we gotta wait."

"We'll just have to tough it out," Gene said.

"Damn, I was counting on it," Dave followed. "Sharon and I wanted to buy a new house out here in hog-heaven."

"It'll only give us more time to refine our plans," added Bob.

"Alright, what are you fools up to?" Butch asked of them.

"Don't worry about it, big troll, we've got everything mapped-out with mathematical precision," John said, continuing to pan the living room. "The four of us and Rol will do all the work. All you gotta do is collect your cut."

"What cut?" Butch demanded, in too serious a tone.

"Okay, flatfoot, I'll come clean," said John, using his best Humphrey Bogart imitation. "We're robbing the bank when you're on midnight. Gene's gonna cause a disturbance at the Exxon station out on Route 55. While you're responding to the call, we hit the bank."

"Sure, I suppose Gene's gonna rob the gas station, too," said Butch, now convinced he was about to become the brunt of their joke.

"No way," said John. "Mean Gene could get arrested if he robbed the gas station. No, we just need him distracting you for ten minutes. Fine him for indecent exposure if you have to. That's peanuts compared to the bank."

"Butch, we got it all figured," Gene rushed to say. "I'll be sitting in my car naked parked at the Exxon station. When I see some woman stop for gas, I'll jump out and start taking a piss in her gas tank. I won't do anything crude. I'll just tell her that my coveralls got doused with gasoline. When she screams, I'll say, 'I'm sorry ma'am, I got mixed-up. I used the wrong hose!'"

Realizing they didn't have much privacy remaining following their raucous burst of laughter, John hurried to explain, "Butch, trust me, it'll go perfect. While you're at the Exxon with Gene, Dave and Rol will disarm the bank's alarm, then Bob and I will dynamite the safe. We'll grab the cash and be gone in five minutes, tops. By the time you get there, we'll be at my house divvying-up the loot. You can stop in the morning to pick up your share."

"Sorry guys, the plan has a flaw," said a smiling Butch.

"What flaw?" said Bob.

"Gene ain't tall enough to piss in the gas tank!" Butch roared.

"Okay, he can use a ladder!" John shouted above their laughter.

As their hilarious antics continued, Vicky Gill sat quietly dismayed at the commotion her date and his pals were causing.

"Boys will be boys," said Diane Cook, as she, Amy, Sharon and Vicky walked towards their men.

Seeing them near, their uproar ceased. "Pipe-down, you guys," said Bob. "We don't want them nagging us the rest of the night."

Diane allowed her husband's comment to pass. "Robert, you're ignoring our other guests. This is the first party we've ever had at this house and I don't want our neighbors thinking we're rude."

"Ah, who cares," he said, though his tone soft enough so only they could hear. "Most of those rich guys are probably embezzlers anyway. They just came here looking for another sucker to swindle."

Diane Cook took hold of his arm. "Let's go, Mr. Attorney. A friend of yours just came in while you were back here clowning around."

Amy and Sharon were next, each wrenching their husband's into the living room. Cautiously Gene drifted the other way–he'd seen Vicky's fiery disposition before.

"Did you come here to carry-on with your friends, or to spend the evening with me?" Vicky puffed, her hands on her shapely hips.

"Calm down, Vick," said John. "We were just having some fun. Hey, you wanna try a Miller Lite? Only ninety-six calories."

"No, thank you."

Eventually Vicky drew him near the living room, where Bob and Diane were participating in a conversation with other individuals. One man appeared completely out of his element with the younger set.

Arthur McNally was a pear-shaped, sixty-something wearing a tawdry, multi-colored sport coat that may have been the style a hundred years ago. Yet he projected a serious countenance, possessing an air of one driven to win. Bob had prefaced his introductions by saying Art was a legal investigator with whom he'd worked with in the past.

During their talk, it became evident to John that most of Bob's other acquaintances–along with his own gang of friends, were growing bored with him. Nevertheless, John remained impressed by him. The man had an unyielding moral compass, never vacillating when a counterpoint was made. McNally was an astute Irishman, the kind who wouldn't go down without a fight. As did the other guests whenever opportunity presented itself, Vicky Gill had politely excused herself. Yet John held sway, taken by McNally's tales of past legal cases he and Bob had been involved in, albeit their roles only periphery.

Near twenty minutes and four shooters of Irish whiskey later, Art said, "Bob, I thank you and your lovely wife for inviting me. Don't want out too late on amateur night."

"Stop anytime, Art," Bob said, shaking his hand. "I'll be in touch if something comes up."

Art smiled as he extended his hand to John. "It was a pleasure meeting you, young man."

"The pleasure was mine, Mr. McNally. I enjoyed speaking with you."

He looked in admiration at John, having encountered too many of his age who didn't have any concept of what courtesy or respect meant.

"Who was that guy?" Gene asked of Bob, as Diane led Art to the door.

"Art McNally. He works for me whenever I need him."

"He's a heck of a nice guy," John added. "Although I admit I'm not particularly fond of his tailor."

"Yeah, Art never did spend much on clothes," said Bob. "But he's still a sharp old guy."

"How'd you meet him?" said Gene.

"When I worked for Tibeau. He used Art exclusively on every big case. Tibeau swore by him." Robert Cook paused, his facial expression projecting resentment. "Should have made him a full-partner, the cases Art's digging won for that selfish prick."

"Does your old boss still use Art?" asked John, as they made their way back to the kitchen counter.

"No, Art and Tibeau really got into it one day, so Art quit for good. Couple months after I went on my own, Art came to my office and said his services were available if I ever needed them. Told me he'd rather starve than work for Walter J. Tibeau & Associates. Man, did I jump at his offer."

"Hopefully he'll help you win a big case someday," John said. "Hey, look at this pair of henpecked jokers."

"We escaped!" Dave crowed, already ducking under the countertop.

"My sister turned off the damn football game so she and another lady could watch some ditzy music show," Butch grumbled, as he reached for another beer.

"Cookie, why don't we move this party downstairs so we can shoot some pool," said John. "I see a few guys we can hustle. Mean Gene, your fish still out there?"

On her way to the refrigerator for more appetizers, Diane overheard. "Forget it, John," she said. "This is a party, not a pool hall. You and Bob aren't going to hustle any of my guests."

"Maybe after midnight," said Bob.

"Robert! No pool."

"Okay, dear," John said, contented that Vicky and the other women were watching television. "No pool tonight."

As before, the guys stayed around the breakfast counter. The activity in the living room had slowed, with what few remaining guests of Bob and Diane's now viewing TV awaiting the midnight celebration. Yet soon after, more outrageous outbursts ensued from the kitchen. As their rowdy antics continued, Vicky Gill looked-on from the sofa.

"Girls, I honestly don't understand how you stand it," she said. "They're acting worse than *The Three Stooges*."

"You just have to put your foot down every now and then," said Sharon Bodette.

"They really aren't so bad once you get used to it," Diane followed.

"That's the problem, Diane. I'll never get used to it."

"Vicky, if you have any hopes of landing John, the most eligible bachelor in Vernon Park, you'd better get used to it, and fast," Amy Gill candidly informed her sister-in-law. "They're inseparable whenever they get together. They've been the best of friends since grade school, and they intend on staying that way."

"All their nonsense" said Vicky. "All the noise they make."
"It's part of who they are," said Diane.
"Vicky, you should look at it our way," Amy said.
"And what way might that be, Amy?"
"Be glad none of them are troublemakers."

CHAPTER EIGHT

"Medical Staff Office," Mary Valone answered her telephone.

"Mary, it's me," spoke the voice of Janet Silva, on her first day back to work.

"Hi, Jan. Everything okay over there?"

"So far."

"How's Tony behaving?"

"Actually he's been fairly quiet this morning, then he went to lunch early. Just before he took-off, he had me contact Dr. Burke and Dr. Cameron to confirm meetings he scheduled with them this afternoon."

Mary hesitated briefly, considering both physicians. "I'd guess Tony just wants to gab with Burke about the medical staff in general. Dr. Cameron—I'm not sure."

"I'm not sure, either. I do know that Dr. Cameron requested the meeting. I'll call you at home tonight and tell you what went on."

"Janet, please be careful. I don't want you getting fired. Tony was in a bad mood yesterday. He was in my office pestering me."

"About what?"

"Nothing in particular. That's just his style of management. The hospital is his kingdom, and he likes reminding me and everyone else that he's the king."

"I really don't care anymore, Mar. This place is becoming a bus stop for a one-way trip to the cemetery. And when it comes to Tony, it disgusts me to even look at the skinny, bald bastard. At least he won't be scratching his pecker when he walks past me from now on. He saves that for Debbie Nichols, his new whore."

"Janet!"

"Mary, there isn't any doubt he's screwing her. Remember my telling you when that pig gave him a blowjob?"

"I remember."

"Listen to what happened this morning. At nine-thirty, Nichols came waddling in. I told her to wait until I buzzed Tony. 'He's expecting me, blondie.' That's what she said to me. She was in his office for over an hour. I heard the door lock after she went in, and that was the last sound I was able to hear until she left. Tony must have taken her into that room behind his office. Pretty easy to guess what they were doing back there, wouldn't you say?"

"With the scruples he has, yes, it's pretty easy."

"She's the first person to walk into his office unannounced ever since I became his secretary. Oh, I was talking with Pam. The latest rumor is that her and Tony started shacking-up on Wednesday's after work. I'm tempted to follow him tonight to see where they stay."

"Don't do it, Janet. As paranoid as Tony is, he'll be looking for someone following him. If he sees you, he'll fire you for sure."

"Hummmhh, that's the only way that fat tramp will ever get my job," said the gregarious Janet. "Pam says that Nichols is by far the worst clerk in the department. While I was suspended, Pam told me their supervisor ordered Debbie to stop taking so many breaks and try concentrating on improving her work. Ten minutes later, Tony called her over here. She hasn't said one word since. Tony must have threatened her job."

"Janet, if she's really that incompetent, there isn't anything for you to be concerned about. You know as well as I that Tony insists we be efficient, and complete our work on time. He isn't about to hand her a difficult job if she's inept. I say he keeps her in Medical Records."

"Don't be too sure about that, Mary."

*****

Dr. Donald Burke arrived promptly at 1 P.M. "Good afternoon, Ms. Silva," he said in well-mannored fashion.

"Doctor," she muttered, her resentment for him intact. "I'll buzz him."

DeTorrio's door opened. "Come in, Don," he said, beckoning towards his office–paying Janet no attention whatsoever.

Anthony DeTorrio was very fond of Dr. Burke. Prior to his seizing control at Carbondale-Mercer Hospital, Dr. Donald Burke was he foremost ally. While DeTorrio was in the midst of overthrowing Kent Flynn, Dr. Burke emerged as his main supporter. Forever popular with his peers, Burke had always wielded tremendous influences among his colleagues, and it was due to his many efforts that his fellow physicians joined to rid themselves of Flynn. Burke had also petitioned friends on the Board of Directors to side with the new man and his innovative ideas for the future.

After his coup succeeded, his domination firmly entrenched, DeTorrio didn't forget the doctor whose support was crucial in the realignment of power. Upon the genesis of Valleyview General Hospital, DeTorrio formed a new position: The President of the Medical Staff. Dr. Burke was awarded the office.

"How are you, Don?" said DeTorrio, once they were seated.

"Just fine, Anthony. Heard you were in Rome over the holidays. Good trip?"

"Could have been better. Rained every day. Incredible city, though."

"Did you go to Vatican City?"

"Yeah, we went. The goddamned Pope wasn't anywhere to be seen."

"Well, maybe next time. At least you got away from here. You certainly deserved a vacation."

DeTorrio sighed. "Had to get stuck taking my wife. All she wanted to do was go sightseeing and eat. I sure could have used some nice young pussy like you've been getting."

Dr. Burke's unblushing smile mirrored his preen. "Yes, Sir, Lisa sure keeps the old ticker going strong. Nothing like walking around all day with a hard-on at my age."

"Lisa sure beats the hell out of that nurse who got caught blowing you in the elevator at the old hospital," laughed DeTorrio. "Christ, she a homely-lookin' bitch with her big beak-nose and her snaggled teeth."

"Ruth Saunders," replied Burke with a smirk. "Gold old Nurse Blowjob we used to call her. I wasn't the only doctor she was sucking, Tony. She was so desperate to marry a doctor, she'd do anything we asked of her. It was before your time, but I remember when she used to blow doctors in their cars. They even caught her fucking an intern near ICU."

"I found out all about her from the Director of Nursing," he said. "That's why I canned her ass before we opened Valleyview. I couldn't let her keep sucking and fucking you guys in the wards or in the parking lots. Too dangerous a risk." As infrequently as they came, Anthony DeTorrio displayed a grin before saying, "It's a shame Nurse Blowjob wasn't a young baby-doll like Lisa. Exceptions could have been made."

Dr. Burke smiled, displaying his stained teeth. "Similar to the exception you made when you were letting that Faddant girl from Admissions clean your pipes. Right, Tony?"

"Don, that was just gossip."

"Come on, Tony boy!" said Burke. "Dr. Cameron saw you registering at The Comfort Inn with her. Admit it, that girl made you feel like a kid again."

DeTorrio grinned and said, "Yes, she sure did."

"Okay, so find yourself another young girl. It'll do wonders for you."

"I just may do that," he chirped between their snickers.

The doctor glanced at the clock above DeTorrio. "What else is new, Tony? I already promised you no more Lisa in the doctors' lounge."

"How does everything look to you in the Staff Office?"

"Everything seems fine," replied the venerable practitioner of medicine, attired in a dark pinstriped suit. "Mrs. Valone's always been an extremely capable employee."

"She's adequate," DeTorrio respond quickly–never the sort to bestow praise upon subordinates. "How about Mancini's numbers on the death-counts?"

"They weren't too bad last year, but I'll redo the statistics to increase the natural-causes like I always do."

"Mr. Nelson? Anything new on him?"

"Not to my knowledge. If the widow was planning on making a fuss, one of us would have heard about it by now." Burke shrugged his shoulders. "If she does pursue it, Lisa will stand by me."

"Excellent," said DeTorrio. "We don't need the County Coroner rummaging through everything looking for skeletons. Both are asses could wind-up in slings."

"Stop worrying, we're safe on Nelson," said Burke, while picking a gray hair from the lapel of his suit. "Tony, I hate to rush you, but is there anything else? Lisa's waiting for me."

"Oh, oh, I can't be holding you from her. Just briefly though, since you mentioned Mary Valone, I keep hearing she may have some sort of issue with her back. Know anything about it?"

"Only that she appears to be in some discomfort at times. Sam Mancini's concerned she may have the beginnings of a degenerative disc, although Mary keeps insisting it's nothing serious. Nevertheless, I think Sam intends to order an MRI for her."

A staid expression immediately spread across Anthony DeTorrio's face. "Fuck. Bad timing if she needs surgery. Real bad timing."

"Why's that?"

"I received word the Joint Commission will be paying us a visit earlier than usual this year. My contact told me to expect them in late March. Mary's the only secretary I have who understands the credentialing requirements and all that other nuisance documentation those cocksuckers always check. Don, what are we going to do if she needs an operation before then?"

"Good question," Burke said. "That's why Sam and I kept telling you that Mary should have an assistant. The woman is overloaded with work as it is now. Maybe it's time you assigned her some help."

"You're right, Don, I'll do just that. For now, I'll have Mary give top priority to the credentials. Oh, and please do me a favor."

"What is it?" said an impatient Dr. Burke.

"If you do find out Mary has a bad disc, try convincing her to hold off surgery until the Joint Commissions' inspection is finished."

"I'll try, but Mancini's the key, not me. Sam's been her doctor ever since I can remember, and she always does as he advises."

*****

Fifteen minutes later, DeTorrio's swung open with such force that it bounced off the wall. "Where the fuck is Cameron!" he shouted at Janet.

"He called to say he's running behind schedule, but he said he'd be here before two-thirty," Janet answered with composure, her eyes fixed upon her computer.

"Why didn't you tell me before?"

"Because you said not to disturb you when Dr. Burke went out."

The megalomaniac snapped his lips. "Pay attention to me, dimwit. I have a business function to attend this evening. I'm going to take a quick shave. Buzz me when Cameron gets here, though tell him I'm on the phone. Think you can handle that?"

"Yes, Sir," she said, though thinking to herself, *"Business function my ass. The only business he has tonight is with his fat slut."*

As he neared his office, Tony DeTorrio came to an abrupt stop. He turned to Janet. "Wait just a damn minute," he said, "Cameron wants to see me. Let him wait. Tell fucking Cameron—"

"Tell fucking Cameron what?" said Dr. Steven Cameron, as he opened the outer door.

"Steve, how are you?" DeTorrio replied coyly, removing his foot from his mouth. "I was about to inquire with Ms. Silva as to when we should be expecting you."

The husky doctor of middle-age with his dark red hair and mustache, decked in a gray, three-piece suit easily perceived the tact DeTorrio was using. Beholding the stupefied expression on the DeTorrio's face was enough for Cameron. "Sorry I'm late," he said. "Hello, Ms. Silva. Tony."

"Hi, Dr. Cameron," said Janet.

"Come in, Steve," followed DeTorrio as he ushered Dr. Cameron into his office. "Anything to accommodate my favorite neurologist."

Once Dr. Cameron had tossed his overcoat onto the chair next to his, DeTorrio went on to say, "Now, what may I do for you?"

From the moment he was informed that Dr. Cameron desired a meeting, DeTorrio had been concerned. The doctor's practice as a neurologist generated huge revenues for the hospital. As Dr. Cameron unlocked his briefcase, Anthony DeTorrio's intuition told him his worst fears were about to materialize.

"Tony, I'm not here to argue with you," he said. "My income's been in decline the past few years. Most of the people from this area are turning to other neurologists, mainly due to the fact they're apprehensive about having surgery performed here. Quite frankly, I can't say that I blame them with the neurosurgeons you have on staff. I've had enough of the situation, and I intend to take immediate action."

"Don't you think you're overreacting a bit? Our neurosurgeons—"

"Aren't worth a damn," Cameron interrupted. "Look, I understand we have an agreement. However I'm the one who is being included in the legal actions patients who were operated on at Valleyview are filing against them for botched surgeries. Tony, I'm sorry. Under the present circumstances, I can't continue like this. Pretty soon I'll be peddling medical supplies."

"Come now, Steve," he said. "Dr. Zimmerman is an excellent neurosurgeon. And I know for a fact that nobody has ever sued him since he's been at Valleyview."

"Zimmerman should have been a butcher," said Dr. Cameron, looking DeTorrio squarely in the eye. "And what's really scary is he's the best of the bunch. Tony, you're certainly aware that when I refer a patient for surgery, I'm held responsible for their aftercare. I've studied too many films taken post-op of Zimmerman's surgical cases. I wouldn't let that cretin operate on my wife's cat, and I can't stand the damn thing. Therefore as of right now, I will not spoon-feed any of my people to any neurosurgeon at this hospital."

Despite his hunch that Dr. Cameron hadn't called the meeting to again convey his usual provocations, the doctor's resolve jolted DeTorrio–it was time for drastic measures. "Dr. Cameron, I give you my word, I will do all I can to replace Zimmerman along with all the other neurosurgeons as soon as possible."

"Tony, be realistic, even you don't have that kind of clout," Cameron said. "You can't revoke their surgical privileges until their contracts expire. As a result, things here will remain status quo. Although it's now irrelevant to me, since I've entered into a business venture that was just too lucrative to let slip by."

While Dr. Cameron's new agenda was certain to decrease profits, Anthony DeTorrio shelved the urge to impart his animosity–not until the doctor had unveiled more of his intentions. "Does this mean you're resigning from the Valleyview General Medical Staff?"

Dr. Cameron pulled a manila envelope from his briefcase. "If that's the way you want it, my letter of resignation is enclosed."

"Steve, please," said DeTorrio. "You're the only neurologist we have on staff right now." Almost a moan. "We're fucked without a neurologist."

"Then out of deference for you, I'll continue to make myself available for consultation," said Cameron. "Albeit with the specific understanding that I will never refer any of my patients to your surgeons."

"Perhaps I'd grasp all of this somewhat better if you would explain a little about your new business venture."

"I'm surprised you haven't heard already," Cameron said. "Tony, I've entered into a limited partnership with an orthopedic, Dr. Harold Elliot. We'll be occupying an office at the Shadydell Heights Hospital Professional Building. We've purchased an MRI and X-Ray unit."

Cameron smiled. "We'll be raking in money hand-over-fist on the films. Judging from the projections my accountant sent me, my income should double this year."

"And your surgical cases? I'd presume Dr. Campbell."

"Duncan Campbell is a gifted neurosurgeon, no doubt about it. However when a patient of mine requires surgery, I intend to refer them to a neurosurgeon who operates exclusively at Shadydell Heights, Dr. Rasheem Nasser."

"The fuck kind of name is Rasheem Nasser!" DeTorrio demanded of him, no longer hiding his acrimony.

Dr. Cameron ignored his frustration. "I believe he's either of Syrian or Lebanese descent."

"What! You're giving all of your surgical cases to some terrorist from the Middle East! Steve, have you lost your marbles! Ever hear of nine-eleven! You'd better have your accountant factor his nationality into your doubling your income!"

"Dr. Nasser isn't a terrorist, he was born in Detroit!" growled Cameron in return. "And regardless of his ethnicity, I've seen him in the OR. It's my opinion, along with my colleagues who have had the opportunity to observe Dr. Nasser that he's an extremely talented neurosurgeon. On par, perhaps even superior to Dr. Campbell. So that's the way it's going to be, whether you like it or not."

With Dr. Cameron having all the leverage–in addition to his recognizing the neurologist's temperament was about to boil-over, Anthony DeTorrio was forced into retreat-mode. "So exactly what will be you commitment towards Valleyview General?"

"I'll do all I can for you," said Cameron, softening his position. "For example, when a doctor puts out a consult for me here, I'll order the films be taken here. I can always request the patient have another set taken at my office. Also, if the patient only needs physical therapy, they can have it here as opposed to Shadydell. How's that sound?"

"I can live with that," DeTorrio said. "But what about the cases you're brought into when the patient's already been admitted to Valleyview? What happens to them when surgery is indicated? You're going to send all of them to the Syrian, whatever the fuck he is."

The doctor frowned while adjusting his tie. "As I stated, any patient of mine who requires surgery, I will be recommending Dr. Nasser."

"That's not fair, Steve!"

"I am prepared to make a final counter-proposal," said Cameron. "If they're welfare or other indigent types, and provided it isn't too serious a condition, I'll leave the choice to them. If they're stupid enough to stay at Valleyview and let Zimmerman operate, he can have them. However, I'm warning you right here and now, the first lawsuit I get hit with due to Zimmerman, I'll steer every last patient away from him."

Anthony DeTorrio let out a heavy sigh and said, "So to summarize, our Physical Therapy Department will continue to treat your patients, and we'll conduct the films on your patients whenever a consult is issued here. But when it comes to the surgical cases, with the exception of the destitute, you'll be pipelining all of my people to some Middle East sandnigger with whom you probably have a kickback arrangement—"

"Hey, Tony!" Cameron interrupted in heated voice. "Lose the attitude or I'll withdraw my offer right now. I feel I'm being more than generous. The entire problem stems from the ineptitude of Valleyview General's neurosurgeons. You're responsible for hiring them, hence your hospital's financial statement will suffer until they're gone."

Dr. Cameron's glare remained indignant awaiting a response. None was offered as DeTorrio sat quietly in thought–a rarity when the tyrant was compelled into submission. Sensing additional hostilities weren't forthcoming, Cameron's past allegiances swayed him to end their meeting on a peaceful note.

"Look at the bright side, Tony," he said. "Eventually you will be able to remove Zimmerman and the rest of those incompetents. Once they're gone and you've found at least one quality replacement, I'll resume keeping some of the locals in need of surgery here. Yes, it is going to hurt Valleyview financially for the time being, though in the long-run it will be better for everyone."

"Perhaps," he sullenly yielded. "I certainly can't fault your logic. The hospital will suffer a monetary hit, yet we'll become a better facility with quality neurosurgeons. And without your referrals, they might all resign anyway before I'm in position to get rid of them. Alright, Valleyview will just have to make due. Although please promise me you'll keep ordering as many films and therapy sessions for your patients as their insurance will allow."

"Tony, nothing will change in that regard," said Cameron. "You're aware that insurance companies are hesitant about questioning neurologists. Every time some bean-counter complains about his firm paying multiple times for a film-study, I simply inform them that I wasn't positive of the results." Dr. Cameron reached for his coat. "That always shuts them up."

With pragmatism his only recourse, Anthony DeTorrio stood to say, "Steve, I wish you success with your practice, and I look forward to seeing you again."

"I'll be around, Tony," said Cameron. "Oh, here's a suggestion that will interest you. Instruct your billing coordinator to start up-coding the welfare and Medicare people a few levels of treatment. They never bother verifying what's submitted. You'll increase revenues with no risk involved."

The autocrat smiled as to show Cameron whose territory he was now treading. "I've been doing that ever since I became Executive Director."

*****

Anthony DeTorrio couldn't dismiss the day's events from his awareness as he drove to The Traveler's Motor Lodge. Dr. Cameron had perturbed to such an extent that he'd taken four Valium to ease his nerves. The irritation of not having any alternative to Cameron ripped at him. Two more tranquilizers were dropped prior to his departure from Valleyview General Hospital, as DeTorrio remained obsessed with how the ramifications of Dr. Cameron's sudden defection would tarnish his icon of efficiency. Despite the Board of Directors being his pawns, he realized a few would make inquiries. And while they would accept his craven excuses why Cameron had gone his own path, DeTorrio feared the grumbles of criticism that would be spoken for his not being able to remedy the Cameron situation. DeTorrio's paranoia was rampant as he pulled his black Lincoln Continental into the motel's parking lot.

As she watched him near, Debra Nichols stood with the door ajar, adorned in a see-through, burgundy negligee that left nothing to the imagination. "Hello, lover," she cooed. "Like my new outfit?"

"Just dandy," he said, slamming the door behind him while holding her at bay. "Christ, this place is a dump. The hotel in Rome was a palace, and I have to come home to this shithole."

"There are a few nicer hotels closer to the hospital," she said. "We'll try one of them next week."

"Not too swift, are you Debbie?" he replied. "I specifically picked this place because of the location. That's all I'd need is for someone to call my wife and ask her why my car's parked at a hotel near the hospital. It'd be all over but the shouting. The bitch would serve me with divorce papers faster than shit through a goose."

"Would that be so bad?"

"Goddamn right it would when you own all I do! I'm not about to let her take my property and pay her alimony on top of that."

Seated on the bed removing his shoes, Debbie dove on top of him. As they tossed about, her hand slid between his legs while she kissed him wildly. Unreceptive to her advances, she rolled off him and hurriedly removed her flimsy garment exposing her plump, nude figure. Her body gave off a quiver of desire.

"Come on, honey, fuck me," she whined, placing his hand on her furry bush.

"Later." DeTorrio hopped from the bed. "Where's the scotch?"

"In my purse," she said in rejected tone of voice.

Debbie watched as he gulped the scotch. "There's water and glasses on the nightstand."

"I don't want any."

"Oh, my poor baby," she said. "Lay down and tell me all your problems. I'll make everything better."

Tony stripped his pants. "The fucking hospital's my problem, what else."

"Something bad happen?"

"Fuckin' doctors. Bunch of greedy bastards."

On her knees, Debbie Nichols' began fondling his limp penis. "Tony, you're not going to be able to get it up if you keep drinking like that."

His brooding endured. "Then get it up for me," he said, pulling her by the base of her neck.

Debbie didn't need any encouragement, as she voraciously engulfed his sexual organ.

Looking down at her, he enjoyed how adept the wench was at performing the act–it was as she'd been born to service him. He savored the sensation of being vigorously sucked dry as he felt his juices ready to flow. Letting out a grunt while ejaculating, he saw glee in her eyes.

After she'd swallowed, Debbie licked at her poorly-endowed lover's member. "He really likes that," she said, her tongue still swirling about. "Fell better now, lover?"

"Believe it, honey," he said, huffing. "Deb, you can sure suck a mean dick."

What hardness he had gone, she lifted from her knees to say, "Tony, I'm starving. How about if I get us something to eat while you're recharging."

"No, I'm going home."

"Your wife's bridge-club lasts until eleven."

"I'm just not in the mood to screw, Deb," he said, while reaching for his pants. "I've got too much on my mind."

"Tony!" she cried, bouncing onto the bed to spread her cellulite thighs. "You can stay longer. Please. Be the best piece of ass you've ever had."

Though enticed by the sight of her finger dipping into her open vagina, he knew all the pills and scotch had added to his inherent sexual deficiencies. "Damn it—I can't stay. Come to my office tomorrow afternoon."

"Tony, what went on at those meetings today?"

"Deb, I don't care to discuss them. That reminds me, though."

"Reminds you of what?" she whimpered, as she pulled the sheet over her torso.

"Friday will be your last day in Medical Records. Monday morning you'll report to Mary Valone." He zipped his pants. "You're her new assistant."

"Assistant! Fire that old lady and make me the Medical Staff Secretary."

"Don't be ridiculous! Debbie, you haven't the slightest idea of all that goes on there. You've had it easy in Records, repeatedly processing the same formatted reports again and again. In the Medical Staff Office, there's plenty for you to learn. Mary knows her job."

"Assign me only the easy jobs," she said. "Make her do everything else."

"I'll let Mary know exactly what duties I want you to learn," he said. "I expect to hear that you're at least trying to learn the job. And don't let me find out that your cockteasing any of the damn doctors."

"You're the only man I want, Tony. I'm not interested in any of the doctors. Just you."

DeTorrio eyed her coldly before saying, "As for Mary being an old lady, she types over a hundred words per minute on her PC, she understands medical terminology just as well as the doctors, and she knows how to use the hospital's complete software package almost as well as I do."

"I'm getting better on the computer every day now."

"Yeah," he said, insultingly. "Before long, you'll be up to five reports per week. Unlike yours, Mary's work is always completed ahead of schedule."

A final drink of scotch. "Oh, and Miss Nichols. Mary's younger than I am. Does that make me an old man?"

"—No."

"Any other questions?"

CHAPTER NINE

"Dr. Mancini, please come in."

"How are you, John?" he said, while warmly shaking the hand of the man he'd delivered at birth.

"I'm worried, Sam," said John. "She keeps telling me she's okay. Then I heard her tell Janet that she had an MRI."

"I understand," he said. "Your mother isn't the complaining type."

"Did you see her MRI report?"

"Yes."

"Is it bad?"

"Is Mary awake? We'll discuss it with her."

"Have a seat, Sam. I'll get her."

While there were other doctors of high character on the staff at Valleyview General Hospital, Dr. Samuel Mancini was of exceptional moral fiber. A trim, handsome man in his mid-fifties with four grown children, nary a wrinkle on his face, his salt-and-pepper hair the only indicator of age. The kind of man who would never stray from his wife, his family and patients his only priorities. With the ink barely dry on his license to practice medicine, Mary Valone had become one of his first patients.

Entering Mary's bedroom, John found her asleep. Nudging her arm, she opened her eyes.

"Is Sam here yet?" she asked.

"He's in the living room."

"Tell him I'll be a minute."

"She'll be right out," John said, dashing through the hallway. "Can I get you a cup of coffee?"

"No, thanks, John."

"Sam, she keeps sayin' its arthritis."

"I'm afraid it's a bit more serious than arthritis."

"What's wrong with her?"

Dr. Mancini held his response, as he and John saw Mary slowly pacing toward them.

"Hello, Sam," she said.

"Hi, Mary," said the doctor, moving to greet her. Dr. Mancini gave her a delicate hug. "How are you feeling this morning?" He guided her to the couch–observing Mary's every movement until she was seated.

"Better than I did earlier," she said. "Sam, my lower back was sore when I woke up, and the left side of my rear-end felt numb. The numbness went away, but I know what causes it. I think my sciatic nerve is becoming impaired."

"That was Dr. Eisen's conclusion as well," said Mancini. "He's of the opinion you do have a bulging, deteriorating disc at the L4-L5 level. It hasn't herniated yet, although Dr. Eisen believes that it's only a matter of time. The pain you're been experiencing is due to the fact that the disc-body is bulging fairly substantially. As a result, it is causing your sciatic nerve to become irritated."

"And it's only going to get worse until the disc eventually does rupture."

"I'm afraid so," said a sincere Dr. Mancini. "Mary, I'm not an expert in orthopedics, but the L4-L5 level is very prone to herniation. It is one of the most common areas of the spine that is susceptible to injury."

Mary Valone wasn't the sort of woman to just fall apart at the seams when given bad news. She had encountered difficult times before. Her intelligence, added to her unabated resolve had always seen her through. It was her nature to rise above adversity. "So I'll need an operation on by spine," she said.

"Dr. Eisen believes it's inevitable," said Mancini. "While your back is stable for now, one wrong movement could cause the disc to herniate. If it does, you'll need immediate surgery."

"Sam, I want Dr. Duncan Campbell from Allegheny Central in Pittsburgh," she spoke out in adamant tone of voice. "He's the best. And I could care less what Tony says, I won't allow anyone from Valleyview to operate on me."

Oh, I couldn't agree with you more. He's the neurosurgeon I'd recommend if any of my patients ever needed spinal surgery." Mancini let out a sigh. "Unfortunately, there's a problem with Dr. Campbell."

"His surgical schedule is probably filled," said Mary.

Mancini nodded. "I took the liberty of telephoning Dr. Campbell's offices when I was in Radiology with Dr. Eisen. Mary, I'm sorry to say this, but his surgical calendar is booked-solid through April."

Although observing her disappointment, the doctor said, "Mary, let's take this one step at a time," he said in a tone exuding a calming influence. "First of all, you're aware that I must refer you to a neurologist."

"Yes."

"Do you want Dr. Cameron, or would you prefer another neurologist from Pittsburgh?"

"Dr. Cameron's fine with me," she said. "But I was speaking with Janet. She told me that Dr. Cameron will be referring all of his patients to another neurosurgeon."

"Janet doesn't miss anything over there," said Mancini, managing a brief smile. "Mary, here's what we'll do. I'll call Dr. Cameron to tell him the facts. And I'll also tell him that you insist on Dr. Campbell so there won't be any misunderstandings. Maybe he has some pull with Dr. Campbell, and he'll be able to operate before April."

"Sounds okay to me."

"Now until you see Dr. Cameron, here's what I want you to do. Regardless of how much Tony complains, I insist you stay home this entire week. Stay in bed as much as possible. I'm concerned about the numbness you felt, and bed-rest is the safest way to prevent it from reoccurring. Obviously you realize that you should not do anything to overexert yourself."

"She won't, Doctor," said John. "I'll be staying home with her."

Dr. Mancini opened his briefcase. "Mary, you' be needing something for pain. I'll give you a prescription—"

"No, thanks, Sam," she said. "I don't want any narcotics. If I feel the pain again, I'll get by on Advil."

"Mary, we're not certain when you're going to be operated on," said Dr. Mancini.

From his briefcase came a box that was placed on the brass-and-glass coffee table. "Here are some Darvocet samples. They're better for pain and inflammation than Advil."

"I know what they are," she said. "I'd rather not take anything prescription-strength."

"At least keep them until you've seen Dr. Cameron. You may need them."

"Alright, Sam," she said with a sigh.

Dr. Mancini looked to John. "You mother can be a very stubborn lady, can't she?"

"Always has been," said John.

They heard a musical sound from downstairs–John sat motionless.

"Answer your cell," said Mary. "It might be Vicky."

"Ah, she can leave a message."

Mary pointed to the stairs. "Go."

"Did Tony tell you yet?" Sam Mancini inquired, once John had left the room.

"Yes, Debbie Nichols," she said. "She's already called here so many times with the most asinine questions, John took the phone off the hook when he saw I was sleeping."

"Mary, you've been overworked too long now. Janet told me all about her. Yes, we know what she is. Nevertheless, I'm glad you'll finally be getting some help."

"She's still Tony's girlfriend. I just don't like the idea of working with someone who'll report my every movement to him."

"What's the difference," said Mancini. "From what Janet told me, she's not even close to being in your league as a medical secretary. Tony may be a lot of things, but he isn't a fool. He knows the Staff Office is going to be in total disarray without you."

"I'm not worried about my job," she said. "If he wants to replace me, so be it. You know that money isn't an issue anymore. Sam, I've been giving this a lot of thought. I had decided to retire by summer. But now with my bulging disc, I'd better stay so I can keep my health insurance intact." Mary paused to say, "I just hope I'm able to tolerate Debbie if and when I do return to work."

"Let's concentrate on your back issues for the time being," said the doctor, taking her by a hand. "Forget the damn hospital. Let Tony do all the worrying for a change."

"Sam, can I be perfectly honest with you about the hospital?"

Mancini smiled. "Go ahead, Mary. Get it off your mind."

"Sam, there are several excellent doctors at Valleyview, yourself included," she said. "But I'm fed up with all the hypocrisy and corruption that goes on over there on a daily basis, and all most people do is hide their heads in the sand like nothing's wrong. I just don't want to deal with it anymore."

CHAPTER TEN

Amy Gill was preparing supper when Butch arrived home. "I thought you were going to watch the first half of the four o'clock game in town," she said.

"Ah, I had enough football today," Butch said, peering about the room. "Where's Kathy?"

"Next door playing. How about Vicky? Is she ready to move yet?"

"Yeah, that last batch of stuff was it," he said. "She told me to thank you for letting her stay with us."

The gorgeous Amy, her strawberry-blonde hair curled *Shirley Temple-esk*, plopped down on the sofa next to her husband. After implanting a kiss on his lips, she said, "I'm glad she's gone. Once Kathy's asleep, you're all mine."

"Sounds like a plan," Butch said, smiling as he massaged Amy's thigh–yet casting a vexed facial expression. "I still can't believe that Vicky wanted to keep tabs on John. He told her that Mary has to have surgery, and was staying home just in case she needed him."

"I pray she's okay," said Amy. "Mary's a terrific lady."

"Damn straight she is. Even though she isn't feeling well, Mary and John still invited Vicky to dinner last night, and yet my dumb sister still had to stop in the bar today just to make sure John wasn't lying to her. Like he'd lie about being concerned about his own mother."

Amy nodded, then said, "I like all the guys, but John's always been my favorite."

"He's a classy guy," said Butch. "Treats people with respect. Polite to everybody. Does anything to help a friend in—"

She observed the sudden shift in Butch's demeanor. "What is it, Butch?

"—Nothing."

"Butch, come on. What's bothering you?"

"—I heard a guy's name in town. Brought back some memories."

"Who is he?"

"I'd rather not talk about him, Amy," he replied in staid tone. "I still have nightmares about that day."

"Butch, I'm your wife. You can tell me."

William Gill let out a heavy sigh–the events he readied to describe forever seared into his consciousness. "It happened when I was a senior in high school, a week before graduation."

Amy could see his reluctance. "Take your time," she said softly.

"Do you remember a George Crawford?"

"No."

"Fat kid, always smelled."

"Butch, I didn't know him. Did he graduate with you?"

Slowly he shook his head. "You're two years younger than I am. That's probably why you don't remember him from school."

"Okay, what about him?"

"I knew him ever since grade school. Nobody liked him. He was a sissy in the first grade and he stayed that way through high school. He stunk and he always acted weird. None of us could stand being in the same room with him—all except for John."

"So George and John are friends?"

"No, Amy," said Butch. "It wasn't that John liked him, but he was polite to George. All the way through junior high, I bullied him every chance I had. Most of the other guys used to slap him for the slightest reason."

"That's awful," said Amy, though mindful of her tone. "Did John ever hit him?"

"Never. John used to encourage us not to hit him. A few of the guys even got into arguments with John whenever he would stop us from hitting him. I used to ask John why he cared about that dirtball and all he'd say was, 'Just leave him alone and he won't bother any of us.' All those years none of us could understand why John defended him."

"I'd guess it was because John couldn't accept what you and the rest of the guys put that boy through."

"That wasn't his only reason, Amy."

"Go on," she said.

"When we started high school, our gang was separated based upon the courses we'd chosen. Bob Cook and John were in the advanced classes, while the rest of us were scattered. Crawford took lower-level courses, so we never saw him unless it was in the halls between classes. Our senior year, we were allowed to pick what day and period we wanted to take physical-education. So we fixed our schedules accordingly so we'd all be together in the same gym class. The first day we were all thrilled about being together—and guess who walked in?"

"George Crawford," she said.

"Yep. While none of us cared to hit him anymore, we always jumped at the chance to poke fun at him."

"Everybody but John."

"Uh-uh. John kept trying to convince us to stop abusing him, but I wouldn't listen. I was 6'2" and there was this fat, dumpy kid who I'd disliked for twelve years. So I kept picking on him, and he'd never fight back."

"How could he? You were bullying a defense weakling who was scared of you."

"You're right," Butch acknowledged with a sad face. "But things sure changed in a hurry."

"Go on."

Drawing a few deep breaths, Butch said, "We were all in the showers after class. George never had taken a shower after gym class, but that day he had to because he had fallen in a mud-puddle. Everyone was howling when he walked into the showers. I yelled, 'Look, it's the Pillsbury Doughboy. George got mad and threw one of his hissy-fits, then he told me to go screw myself. Instead of gaining an ounce of respect for him standing up to me for the first time his life, I punched him in the mouth."

"Did you get punished for hitting him?"

"No, he didn't report me to Mr. Schnell, our gym teacher. George went by his locker. He got dressed and never said anything. Then he came up to me and told me—he was going to kill me before we graduated. I didn't take him seriously, but from that day I figured enough was enough."

"It sure took long enough for you to realize that you'd been treating that boy like dirt," Amy insisted. "You've always been such a good guy, Butch, I'm really surprised at all this."

He shrugged, the corners of his mouth pointed downward. "I was young and stupid back then. Anyhow, for the rest of the year, I let him alone. I even tried to apologize but he ignored me. He ignored everyone, expect for when he would occasionally speak with John."

"So what has you so nervous?"

Butch's facial expression readily communicated his uneasiness as he said, "After our final gym class, we were around our lockers getting dressed. George was sitting nearby. He sure picked the right time, because nobody saw him take a gun from his gym-bag and point it at me. He pulled me over to where his back was against his locker. No one dared make an attempt to rush him. 'Today's the day, asshole,' he'd shouted in my ear. Amy, I shuddered when he put that pistol against my head."

Butch wiped the perspiration from his brow. "Mr. Schell tried talking sense to him, but George shot at ceiling. He kept ranting about how I'd mistreated him, and he was going to kill me and anyone else if they tried to rush him."

"Where was John?"

"He was in the bathroom when he heard the shot. When he ran out and saw what was going on, he yelled for everyone to stand back. Schnell told John he was in charge, but John shoved him at Bob and Rol, and told them to hold him. Then John asked George if they could talk. George demanded everyone get out of reach, and ordered John to sit on the bench in front of us. He told John if he or anyone else tried something, we'd both die. John stayed calm as could be while talking to a lunatic who'd kept pointing a gun at his face. I was trembling to beat all hell and so help me, Amy, I never saw one sign of fear in John. He kept telling George to calm down, that he wouldn't get into any trouble for shooting his gun."

Feeling his pulse quicken, Butch drew several deep breaths. "Then Mr. Schnell tried to pull away from Bob and Rol, insisting he was obligated to call the police. So John asked George's permission to get up. He, Bob and Rol muscled Mr. Schnell against the wall. They told me later that John had whispered to Schnell that if he didn't shut up, he would personally shoot him if I was killed."

"Wow," she said. "John took a big gamble with both of your lives. All of your lives."

"Yes, he did. John told us later that he felt George was really capable of killing, especially if the police came, so he did what he could to buy more time."

"Then what?"

"Finally John was able to persuade George into letting me go. But George told him that the only way he release me was if he was assured of escaping the locker room. So John talked him into trading places with me. John slid on the floor next to me, and George put the gun to his head before allowing me to move. While he kept the pistol pointed at John, that's when they walked out of the locker room. Maybe two minutes after, John came back in and said George had just torn-out of the parking lot."

"Did the police catch him?"

Butch sat with his teeth clenched, grimacing. "The police went to George's house. They found him dead—hanging in the attic."

"Oh, God," she whispered.

He sighed before saying, "A couple days later we read that there was a history of mental illness in Crawford's family. His brother was bi-polar, his mother was in an institution, and his father had committed suicide years before. John told me that he'd remembered reading about Mr. Crawford. That was the main reason he never wanted any of us tormenting him."

"Why didn't John say something sooner?"

"He thought it was possible George was mentally-deranged, but he was scared to say anything because of the way we were back then. He was afraid the guys might use it to agitate George even more."

His eyes tearing, Butch wrapped an arm around her. "Amy, neither Kathy nor I would be alive today if John hadn't saved my ass. Crawford would have killed me if it weren't for John. That's why until the day I die, I'll forever be in his debt."

The room remained hushed until Amy moved to stand. "Make sure the potatoes are cooked. I'm going to get Kathy." Briskly rubbing at her arms covered by her Pittsburgh Steelers' sweatshirt, Amy was shivering. "Damn, Butch, I'll probably start having nightmares. If Crawford was crazy enough to hang himself, he certainly wouldn't have thought twice before killing you. You're right, you really are lucky to be alive."

"No, Amy, I wasn't lucky," he said somberly. "I was blessed. Blessed that I have a friend like John who was looking out for me."

"It sure took a lot of guts for John to do what he did."

"Balls, Amy. Balls of steel."

CHAPTER ELEVEN

"Cameron," said the doctor–speaking on his cell phone.

"Steve, Anthony DeTorrio. Where are you?"

"I'm on my way now. I'm meeting Mary Valone in Radiology at noon."

"Yes, the woman at your office said she thought you were heading here. Steve, I want to personally thank you for seeing Mary on such short notice."

"My pleasure. Mary's always been very helpful to me. Also, Dr. Mancini asked me to evaluate her condition as quickly as I could."

"Did you have a chance to speak with Dr. Eisen?"

"Yes. Based on his findings, surgery seems indicated."

"Yeah, Mancini told me the same. He had Mary take off work all this week until he learned your opinion on her."

"Just from listening to Dr. Eisen, it sounds like an ordinary degeneration of a disc. I'll study the films, although Dr. Eisen's opinions are usually spot-on. If so, Mary's surgery shouldn't be all that intricate."

"Steve, let's discuss Mary's surgery. Did Mancini tell you that she's insisting on Dr. Campbell at Allegheny Central?"

"He did."

"And that Campbell's already booked through April?"

"So I've been told."

"Can you pull a few strings so she can be operated on sooner?"

"I don't think he'd go for it, Tony. While Dr. Campbell and I get along, I haven't been referring patients to him lately. I don't see him doing me any favors. Maybe if her condition were life-threatening he'd squeeze her in, although in Mary's situation, I'd tend to doubt it."

"Would you reconsider recommending Dr. Zimmerman?"

"Forget it, Tony. Even if I did suggest Zimmerman, Mary wouldn't have him. No, I'll be recommending Dr. Nasser, then it's totally up to Mary. If for some reason she doesn't want him, there are several other well-qualified neurosurgeons in Pittsburgh."

"Could Nasser operate on her soon?"

"I would guesstimate the latter part of January at the earliest. Why? What's your hurry?"

"I need Mary at the office, Steve. We have a state inspection coming soon. Mary's the only secretary here who knows how to organize all of the doctors credentials. So I need her to either have the surgery asap and return to work by at least the first week in March, or hold-off the operation until the inspection's finished. It has to be one or the other. Fucking Mancini has his way, she'll stay on sick-leave waiting for Campbell. Then I'm really screwed. Christ, she's been off a week now and the office is so fucked-up, I'm ready to go over there and start shitcanning everything."

"Calm down, Tony. Let me review her films, and I'll see what I can do to help you out. Although judging from what I've been told, Mary's been experiencing some sciatic pain—"

"I don't give a flying fuck about her pain! Just get her operated on now, or convince her and fucking Mancini she can come back to work!"

*****

Less than an hour later, Dr. Cameron stood in a darkened room, the only light from an illuminated board that displayed Mary's films. Having conferred with Dr. Ralph Eisen, the head radiologist of Valleyview General Hospital, he, Dr. Mancini, and Mary Valone were seated within viewing distance. John Valone stood propped against the wall behind his mother, his forearms folded across his chest.

Using a light-wand to better illustrate for his audience, Dr. Cameron directed their attention to the bottom portion of the MRI. "Mary, Dr. Eisen is correct," he declared. "You do have a degenerative disc at the L4-L5 level. At the moment, the condition of the vertebral-body itself isn't too serious. However, based upon the type of pain you described to me earlier, and despite any herniation of the disc not being visual on the MRI, it is my belief that a fragment has broken away from the disc-body and is lodged in the vicinity of your sciatic nerve. Trust me on this, I've encountered this exact symptomology countless times. Now in your case, again based upon the sensation of pain you've been encountering on an intermittent basis, I must conclude that for the time being, you're in no immediate danger. I say that simply due to the fact that if the fragment were impairing the sciatic nerve to greater extent, you would be in constant pain, possibly to the point of not being able to walk. So I'm thankful it isn't. Nevertheless the fact remains that the disc will only continue to deteriorate. Naturally, that event will further complicate the issue. Therefore, it's my opinion that surgery is your only recourse. A portion of the disc, perhaps the entire disc-body itself, as well as the fragment encroaching upon your sciatic must be removed."

Cameron tucked his bi-focals into his pocket. "Dr. Eisen, do you concur?"

"Oh, absolutely," he said. "My main concerns pertained to the stability of Mary's spine."

"True, Doctor, the disc is bulging anteriorly to a small degree, though in my opinion it doesn't pose any meaningful risk at this time," said Cameron, his tone remaining meek, yet obviously enjoying his role as the oracle. "The main priorities are to remove whatever portion of the disc is necessary and retrieve the fragment, thereby eliminating Mary's sciatic pain altogether. Once accomplished, a piece of bone from the bone-bank may be fused into the vacated area between the vertebrae if necessary, thus assuring spinal stability."

Dr. Cameron looked to Mary. "The bottom-line is simple, Mary. You should have the operation performed in the very near future before the disc erodes any further. As I'm sure you're aware, you may lose only some minor flexibility in the lumbar region. Generally most patients don't even notice a difference three months post-op. That's the only negative. On the positive side, your spine will be far more stabilized, and of course you will be pain-free and able to live your life without any limitations whatsoever."

Silence ensued as Dr. Cameron turned on the lights. "Any questions, Mary?"

"No, Doctor," she said. "Dr. Eisen, Dr. Mancini, and I have discussed my situation. I realize I need surgery. My only concern is Dr. Campbell."

"I can appreciate that. As Sam mentioned, Dr. Campbell's OR schedule is filled through April. Now if it's your decision to wait until May, possibly even June, assuming your sciatic distress doesn't increase to the level I've described, then by all means try to hold-off surgery until Dr. Campbell can take you. I just hate to see you suffer needlessly, as well as living in fear of your disc."

"What other choice do I have?" asked Mary–always respectful in the company of doctors, she opted against degrading any surgeon on the Valleyview Hospital staff.

"There is a viable alternative," stated Dr. Cameron, his inflection expressing he understood what had just gone unspoken. "Mary, I would recommend Dr. Rasheem Nasser. For almost a year now, he's been practicing neurosurgery exclusively at Shadydell Heights."

Able to survey her apprehension, Cameron went on to say, "Mary, believe me, this man is a top-notch neurosurgeon. Graduated with honors from Northwestern Med. He's an extremely gifted surgeon. Extremely meticulous, doesn't leave anything to chance. Trust me, I know. I've examined many of his surgical cases post-op. All of his patients I have followed-up with are doing quite nicely today."

With Mary remaining silent, Dr. Mancini said, "Dr. Cameron, do you have any idea when Dr. Nasser would be able to perform Mary's surgery?"

"On my way over here, I phoned Dr. Nasser's office to inquire about his OR schedule," said Cameron. "The tentative date given was Thursday, January 31st. Mary, if you decide to have him, you would be admitted on Tuesday the 29th, have the usual tests, and you would be operated on by Thursday, Friday at the latest. In all likelihood, you'd be discharged by Sunday. Three, four weeks recovery-time, you'll be as good as new."

"Dr. Cameron, I believe you when you say how talented this Dr. Nasser is," said Mary. "It's just that I've never heard of him."

"He's relatively new to the Pittsburgh area," Cameron said. "Dr. Nasser spent the first fourteen years of his surgical career working in Detroit."

"Why did he leave Detroit?"

"Just that needed a change of pace, that Detroit was becoming too much of a hassle. Dr. Nasser came to Pittsburgh for a medical conference, decided he liked the area, so he relocated here. Believe me, the people at Shadydell Heights are happy he did. I haven't heard anything but praise for Dr. Nasser since he joined their staff."

"About how old is he?"

"Early forties."

"Does he have surgical privileges at other Pittsburgh hospitals?"

"Mary, I'm not sure if he's ever applied to another hospital other than Shadydell. Dr. Nasser mentioned to me when I first met him that he didn't prefer traveling into downtown Pittsburgh on a daily basis, and he only lives a few miles from Shadydell."

"Is he a board-certified neurosurgeon?"

Cameron grinned at her medical knowledge. "Yes, Mary, of course he is. I wouldn't be recommending him to you if he wasn't certified. You know me better than that. All I can say is I have complete faith in Dr. Nasser's abilities. Mark my words, before long Dr. Nasser will be just as sought after as Dr. Campbell is now."

His audience remaining mum led Dr. Cameron to say, "Mary, I know you wanted Dr. Campbell. Although in all candor, with Dr. Nasser as your surgeon, you'll be just fine."

Immediately she faced Dr. Mancini. "What do you think?"

"It's your choice, Mary," he said. "If Dr. Nasser's the caliber of neurosurgeon Dr. Cameron's believes, you really should consider him. As Dr. Cameron, I hate seeing you suffer until Dr. Campbell can operate on you."

Mary turned to her son. "John, what should I do?"

"All I know is that you're in more pain than you've been letting on, and May's a long time away," he said.

Mary Valone remained silent, her intuition suggesting she wait for Dr. Campbell–her back pain urging otherwise. Following a sigh, she said, "Alright, Dr. Cameron, I trust your opinion. Call Dr. Nasser."

"You've made the best decision, Mary," said Cameron, smiling in satisfaction. "Now don't worry about anything, I'll make all of the arrangements. You're to be at Shadydell on—"

"Mary, I'm so happy I found you! Anthony DeTorrio startled all by charging into the room. "Hello, Dr. Cameron. Dr. Mancini. Dr. Eisen. Mary." He looked to John. "Who's the young man?"

"My son, John," said Mary.

Ever so slightly, John nodded his head while looking him over. Along with his tightening his hands causing the muscles of his forearms to ripple, there was a cold glare cast from his brown eyes forewarning DeTorrio not to approach him. Remaining sedate, his thoughts rushed, *"So this little worm is DeTorrio. This is the bigshot who abuses Janet. What a scumbag."*

DeTorrio's radar was functioning at peak efficiency sensing the hostility being emitted his way. Wisely breaking off eye-contact, he said to Cameron," Doctor, have Mary's films revealed anything significant?"

"Surgery is indicated."

"I'm so sorry to hear that, Mary," DeTorrio followed. "Who is going to perform the operation?"

"Dr. Rasheem Nasser at Shadydell Heights," Dr. Cameron answered instead.

"Is the procedure scheduled yet?" said DeTorrio.

"Tentatively for the last week of January," said Cameron.

"Mary, I wish you all the best," said a sincere DeTorrio. "Dr. Cameron has told me how proficient Dr. Nasser is. Sounds to me as if you'll be in excellent hands."

"Thank you, Mr. DeTorrio," said Mary while extending him a smile.

In spite of his not having any true confidants in the room, the upcoming JC inspection compelled Anthony DeTorrio to say, "Mary, I realize this is a stressful time for you, but do you think it possible to work on a limited basis? The staff credentialing must be completed by mid-March at the very latest."

"No, Tony," declared Dr. Mancini. "I won't have Mary overextending herself."

"Just on a part-time basis, Sam," said DeTorrio. "I already have Miss Nichols and another secretary performing some of Mary's routine job duties. All I ask is that Mary work solely on the doctors credentials, and perhaps show Miss Nichols some of her other job functions. Mary can work at her own pace."

"Tony, I'm sorry," said Mancini. "Mary's health comes first to me. The credentials will have to wait until after Mary's surgery."

"At least if Mary were—"

"Hey, bub!" John broke in, his tone rude. "You deaf? The answer's no. My mother isn't working at all until she's completely recovered from her operation. Did you hear that time?"

DeTorrio didn't take to his snide retort. A false smile masking his annoyance, he measured John's resentment towards him increased due to his efforts to sway. Helplessly he remained silent.

It was Mary who said, "Mr. DeTorrio I'd like to apologize for my son's behavior."

"Not an issue," said a placid DeTorrio, holding up a hand. "Your son's concerns are perfectly understandable."

Mary nodded in thanks. "Sir, while I wouldn't mind trying to work on the credentials, it's my understanding that Miss Nichols has limited work-experience. All things considered, Dr. Mancini feels it could place too much of a burden upon me."

Sensing a ray of hope, DeTorrio chose to sweeten his offer. "Mary, I appreciate your position," he said. "We'll have Janet work in your office with you and Miss Nichols. Janet has some knowledge of the credentialing process, and she would be able to train and assist Miss Nichols with some of your other job functions. All I'm asking of you, and again, you may work on a limited basis, is that you get Janet familiarized with the credentials. Then during your convalesce-period, Janet and Miss Nichols will continue on in your position until you return. How does that sound to you?"

Mary turned to Dr. Mancini. "Sam, if would only be for a few weeks. With Janet there to help me, I think I can manage until I'm operated on."

"It could put you at further jeopardy," said Mancini. "Sitting wouldn't hurt your back, but when typing most people tend to lurch forward. In my opinion, it could place too much strain on her lower spine."

"Dr. Mancini," intervened Cameron, "you are correct that lurching forward could place some strain on Mary's disc. However in her present condition, Mary would feel any excess strain faster than a person with a healthy L4-L5. So I would suggest to you, if Mary is willing to return to her job under the conditions Mr. DeTorrio outlined, she could, just as long as Mary understands that at the first hint of pain, she should cease typing. Although in all honesty, it's my opinion that if Mary just takes it slow and is aware not to lean forward while typing, it's highly unlikely she would place herself at further impairment."

"Sorry, Dr. Cameron," said Sam Mancini. "I still don't like it."

Anthony DeTorrio felt powerless as he stood hushed. He could feel his anger simmering, yet he knew it would prove futile to protest. They had been in many distasteful battles over the years. Sam Mancini wasn't of the nature to ever shy-away when it came to issues of principle or morality. He was a man of honor and integrity–a physician Tony DeTorrio could not utilize his sword of mastery against. He held nothing to dangle of his head. Then there was Mary's son, his eyes burning brighter.

Finally Mary said, "Sam, if Janet's there to help me, I'm willing to try. It would only be for a few weeks, and I promise I'll be careful not to place any strain on my lower back."

Having worked with Mary when he was the Staff President, Dr. Mancini realized how strong her work-ethic was–her dedication to her job had always taken precedence. "Alright, Mary," he said after a sigh. "Please promise you'll take it easy."

"I will, Sam."

Mancini turned to John. "If you see it's too much for her, call me immediately. Knowing your mother, she won't tell me if her pain's getting worse."

"Count on it, Doctor."

CHAPTER TWELVE

"Can I get you something to drink?" Vicky Gill asked of John, upon their arrival at her apartment.

"Pepsi or Mountain Dew's good."

"I'm having a glass of sherry. You want some?"

"No, Vick, I never liked that stuff. Tastes like cough syrup."

When Vicky returned with their drinks, she sat on the sofa besides him.

"You've been pretty reserved ever since you picked me up tonight," she said.

"I could say the same about you."

"John, I haven't been reserved. I didn't care to talk about our personal relationship in the restaurant. I wanted to wait until we got here."

John fixed his eyes upon her–knowing this a moment in time that could forever alter his life. "Okay then, let's talk."

"I know you were about ready to ask me to get married before I lost my temper that night at the bar. Am I right?"

Taken by her straightforwardness, his eyebrows lifted. During their previous go-around, Vicky's normal approach had been to bandy-about a touchy subject, never posing such a direct question. Only when she'd become agitated was it her custom not to mince words. He chose to be straightforward as well. "The answer's yes," he said. "I still have the ring."

"John, I admit that I overreacted, and I've regretted it ever since. After your dad's funeral, Butch kept urging me to call you, but my childish pride wouldn't allow it. A month or so later, I called my brother. Butch said you refused to speak about me with him, so I thought it best to let some more time pass. I wanted to call you so many times after that, but I just didn't know what to say, since I knew your attitude towards me would be bitter because I had hurt you."

"You hurt me real bad, Vicky," he said in somber tone. "I was a basket-case for longer than I care to admit. I couldn't sleep. I was forcing myself to eat. I was so depressed that I could barely stand being around people."

She frowned at his words. "Butch told me. He said you were doing your best to pretend it didn't matter, but he saw how upset you were. Truthfully, I was depressed, too."

"That's because we were in love."

Vicky nodded as she dabbed a teardrop. "Anyhow, the time kept passing. Butch, even Amy, kept encouraging me to call you, but I didn't have the nerve. Then I got the job in Harrisburg. I thought by then it was too late, that I'd just have to forget about you, and move on with my life without you."

He twirled the cola around the glass, remaining silent for a prolonged period. "Yeah, well, maybe I should have called you. I had the most beautiful girl in the world, the love of my life just waiting for me to marry her. Maybe I took too much for granted."

She drew a deep breath before saying, "Would you like to get back together for good?"

John took hold of her hand. "Of course I would. Vicky, I've been in love with you ever since the day I met you, and I'll love you until the day I die."

He barely managed to set his glass down as Vicky embraced him. Several passionate kisses later, John said, "Vicky, as much as I love you, as much as I want to spend the rest of my life with you, we have to get it straight right now that while I can accept the things you like doing, you can't be so stringent about my friends. There isn't anything wrong with my having a few beers bullshitting and reminiscing with them once in a while. If we can agree on that, I promise everything will go great for us."

"That's fine by me," she said. "Just so you don't stay out all night."

"Are you kidding? Maybe when I was younger I overdid it a little. Now I never stay out late anymore. Five in the morning comes around too fast when I have to work. That should tell you something else about me. If I wanted, I could quit working tomorrow,"

"It does, honey," she said, seductively placing her leg across his thighs while pulling at his hand. "Take me into the bedroom. I want you so bad I can't stand it."

For Vicky, the lovemaking wasn't as it had been before. John wasn't as affectionate as he'd been in their previous times–as if he were still on guard against her, still protecting his emotional well-being. Yet she gave no hint about his performance. She believed that through some idiosyncrasy of nature, men were more sensitive to a situation such as theirs. Still, she found making love with him even after such a long absence the most natural thing in the world. It was almost as if they'd never been apart, the incidents of their past soon to become a distant memory.

"How many other girls have you slept with since me?" she asked, while nestling against him afterwards. "Butch told me he's seen you discourage quite a few of them at the bar."

"Just one Butch never knew of," he replied, a demure facial expression about him.

"I hope you—"

"Yes, Vicky, I always used a rubber with her. When I met her, I was so horny from missing you, I needed to get laid. I only wanted sex. I certainly didn't want to knock her up."

"Who was she?"

"Ah, she didn't mean anything to me."

"Oh, come on. Tell me about her."

"Her first name was Grace. I never asked her last name."

"Was she from Vernon Park?"

"No. She lives in some dinky town on the way to Altoona."

"How'd you meet her?"

"On business. She works for some guy named Darren who owns a manufacturing company."

"So how did you happen to meet her?"

"I was doing some consulting for Darren's company. When I was getting ready to leave one night, she practically threw herself at me. So we went to a motel and had sex."

"Was she pretty?" asked Vicky, holding the jealously from her tone.

As he laced his fingers through her golden hair, he kissed her full-lips. "She was a dog next to you."

"So why didn't you keep seeing her? Sounds like she was easy."

"Too easy," he said. "And I found out why."

"What'd she do?"

"For the next couple months I drove there every Sunday morning and met her at the same motel. She never wanted to leave the room, so it was practically non-stop sex the whole time we were there. Whatever I wanted, she did. Whatever she wanted, I did." A sigh of disgust. "She must have thought I was putty in her hands when she asked me for a loan."

"How much did she want?"

"Twenty thousand."

"For what?"

"Told me she wanted to buy a new trailer so she could get away from her husband."

"You're joking?"

"Nope." John shook his head and said, "Shows how lonely and naïve I was. There I was having an affair with a married woman who was nothing but trailer-park trash."

"What happened then?"

"I put my clothes on and I dropped a hundred dollar bill on the bed. I told her that was my going-rate for whores."

"That sure sounds like something you'd do," said Vicky, giggling.

"You know me, Vicky. I try to be a good guy, but I can be a nasty son of a gun whenever I get mad." Shifting onto his side, he cradled his head. "Okay, your turn."

"Honestly, John, there haven't been any other men in my life since you. I had plenty of them chasing me, but there was only one guy that I was even remotely interested in. Seemed like such a polite sort, so I invited him over for supper one evening. As soon as we were done eating, he threw a bag of cocaine on the table and began unzipping his pants."

"Real bashful type, huh?"

"I didn't find it so damn funny!" she chirped, punching his stomach. "I thought he was going to rape me. I told him to get out before I called the police."

Soon thereafter, John excused himself and stepped into the adjoining bathroom. Returning to the bedroom, he found Vicky had turned off the night-light. His eyes adjusting to the darkness, he could see the outline of her body under the covers. He slipped naked between the sheets, reaching to touch her glistening skin. Vicky turned rapidly, his hands now upon her soft, full breasts. She was in his grasp so quickly that their bodies came together with a burst of silken electricity. Tightly he wrapped his arms around her, kissing her warm mouth deeply, squeezing her body against his while rolling atop. Her flesh hot, her hair taut silk, all of her erotic eagerness wildly rushed against him. When he entered her, she gave a slight gasp. With a forward thrust of her pelvis, she locked her ankles around his hips. Their primordial urges gushing, they surged against each other in an unbridled frenzy. When they came to an end, they were bound together so fiercely that both trembled while separating for the others' arms.

Both lying quietly savoring the moment, Vicky raked her fingers through his chest-hair. "Darling, that was the same kind of passion we used to always enjoy."

Softly he sighed in the darkness. "I thought it was all over for us. Damn, I'm glad I was wrong. I love you so much."

"And I'll always love you," she said, before tenderly kissing him.

They lay in bed a while longer, caressing and fondling each other. Vicky was first to break their silence. "Let's get up for a minute, babe. I want to change the sheets."

He bounded from the bed and grabbed his shorts. "I could use a drink after all that," he said.

Vicky was smiling spicily as he left the room.

While sitting in the living room sipping a bottle of water, his eyes became transfixed on Vicky as she walked nude into the room and sat at the opposite side of the couch. John lifted her legs, and watched her toes enter the slit in his boxer-shorts.

"Enjoying yourself, Miss Gill?" he asked flirtatiously, as she continued to wiggle her toes, delighted with the arousal she was stimulating.

"For sure," she said with a giggle. "Things are definitely looking up."

Removing her foot, he wrestled her breathtaking naked body atop his. A long, passionate kiss ensued. "Oh well, I suppose I can manage to satisfy you one more time," he said, as he began nuzzling her breasts.

"Honey, it's only eight-thirty and I'm off tomorrow. You'd better be prepared to satisfy me more than once. We've got lots of time to make up for."

CHAPTER THIRTEEN

Mary Valone was at her desk at her normal 8 A.M. starting time the following Monday. Seated along side was Janet Silva–elated to be out of Anthony DeTorrio's shouting range. At a smaller desk stationed next to theirs was Debra Nichols. Immediately upon learning of Mary's willingness to return, DeTorrio had a crew revamp the office so they could work as a team.

With her priority being the doctors' credentials, Mary spent most of the morning showing Janet exactly what was mandated by the state. Since Janet did have some background on the documentation, she caught-on easily and felt able to handle the task with near the same competency Mary had always displayed. Once Janet felt at ease with the task, Mary then began to review to both Janet and Debbie some of the numerous responsibilities that she was held accountable for. As before, Janet had caught on quickly–stunned with all the work Mary had been able to accomplish unassisted for so many years.

Conversely it was obvious to both women that Debra Nichols could care less about her new assignment. Even the most basic functions of the medical staff seemed beyond her grasp. As Mary sorted through some of the files on her PC, she noted many to be in complete disarray–a product of Nichols' efforts from the week previous.

After lunch, Mary began an attempt to better familiarize them with her job by outlining her obligations. Janet, the professional she was, took detailed notes, stopping Mary on occasion to verify something she wasn't certain of. All the while, Debbie sat head-in-hand, uninterested. Both tried to ignore the obese girl as she constantly reached into her desk for another piece of candy or a donut. She caused further disruption by leaving the office throughout the afternoon for whatever reason she could conjure.

During one of her breaks, Mary and Janet acquiesced to the fact they were fighting a losing proposition as it pertained to Nichols. It was blatantly obvious that Debbie Nichols had no interest whatsoever in learning even the most basil functions of the Medical Staff Office. The final straw came late that afternoon. While Mary and Janet reviewed a report they had generated, Mary asked Nichols if she understood at least the basics as to how she would be able to perform the same task–Nichols' responded with a scornful facial expression.

It was an extremely stressful day in the Staff Office. Debra Nichols' laziness, along with her unwillingness to learn permeated the air with animosity. Even Dr. Burke couldn't help but sense the hostility when he stopped by, and had soon thereafter made a rapid departure. The office held the atmosphere of a battlefield, with the female combatants just waiting for the heated words Mary sensed Janet was prepared to use with Debbie. In spite of Mary's feeling some soreness in her back, she had elected to stay until 4 P.M. She knew Janet's temperament, and feared the worst if she had left them alone.

To Mary and Janet's amazement, Debbie Nichols arrived at work the following morning to cheerfully greet them–diametrically opposed to yesterdays snarl. It shocked even further when Debbie said, "Mary, Janet, I apologize for the way I behaved yesterday. My conduct was unprofessional and I'm sorry. It's just that I've been under a lot of pressure here and at home. If we can, I'd like to start fresh. I promise you both that I'll try very hard hold up my share of the work."

After they'd graciously accepted her apology, relieved to be putting an end to the hostilities, Mary said, "Debbie, we all have our problems. I understand this job can seem too much at times."

Happily Mary spent the remainder of the morning reviewing many of the incidentals that Debbie hadn't attempted to comprehend the day prior. It pleased her that Debbie was paying attention and asking pertinent questions. With Janet working on the credentials, Mary moved her chair next to Debbie's and started demonstrating some of the workload she would need to understand during her absence.

Their afternoon was spent working in harmony as Nichols kept at her PC, only pausing to briefly chat with either of her co-workers. At three o'clock, Mary said, "Debbie, why don't you take a break. You haven't stopped since lunch."

"You have done a lot today," added Janet.

"Thank you, but I've just started on something," she said. "Mary, I'm hoping to have it finished and have you review it before the end of the day."

Without another word, Nichols kept typing, her pudgy fingers furiously tapping at the keyboard. Janet and Mary exchanged glances– both dumbfounded at Nichols' transformation.

It was approaching 4 P.M. when Mary and Janet shutdown their computers. Debbie continued to type, having never lifted her eyes from her PC screen.

"Come on, Deb, that's enough for today," said Mary. "Do a file-save. We'll review it tomorrow."

"I'm almost done," she said. "I'm so far behind, I'd like to finish this and have you review it in the morning. You and Janet go ahead, I have my office key. I'll lock-up."

"My Lord, today sure was a change for the better," said Mary to Janet, as they walked to their cars. "I'm so glad she decided to decided to work instead of loafing all day."

Janet Silva eyed Mary, her skepticism evident. "Mary, I don't give a damn how she behaved today, I still don't trust her. That fat slut didn't change overnight. I'm telling you, that girl's nothing but trouble." Seeing other hospital workers in the parking lot within earshot, Janet went on to say, "Let's talk in my car."

"Jan, at least give her a chance," Mary urged of her. "The way it looks now, you're going to take over my office until I return. Tony knows she can't handle all the work herself. At least if she does the simple things, you won't be so swamped with the workload."

"Helluva choice I have," Janet said abruptly. "Being stuck with her lazy ass and Burke, or with that little schmuck over there."

"Janet, the point is you'll be in charge of the office. While I'm gone, let Tony know exactly what is expected of her. Then if she starts loafing again, he won't have anyone to blame but her."

"It's not the work that bothers me, Mary," Janet said. "I'm telling you, she's up to no- good."

Mary let out a sigh. Alike herself, Janet Silva was difficult to sway once her convictions were set. "Let's see how she acts tomorrow."

"Did you hear that we're supposed to get some freezing rain and eight to ten inches of snow by morning? Let's call-off tomorrow."

"I can't, Jan, all of my files are a mess. I want to keep her working on the simple things until I can get the more complex files corrected for you."

"Too damn dedicated, Mary," Janet huffed. "Alright, if you're coming in, I guess I have to as well."

"John's off all this week. I'll ask him to drive us."

"Thanks, Mary," she said. "If you want to leave early, I'll catch a ride home with Pam or someone else."

"We'll pick you up before seven-thirty."

*****

Janet's warning to Mary was about to prove itself true. After waiting only minutes after they'd gone, Debra Nichols looked outside the office door, making certain there wasn't anybody lingering in the hallway. She then locked the door, and made her way behind the desk both Mary and Janet were sharing. Seated on the floor, she dug into her purse for a wrench. The bolt that supported the back-rest portion of the seat to the frame of Janet Silva's chair was her objective. Not adept with tools, she struggled to loosen it–unaware that she was chipping paint from the bolt-head and surrounding areas. Perspiration dripped from her pasty skin as she fought to twist the bolt. Several minutes passed before she removed the bolt from its slot, causing the back-rest to topple to the floor. Having accomplished her goal, Debbie held the fallen section as she realigned it with the frame. Carefully she positioned the bolt at such an angle, enabling enough support to keep the back-rest in place. Watchful not to bump it as she made her way around, Debbie Nichols tucked the wrench into her purse and made her way out.

*****

When Gene Polachek opened his garage door early the following morning with a snow-blower in tow, he saw John shoveling the more than eleven inches of snow that had accumulated overnight. "Why don't you buy one of these gizmos, ya tightwad?" he yelled to John.

"Its good exercise shoveling," said John, not breathing heavily. "Why you up so early?"

"Ah, I gotta go out three-to-eleven, so it was get the snow now or later," said Gene, as he trudged through the narrow strip of snow-covered lawn that separated their parallel driveways. "How's your mom doing?"

"She's feeling okay."

"When's her operation?"

"Not next week, the week after. What's up with you?"

"Same old shit." Gene smiled. "You and Butch's sister must be gettin' along pretty good again. I heard your garage door opening late couple nights ago."

John paused to grin at his friend. "Pal, she wore me out that night." In good-humored fashion, he shoveled snow onto Gene's driveway. "Hey, keep chasing Allison. She'll let you jump her one of these nights."

"Ah, she's just nice to me so I'll give her a tip."

"We almost ready?" they heard Mary calling from the garage.

"Just about, Ma."

"Okay. Hi, Gene."

"Morning, Mrs. Valone," said Gene, waving to her. "How are you?"

"Pretty well today. How's your dad?"

"Okay."

"Tell him I said hello," said Mary.

"I will. Take care of yourself. If I can ever help you with anything, please call me."

"Thank you, Gene. I appreciate that."

"Ma, I'm almost done," said John. "Get the Caddy started."

"Sure you don't want to take the Taurus or my car?"

"No, the Cadillac's heavier. It'll hold the road better."

"Want me to finish to top part of your driveway?" Gene asked.

"Nah, I get it when I come home," John said. "Tell you what. If you want, we'll go into town for lunch. Maybe Allison's cooking today."

"I'll try," he said. "Depends on what time my aunt gets here to stay with my dad."

Gene had his snow blower spraying full-throttle when the Valone's pulled away. The road-crews hadn't even started clearing the residential areas, and navigating the snow covered road proved difficult.

Janet stood waiting on her porch. While John used the cul-de-sac above her home to turn around, she plodded through her lawn towards Pinewood Lane.

"Isn't this terrible," she said, once inside the car. "Hi, Mar. And hello, cutie pie."

"Hi there, pretty lady," said John.

With Mary and Janet gabbing about their upcoming day, John kept attention on the drive to Valleyview Hospital. The conditions improved somewhat on the main roads, yet the patches of ice that remained on the roadways had made it a tenuous trip when arrived at the hospital's main entrance. Once he'd helped Mary from the car and ushered both ladies inside the building, he said, "I'm gonna grab a cup of coffee. Ma, if you want to quit early today, call the cell. Jan, if you need a ride home, I'll come get you."

As the two women walked the corridor leading to the Staff Office, John went into a nearby gift shop. Stopping momentarily to look at a magazine, he heard a shriek, followed by Janet racing towards him.

"John, come quick!" she yelled. "Your mother's had an accident!"

As he sprinted the hallway, Janet hurried into the office. John charged into the office to find Mary sprawled on the floor behind her desk, with Janet holding a hand under Mary's head. The expression on

Mary's face was one of anguish. "Get some help in here!" he shouted to the top of his lungs.

"What the hell happened?" he demanded of Janet, while kneeling beside his fallen mother.

"John, I saw Mary sit on my chair," said Janet, her voice quaking. "Next thing I knew, she was on the floor."

"Mary, talk to me," he said, wincing at the sight of her being in agony. "Where does it hurt?"

"My back's killing me," she said. "Have Sam paged."

"I already did, Mary," said a shaken Janet.

They heard a voice on the intercom announce, "Dr. Mancini, any ER personnel to the Medical Staff Office. STAT!"

"Ma, please stay down," said John, seeing her trying to arise. "Just lay still. Help's on the way."

"They'll be here any minute," Janet said, her hand remaining cupped under Mary's head.

"Are you sure Sam's here?"

"He always does his rounds this time of morning," said Janet.

John nodded in thanks. Looking to the floor at the broken chair, he said, "Jan, please keep holding her head. Lay still, Ma."

He slid near the crumbled chair, while Janet did her best comfort Mary. Examining the two disjointed sections, he noticed the scraped paint around the slot as it flecked onto his thumb. Looking down, he spotted the bolt. Retrieving it, he could feel the scratched surfaces of the bolt's octagon-shaped head. After he'd tucked the bolt into his pocket, John hoisted both pieces atop Mary and Janet's desk, his eyes showing a choleric rage.

"How many people have keys to this office?" he asked Janet.

"Your mother, me, Debbie Nichols, and the Housekeeping people," she replied, watching as the vile guise continued to spread across his face.

"Somebody deliberately arranged for this chair to break. I want to know who."

"Goodness gracious!" they heard Debra Nichols cry out. "What happened?"

"You're Debbie?" he fumed–despised at the sight of her.

"Yes. Is Mary alright?"

"Her chair collapsed."

"Honest, I don't know how the bolt could have popped-out," she said.

"Who said the bolt popped-out!" John growled.

Nichols' foolish denial, added to her uncaring facial expression had him convinced.

"Well—isn't that—I mean—that's how a chair usually breaks, isn't it?" she managed to stammer.

"Especially when the fucking bolt has been arranged to fall out! And I think you did it!"

"I don't have to stand here and listen to your accusations! I'm calling Mr. DeTorrio," she said in a huff, then fled the room–nearly colliding with the gurney being wheeled in by the Emergency Room crew.

"Call a fuckin' SWAT team!" John screamed at her.

"Please step back, Sir," requested the young doctor, circumspect of what he'd just heard. "We'll take care of Mrs. Valone."

"Be careful with her," said John.

The ER crew took every precaution before readying to assist Mary upon the gurney. "Easy now, Mrs. Valone," said the doctor. "We're taking you to ER."

"Take your time with her," said John. "She's got a bad back."

He looked to Janet. "When could that bitch have done this? Mary told me the three of you have worked together this week. You all take lunch together. You all leave together. When could she have fucked with my mother's chair?"

"She stayed late yesterday after your mom and I left." Janet eyed him with an apologetic face. "John, that's not you mom's chair. It's mine."

Although perplexed, he said, "What about the cleaning people? Could they have done this?"

"They only clean this office on Friday's," she said. "John, I'm positive it was her."

He glared in anger. "So am I."

The Emergency Room staff had Mary fastened to the gurney and began wheeling her out. Janet and John were somewhat relieved when

Mary smiled at them. As they moved through the corridor, John said, "Janet, I'm going with my mother, but I'll be back."

Dr. Mancini arrived in the ER to find Mary alert, though the pain he observed on her face frightened him. She'd been fortunate to only suffer a bump on her head–however Sam Mancini knew the consequences of her fall were far more grim. "Mary, can you sit up for me?" he said.

As Mary bent forward, Dr. Mancini and John noted her clutching her left leg.

"Sam, I've never felt a pain like this before," she said. "My leg feels like it's burning and numb."

Mancini sighed, then said to John, "Was she hurting as badly before she fell?"

"Not at all, Doctor. Before this morning, she's been feeling fairly well."

"Damn, the fall brought this about," said Mancini. "Mary, I'm calling Dr. Cameron. You can't wait any longer. You need surgery."

"We'll take good care of her, Dr. Mancini," insisted the attending nurse. "Come now, Mrs. Valone. Just lay still and try to relax."

Without another word, John stalked down the hallway, malevolence stamped on his face. He charged into the Staff Office where Janet, Anthony DeTorrio, and Debra Nichols were discussing the circumstances.

"There he is, Tony," she said, pointing at John. "He's the one who accused me of breaking the chair."

Already familiar with the hostility of John's character, DeTorrio sought a mild approach. "I'm sorry what happened here, son."

"I'm not your son, jerkoff," he said maliciously, while advancing towards the desk where the broken chair remained. "I want to know what you're going to do about this."

"There could be several possible reasons why the chair broke, Mr. Valone," he calmly said.

"Bullshit! Look at this chair. Any idiot can see it was tampered with. What the fuck are you going to do about it?"

"Mr. Valone, please watch your language," said DeTorrio. "There are ladies present."

"Correction, asshole!" thundered John Valone, his emotions heightening by the second. He pointed to Janet and said, "She is a lady. That thing standing next to you is a fat, greasy pig who deliberately arranged for the fucking chair to break."

"I should slap your goddamned face," Nichols threatened, venturing a step closer before being halted by DeTorrio.

"Try it, dickbreath," said John. "See what happens."

Though incensed by John's retort, Anthony DeTorrio maintained his composure to say, "Debra, please call Security and the police. Ms. Silva, I think it best if you left the office, too."

With Nichols gone and Janet only a few steps outside, DeTorrio faced John–grateful the desk separated them. "Mr. Valone, I realize you're angry, but please calm down. Now as to the chair, it was just placed in this office last weekend for Ms. Silva's use, not your mother's. It's a brand-new chair. The bolt could have been a factory defect, or perhaps someone from Maintence failed to properly assemble it. I assure you this wasn't deliberate."

"Your fulla shit," said John. He took the bolt from his pocket, then smashed it atop the desk. "Tell me how this steel bolt is defective. C'mon you fuckin' weasel, tell me!"

"I didn't say the fucking bolt was defective!" DeTorrio screamed in retaliation, having tolerated enough insolence. "I said it could have been defective."

"Yeah? Try explaining the chipped paint on the shaft where the bolt inserts."

"It could have came that way from the factory."

His justifications pushed John over the brink. DeTorrio sensed it, as he immediately began giving ground. Mary Valone's son had the expression of an insane man.

"You're a fuckin' moron!" roared John. "Here, asshole, take a closer look!"

With one continuous motion, he lifted the bottom portion of the chair and flung it across the room, forcing Anthony DeTorrio to hurriedly dart from the projectile's path.

Sam Mancini and a security guard rushed in. "John!" yelled Mancini. "Stop it!"

"You sonofabitch!" Tony bellowed. "I'll kill you!"

Dr. Mancini jumped in front of John, forcibly restraining the powerful young man before he could get his hands on DeTorrio. "Damn it, John, settle down."

"Get outta my way, Sam, that little punk just said he's going to kill me," said John, the veins protruding from his neck. "C'mon, tough guy, I'll give you the first punch. Fuck you, I'll give you the first ten punches. I'll kick your fuckin' ass like it's never been kicked before!"

Moving towards the doorway, the tyrant was through attempting to reason. "Guard, hold him here until the police arrive."

"They're on their way, Mr. DeTorrio," said the guard, the name Ken inscribed on the label of his coat.

"I want the police to see this, you fuckin' pussy!" John shouted to DeTorrio.

"Okay, just slow down now," said the guard. "Get against the wall by the window. Stand there and don't move."

John ignored the guard while facing Dr. Mancini, "That fat bitch did this, Sam. I know it. Janet knows it. That little mope over there knows it."

"Maybe she did, but right now we have to think of Mary," said the doctor. "You can't help her if you attack him and get thrown in jail."

"What about my mother?"

"The fall did aggravate her condition," he said. "But I just got off the phone with Dr. Cameron. He wants Mary at Shadydell Heights today. Dr. Cameron promised me that Dr. Nasser will operate on your mom as soon as possible. Okay? Now please calm yourself."

Dr. Mancini was thankful when he felt the push begin to ebb from John's muscular biceps, yet released him gradually–just in case. John pocketed the bolt and said, "Alright, Sam, I'm good. Let's go see my mother."

"Just a damn minute!" barked the pit-bull. "You're not going anywhere until the police get here. And give me the bolt. That's hospital property."

"Come and get it, tough guy," John taunted him.

Fearful of another uprising, Mancini blocked his path. "Tony, forget the damn bolt. His mother's in the ER. He has every right to be upset."

Refusing to knuckle-under, DeTorrio said, "Guard, I want that bolt."

"Fuck you," said John. "I'm giving it to the police."

"Guard, if you expect to keep your job, make him give you the bolt!" shouted DeTorrio.

Immediately the guard drew his gun. "Now listen, we don't want any more trouble. Put the bolt on the desk, and step back against the wall."

"No, Ken," said John. "I'll give it to the police."

Without further prompting, Ken pointed his pistol at John's chest. "The bolt on the desk. Now!"

Quickly Sam Mancini moved in front of John. "Put the gun away, Ken," he said. "We'll all wait for the police."

"On the floor, facedown," the guard ordered, waving his pistol downward.

"No, Ken," replied John with hard defiance–stepping to the side of Dr. Mancini. "I'm standing right here until the police come."

As many of the hospital employees whom were gathered outside the office kept imploring the security guard to put his gun away, Ken refused. Despite his being of similar diminutive stature as DeTorrio, he imposing glared at John Valone, waiting for his knees to buckle in fear of his .38 caliber revolver. Yet his target stood steadfast.

"I'm telling you for the last time, boy," said Ken. "On the floor."

John smiled at him, while pointing to the people in the hallway. "My, my, you've got quite an audience out there, Kenny." He held open his black leather jacket. "Go ahead, pull the trigger if you got the stones. Or you just waiting for someone to take your fuckin' picture?"

The silence brought about by John's bold reply was suddenly interrupted as a Vernon Park police officer came rushing through the crowd. "Guard, holster your weapon right now," said the big man dressed in full police uniform blue.

"Officer, this man was ready to assault Mr. Anthony—"

"I'm in command of the situation," said the police officer. "Holster your weapon."

"He also threw a chair at Mr. DeTorrio."

Without additional response, the policeman moved between Ken and John, brandishing a menacing gloss as he released the strap that secured his own weapon. Ken swallowed hard as the officer placed his hand on the handle of his own firearm.

"Guard, holster your weapon! I won't say it again."

Quickly, Ken did so.

Now entirely in control of the scene, the officer pulled his radio from his belt. In communication with his command-center, he requested for any available police assistance. Having received response another police-unit was nearing the hospital, he fiercely grabbed John's arm and said, "Guard, another unit will be here shortly. Coordinate with them. Get written statements from anyone who can attest to what happened here. I'm taking this man to the station for his statement."

DeTorrio made his way forward. "I'm pressing charges against you, you cocksucker!" he shouted. "I'll be seeing you again."

John Valone stared with predatorial eyes. His handsome face was turned into a portrait of evil. The hatred they bore each other galvanized all in observance. "Pray that you don't."

CHAPTER FOURTEEN

"You stupid cunt!" Anthony DeTorrio screamed at Debra Nichols later that morning in the privacy of his own office. "How in the fuck could you even think of pulling such a dumb stunt like that?"

"I meant for that blonde bitch to fall," she said. "Not Mary."

"Why?"

"I want to be your secretary. If Janet had gotten hurt, you could have promoted me."

"Are you out of your fucking mind! The woman I pulled out of Admissions is a damn good secretary and she's been struggling to keep up with Janet's work. As incompetent as you are, you'd never even come close."

"But lover—"

"Don't lover me, you silly twit. I put you in the Staff Office to help Mary and Janet, not to fuck around with the furniture. They're the two best secretaries I've got. I hoped you'd try to learn from them, not just sit on your ass all day like some lazy bitch."

"Why don't you make Janet the Medical Staff Secretary while I'll learn how to be your secretary?"

DeTorrio cast an unapproving glare as he reached into his desk for a pharmacy bottle. "What about Mary?"

"Fire her."

"Fire her! I should fire you! Debbie, you were in her office. You saw for yourself how much work she's responsible for."

"Tony, if you really wanted to, you could fix it so Janet stays over there for good and I'm trained to be your secretary." Nichols displayed her tongue. "Just think, we could have sex every day."

"You really don't understand, do you?" said DeTorrio with disgust.

"I'll try my best to learn—"

"Debbie, shut your fucking mouth!" he yelled. "Do you actually believe that just because I let you suck my dick that I'd put you in a job where you're totally inadequate? Now listen to me, bubblehead. As much as neither of us cares for Janet, I can't fire her without cause. As for Mary, she is by far the best secretary at Valleyview. You may not give a shit, but I do. I've had Mary do sixty, seventy page detailed reports for me many times. I asked her to try to have them done before the end of the day, even work overtime if she needed to. Take a guess when she'd always email the reports to me."

"Umm—"

"By lunch at the very latest. Fuck, it would take you a month to accomplish what Mary does in half a day."

"Tony, that isn't very fair."

"I don't give a fiddler's fuck about fair! Shut up. Next, gossip has it that Mary might retire soon. And after today, you may very well have convinced her to. So even if I did want Mary out, why should I risk antagonizing her, especially now with her set for surgery. Only someone with the IQ of a fucking cucumber like you would even think of doing something so idiotic."

"I didn't know Mary was thinking of quitting—"

"Whoop-de-do, you didn't know something! Debbie, let me tell you, that isn't any real newsflash. Fuck, the sum of everything you don't know would fill the Atlantic Ocean."

"Tony!"

"Shut up! Another point you might be able to comprehend. If I were as stupid as you and did terminate any employee with a pre-existing medical condition, every bleeding-heart agency dealing with employee rights would be blowing fire up my ass until I reinstated them. I don't need that kind of hassle. But what outweighs all else, because of your incredible stupidity I have to take into account Mary's accident as well as her son."

"Her son's a lunatic," she said.

"Yeah, he's got a big mouth, but I've been told he's very protective of Mary, and he's an intelligent kid." DeTorrio leaned back and said, "No, the smart play here is to be nothing but nice to both Mary and her son."

"Why be nice to him?"

"Stupid cunt," he snapped at her. "Because after Mary's recovered from surgery, if she wants to return to work, fine. Or if she wants to retire, fine. Either way, she'll be doing what she wants. Most importantly, I can only hope her son is less-inclined to pursue the debacle you caused today."

"Tony, I'm sorry, I thought—"

"Stop thinking! If you had an ounce of common sense, you would have realized what a dimwitted thing that was to do! Now hear me good, Debbie. Janet was here right after the police took Mary's son. She refuses to work with you. So since I'm forced to keep her in the Staff Office for the time being, you're going back to Medical Records as of right now. And I'm warning you that if I hear even one peep about your not trying to improve your work, the only job you'll ever have around here will be scrubbing the fucking toilets. Understand?!"

"Yes," she said in a stilled tone.

DeTorrio sat quiet–his cruel temperate finally appeased for the first time of the day. He pointed to the door and said, "I'm not paying you to sit there. Records is on the bottom floor of the hospital. Get over there."

"What about tonight?"

"No, Debbie, after all you put me through today, I'm not in the mood. Once this all blows over, then we'll see."

*****

"Okay, John," said Officer William Gill, closing the door behind him. "I listened to your version all the way back here. Now that you're in a better frame of mind, I want to hear it again for my report."

"Gee, Officer, I don't know," John said, smiling. "Maybe I should call Robert W. Cook, Attorney at Law."

"Be glad I was first on the scene. You might be needing Bob."

"If this is an official interrogation, then you'd better read me my Miranda Rights. I watch *Law and Order* reruns. Your case could get tossed on a technicality if you fail to read me my rights."

"Stop it, ya fuck," said Butch. "Just run everything by me again."

"Long or short version, Officer Gill?"

"Oh, jeez," Butch mumbled. "Short."

"The fat sow arranged for a chair to break in Mary's office, my mother sat on it and fell, I went in and saw the chair had been tampered with, the scumbag who runs the hospital tried to feed me a line of bullshit about it not being intentional, so I threw the chair at him. Then the—"

"Okay, okay," said Butch, his face projecting concern as he continued to roll the stripped bolt atop his desk. "I got the picture." A brief pause. "How about your mom?"

"She's being ambulanced to Shadydell Hospital where they're going to operate on her. Butch, no disrespect, but I'd like to get this over with so I can go home and pack some stuff and get down there with her."

"Was she badly injured by the fall?"

"Bad enough that they've moved her surgery up to sometime the next couple days."

"Yeah, I heard you talking with a doctor on the way here. What's he think about Mary?"

"That was Dr. Cameron, Mary's neurologist. Judging from what Dr. Mancini told him, Dr. Cameron thinks she'll be okay after the operation."

"Glad to hear it. Tell your mom Amy, Kathy, and I are pulling for her."

John smiled in thanks, then said, "Butch, I gotta get moving pretty soon. Dr. Cameron told me he would be seeing Mary later this afternoon, and the surgeon would be with him."

"Alright, just a few more minutes." Despite his attempting not to, Butch grinned. "I still can't believe you threw a chair at Anthony DeTorrio. That guy's got a lot of juice around here."

"Why not? Remember when Bobby Knight threw a chair at the ref? We both thought that was hysterical."

"C'mon, John, this ain't no laughing matter. Considering the circumstances, everything you did can be justified except for your throwing the chair at DeTorrio."

"He's lucky Dr. Mancini and that rent-a-cop showed when they did, because I woulda beat that little scumbag silly."

"No, you were lucky they were there to stop you," Butch implored. "If you'd put a hand on him, that's assault just for starters."

"Butch, we've been best friends for a long time now, and you don't have any idea how much I can't wait to have you for a brother-in-law," said John. "But when it comes to my mother, anyone fucks with her, their ass is mine. Fuck assault. Their ass is mine."

"Look, don't get me wrong, I would have been just as pissed as you were if something like that would have happened to Amy or my mother. But, John, you gotta understand, we ain't kids anymore. Sure when we were younger, somebody got into a fight it wasn't a big deal back then. Maybe we got sent to bed without supper. Maybe we got a slap on the wrist. But not anymore. Hey, I learned the hard way with Crawford."

"Please don't remind me of him."

"Yeah, I hate thinking about him myself, but I'm trying to make you understand the way it is. Granted you had every right to be angry today, but you've gotta learn how to control your temper."

"Who, me?" said John, smiling. "C'mon, Butch, you know me. I'm a sweetheart."

"You can be, but like you just said, I know you. I remember all the fights you were in back in school. I remember in Hershey when you were ready to fight Denny Perella. He was—"

"Ah, we didn't fight—"

"Let me finish," Butch interrupted in resonating tone. "You didn't get into it with Denny because we were there to stop you. Then you went a few years without getting into a fight. I still remember thinking, 'he's finally mellowing-out.' Then Gene told me and the guys about how you beat the hell outta your cousin."

"He insulted Mary," said John matter-of-factly.

"Okay, maybe he did deserve to get slapped around a little," Butch said. "Gene told us you beat the guy to a pulp. Even after you'd knocked him down, you put your knees on his arms and kept swinging until Mary, Gene, and some of your neighbors finally were able to pull you off him."

John shrugged his shoulders. "That's over and done with. I want to know what you're planning on doing about the chair. I want a full investigation conducted."

"Officer Luzanski brought it in," Butch said. "We don't have a crime lab in Vernon Park, so it'll be sent to Westlake County for examination. Although I have to tell you, John, I wouldn't expect too much."

"Why not?"

"Other than somebody actually seeing her messing with the car, the only possible way a case could be made against Nichols would be through fingerprints. Forget the bolt, we've both handled it. As for the chair, considering you, Janet, DeTorrio, and whoever else may have had their hands on the area that connected the back-rest to the seat, chances are all they'll end-up with are smudges."

"But she was in the office alone the night before! I'm telling you, Butch, that's when she did it."

"John, I believe you. I'll call the Westland DA's office and find out what they think. I'll even go to Valleyview myself and ask around. All I'm saying is, don't get your hopes up."

"Fuckin' bitch," said John, gritting his teeth. "Fat hog should enter an ugly contest. What about DeTorrio? You heard anything from him yet?"

"Not yet," said Butch. "If he does press charges, you'll get a notice by mail from the Magistrate's Office. Although once the Magistrate reads my incident-report, most you'd get would be a Summary Offense that would require you to pay for any damages."

"Thanks, Butch. Okay, anything else? I gotta go see Mary."

"Just one last thing," Butch replied, casting rueful eyes. "John, as you said, we've been best friends for a long time and like you, I can't wait for the day when one of your and Vicky's kids calls me 'Uncle Butch.' Just please remember, do all you can to better control your temper."

CHAPTER FIFTEEN

"Mary, I'd like for you and John to meet someone," Dr. Cameron proudly announced, as he and another man approached her hospital bed. "This is Dr. Rasheem Nasser."

From the moment they'd made his introduction, the Valone's recognized the doctor to be a unique individual. For a man of common height and build, there was an incandescing aura about Dr. Nasser that revealed itself without reservation. His tanned face, though not unduly handsome, was the kind that caused people to stare at him–almost as if they were on the periphery of a trance. His full head of premature silvery-white hair glistened, casting a reflecting shine upon the shoulder-line of the double-breasted, charcoal-gray suit he was clad in. His comportment expressed extreme intellect. His presence suggested royalty.

"Mrs. Valone, Dr. Cameron and I have reviewed your MRI," he said without any trace of an accent. "The erosion of L4-L5 is very common with its fragmentation being minor. Your surgery will be a routine case."

"Dr. Nasser, do you anticipate any problems with my operation?" Mary asked.

"None whatsoever, Ma'am. If I may, I'll outline what your surgery will entail."

"Please do, Dr. Nasser," said Mary–already taken by his charms.

"At the intersection of your waistline and spine, I shall make a vertical incision. I'll remove any or all of L4-L5 that has become diminished. In the region vacated, I shall insert a section of bone to replace it. I will then probe the area near your sciatic nerve and remove the fragment that has been bringing about your pain. Any questions so far?"

"I understand the procedure, Doctor. About what time tomorrow?"

"You're scheduled for 7 A.M. You'll be in the Recovery Room before 9 A.M. altogether free of sciatic pain when you awaken. Once the anesthetic wears off, you may encounter some minor discomfort in the general vicinity of your incision simply as a result of surgical invasion.

That will subside within a few days. You may also incur a bit of innocuous stiffness in your lower back due to the bone-graft, though that too shall quickly abate. That's about it. You'll be up-and-about by Friday and I expect to discharge you by Sunday, perhaps even Saturday if Dr. Cameron and I feel you're prepared to go home."

"And afterwards, I want you to take at least five weeks off from work to fully recover, even though you'll be able to return much sooner," added Dr. Cameron. "You certainly deserve an extended vacation from the hospital and Tony. I'll go into greater detail concerning your post-operative care when you're discharged."

"Mrs. Valone, I must be leaving," said Dr. Nasser. "Please rest easy tonight. Place the operation completely out of mind. Honestly, your surgery will not pose any difficulties. It was a pleasure meeting with you and your son. I'll see you both in the morning."

"I must be leaving as well," said Dr. Cameron. "Mary, I'll stop by tomorrow afternoon. Now don't worry. Dr. Nasser is the very best."

Mary looked to John once they'd departed. "Well, what did you think of him?"

"He impressed me," said John. "I was expecting some guy wearing a turban and a toga. Wasn't I wrong. That is one very impressive man. Let's just hope he's as good as he thinks he is."

*****

The following morning John anxiously awaited news of his mother's surgery. The first hour had passed quickly, though he was now at the point of peeking at his wristwatch every other minute while he sat with his eyes riveted upon the doorway where Dr. Nasser would emerge. Still he wondered why Vicky hadn't arrived as she'd promised.

As imperilous as Dr. Nasser had made her operation sound, Mary had spent the previous evening concerned about her future. Her knowledge of the many botched surgical cases at Valleyview General Hospital had brought about a sense of anxiety overriding Nasser's assurances. The expression of fear that blanketed her face as she was being wheeled into the operating room lingered with John, as he crossed his forearms and continued to wait.

A short time later, the door opened. Dr. Nasser approached, still in surgical garb flashing a smile of confidence. "Mr. Valone, your mother's doing just fine," he said. "The operation went perfectly."

John vaulted to his feet. "No problems at all, Doctor?"

"None whatsoever," said Dr. Nasser. "As Dr. Cameron and I had deduced, the fragment was relatively easy to extract. It was lodged at the sciatic nerve, however I wasn't able to ascertain any impairment of the nerve itself. What remains of her L4-L5 disc-body is healthy tissue not presenting the slightest inclination of any further degeneration. In addition, the bone-fusion went perfectly. Young man, without any doubt, your mother will make an unequivocal recovery."

"Dr. Nasser," he said, obviously relieved while shaking his hand, "I appreciate all of your expertise and diligence on behalf of my mother. Sir, from the bottom of my heart, thank you very much."

"Mr. Valone, it was my pleasure," he replied humbly. "Dr. Cameron speaks very highly of Mary. He's told me what a splendid lady she is. I'm proud to have been of service."

"Very kind of Dr. Cameron and yourself, Doctor. Thank you."

"You're most welcome. Now your mother's still unconscious in the recovery room. I have another surgery to perform, so I'll be checking on her in an hour or so. She'll be taken back to her room afterwards. Why don't you get some breakfast and unwind a bit. I'll stop by to see your mother later today."

*****

"Mrs. Valone," Dr. Nasser whispered softly, waking Mary from an anesthetic fog. "Welcome back."

"I made it, Doctor," she said in a raspy voice.

Dr. Nasser flashed a smile of confidence. "Of course you did. Are you coherent enough to understand me?"

"I think so," she said, her hazel-green eyes wide open.

"Alright, now without moving, tell me if there's any sensation of pain in your back or leg."

"None at all, Dr. Nasser. I feel fantastic."

"Fine. Now gently flex your legs. Do you feel any pain whatsoever?"

The joyous expression that brightened Mary's face answered his question. "Dr. Nasser, that terrible burning pain is gone. Thank God."

"No, Mrs. Valone. Thank me."

*****

"You ready, Ma?" said John, as he and Vicky walked into her room Saturday morning after Dr. Cameron had given Mary a final examination. "Let's get outta this joint. I hate the smell of hospitals."

"Yes, Dr. Cameron signed my discharge papers. The nurse sent for someone to wheel me out."

"Ah, baloney. You don't need a wheelchair. C'mon, let's go."

"Hospital policy, John," she said. "Why don't you bring the car around to the front entrance, and we'll meet you there."

John's happiness was outward when Mary quickly lifted herself from the wheelchair and effortlessly walked to the car, declining any assistance he and the nurse offered. Considering Mary's condition prior to surgery, her recovery was nothing short of remarkable.

Both Doctors' Nasser and Cameron had marveled at the resilience Mary Valone displayed during her short stay at Shadydell Heights. She was walking without support the evening of her operation; her incisional pain had dissipated by Friday; the minor stiffness of her lower back regions Dr. Nasser had forewarned never came to be. When Dr. Cameron had offered to prescribe a painkiller for Mary that morning, she'd declined, informing the doctor she had the Darvocet that Dr. Mancini had given her.

"Mary, you've been an exceptional patient," Dr. Cameron had said prior. "Dr. Nasser and I are amazed at your recuperative powers. Be that as it may, I still insist you refrain from any form of physical exertion for at least a month. I'll have my secretary call you to schedule an appointment early in March. If you need anything or have any concerns whatsoever, please do not hesitate to call either Dr. Nasser or I. If Tony asks why you're not back at work before you see me, tell him to call me. Now go home and enjoy your vacation."

Vicky spent the ride back to Vernon Park speaking with Mary about how flawlessly her operation had gone, as well as all the many visitors she had received during her brief stay at the hospital. She also kept insisting that she and John were to be wed.

Immediately upon their arrival home, Mary observed the house wasn't up to her standards. "John," she said, "this place is a mess."

"I spent fifteen minutes cleaning this morning."

"Wow, fifteen minutes. You poor thing. You must be exhausted."

"Come on, Mary, I'll be glad to help," said Vicky. "And you're going to help too, buster."

"What the heck do I know about cleaning?" said John, holding his palms upward. "Can I help it if I'm a slob."

"It's about time you learned."

"You tell him, Vicky," said Mary. "John, you can start by running the sweeper over the entire house, including the basement. And do under the pool table."

"And when you're done with that, I'll have lots more for you," added Vicky. "So get busy."

"Nag, nag, nag," he said in jest, with the telephone sounding from the kitchen. "Now I'm getting' nagged in stereo. Alright, I give up, I'm outnumbered. But Ma, you're not doing anything except supervising."

While carrying the vacuum into the living room, he overheard Mary speaking, "Thank you, Gene. I feel much better. Hold on, he's right here."

"Get over here and help me clean!" John said to Gene. "These two women are trying to turn me neat."

"Can't help you there, pal," said Gene. "Glad to hear Mary's okay."

"Thanks, Gene. Yeah, everything went great with her surgery. What's up?"

"The whole gang's going to Wheeling tonight. Think you can make it?"

"I'm not sure, Gene. Depends on how Mary's doing and if Janet's coming over. I'll let you know for sure later."

*****

"Where is he?" Vicky asked of Mary, returning to the living room after she had showered and changed clothes. "It's almost five-thirty."

"He has to be next door with Gene," said Mary, resting comfortably on the white living room couch watching television. "You'd better go get him."

When Vicky stepped outside, she saw Gene's car pulling from his driveway as John walked towards her. "We're going to be late if you don't hurry," she said.

"Vicky, I'm sorry, I think we should stay here tonight."

"You said we were going out. Why'd you change your mind?"

"Because Janet can't make it tonight. She thought Mary wouldn't be home until tomorrow, so she made other plans."

"Honey, your mother's doing just fine," she said. "You've been with her ever since her operation. You even stayed overnight at the hospital the night after she was operated on. You know there isn't anything bothering her. Now come on. Mary wants us to go out tonight and have some fun."

"I can't leave her alone only after a few hours after she was discharged. Who knows what might happen. Plus I'd bet the minute we walked out, she'd be on her hands and knees scrubbing the kitchen and bathroom floors."

"Don't be silly. Mary wouldn't do that."

"Ha! You don't know how stubborn she can be. I'm gonna have a professional cleaner do every floor and carpet in this house. Dr. Cameron said for her not to overextend herself, and I intend to see that she follows his orders."

"Aren't any of her other friends stopping by?"

"Not until tomorrow," said John.

"What about the lady with that little dog who stopped by earlier?"

"That was Nancy Schriver. Vicky, I can't just call her and ask her to stay with Mary tonight."

"So that's it!" she snapped in an unbecoming inflection.

Vicky eyed him with a look reminiscent of their past. "Tell me something, John. Exactly how much longer will you be babysitting your mother? Another week? A month?"

"Sweetie, please don't be like that," he said. "I just can't leave Mary home alone her first night out of the hospital. It isn't right. I'd like for us to go to Wheeling, but we'll just have to wait for another night. Next weekend, I'll take you wherever you'd like."

"Alright then, I guess that's the way it's going to be. Although I still think you're being entirely unreasonable about Mary."

*****

Tuesday morning, a cleaning-service spent hours making the Valone's home sparkle; polishing all the furniture; steam-cleaning the plush mauve carpeting; waxing the marble of the kitchen, laundry, and three bathrooms floors–with Mary hot on their heels in observance.

After the cleaning crew had gone, Mary went to the basement to find John seated on the leather couch staring at a dark television screen.

"They do a good job?" he asked.

"Very good. Everything's spotless."

"Glad you're happy. Ma, sit down. There's a couple things I'd like to discuss with you."

"I thought there was something on your mind," said Mary, as she sat next to him. "You have that look on your face."

"It shows, huh?"

"I can usually tell when something's bothering you."

John shifted his position to face her. "What are you planning to do about the hospital?"

"I haven't made up my mind yet. I'd planned to resign this summer, but something inside me keeps telling me not to. I suppose it's the fear we all have of growing old. I've seen too many people retire from their jobs and before long, I see their name in the obituaries."

"What does Dr. Mancini think?"

"Sam keeps encouraging me to come back. I'm not sure, John. I think I'm just going to use my sick-days until Dr. Cameron clears me to return. I'll make my decision then."

"What about that DeTorrio jerk? He'll probably try to make your life miserable if you go back to work."

"Not according to Dr. Mancini," she said. "Sam told me that Tony is actually hoping I return to my job, so Janet can return to hers. And for his trying to make my life miserable, he tries to make everybody's life miserable. Anthony DeTorrio isn't happy unless he's yelling or belittling someone." Mary shook her head and grinned. "That's why I wasn't upset with you when Janet told me how you'd screamed at him."

While her commentary on DeTorrio annoyed him, he let it pass. Yet he said, "I don't want you working anywhere near that Nichols—girl again."

"Don't worry about her, Janet has her friend Pam as her assistant now. Nichols is back in Medical Records supposedly behaving herself."

"Yeah, probably doing nothin' but feeding her fat face. Okay, for arguments sake, let's say you do decide to retire. What are the possibilities of DeTorrio messing around with your pension?"

"He can't," Mary said. "Janet knows the administrative side better than I do. She insists Valleyview's pension-plan is guaranteed by an independent holding company in Iowa."

"So Janet's sure DeTorrio can't monkey-around with your pension?"

"Absolutely sure. Tony knows better than to try something foolish. He wouldn't dare create waves that would result in a public investigation against the hospital that he couldn't fix."

"That's a relief," he said. "Well, regardless of that little worm, you know that I'd like for you to retire. Nevertheless I understand your reasoning, so it's your decision."

"Come on, what else is on your mind?" said Mary, as she continued to watch his eyes dart aimlessly about the room.

"What do you really think about Vicky?"

"I liked Vicky the very first time I met her. She's a gorgeous, sweet, intelligent girl who loves you dearly. Don't you love her?"

"I do, but—"

"Son, there aren't any buts about it. If you love her, ask her to marry you. Beautiful single girls like Vicky are few and far between. I remember how heartbroken you were the last time. So here you are in love with her again and from what I've seen, she loves you just as much. If you truly love her, marry her. Don't risk losing her again."

"Vicky keeps pushing me to purpose. She wants to get married." A brief pause. "I don't know yet. I'm just not sure."

Mary sighed and said, "John, I can't help you make up your mind. Do what your heart tells you. Although in my opinion, if you do something that makes her reject you again, you won't get another opportunity."

"Ma, I realize that. I'm just worried that after we got married, she'd revert back to her old self, trying to constantly impose her will upon me. Sure I understand the necessities of compromise. It's just—it's just that I've noticed some subtle things about her that concern me."

"Like what?"

"For example, when you came home from Shadydell and I decided we shouldn't go out, she got upset with me."

"She didn't seem that upset to me."

"Oh, she was. Sure she was polite the whole night in front of you, but I could tell she was pouting."

"John, don't criticize her for that night. Vicky was disappointed because she wanted to go to Wheeling with you and your friends."

"But that's my point, Ma. Ever since we started dating again, every time I offer to take her to someplace where the guys were going to be, she was always against it. But the one night when I thought it best to stay home with you, all of a sudden she wants to go. See the contradiction?"

"That's silly," Mary insisted. "Vicky just needed a night out with you and your friends. You can't fault her for that."

"Not with my friends she didn't. Ma, let me explain something to you. Vicky puts-up with Butch. She gets along with Amy, Bob Cook, and his wife, Diane. As for the rest of the guys and even some of their wives, I'd say they fall somewhere between moderately disliked and totally unacceptable to her."

"Sometimes you and your pals do get carried-away a little too much." Mary smiled. "I almost wet the bed at Shadydell when Gene asked Janet if she wanted to go out on a date."

"Ma, it isn't only Vicky's attitude about my friends that scares me. I've noticed other little nuances about her that have me worried. I just don't want to rush into marriage until I'm completely certain about her."

"You can be just as stubborn as I am, can't you?"

John grinned to say, "Hey, I inherited being stubborn from you."

"Yes, you sure did," she said. "John, all I can say is do what you think is best. Just remember though, if Vicky's heart is set on getting married and she sees yours isn't, you may lose her forever."

Mary reached to rub her lower back.

"What's wrong?" asked John.

"It's nothing. My back's a little sore. Dr. Nasser and Dr. Cameron said I may develop some stiffness post-op."

CHAPTER SIXTEEN

By the second week of February, it had become very evident to Mary Valone that something was wrong. The pain and stiffness in her lower back kept increasing, resulting in a constant throbbing ache at her surgical scar. The box of Darvocet samples Dr. Mancini had given her were gone. Although her scheduled appointment with Dr. Cameron remained some two weeks away, she was desperate when she called his office as soon as John had departed for a new consulting assignment.

Dr. Cameron was congenial with Mary when he arranged to squeeze her into his overcrowded schedule. Cameron appeared sincere while listening to her complaints, then stated his opinion. "Mary, this type of discomfort is somewhat common with patients around your age who have had back surgery. Honestly, I've seen it many times before."

"But Dr. Cameron, why didn't I feel this pain immediately after my operation?" Mary asked of him. "I could be infected. I'd like for you to order a sed-rate for me."

"No, Mary," he said. "Trust me, you're not infected. Your system was probably just a bit hypersensitive to surgical evasion, thus your body simply had a delayed reaction. Mary, this is what I think we should do. I'd like for you to do some mild stretching exercise in an attempt to alleviate this problem. Nothing too strenuous, mind you. Just leg-lifts and various types of other movements that should help alleviate your back stiffness. My secretary will give you a booklet that illustrates exactly what kind of exercises I'd like you to perform. Also, I'll give you a script for Percocet."

"Doctor, I've never taken Percocet, but I know they're strong."

"Don't worry, you won't be on them very long. Let's try this course for the time being."

For the next week, Mary followed Dr. Cameron's advice by exercising daily–it only seemed to heighten the rigidity of her lower back. Although the Percocet did offer some relief, she could feel her pain growing progressively worse, as her array of discomforts were now compounded by burning sensations along with muscle spasms. She took the last pill Dr. Cameron had given her when she arrived at his office for her appointment. Her mistake: Mary had been continuously telling John that she was beginning to feel better, and there wasn't any need for him to accompany her to Dr. Cameron's office.

There Dr. Cameron had Mary undergo an MRI. The disc that had caused the initial problem showed no additional degeneration. Her bone fused to the region appeared healthy. Yet Cameron noted some sort of abnormality.

As the doctor was opening the door to her examination room, Mary said, "Did you find anything, Dr. Cameron?"

"I'm afraid not, Mary. I compared this MRI to the set I took at Shadydell. Other than the bone-graft, there aren't any physiological changes at the L4-L5 level."

"Then what's causing my pain, Dr. Cameron?"

"I believe your body needs a little more time to recover," said Cameron. "However, since I'm convinced your problem is not neurologically related, it's now my concern that you pain could be of an orthopedic nature. So I'll arrange for you to see my partner, Dr. Harold Elliot. Perhaps with his input, we'll be able to better ascertain what is causing your discomfort."

"Doctor, could I have an infection?" she asked.

"No, Mary, there isn't the slightest trace of redness or swelling at your incision that would specify the potential of infection. Nor is there anything depicted on your MRI that would even remotely indicate the possibility. In addition, Dr. Nasser's surgical record is unsurpassed for his patient's not ever incurring any type of infection."

"Shouldn't you order a sed-rate to make certain?"

"It isn't necessary, Mary," said Cameron. "There isn't any hint of infection represented on your MRI. I can see that you're in pain, but I assure you it isn't as a result of infection."

"Then what should I do? The exercise regiment is only aggravating my pain."

"Discontinue the exercise program. I'll have my secretary schedule another appointment. Just stay here a few minutes, Mary. Dr. Elliot will see you. Perhaps he can help."

"I hope so, Doctor. Oh, Dr. Cameron, I need more Percocet."

"Certainly," he said, taking a script-pad from his suit pocket. "Mary, don't worry. You're going to get over this setback before much longer."

Moments later, a balding man of middle-age wearing a white coat to his knees entered her room. "Mrs. Valone, I'm Dr. Elliot," he said. "Dr. Cameron asked me to speak with you."

"Hello, Doctor," she said.

After Mary had detailed her circumstances, Dr. Elliot said, "Mrs. Valone, as you're aware, I'm an orthopedic. Dr. Cameron believes your condition could be orthopedic as opposed to neurologic. Now please understand, since I'm not a radiologist, nor do I claim to know all the particulars of your medical history, I can only presume that the pain you've been experiencing is a result of what is known as 'mechanical back syndrome.'"

"What causes mechanical back syndrome, Dr. Elliot?"

"Ma'am, it could result from any number of reasons. It is a fairly-rare occurrence. However, just based upon the information Dr. Cameron and yourself have provided me, at this time mechanical back syndrome is my only assumption. I suggest you continue to treat with Dr. Cameron, and continue to follow his instructions."

Later that afternoon, Dr. Elliot stepped through the adjoining door that connected their offices to find Dr. Cameron viewing Mary's films.

"One of yours or mine?" said Elliot.

"Mine. Mary Valone. The lady I asked you to see today."

"Yes, the lady Dr. Nasser operated on. Pain, back spasms, rigidity of her lower spine."

"So she says," followed Cameron, a hint of cynicism in his tone of voice.

Dr. Elliot stood next to him while they studied her MRI. Warily Elliot pointed and said, "What's this shadow near the anterior of L4-L5?"

"Just ignore that," said Cameron. "Nasser did a bone-fusion at L4-L5. That's what he attributes it to."

"Maybe you should seek Dr. Schmidt's opinion."

"No," said Dr. Cameron. "Lately Schmidt's been trying to convince me to hire one of his residents for our office. We don't need him cutting into our profit-margin."

Dr. Elliot's attentions returned to the MRI. Upon further study, he said, "Steve, I'm not sure what to make of her condition. I suggested mechanical back syndrome, although I'm not certain of all the facts of her case. What do you believe is causing her pain?"

"I'm not sure, either. Nasser feels there are a number of possibilities. She's about the age when females go through the change of life. Perhaps she has an estrogen imbalance that's boosting her spasms. Maybe she's in the early stages of arthritis. Or maybe Mary isn't hurting as badly as she's letting-on because she wants more time away from her job."

"Any of which are possible," said Elliot.

"There is one other possibility," Dr. Cameron said. "Maybe she's growing fond of opiates."

On February 26th, her level of pain continuing to mount, Mary arrived at Dr. Nassar's office–without an appointment. Begrudgingly he agreed to see her. Appearing bored as she described her symptoms, he interrupted before she could finish. "Mrs. Valone, there isn't anything wrong other than what you've been told by Dr. Cameron. Stop acting like a child. Keep taking your medications and you'll be fine."

"Dr. Nasser, I'd like for you to order a sed-rate for me."

"Mrs. Valone, that ridiculous!" he jeered. "My patient's don't get infections. It simply takes time for one's body to recover from the shock of surgery. I've looked at your surgical site and all appears normal. Now if you'll please excuse me, I have patients to see." He halted in midstride. "And Mrs. Valone, all of your future examinations should be conducted by Dr. Cameron. I don't have time for patients with petty post-operative discomforts."

Now almost seven weeks removed from her operation, Mary returned to Dr. Cameron on March 3rd. Following yet another MRI, Mary kept informing Dr. Cameron that her pain was growing intolerable, though was extended the same rationalizations she had received two weeks prior. Again she requested a blood analysis–again she was refused.

From the first day Mary had informed him of her post-operative pain, Dr. Sam Mancini was deeply concerned. As her pain had continued to intensify, he'd kept insisting she have a blood test in order to establish her sed-rate. He'd urged Mary to go to the Valleyview Hospital laboratory where they could perform the blood test–despite knowing Dr. Cameron's urbane admonitions that he was always in charge of his patient's post-operative care. Mary understood the protocols in the world of medicine. Despite her pain, she'd continued to shy-away from Mancini's advice, instead promising she would have her blood tested soon, with or without Dr. Cameron's permission. She also had promised Mancini it was time for drastic measures–John needed to be informed of all the facts they had been reluctant to disclose.

All throughout this time, John Valone's distress burgeoned on a daily basis. It would tear him apart when he'd see Mary staggering around the house in a stupor from the codeine-based narcotics she was dependant upon. He had continually urged Mary to be re-admitted to the hospital, yet she would always respond by asking him to wait until tomorrow.

He arrived home on March 3rd in the evening. The house was dark when he came through the garage. Instantly he rushed into Mary's bedroom. To his absolute appall, he found Mary crawling on the floor as if she were a wounded animal, whimpering in pain.

"Dr. Mancini, this is John Valone," his voice boomed into his cell phone.

"How is she, John?"

"Sam, she's in bad shape! I just lifted her off the floor. She was crawling to her bed. Sam, I'm tired of all the crap those doctors have been giving her about her pain being normal. My God, she's going to be dead pretty soon if something isn't done!"

"John, take her to the Shadydell Heights Emergency Room, right now! Have her admitted to Dr. Cameron. Do you know if Mary's had a sed-rate conducted?"

"What the hell's that?!"

"It's a blood analysis to determine infection. I've been telling her to have it taken."

"Damn it, Sam, she never mentioned it to me! You shoulda told me she needed it."

"I'm sorry, I wish I had, but your mother didn't want you to worry. John, demand Dr. Cameron or Dr. Nasser order a complete blood analysis. Make sure it gets done. Don't take no from either of them."

"Oh, it'll get done, Sam. No matter what, it'll get done."

*****

John awoke the next morning on a chair beside her Mary's hospital bed. Mary had passed-out moments after the ER doctor had deemed it necessary to alleviate her pain with an injection of Demerol. She remained unconscious, now ten hours later.

While observing his mother, he noticed Mary stirring. The medication she had received last night had stopped masking her pain. Instantly he saw her anguish.

"Where am I?" she said.

"Shadydell Hospital, Ma. Dr. Mancini told me to bring you." John looked to the door before handing her three Percocet. "Here, take these. The doctor in the Emergency Room isn't permitted to order anything else for you."

With a drink from her hospital water-bottle, she swallowed the pills. Mary soon said, "I'm glad you brought them. Who knows when Cameron or Nasser will get here. John, I don't know what I'm going to do. I can't stand this pain much longer."

"Why didn't you tell me about the sed-rate?"

"A lot of reasons you wouldn't understand."

"Name one."

"Not now."

He could only snap his lips in disgust.

Dr. Rasheem Nasser sauntered into Room 923 a few hours later. "Mrs. Valone, I see your son had you admitted last night," he said, an air of nonchalance about him. "What seems to be your problem?"

"You know damn well what my problem is," she replied. "Doctor, this pain isn't from muscle spasms. Dr. Mancini and I believe I'm infected. Why can't you accept that possibility?"

"Mrs. Valone, please. You're willing to trust the opinion of a general practitioner from some two-mule town over mine? That's preposterous. All that's required is a stronger pain medication to help you withstand the effects of your infirmity until it starts to slacken. I've notified the nursing staff to continue you on Demerol. You should be receiving your dosage shortly."

"Why won't you order the sed-rate, Doctor? With the results, at least you'd be able to rule out the possibility of infection."

"I'll tell you why," he said, the pitch of his voice raised at first–then tapered down as he glanced at John. While he wasn't looming, a nefarious shadow had descended over his face. "Mrs. Valone, as I informed you at my office, the site about your surgical incision doesn't present the slightest bit of infection. Also as I've told you, never in my entire career have I had a patient plagued by any sort of infectious process. Ma'am, I'm very proud of that fact. Nevertheless if I thought there was a one-in-a-million chance you could have an infection, I would have ordered the test for you weeks ago."

"Dr. Nasser, please, for my peace of mind."

'Mrs. Valone, for the last time, I don't get infections. It shouldn't be much longer before your spasms abate."

"So what you're saying is that you care more about your unblemished reputation than you do my pain!" Mary shouted–her respect for him no longer existent. "That's so damn revolting, it nauseates me! You nauseate me!"

As Nasser pondered his response, a nurse entered the room.

"Sorry for the intrusion, Doctor," she said. "I have Mrs. Valone's medication. I'll come back if you'd prefer."

"That's okay, Nurse," said John, sporting a broad smile as he approached. "My mom needs her medicine. Dr. Nasser, my I please speak with you alone for a moment. I promise it won't take long."

Nasser eyed him cautiously, yet no fears were alerted since there wasn't a grain of malice on John's face. "Just for a minute, though," he said, "I have rounds to make."

"Thank you so much, Doctor," said John most graciously.

Nasser momentarily turned his attention to Mary and said, "Mrs. Valone, Dr. Cameron should be stopping by soon. Trust me, you're going to be fine before much longer."

"What may I do for you?" he asked of John, out in the hallway.

"Dr. Nasser, I'll ask you nice. I want my mother's sed-rate taken right now."

"Mr. Valone, as I've said—no—don't—ughhhhhh—"

His words were abruptly discontinued as John grabbed his throat, and slammed him against the wall. Dr. Nasser jostled briefly to free himself, though John's locked fist as well as his easing his grip just enough to enable him to gasp for breath persuaded him otherwise.

"Listen to me real good, you pompous fucker," whispered John, his face flush, his eyes burning with rage. "I'm only going say this once. I don't give a fuck about your reputation or any of your other bullshit. You order my mother's blood test, or so help me by everything that's holy, I'll kill you right now."

Helplessly Nasser peered down the corridor–hoping help was on the way. Immediately John strengthened his hold on the doctor's esophagus.

"The cavalry won't get here in time, Doc. See the window behind me. If I see anybody coming, you'd better be able to sprout wings because so help me, I'll throw your fuckin' ass straight out the window before they can stop me." He squeezed as tightly as he could, then softly said, "Make up your mind. What's it gonna be, one blood test or someone scraping your dead ass off the sidewalk?"

"You win," Nasser quickly relented, wheezing for air. "It—it might take an hour—"

"No!" he charged, deliberately bashing the doctor's head against the wall. "You got ten minutes to draw my mother's blood. Ten fuckin' minutes or else you're dead meat."

"Alright," he said docilely, trying to regain moisture in his mouth. "I'll make the call to the lab myself."

"Don't even think about playin' fuckin' games with me," John said, again tightening his stranglehold. "If somebody isn't up here in ten minutes, I'll kill your motherfuckin' ass. You might sneak outta here, but I'll find you. I promise you, you'll be dead before the sun goes down."

"I'll call the lab right now."

"Wise choice, Doc,"

Upon releasing him, John began fixing Dr. Nasser's badly mangled necktie and jacket lapel. "Hey, nice suit. Armani or Brione?"

"Armani."

"Thought so," said John, as he brushed his knuckles upon the lapel. "I got a few of them, but I like Brione's better." His thumb and index finger pinched Nasser's cheek, leaving impressions of his fingernails. "Now get your ass in gear. Oh, and Doc, you'd better pray to Allah or whoever the fuck you pray to that she doesn't have an infection."

Dr. Nasser's eyes conveyed his dread. "And if she does?"

His answer came in the form of an evil scowl.

Having dispatched Nasser, John returned into Mary's room to find her sitting-up in bed. "John, please go to the nurse's station and have Dr. Cameron paged. If he won't order my blood test, I'm going to ask for another neurologist. Lord, I thought Valleyview was bad!"

"Easy, Ma, Dr. Nasser's calling the lab. He decided to order your sed-rate."

"How in the hell did you persuade that egotistical son of a bitch to change his mind?"

Barely a shrug. "All it took was a polite negotiation."

*****

"Mary," Dr. Cameron uttered, as he and Dr. Nasser slowly paced into her room later that same morning. Cameron had a somber expression about him–Nasser appeared even more dismal than his colleague, only stealing a quick glance at them before dipping his head. "Your results are in from the lab."

"Well?!" she said rudely, the days of sequestering her acrimony gone.

"I just got off the phone with Dr. Mancini," said Cameron–seemingly searching for his next words. "I inquired if he'd ever recorded your sed-rate."

"Yes, he has. I have a physical every year. I specifically recall when we were reviewing the results during my last exam that Dr. Mancini commented my sed-rate was below the normal range."

"You're correct. Your last reading registered eight. Acceptable parameters are between twelve and twenty."

"Get to the point, Dr. Cameron. What is it now?"

"Your sedimentation-rate is—it's—forty-four."

With John by her side glaring at them, Mary erupted to say, "I've been telling both of you that something was wrong! Dr. Cameron, I was at your office three times after my surgery! Why in the hell wasn't my infection found?!"

"Mary, I'm sorry. It didn't depict itself on the MRI's."

"And you!" she screamed at Nasser. "I begged you to take my sed-rate, but you wouldn't! All you were concerned about was your damned prestige. All I heard was, 'Mrs. Valone, I don't get infections. Mrs. Valone, you'll be fine.' You were wrong, weren't you, you arrogant son of a bitch!"

"Mrs. Valone, I truly am sorry," said Dr. Nasser, his words barely audible. "If you'll please excuse me, Dr. Cameron will inform you as to our intentions how to countermeasure your infection."

"Miserable bastard!" she shouted as loudly as she could.

John squeezed her hand. "Mother, calm down. Let's hear how Dr. Cameron's planning to deal with this." A sinister facial expression ensued. "And it'd better be good."

Dr. Cameron eyed them gingerly. "Mary, I'm terribly sorry. Although as you're aware, the chance of infection is always prevalent in any type of surgical procedure. Unfortunately it happens. It wasn't Dr. Nasser's fault. It wasn't anyone's fault."

"Spare me the lecture," she laconically replied. "I never want to see that egotistical ass again. I want to know how you're planning on fighting my infection."

"I've put out a consult to Dr. Lorraine Yoder. She specializes in infectious disease. She's an extremely intelligent and devoted physician."

"You told me the same damn thing about Nasser!"

CHAPTER SEVENTEEN

As evening approached, Mary and John Valone heard a tap on the door. "Mrs. Valone, it's Dr. Lorraine Yoder."

"Please come in," said John, springing from his chair.

Once the petite brunette clad in hospital whites was seated, she opened her laptop computer and said, "Mary, I hope all the tests I put you through this afternoon weren't too uncomfortable for you."

"Just the MRI," she said. "It was difficult to remain still because of my pain."

"Well, you did just fine, Mary. The images aren't blurred at all." Dr. Yoder took a moment on her PC, then said, "Mary, Dr. Cameron tells me that you're a medical secretary."

"Yes, I am."

"Then please don't allow what I'm about to say frighten you," Dr. Yoder said, her sympathy for Mary unmistakable. "Upon reviewing your bloodwork, I wasn't able to determine exactly what specific type of infection you have. I'm certain it's a Group B, Streptococcus type of strain. However without actually taking a biopsy of the infected tissue, I won't be able to pinpoint the precise pathogenic family."

Appreciative of her honesty, Mary managed a smile. "Dr. Yoder, after all I've been through, I wouldn't mind having a biopsy."

"Yes, it would make things easier. However in all my encounters with this type of microorganism, the broad-spectrum antibiotic approach is always indicated. There's another factor that we must take into consideration. I, along with the head of Radiology, reviewed your latest films. Neither of us believes a biopsy should be conducted."

"Why is that?" said Mary.

Dr. Yoder sighed. "The MRI clearly defines the infectious boundaries. It is one, very distinct region of tissue. However I won't risk a biopsy because your aorta is in close proximity. A misguided punch of one-quarter centimeter could perforate the aorta, resulting in your bleeding to death."

"My God," said John, his voice hushed.

In spite of what she'd been informed, Mary Valone's intrepid eyes showed courage as she said, "Dr. Yoder, were you able to detect if the infection will affect any of my bodily functions?"

"To some extent," she said. "Provided we begin putting a halt to the infection spreading any further, I'm positive all of your major organs will not be damaged. Your gastro-intestinal system doesn't appear to be at issue." A slight pause. "However, the site of the infection is spread anterior to the disc-space where you had the bone-fusion."

"That's why my incision never became inflamed or began seeping any puss," said Mary.

"Correct," said Dr. Yoder. "Now at the moment, while there doesn't appear to be any further bone erosion of the L4 or L5 vertebrae, numerous nerve junctures originate from this region. As to how the infection will affect the nerve-roots themselves, I can only speculate."

"Alright, Dr. Yoder, I trust your judgment," Mary said. "I'll go with the broad-spectrum approach. When can we start?"

"Immediately," she replied. "All I have you on now are oral antibiotics. You'll be placed on two antibiotics intravenously. Being a medical secretary, perhaps you're acquainted with Vancomycin and Claforan."

"Yes, I'm familiar with them."

"Mary, I realize there are newer antibiotics available. However since I've always had success with Vancomycin and Claforan, it's my preference to stay with them."

"I respect your opinion, Doctor. About how long will I be on the antibiotics?"

"At least sixty days. I realize it's a long time, yet I assure you the infection will be eliminated."

Dr. Yoder closed her laptop and said, "Mary, this course requires a very regimented program. The Vancomycin must be administered four times per day, every six hours. The Claforan must be administered three times per day, every eight hours. The only good news is, once I'm certain the infection is diminishing after thirty days, you may go home. You can continue having the antibiotics given to you by a home-nursing service. Your insurance carrier will be more than happy to cover their costs since it will be cheaper to pay nurses to come to your home as opposed to your remaining here."

Dr. Yoder awaited a response, yet Mary and John remained quiet. Finally she said, "Is there a problem?"

"Well, kinda," said John.

"I'd prefer not to stay in this hospital, Dr. Yoder," Mary said. "Dr. Cameron came to see me earlier. To be perfectly honest with you, I can't stand the sight of him anymore."

"And neither can I," added John. "I've already told him he's not my mother's doctor anymore, and not to step foot into this room again. You're in charge now."

"Do you have privileges at any of the Pittsburgh hospitals?" Mary asked of her.

"No, I work primarily out of my office at the Professional Building adjacent to here." Dr. Yoder took a moment to think and said, "I could recommend another neurologist from Shadydell if you'd like."

Vehemently they shook their heads.

"Dr. Yoder, don't get me wrong," said Mary, "I like you, and I'm all for your continuing to treat me. Nevertheless, both my son and I feel it best that I go elsewhere."

"You could be transferred to the hospital where you work if—"

"Excuse me, Dr. Yoder, that's out of the question," said Mary. "Dr. Cameron's the only neurologist with privileges there."

"—I honestly don't know what else to tell you," said the doctor.

"I have a suggestion," Mary said. "You mentioned that after thirty days I could go home, provided you were certain I was healing."

"Yes, but I would require bi-weekly blood samples along with their being analyzed in order to confirm the fact that you were indeed making progress."

"My family doctor, Dr. Samuel Mancini, would provide them for you. He's already agreed to draw my blood, send it to a laboratory, and fax you the results. If you felt it necessary for whatever reason, then I'd have no other alternative but to be re-admitted here."

Dr. Yoder contemplated before saying, "I suppose Dr. Mancini and I could coordinate the details. However it is of the utmost importance that you begin the antibiotics immediately. As I mentioned, I'm worried about the proximity of the infection. It's dangerously close to your aorta. We can't risk it spreading any further."

"Oh, that's fine with me," said Mary. "The sooner I start on antibiotics, the sooner this horrible pain I have will begin to ease."

Dr. Lorraine Yoder pressed a button on the console along Mary's bed. "Please send a phlebotomist to Room 923, STAT," she said to the nurse who'd answered.

She looked at Mary. "I'll go to the lab and bring your first IV with me."

The initial bag of Vancomycin was soon flowing through Mary's veins. John observed closely as the phlebotomist had inserted the needle in Mary's arm. As Dr. Yoder was writing on Mary's chart, John said, "Dr. Yoder, couldn't I give my mother her antibiotics when she comes home?"

"I suppose so, but you would need to be instructed on how to insert the needle into her veins. Unfortunately these antibiotics are somewhat caustic and will induce your mother's veins to weaken, necessitating the placement be changed whenever the site starts to display discoloration. Do you become queasy at the sight of blood, John?"

"Not at all, Doctor. Is the training very involved?"

"No," she said. "Shadydell Heights promotes their lab technicians into such jobs. Once they've proven they can handle it on their own, they're assigned to the job."

"If they can do it, so can I," he said. "At least I'll be positive my mother is receiving her dosages at the proper times."

"No, John," said Mary. "Let the visiting nurses give them to me."

"What happens if they have car trouble, if it snows again—whatever? No, Ma, no more chances. Go ahead, Dr. Yoder, anything else about the needles?"

"John, I'm sure you wouldn't have any trouble with inserting the needle, although there are other factors involved," said Dr. Yoder. "You must understand that you'll be hooking-up seven IV's per day for sixty consecutive days, and it's absolutely imperative they be administered on an exact timetable. Since the IV's must be staggered, it will be extremely demanding upon you. You won't be able to sleep or leave home for any longer than a five-hour period during the entire time." Dr. Yoder smiled at him. "Are you absolutely positive that you wish to undertake such a formidable schedule?"

"Yes, Dr. Yoder, I can handle it," he said in convincing tone. "I'm sure the nurses would try to do their best, but I prefer to trust myself."

Dr. Yoder looked to the chart and said, "Alright then, we'll plan on it that way for now. You can always call the nursing agency if you change your mind."

"I won't change my mind, Doctor," he said. "I want the responsibility. I want my mother to get better. She's already suffered enough because of all this."

"John, I appreciate your offering to do this for me," said Mary. "But what about the job you're currently working on?"

"I can finish it at home and email them everything they need."

"And what about Vicky? You won't have much time for her."

"She'll understand."

*****

"Rasheem, its Steve," said Dr. Cameron.

"I can barely hear you, Steve. Where are you?"

"I'm still at the hospital at the 9th floor nurses station."

"Why aren't you calling me on your cell phone?"

"I don't want anyone being able to trace this call to my cell."

"Why are you whispering?"

"Be quiet and just listen before the nurses get back from passing meds. I just saw Mary Valone's chart. Yoder didn't go for it. She recommended the broad-spectrum and Valone agreed."

"Did you try to persuade her Yoder was incorrect?"

"I never got the chance. I went to see her before Yoder arrived. Her fucking son told me to leave before he threw me out of the window."

"—Then Dr. Abdulaz won't have an opportunity to do the biopsy."

"No."

Dr. Cameron overheard Nasser cursing in the background before he said, "Damn you, Steve! Dr. Abdulaz was our best chance!"

"Don't blame me. You're the one who was convinced she'd die before they found it."

CHAPTER EIGHTEEN

Mary Valone had bravely endured the following two months while receiving her intravenous dosages of antibiotics at home. Under the strict guidelines of Dr. Mancini, she was only permitted out of bed whenever she needed to use the bathroom. In spite of her stubbornness, Mancini did not want her moving about the house. Even when Mary wasn't receiving the antibiotics, his concern was Mary could fall due to the wooziness her pain medication brought about.

John had been relentless in adhering to Dr. Lorraine Yoder's roster as to when Mary received her antibiotics. As Dr. Yoder had forewarned, the Vancomycin and Claforan were caustic drugs that were making the thin veins in Mary's forearms swell and become discolored. It sickened him to see Mary's arms taking on the appearance as a heroin junkie's might. In an attempt to avoid further damage, he had re-positioned the feeding-needle every day.

Mary was delighted when Vicky Gill showed the diamond ring John had given her. Whenever Vicky had made one of her infrequent visits during Mary's convalescence, the main topic of conversation always revolved around potential arrangements for their wedding day. All throughout this period, John had come to accept Vicky's pressuring him into selecting a date for the ceremony. Though the fact that continued to bring about his disfavor was Vicky's unwillingness to spend only an hour or so at the house–despite both his and Mary's urging she stay over on weekends. He couldn't help but intuit that his future wife was skittish with Mary's illness.

On a Monday evening in early May, John bolted down the stairs when he heard the doorbell–knowing it was Dr. Mancini. The smile he observed on the kindhearted physician's face came as a welcomed relief.

"Sam, what is it now?" Mary asked of him, from the top step.

"Eighteen," he replied, beaming as he gave her a warm hug. "It's not as low as it used to be, but it's still within the normal range. Mary, you're recovering well. I pray the worst is over."

"Thank God for Dr. Yoder," she said.

"Even more good news," said the doctor. "I just spoke with Dr. Yoder. She advised me to have you finish what remains of your IV's and prescribe an antibiotic that you can start taking orally just as an extra precaution."

As they moved towards the couch, Dr. Mancini said, "How's your back feeling today?"

"There's still some pain, but not nearly as much as I had."

"Are you still feeling a burning sensation?"

"No, the burning and the spasms have stopped. What I'm feeling now is more like a pulling, a tightening sensation. Have you found another neurologist who'd be willing to see me?"

"No, Mary, I'm sorry," he said, frowning. "You know as well as I do that most neurologists won't touch another's mistake. Dr. Yoder believes that Dr. Cameron has informed all of the Pittsburgh area neurologists to avoid you."

Mary offered a subtle nod of acceptance and said, "What should I do, Sam?"

"I'll keep inquiring, although it seems all we can do is look outside of the area. I'll be seeing Dr. Eisen tomorrow at the hospital to learn his opinion on your latest MRI. Maybe he can recommend a neurologist for you."

"Speaking of the hospital, how's that little DeTorrio weasel?" John wryly said.

"Never mind him," said Mary. "Even though he didn't press any charges against you, I just hope he gives me my job back when Sam thinks I can return."

"Mary, I wouldn't be too concerned about that," said Dr. Mancini– vying to keep a straight-face. "Tony, Dr. Burke, and I had a discussion recently. Tony told me that you can return to work whenever we feel you're ready, and Pam will stay as your assistant. Even though Janet and Pam are doing okay, Tony and Dr. Burke are actually hoping that you do return."

"That's good to know, Sam," said Mary. "I was planning to retire, but because of my back, I've decided against it mainly so I'll be able to keep my health insurance."

"The heck on your health insurance," said John. "I'll pay for you to get new health insurance."

"With a pre-existing condition like I have!" Mary said. "John, it's not a question of money. I'd never find another insurance carrier that would accept me. Forget it. I can't retire until I'm certain about my back."

"She's right, John," said Dr. Mancini. "The way health-costs keep escalating today, most insurance carriers won't take patients with a pre-existing condition such as your mother's, regardless of the premium."

As John looked to the ceiling, Dr. Mancini said, "Mary, keep using your sick-days. We'll see how you're progressing in another month."

*****

Dr. Mancini went into Dr. Ralph Eisen's office the following morning. Sam Mancini could sense the radiologist's apprehension as he said, "Well, Dr. Eisen, you know why I'm here. What do you think about Mary's MRI?"

Dr. Eisen turned to the illuminated panel that displayed the images taken at a facility near Valleyview General Hospital, along with those conducted while she was in Shadydell Heights. He'd circled the area in question on each set. "Compare Mary's L5 in the newer film as opposed to those taken at Shadydell," he said. "It's obvious there's only slight deterioration of the vertebral body. Although if you'll notice the lighter appearance at appearance along the lower edge of the vertebra in the newer image, this delineates L5 beginning to calcify."

"Do you perceive any future issues for Mary in this aspect of her recovery?"

"In my opinion, no. The MRI distinctly indicates that bone is being re-established at the eroded region. In addition, the bone-fusion enhances Mary's spinal stability. You may encounter an orthopedic surgeon who disagrees, yet considering what will most certainly be her pre-eminent difficulty, I would strongly implore of Mary never to have any further back surgery."

"That sounds rather bleak, Doctor."

"Sam, it my intention to startle you," said Dr. Eisen, in earnest. "The previous time we spoke, you mentioned that before Mary dismissed Dr. Cameron, he'd assured Mary that after her antibiotic therapy, she'd soon be at or near one-hundred percent. True?"

"So I've been told."

"Well then, let's just say Dr. Cameron wasn't totally forthcoming with Mary."

"Doesn't surprise me, Ralph. As you, I've known Dr. Cameron for years. While he's very competent, he's also quite adept at covering his ass when a patient develops a problem."

Dr. Eisen nodded. "Has Mary related to you any changes in her pain symptoms?"

"Yes, I spoke with her yesterday. Mary said the burning sensation is gone. However she's now experiencing a tightening or pulling of her lower back."

"Sam," Dr. Eisen said with a sigh, "Mary's symptomology correlates with what is represented in her latest MRI. Note the area of propinquity to L4-L5."

"It appears darker than the surrounding tissues."

"Unfortunately so. Doctor, there isn't any question that the shaded region denotes scar tissue. It represents no real peril to Mary, yet it is inevitable that many nerves are entrapped within. This mass of scar tissue is the current source of Mary's pain. What has occurred is the infection has damaged inner tissue. The human body's inner tissues always re-bond in an unorthodox manner whenever they've been injured. This isn't the best analogy, but let's says a person severely gashes their arm. With stitches, they'll have a scar. However without stitches, while the cut will eventually heal, the scar will be more uneven and will exhibit a protuberance texture about it. Regrettably this has occurred to the tissues of Mary's back. Yet of far greater significance, there are nerves enmeshed within the tissue mass. The tightening or pulling sensations she's experiencing are a result of scar tissue sealing the nerves within. Naturally as the scar tissue grows more snug, the more pressure they exude upon the entrapped nerves. Has Mary ever disclosed any loss of bodily functions?"

"No, she's fortunate in that regard."

"Very fortunate," said Dr. Eisen. "However that's why I implore of Mary never to have another back operation unless there isn't absolutely any other alternative. Because if a surgeon were to make an incision in this region, he or she might actually sever a nerve. Your guess would be as good as mine as to what bodily function might be affected or quite frankly, lost."

"Dr. Eisen, is there any possible solution to the scarred region?"

"None that I'm cognizant of. Most patients with inner scar tissue are placed on conventional therapy programs such as swimming or other forms of mild exercises. The practical theory is this sort of therapy will aid the body in adapting to its condition, hence decreasing the level of pain. Of course my knowledge of this type of ailment isn't complete. I'm sure there are neurologists out there whom may have other ideas on the subject."

"Can you recommend another neurologist for Mary?"

"I presume you're referring to outside of the Pittsburgh area."

"Yes, Ralph. Dr. Cameron's already spread the word about Mary."

Eisen shook his head and said, "Unfortunately, I can't. Sam, I'm sorry. I wish I could have given greater cause for optimism. All we can hope for is that Mary's presently experiencing the apex of her pain-level, and it will begin to diminish as her body acclimates itself."

"Damn it," said Dr. Mancini. "I had a hunch she was hurting more than she was letting-on. I should have told her son about the sed-rate."

"In hindsight, yes, you should have," said Dr. Eisen. "Although my belief is Dr. Cameron banked on your adhering to the policy of non-intervention. Had you challenged him, anytime you may have had another patient who needed a neurological consult, Dr. Cameron would have refused to see them. He's done it before, Sam. I understand."

Dr. Eisen pointed towards Mary's films. "Sam, regardless of the sed-rate, Dr. Cameron had to know Mary was infected. Look at this film taken at Shadydell. The infection is as plain as day."

Dr. Mancini sighed before he said, "I see it. Yet Mary told me Cameron assured her nothing was visible on either MRI he took at his office."

"Nonsense," replied Dr. Eisen. "Do you recall when Dr. Cameron performed the latter MRI at his office?"

"One day before the MRI at Shadydell."

"He had to see it!" said Eisen in charged tone of voice. "It's so obvious that a first-year pre-med student would have seen it. Sam, I hate saying this, but Dr. Cameron and probably the neurosurgeon didn't want her infection found. That is, not until autopsy."

The stupefied expression remained on Mancini's face. "But why Mary?"

"Because the dead can't testify."

CHAPTER NINETEEN

The erotic energy between them remained intact as Vicky and John locked their lips together for many wet kisses the moment he stepped into Vicky's apartment. Releasing her, John began running anxious hands along the sides of the tight-fitting blue blouse she was wearing that accentuated her sultry figure. "Did you miss me, Miss Gill?" he asked–beginning to tug her towards the bedroom.

"More than you'll never know," she said in seducing voice.

Despite her seeming equally eager, John sensed her hesitation. "What is it, Vick?"

"Are you done giving Mary her antibiotics?"

"Last bag was yesterday afternoon."

"Is she better now?"

"The infection's gone." He placed a hand between her upper-thighs. "C'mom, I'm ready to shoot in my pants."

"You promise you'll make all of this up to me?"

"You know I will."

Her teasing stopped. "Let's get started, hon. I'm hornier than you are."

She raced into the bedroom, flinging her blouse behind her. Vicky felt the flesh between her legs twitching as she hurried removed her shorts and panties. Turning to face him, she saw John standing naked holding a condom.

"Do I need this?" he whispered.

"Please."

"Her legs went weak as John clutched her. He then placed his hands beneath her bare buttocks and lifted her onto the bed. He began softly kissing her firm nipples while caressing her clitoris. With Vicky moaning in ecstasy, he moved down and started licking her already damp vagina, his tongue only stimulating her craven lust as he continued to reach deep inside her.

"John—stop it," she groaned, "I'm almost ready to cum."

"Go 'head, I love tasting you."

"No, I want your stiff cock inside me. Fuck me, John. Fuck me hard."

Quickly he moved atop her voluptuous naked body. As she guided him, her fingers felt a pulsating pole of muscle. Nearly sobbing in delight, the force of his entry made her puff with euphoria. In spite of his hands being locked behind her head for protection, she quivered as his vigorous surges caused her to bump against the headboard. Salaciously he persisted with powerful yet affectionate thrusts while they groaned until a passionate climax was achieved.

Remaining inside her, he rolled Vicky atop of him. As he gasped to regain his breath, Vicky said, "Am I a better lay than that Grace girl?"

"Vicky—forget about her." A few more deep breaths. "She was so loose, she'd probably screwed every guy in that hick town. I'm lucky I never caught anything from her."

Softly she kissed him.

Hours later, after they'd finished making love for the fourth time, Vicky rolled of the bed to see an uncharacteristic grin across his appealing face.

"After all that, you'd better be smiling," she said. "I'm sore all-over. My ass has brush-burns because of the way you hammered me."

"Vicky, tonight was beyond fantastic," he said. "C'mon, let's take a shower."

"Let me pee first, then I'll get the water running."

"Sure."

It wasn't only the wanton sex that effectuated John to glimmer for joy. He'd felt a special ambiance possessing his inner-self the moment Vicky Gill had arrived at his door last December. And despite any lingering doubts about her, John had come to the realization they were indeed born for each other. Soon she would be his wife and a lifetime of happiness, companionship, and romance awaited him. The woman he loved with all his mind, heart, and soul was to be his forever. *"Mary a grandmother and Uncle Butch."* he kept thinking to himself.

*****

Throughout the remainder of May and all of June–despite her knowledge that she was now a victim of a noted medical axiom being invoked against her, Mary and John Valone traveled to various cities in Western Pennsylvania and Ohio to see different specialist May had made appointments with. Upon each visit, Mary would receive rapid prognostications that nothing could be done for her. What astounded her was that not one had bothered to give her an examination. At most they would take a quick glance at her MRI's before politely bowing-out. None of these intellectual physicians, who'd be billing her insurance for as much a thousand dollars for the evaluations refused to proffer even a remote opinion as to how her lasting soreness could be remedied.

Dr. Lorraine Yoder amiably responded to Mary's request for an office visit in early July. Although she wasn't able to put forth any new ideas, she was curious as to what–if anything–other doctors had recommended. As the two ladies came through the door leading into the empty waiting room where John was seated, Mary expressed to forlorn. "Dr. Yoder, what should I do? My back is hurting and nobody wants to help me."

"Mary, all of the neurologists I know follow the old-school standards not to intercede," said Dr. Yoder. "However there is one man with whom I've recently met. His name's Dr. Wayne Jennson. He's fresh-out of residency. His office is on the north shore of Pittsburgh. Perhaps he'd be willing to examine you."

"Thank you, Dr. Yoder," said Mary. "I'll call him first thing in the morning."

"He seems like a very caring and intelligent young man," added Dr. Yoder. "I hope he can help your pain."

"So do I, Dr. Yoder. Anything else you can suggest?"

"Find yourself a good lawyer. You have a major lawsuit against Cameron and Nasser."

They'd barely made their way out of Dr. Yoder's office when Mary eyed John, her lovely face scathing in anger. "John, I'd like for you to do something for me tomorrow morning. I want you to go get my films from Dr. Cameron's office. Normally he doesn't get there until noon, so you'll need to be there before he does. His secretary's name is Agnes. Ask her to get them for you. If she asks why, say that my new doctor requested them, and you'll return them as soon as you can. And whatever you do, don't mention one word about Dr. Jennson."

"No problem. Want me to give Bob Cook a call?"

"Not until I've seen Dr. Jennson. If I were to file a lawsuit now, word would get around fast. Dr. Jennson wouldn't dare see me."

"Okay, Ma, we'll wait," he said. "But I promise you, those two low-life's aren't gonna away with what they did to you."

"Oh, I am going to sue those two rotten bastards. That's why I want you to get my MRI's before they mysteriously disappear from Cameron's office. Believe me, when the time's right, we'll let Bob know."

*****

John arrived home the following morning with her films. "Ma, I got 'em!"

Mary sat waiting on the couch. "Any problems?"

"Nah, Agnes never asked why I wanted them."

"Did you see Dr. Cameron?"

"Agnes said he was at the hospital. Did you get in touch with Dr. Jennson yet?"

"My appointment's next Monday at four o'clock."

"Great. Let's hope he can do something to help you."

*****

As Mary was drinking a cup of coffee the following Monday, the telephone rang. "Probably Janet," she said aloud as she reached for the phone.

"Mrs. Valone," she heard, "this is Dr. Jennson."

"Hello, Dr. Jennson. I was about to start getting ready for our appointment."

"Mrs. Valone, I'm positive I would not be able to help you. Your appointment's cancelled."

"But Dr. Jennson, the least you could do is examine me."

"I'm convinced it would be a waste of time."

"Dr. Jennson, please—"

"Sorry, Mrs. Valone, I can't help you. Please don't call again. Goodbye."

Mary slammed the phone down. "John!"

He rushed up the stairs towards her. "What's wrong?"

"Call Bob Cook right now."

"I thought you wanted to wait until you saw Dr. Jennson?"

"Fuck Dr. Jennson," she said, her face filled with a cold, majestic contempt he had never observed before. "Call Bob Cook. We're not waiting any longer."

CHAPTER TWENTY

"Why didn't you leave a message?" Bob Cook greeted John later that evening at his home. "Get in here. You wanna drink, shoot pool, or both?"

"Diane around?" John asked, as they made their way into Bob's living room.

"Nah, she's out visiting some rich people down the street. Damn, it's been too long since we've seen each other. How've you been?"

"Okay. Thanks for the flowers you and Diane sent."

"Anytime," said Bob. "How's your mom been?"

"Better than she was," he said, forcing a smile.

"The guys told me what happened after her operation."

"Bob, her operation went perfect, but she caught an infection and they ignored her. I had to jack Mary's surgeon against the wall before he finally agreed to even test her for infection."

"I heard. Gene told us everything. Pal, you should be damn proud of yourself. Not many guys our age would have taken care of a parent like you did."

"Thanks, Bob."

Robert Cook remained silent. He observed that while John was attempting to appear stoic, he easily sensed the anger that brewed within. *"Should I ask him?"* he thought before saying, "Well, tell Mary that Diane and I will be stopping by this weekend to see her."

"If you got time, you'll be seeing her before the weekend," said John. "Mary and I would like for you to represent her in filing a lawsuit against those fucking doctors."

Cook's eyebrows lifted. Quickly he muted the television. "John, I'm flattered that you and Mary want me. I haven't had a significant case for a long time now." Putting his exuberance on hold, Bob gathered his composure to say, "I'll be more than happy to represent your mother, although I'll need to find another attorney to help me."

"Why? You that busy?"

"I wish," said Bob. "As of today, I have a total of five cases pending, none of them worth baloney."

"Then you can handle Mary's case by yourself."

"Oh, I'd love to go at it solo, except costs mount too quickly in malpractice cases. I saw the bills when I worked at Tibeau's firm. There's filing fees, depositions, expert witnesses, incidentals, et cetera, et cetera. John, to be perfectly honest, I just can't afford that kind of money right now."

"Alright, how much you need?"

"Ballpark estimate of the costs I'd incur before we'd get to trial would be somewhere around thirty grand," Bob said. "If I were to bring a partner, I could make a deal with them to pay the brunt of the costs. I know a guy in Pittsburgh—"

"No way, Bob!" John sharply interrupted him. "Dr. Cameron has too many bigshot connections in Pittsburgh, No Pittsburgh attorneys on our side. I don't care how well you know him, there isn't any way we could be positive of his allegiances. How can you be sure the guy doesn't know those two scumbags? Maybe he belongs to the same country club or fraternizes with them someplace else. No way, I've read too many stories about lawyers selling-out their own client, and it ain't gonna to happen to my mother. I trust you and you alone. You decide to take the case, I'll pay all the expenses up-front."

He reached for his checkbook. "Thirty thousand, right?"

"That should cover it," said Bob in soft tone–stunned by his good fate.

Soon a check floated atop the coffee table. "There's a hundred," John said. "Bob, don't spare any expenses. You need more, you got it. I don't care what it takes, just win Mary's case. Deal?"

"Oh, it's a deal alright," said Bob while shaking John's hand. "Bring Mary in tomorrow morning. We'll sign a contract and start at square-one. Pal, you may not realize it, but a lawsuit of this magnitude could be worth millions."

"Bob, my mother deserves a big settlement, and I want her to have it. You've no idea what that woman's been through. But to be perfectly honest with you, I really don't give a fuck about the money. All I know is my mother's going to have justice."

*****

Mary Valone was always assigned the final appointment of the day with Dr Mancini.

His examination of her complete, he said, "Mary, comparing as to how your pain was after your antibiotics had been concluded as opposed to now, how does your back feel?"

"Still about the same," she said. "My back aches, Sam. Some days not as severe as others, but the pain's still there."

"How are you spending your days?"

"I'm bored sitting around the house all day thinking about my pain."

Mancini paged-through a stack of forms relating to her medical history as he said, "I told you Dr. Eisen's opinion. He believes your spinal stability isn't at risk. Maybe, just maybe, returning to work might be the best possible therapy for you, provided you don't overdo it. Perhaps by focusing on your job, it would help take your mind off the pain."

"I've had the same thought many times," she said. "I would like to go back to my job."

Mancini sighed. "I'm just not certain you're up to it."

"Please, Sam, at least let me try. Remember when you mentioned that Tony wants me to return? Does that still apply?"

"Definitely. As you know, Janet went back to his office, and Tony has Pam and two other women from Administration in the Staff Office.

From what Dr. Burke tells me, all Tony does is complain because they're not as efficient as you were."

"What about John? Even though Tony never pressed any charges, he still must be mad as hell at him."

"John really embarrassed Tony that day," said Mancini, chuckling. "Yet from all of Tony's indications to me, he's willing to put it aside. Ever since your absence, he's finally realized just how important an employee you are."

"My son's another reason why I want to go back to work," Mary said. "Sam, ever since John saw I was having pain post-op, he's been depressed. He never seems to have much of an appetite, nor is he sleeping very well. He isn't seeing enough of his fiancé and they wanted to get married later this year. Even some of his friends have told me that John hasn't been the same."

"Mary, your son's a very dynamic young man with strong emotional conceptions," said Dr. Mancini. "John's concerns for you have caused him to neglect himself to some extent. Don't worry, John's a resilient young man. He'll bounce-back before you know it."

"I keep thinking that if John sees I'm at least capable of working, it would take some of the stress off his mind."

"True, it would be a huge psychological lift for him," said the doctor. "When one's mind is suffering, the body suffers as well."

"Sam, I want you to authorize my return to work," she said forcefully. "I owe it to John."

Sam Mancini gazed at the ceiling and huffed. He understood Mary's determination. "We could debate this all night, and there still wouldn't be anything I could say to convince you otherwise, is there?"

"No."

Another sigh before he said, "Alright, Mary, I'll let Tony know you'll be returning to work next week, provided he keeps Pam as your assistant. However, if I see it's too difficult on you, you're going on short-term disability. Agreed?"

"Agreed."

"How's your Vicodin supply?"

"I still have plenty of them, Sam," she said, while sliding off the examination table. "I just pray for the day when I can throw the damn things away."

"I know you do, Mary," he said, taking her hands. "So do I."

"Sam, one more thing. My attorney recently filed a lawsuit against Nasser and Cameron. Please don't tell anyone."

"I won't and good for you," he said. "Mary, I'll be more than happy to testify on your behalf, and I don't give a damn who gets mad about it. Their negligence against you is without question."

CHAPTER TWENTY ONE

"I still don't believe Sam okayed you!" Janet Silva joyfully exclaimed, rounding her desk to embrace Mary.

"I'm a little sore, Jan, but the pills help take the edge off the pain," she said.

Janet plainly marked the wariness Mary's eyes projected as she peered at DeTorrio's door. "Relax, the little putz went over to the hospital."

"How's he been treating you?"

"Not too bad," said Janet. Her effervescent face suddenly reverted to grim. "I didn't want to tell you this over the weekend, but what scares me is that ever since Sam informed him that you'd be here today, Tony's been relatively pleasant. Too damn pleasant. Mary, I'm nervous."

"Why, Jan?"

"Tony was smiling like the cat that ate the canary when he told me to have you stop here today. Watch yourself in there."

As Mary readied to answer, the sound of footsteps in the outer corridor stopped her.

In trod Anthony DeTorrio, attired dapperly in a pale blue suit. "Mary, it's wonderful seeing you again," he said most courteously.

"Thank you, Mr. DeTorrio. I'm happy to be back to work."

"Mary, I sorry I had to ask you to stop here today," he said. "There's just so much trivial documentation that must be processed before you're allowed to resume your job. Please, it's all in my office. Janet, please hold my calls."

Before she was seated, DeTorrio handed Mary a paper-clipped stack of forms. "Mary, I don't mean to rush you, but I'm running late. Those are just the usual insurance releases along with some of the other mandatory items that require your signature. I would appreciate your signing them as quickly as possible."

"Mr. DeTorrio, before I do, I would like to apologize for my son's behavior."

"Oh, it was completely understandable on his part. Let's forget it ever happened. Please start signing."

His polite reply caused Mary to shift uneasily in her chair, a shiver tingling round. Anthony DeTorrio's mannerisms were entirely opposite his normal persona. *"Jan's right. He's up to something,"* she thought, while doing her best to convince Tony she was hurrying–though scrutinizing each document.

DeTorrio sat motionless. The warm smile he displayed immediately dissipated as Mary removed a page. "Something wrong?" he asked.

"Mr. DeTorrio, this form states that I must undergo a prerequisite drug-test once per week."

"We don't enforce it," he said in calm fashion.

"Sir, I'm aware of the hospital's drug policies. This document goes way beyond them. It clearly states that if an employee tests positive for any form of narcotics, they're subject to termination for cause. I'm presently taking Vicodin prescribed for me by Dr. Mancini. I'm not signing this."

"Honestly, Mary, it's only a formality."

"Then there isn't any need for my signature."

His plot foiled, Anthony DeTorrio's facial expression instantly turned cruel. "Fucking cocksucker! Did you actually think I'd ever allow you to work at my hospital again?!"

"You little bastard!" she shouted in return. "If I'd have signed that form, you would have fired me!"

"Your ass would've been out on the street before lunch!"

Mary Valone vaulted to her feet. "Tell me something before I go. Is it because my son dared to put you in your place?"

"Not entirely," was his reply, his face now cast in stone. "If you thought for one minute that I'd ever allow some cunt working at my hospital who filed for malpractice, you're out of your fucking mind."

"You always were an evil son of a bitch," said Mary.

"What the fuck do you want, kike slut!" he shouted at Janet, upon her flinging his office door open.

"Drop dead!" she yelled, venting her years of animosity. "You've screamed at me for the last time! Make one move towards either of us, and kick you right in the balls!"

Their defiance had set a precedent, forever insulting his vainglory–perfect outlets awaiting humiliation. "Janet, you're fired. I want your desk cleared now. As for you, Mrs. Mary Valone, go home and suffer. I hope you have fucking pain until the day you die!"

*****

"Jan, you need an attorney, too," said Mary, as they and John continued discussing the events of the previous day.

"I've already called several," said Janet. "The lady that was recommended to me only handles work-related grievances. She told me that my winning any legal action against him are slim and none. They gave me my termination papers this morning when I went to apply for my pension. I was fired for insubordination. When I told her what happened and about all the ethnic slurs, she said that without witnesses to corroborate my allegations, it was useless. She believes I'd just be perceived as another disgruntled employee trying to get back at their supervisor."

"I heard what he called you," said Mary. "Did you tell her that?"

"Yes. She wasn't very impressed with the fact that only one person who's my best friend could attest to one instance on the same day I was fired."

"Did Pam ever hear him swear at you?"

"No, Mary," she said. "That's the main reason why she told me I couldn't win. Tony was shrewd. Whenever I was with Pam, he was polite with us. So if I were to file, Pam would have to testify that she never heard him say anything of the kind."

"Jan, if it's a question of money, John and I are willing to help you find someone who would help you file a complaint against him."

Janet shook her head and said, "No, the lady I spoke with was highly recommended to me. She suggested I put the hospital behind me, and that's what I intend to do. The more I think about it, I'm happy to be out of there. I need some sanity back in my life." A gulp of wine. "It just scalds me when I think of how he had everything planned in advance."

"I talked with Sam last night," Mary said. "An hour after we were escorted off the premises, a woman from Pittsburgh came in and Tony gave her my job. Sam told me he charged into Tony's office and was ready to punch him. Tony just laughed at him. I really don't care about myself, but what really pisses me off was that he gave Debbie Nichols your job."

"So help me, I'll get that whoremongering little prick," said Janet.

"How?" asked John, passively.

"Tomorrow I'm following him from work for his weekly shack-up with that cow," said Janet. "Rumor has it they stay at the same motel about ten miles from the hospital. When I find what room they're in, I'm calling his wife and telling her exactly where and with whom he's with. She'll enjoy learning that her loving husband is screwing his new secretary."

"Jan, it isn't a bad idea," said John. "But you'd better let some time pass before you try.

"If he does go a motel that far away from the hospital, I guarantee he'll spot your car if you tail him for that long a distance."

Janet sported a resentful face when she said, "Sweetheart, as much as I adore you, I must admit that your reactions to all you've heard about how that little fucker belittled your mother and I have me confused. When Mary told you about his vulgar insults, you told her to be happy she was out of there for good. I'm not saying that you should go barging into his office, but I never expected you to say I should wait before trying to get him into trouble. I've met his wife. When she learns the truth, she'll divorce him."

"Janet, I'm sorry for all the years of abuse you took from that man," he said. "I really am. Believe me, I understand just how badly you want to retaliate against him, but consider how paranoid he must be right now. I'd bet every time he drives anywhere, he always keeps a close-eye on the rear-view mirror. So now it's only logical to think that he's going to be even more cautious that he's not followed to any motel until things cool down. If he spots you tailing him, he'll just turn around and go home. Then what would you do, follow him every night after work? Trust me on this, Jan, I'd love seeing his wife take his money just as much as you would. But I'm telling you, the best move is to wait."

"For how long?"

"At least a month," said John. "Let him relax a bit. Let him figure he's safe. Then the three of us will take my car and follow him to the motel. Once he's inside, you can personally call his wife with all the details. Sound good?"

"A month, huh?"

"No longer."

"I think he's right, Jan," said Mary. "Tony's as paranoid as they come. We should wait."

Janet sulked with another swallow of wine. "Yes, damn it, so do I."

"And Janet, dear," John said in a tone meant to console. "As for what he called you and my mother, they were just words spoken by an ignorant man. As much as I'd like to, I can't go over to the hospital and beat him senseless. I'm sorry, it's just not worth it. I promise you we'll catch him and Nichols at the motel. Just please don't get impatient."

*****

As Janet was saying her farewells later, John stood enamored with the deception he'd carried off. He'd reached his flashpoint when Mary had confided what had occurred yesterday. Enraged ever since, the outpouring of hatred he bore Anthony DeTorrio continued to increase. And now, out of the blue, Janet Silva had unknowingly supplied a major piece to the puzzle fulfilling his visions. Only a few stumbling blocks remained–stumbling blocks that could be overcome.

*****

The rowdies at Mike's Pub were elated when Vicky and John walked in Saturday evening. John warmly greeted them, thanking all for the many cards and flowers they had sent Mary. He also apologized for his unpleasantness during the past few months. His overall demeanor along with his somewhat optimistic answers to their questions concerning Mary's health led them to believe John had finally overcome the distraught he had been trapped in.

All evening Vicky and Amy Gill drank with John, Butch, and their boisterous friends, astutely mindful that John deserved a festive reunion with the gang.

"He seems to have gotten over his mom's health problems," Amy Gill whispered to Vicky.

"I hope so, Amy," she said. "Although he seems different tonight. On the way here, one minute we were talking about our future. Then all of a sudden he'd become disassociated—almost like he was in some kind of trance."

"Vicky, everything's going to be fine between you and John," said Amy. "He's too sweet a guy for it not to."

A few minutes later, Vicky saw John standing behind David Bodette and Gary Rowland. She waited for the moment until she whispered into his ear, "Let's go to my place, big boy. I'm on top tonight."

*****

The following morning, finding Dennis Perella's home was John's ambition as he drove through the rural outskirts of Vernon Park. He hadn't been to Denny's house in years–the countryside was full of nature's growths. Slowly he coasted down the winding country road seeking any hints of his whereabouts. All he continued to see was an extended corn field on his right side and a few deserted shacks along the left.

"That's it," he said aloud, viewing a green aluminum-sided house in front of a wooden building and several cars parked beside it. While pulling onto the cobblestone driveway, he saw a man dressed in bib-overalls and a welder's mask looking to him from the garage.

"What are you doin' out here in the wilderness?" Denny bellowed, while ambling his way.

"Just out for a Sunday drive," he said as they shook hands. "Hey, Den, where's the creek? Maybe I'll get to see Burt Reynolds and his pals rafting downstream. And where's the kid with the banjo?"

"Still a fuckin' wiseguy. C'mon, let's go inside. I'm thirsty."

*****

"John, we've been bullshittin' for five beers now," said Denny. "When you first got here, it seemed like you were okay. But why is it the more we talk, the more I think something's eating at you besides your mom's health."

"There is, Den. I need to ask you a big favor."

"Name it. It's yours."

"What I'm about to ask is pretty heavy."

"Kid, I've been telling you for years that I owed you. I wasn't just jerking you around. I meant it. C'mon, what's the problem?"

"Did you hear about the guy I almost got into a fight with at the hospital where my mother used to work?"

Denny's laughter burst throughout the garage. "Oh yeah, Mike told me all about it. Best part was your pal Butch the cop made it look like you were under arrest."

"He's my problem."

"I get it, you want me to fuck'em up. Hey, I'll be glad to pull a bag-job on him. I'll pulverize his face into mush for you."

"No, Den, that ain't enough," said John in emphatic voice.

Dennis Perella remained hushed, his rock-solid jaw constantly dropping to his chest as John summarized the events of the past months. After the recap was concluded, he understood why John so despised the man. Anthony DeTorrio's total lack of respect towards Mary Valone cried out for vengeance. Yet the burly ex-marine sat reserved, rubbing the stubble on his grizzled face before venturing to say, "You know, it almost sounds like you want me to kill this guy for you."

John eyed him with a poker-face. "Denny, I'd never ask that of anyone. No, I'll kill that motherfucker and the girl myself. All I'm asking is your help with some of the details."

Denny leaned backwards, barely able to fold his arms across his broad chest. "Kid, you'd better realize what you're saying. I know you got heart, but you'd better think awful hard about this. Are you willing to risk everything and stand trial for Murder One for revenge? I don't care how clean your record is, chances are you'll get sentenced to death if you get caught."

"Yes, I am," said John, his tone without fear. "Denny, there are people in this world who don't think twice before they shit all over someone else. People without any moral values whatsoever. Like it's their God-given right to take full-advantage of other people. These two assholes are perfect cases in point. And right now at this exact moment in time, I've got the ideal opportunity to put a stop to them. That's what life is, Den, a series of opportunities. I'll never get a better opportunity than this."

Through the lens of familiarity, Denny viewed an expression of unabashed malice he understood all too well. He'd seen it innumerable times in Vietnam. It was of a kind he used to brandish. "John, you're a sharp kid," he said. "Think real good now. And I mean real good. Are you sure you want to risk it? This is life or death we're talkin' here."

"Dennis, I can assure you that scumbag and his fat cunt of his are going to die, preferably within the next three weeks before Mary's friend gets in my way. All I keep thinking about is how he mistreated my mother and what that bitch did to her chair. Oh, they're goin' down, whether you help me or not. But with your help, I figure my chances of not getting caught increase tremendously."

"Okay, okay, enough already," he grumbled. "If either of them had done something like that to my mother, I'd want to whack the fuckers myself. What do you want me to do?"

"Ever been to the Traveler's Motor Lodge?"

"Drove past it. Never stayed there."

"I tailed DeTorrio there last Wednesday. I didn't follow him into the parking lot, but later on I rode through and saw his car parked in the back of the motel by Room 13. I've been told they stay there every Wednesday evening, and it's my guess he has thirteen reserved for Wednesday's because the room's a perfect hideaway. The motel's old, Den. It's a single-story rectangle. The office is in front. There are twelve rooms along each side, and thirteen's in the back. It's secluded from the other rooms, and their cars can't be seen from the road. I know that's the room I'd want if I were him."

"That's a tactical advantage," said Denny. "Less chance of anyone seeing you."

"Den, what I'd like you to do is go there Wednesday. Make sure his car is parked by Room 13 again. It's a late-model, black Lincoln with the license plate ALD-1. If I'm right, the first step is to get a key for his room."

"I'll take care of the key. How 'bout the girl's car? Was it parked next to his?"

"Uh-uh. An older, purple Subaru."

"Okay, what else?"

"A pistol with a silencer."

"No problem. I got one that's untraceable."

"How about a car?"

Denny grinned. "I got a bunch of 'em outside."

John offered a smile in return. "Thanks, Den. This means a lot to me."

Dennis Perella eyed him sternly. "John, murder is damn tough to get away with unless every last detail is planned and carried out flawlessly. The slightest fuckup will get you convicted, and you'd better realize Butch won't be able to help you. Homicide cases are under the jurisdiction of the county with help from the state police."

"I know, Den. Okay, what do we do next?"

"Today, nothin'. My boy's gonna be here pretty soon, so we'd better not risk his seeing us together. Go home. Leave everything to me. Call me Friday and I'll let you know what I think. If it's a go for the next Wednesday or the Wednesday after that, we'll have plenty of time to make all the preparations. Now remember this. When you call me, use a pay phone. If you get arrested, I don't want the cops connecting us through the phone company."

"I understand," said John. "Last thing I'd ever want is to drag you down with me."

"Don't worry, pal. If the setup's as good as it sounds and if you do exactly as I say, with a little luck they won't have didley-shit on you."

*****

"I'd say you overdid it on the wax, kid," said Denny, as John was changing into a black jogging suit and a pair of boots Denny had provided him.

"Hey, you told me to have a good alibi ready if the police ask," John said.

"You mean when they ask. Okay, we still got time, so let's go over everything again. First of all, did your mom and her friend leave for Aruba yesterday?"

"Yep," said John. "Ever since the thing at the hospital, they've been talkin' about taking a vacation together, so I booked them a trip. Timing couldn't have been better."

"You weren't going tonight if they hadn't," Denny said. He motioned to the side. "How's it look?"

"I can't even tell what make it is."

"That's the idea, kid. It's that old Chevy Malibu the guy brought in for bodywork and a paint job. I fixed the rust spots and painted it flat-black last night. Unless they're some car fanatic, nobody will be able to tell what model it is."

"CB's hooked-up."

"Check out the antenna, it's glued to the roof," Denny grinned. "Okay, while you're gone, I'll be listening to the police-bands. If anything's broadcast concerning the motel, maybe there'll be some piece of info I give you. Alright, here's the plan and the timetable one last time. You're not sure of somethin', ask. You're gonna leave here at eight-thirty. It's a twenty minute drive via Ridge Road and Bray Hollow. Don't speed either going or comin' back. You'd be surprised how many guys get stopped by the cops while speeding away from a crime."

"I won't speed."

"Here's the key," said Denny, tossing it. "The door has a chain-lock, but I loosened the screws. Put a shoulder into the door, it'll pop right out. Okay, you'll be there at eight-fifty. It'll be dark by then. Park in back by the hillside, but make sure to turn off the headlights before you go around the bend. We don't want the lights shining on their window. Make sure nobody's around when you get there. Even if someone's out in the lot when you drive in, don't risk it. But if the coast is clear, get in, get it done quick, and get out. Okay?"

"I'm with you, Den."

"Okay, put on your gloves and tossel, and get in. The gun's on the seat."

Once John was inside with the gun in hand, Denny said, "Ain't it a beauty?"

"Yeah, it shoots nice. When I was practicing with it, I could barely feel any recoil. You sure it's a big enough caliber?"

"Whattafuck'd you want, a fuckin' cannon!" Denny roared. "You wanna blow holes in the walls! That's a .22 caliber, semi-automatic, twelve-shot clip loaded with dumb-dumb bullets. Sure you can handle it?"

"Yes, Denny, it's shoots easy."

"Good enough," he said, looking at his wristwatch. "Now put down the gun and listen. Remember, shoot the girl first, regardless of her position. If you have to, aim for her chest just to put her down, then zap her in the head. Women almost always scream when confronted with danger and men usually freeze, so shoot her first. John, this is important. You've got twelve shots. I don't care how many you put into them at first, just make damn sure they each end-up with at least three slugs in the head. We don't want any miraculous recoveries. At least three each in the head, then drop the gun. Okay, they're dead. What are you gonna do next?"

"Take his wallet and her purse."

"Don't fuckin' forget!" Denny urged of him. "John, you're gonna be a little shaky after you kill them, but don't forget the wallet and purse. You don't make it look like a robbery, the police will know for sure it was personal. Got it?"

"Got it."

"Now there's one last thing we planned, assuming everything goes smooth and you don't have to make a fast getaway. Remember what it is?"

"The hair we talked about," said John, pointing to a plastic bag in the ashtray. "Den, this is a great idea."

"Hey, I know what I'm doing," he said. "I used to watch the O.J. trial. Put it on the bed they were using. When the cops find it, they'll tag it as evidence. Once they determine it doesn't match-up with the victims, they'll assume it came from the killer. With all these fancy DNA tests today, and if they don't have any witnesses, the hair alone should make that sap Dague pull his people off you."

John laughed. "Damn, Denny, you did learn a lot watching O.J."

"Yeah, well, let's not talk shit yet," said Denny. "Okay, back to the timetable. You'll get there at eight-fifty. That puts you outta there by eight-fifty-five at the very latest. Just answer the CB like we said. Don't mention any names or locations. No bragging. No swearing. Alright, say everything goes as planned. That means you'll be here close to nine-twenty. You'll be outta here before nine-forty. On your way home, you're stopping at the Burger Chef close to your house and buying something at the drive-thru. You should be home by ten o'clock, tops."

"I am hungry," he said. "I was so busy today with the cars, I didn't eat anything."

"Pal, you ain't gonna have an appetite later."

Denny glanced at his wristwatch. "John, last chance. Are you absolutely sure you want to go through with this?" he asked in a fatherly tone. "Don't be ashamed to change your mind. I'll understand."

"No choice, Den," he replied. "I won't ever be able to look myself in the mirror again if I don't. I want that scumbag and his whore dead."

"Alright then," said Dennis. "Just remember to trust your instincts. If you sense even the slightest problem before you get into their room, regardless of what, bail-out quick."

"I will, Den. I promise."

"Okay, kid, you're on. Remember everything we talked about. Be careful. No mistakes."

*****

Cloaked by the darkness, John drove into the Traveler's Motor Lodge parking lot. Passing the office, he dimmed the lights. As he parked behind the Lincoln and Subaru, he could feel the goose-bumps prancing about his skin. After gently closing the car door, he took a cautious peek around both sides of the building. All near the office, only four cars surrounded the dreary motel without anyone stirring outside. The hillside that contoured the rear section of the motel shielded him from the street behind the property. Securing his weapon, he stalked towards the door with the unlucky number attached. His heart racing, he slid the key into the lock. Turning it slowly, it made a click that didn't cause any warning of distress to resound inside. Payback time had arrived.

The door ajar, the chain-lock unfastened, John saw the crack of Debra Nichols' bare ass as she stood between the beds toweling herself. The bathroom door open, the sound of water indicated where Anthony DeTorrio was. He stepped inside as if he were walking on eggshells, sensing he was in a tunnel being guided by a force of nature beyond him.

His mind filled with an insatiable rage, John fired three bullets into Debbie's back, cascading her onto the bed like a sack of bricks, the cheap striped wallpaper painted in blood. Though beholding her shiver of death, he held the gun against her temple and discharged it three more times. The impact of the shots amazed, as they resulted in chunks of scalp and gooey brain spraying about the room.

"Be right out, Deb," he heard DeTorrio call. "Get kitty all buttered-up."

His adrenalin coursing, John stood behind the outer wall of the bathroom. DeTorrio wasn't about to die in the same rapid fashion that had been Nichols' fate. He wanted Tony bound for his grave knowing who had done him in. Even more obligatory, John yearned to terrorize and degrade him before a macabre death.

DeTorrio emerged from the bathroom naked. A ferocious shove catapulted him against the wall before he toppled onto the floor. Before he could make a sound, he was shot twice in the stomach, producing deep-red blood to gush from his wounds.

Quickly jamming the gun barrel into DeTorrio's mouth, he seemed nearer to death than John desired, as he observed the candles of Tony's eyes beginning to grow faint.

"Remember me, tough guy?" said John. "How's it goin'. Awl, not so good, huh. Take a look at your sow over there. Fuckin' devil's probably rammin' her kitty right now. Maybe he'll let you have sloppy seconds."

John gave an icy grin at the sheer horror Tony DeTorrio's face revealed. "Know something before you die, scumbag. The last time you saw my mother, you called her a cocksucker. The last time we saw each other, you called me a cocksucker. Guess what, when the police find your dead body, they're gonna have a real good reason to remember you as the cocksucker."

As DeTorrio gasped, John eased the pistol to Tony's lips as he said, "Choose your next words carefully, tough guy. They may be your last."

Anthony DeTorrio accepted he was bound for oblivion. "Cocksucker, I'll be—waiting for you in hell," he managed to gag.

"Very well spoken, Mr. Anthony DeTorrio, sir," said John in faint praise. "Perfect last words for a pathetic piece of garbage like you. I'll personally inscribe them on your tombstone after I'm done taking a piss on your grave."

Without further ado, John Valone tilted the barrel upward and squeezed the trigger twice. The hollow-point bullets smashing force caused the crown of DeTorrio's head to explode before he slumped onto his side. Clumps of sticky brain-matter and bloody fragments of scalp and bone splattered about, further pasting John's face and jogging suit.

"No open-coffin for you, scumbag," he muttered, then fired his two remaining bullets into DeTorrio's face. The shots resulted in an eyeball detaching from its socket, falling to the carpet by the corpse.

Confident his primal actions hadn't been overheard, John flung the gun onto the bed. He pulled the plastic bag from his jacket's pouch. The hair stuck to his glove until it finally fluttered onto a spot on the bed unstained by Debbie Nichols' blood. Not chancing to lose the bag, he pushed it into his left sock. Reaching into his right sock, he drew a pocket-knife he'd brought–without Denny's knowledge. While straddling DeTorrio's body, he exposed the blade. John grabbed the dead man's penis, pulling it to stricture. The bantam member easily severed. With Gothic horror, he sadistically stuffed the detached organ into the hole in Anthony DeTorrio's face that had been his mouth.

With DeTorrio's wallet inside Nichols' purse tucked under his arm, an evil countenance darkened John Valone's face as he readied to depart the room. He felt no guilt, no remorse. Instead he was overcome with the marvel of unequivocal power. In a few moments, he had taken the lives of his venomous enemy and the woman who had schemed to injure his mother. Neither would scheme again.

Stillness remained outside as he started the Chevy. He drove slowly around the building, and pulled from the lot. In his side-view mirror, John saw the counter of the motel's office. Nobody was visible.

Citizen's Band Channel 29 spewed nothing but static as John neared the junction of Bray Hollow and Ridge Road, until he heard Denny's voice say, "All clear."

"Clear."

Turning onto the cobblestones moments later, he saw the garage door opening.

"Stay the fuck in there!" said Denny, while directing him into the garage.

As Dennis unfolded a blanket atop the concrete floor, John said, "Anything on the police bands?"

"Nothin'. Hurry up, on the blanket and strip. Give it to me, quick."

"It went like clockwork, Den," he said. "When I got in, the girl's back was to me and he was in the bathroom. I put three into her back and three more into her head. Then he came out. I popped him twice in the belly and four more in the head. If was so fuckin' beautiful how their brains were slopped all over the walls."

"Their brains are also slopped all over you. Where's their stuff?"

"Front seat."

"Put the hair where they'll find it?"

"They'd have to be blind not to," he said, already peeling-off his pants. "It's on the bed next to the fat bitch."

"Your knees and shins got blood on them. How'd you do that?"

"Well, Den, I'll tell ya," said John with a chuckle. "I decided DeTorrio needed an amputation of an external body-part." His socks off, he placed the plastic bag and knife into Denny's outstretched hand. "Here's my scalpel."

"You didn't?"

"The fuck I didn't. He used to call everyone a cocksucker. Now he's the one with a dick in his mouth."

"Oh, fuck," said Denny. "Okay, we'll talk about this some other time. You gotta get home. Jump in the shower and scrub yourself good, especially your face and legs. I'll take care of all this stuff."

As John arose from the blanket, he saw Denny clutching at his flank. "Den, you okay?"

"Yes. My side hurts once in a while because of the kidney I lost in Nam. Get moving."

After he'd showered and put on his wax-covered clothing, John slid an envelope across the hood of the Chevy Malibu and said, "Dennis, I thank you for all of your help. That's a small token of my gratitude."

As Denny thumbed through the envelope, he said, "Hey, John, I don't want all this money. This was a favor to you."

"Den, it's only forty grand. You earned it, pal."

"You'd better not have just taken this outta the bank."

"Nah, I gotta slush-fund stashed away in my basement."

"Must be nice," Denny said. "Thanks, John. I'll keep this for my boy. Listen, couple quick reminders. Make sure you keep the Burger Chef receipt for when the cops come nosin' around. First thing when you get home, call someone on your landline to establish the time. And when the police show, don't give them any shit. That kind of attitude pisses them off, and only makes them search harder into your background."

"That, I know," said John. "That's how I got us out of the beef at Hershey."

Dennis Perella smiled at the memory. "Just make sure you don't forget. One last thing. Whatever you do, don't let on to anyone, and I mean anyone, that you know anything about the killings except for what's in the papers or on TV. I know you're smart enough to realize it, but I'm afraid you might unintentionally mention something about the hair when the police grill you. The DA's office won't tell the media about any of their evidence. So when they question you, don't mention the hair. You do, even if they never find any hard-proof against you, they'll still know it was you. So keep your mouth shut about everything. Don't trust nobody."

CHAPTER TWENTY TWO

The Valone doorbell chimed early Friday morning.

"Butch, you big troll," said John. "Man, that new chief's uniform really looks great on you. What's up?"

"John, by now I'm sure you know about DeTorrio and Nichols," Butch said in a tone of voice John had never heard before.

"Sure did. Butch, I'm not going to lie to you, it couldn't have happened to two nicer people. But what does it have to do with me?"

Gill lifted his eyes from the sidewalk. "I've got some bad news for you. Two Westland County detectives are on their way here. They have a search warrant."

"Why? I had nothing to do with it."

"I believe you, but I've been with these guys since yesterday morning when the motel manager discovered the bodies. They've put a preliminary list of possible suspects together and everyone's going to be questioned. Your name's near the top of the list. Where's Mary?"

"She's on vacation in Aruba with her pal Janet. They left Tuesday."

"Good," said Butch. "They're both high on the list, too."

Soon thereafter, they observed the county detective's car entering the driveway.

"John, listen to me," urged Butch. "Cooperate with these guys. Just answer their questions honestly and you'll be okay. There haven't been any homicides in Westland County for over a year, and the murder of such a prominent man as DeTorrio has generated tremendous pressures on everyone."

"Prominent scumbag is more like it."

"John, please cooperate."

"Okay, Chief Troll," he said with a grin. "I'll behave."

Butch held the door opened as the two detectives clad in dark sport coats approached. The older man said, "Sir, are you John K. Valone?"

"Yes, Sir."

"Mr. Valone, I'm Detective Louis Indoff. This is my partner, Detective Tom Neupaver."

Indoff unfolded a document with a gold seal affixed. "This is a search warrant giving us the authority to inspect the premises and all contents located within, including any and all automobiles currently on the property."

"Come on in, fellas," said John.

Once they were all standing near the living room, Indoff said, "Mr. Valone, I understand Mary Valone's your mother. Is she available?"

"No, Sir, she's on vacation. She won't be home until late next week."

"He informed me before you and Detective Neupaver arrived that Mrs. Valone and Ms. Janet Silva have been out of the country since Tuesday," Butch interposed.

"Thank you, Chief Gill, that will be easy to confirm," said Indoff. "Mr. Valone, do you own a gun?"

"No, Sir. Detective, may I inquire as to what you're looking for?" he asked–his bewilderment appearing authentic.

"I'm not at liberty to disclose that," Indoff said in return.

Offering only a respectful nod, John moved to the couch. Indoff then said, "Tom, take the upstairs. Chief, downstairs."

With Neupaver and Butch out of sight, Indoff said, "Mr. Valone, I have some questions for you, however it is within your constitutional rights not to answer. You may also contact an attorney if you so choose."

"Detective, I don't need an attorney. I'm more than willing to answer your questions." John appeared at ease on the couch. "Please, Sir, have a seat."

Eventually Indoff drew near. "Mr. Valone, before we begin you should know there's a criminologist on his way to perform some various testing of your home. Afterwards, I must ask you to accompany us to Westland. We'll need a set of your fingerprints. Also my superior may ask your permission to have the county doctor extract a small blood sample for DNA analysis. If you refuse, I'll have a Court Order here tomorrow that will compel you to do as I say."

"Detective Indoff, I'm completely willing to do anything your department asks of me. I had no part in the crime. Please, ask whatever you'd like."

"Very well then. I'd like a complete accounting of your whereabouts this past Wednesday, from noon through midnight, along with the names of any individuals who would be able to confirm what you're about to say."

"I was home pretty much the entire day washing and waxing our three cars," said John. "I only went out one time that evening to Burger Chef."

"Be more specific with the times, Mr. Valone."

"I'll try." After a quick pause, he said, "Okay, I spent most of the morning washing the cars. I'd guess I started waxing my mother's Mercury at noon. Once I'd finished it, I began on my Taurus. I'd say I was done waxing it by five o'clock."

"Please continue."

"I took a break after the Taurus. I came inside and drank a bottle of Gatorade."

"Were all three of your garage doors opened during this time?"

"Yes."

"Please continue."

"Okay, I'd say that I began waxing my Cadillac at five-thirty. Around seven o'clock, my neighbor, Gene Polachek, came over to see me. We spent, oh, fifteen minutes talking."

"Where does Mr. Polachek live?"

"Next door, first house on the right."

"Continue," said Indoff, while jotting on his note-pad.

"I finished the Cadillac about nine-thirty. I came inside, grabbed another Gatorade and went to Burger Chef. When I got home, I took a shower and called my fiancé. We were on the phone until about eleven. That's it, Detective. After that, I went to sleep."

"What's your fiancés name?"

"Vicky Gill. She's Chief Gill's sister," said John–resulting in Lou Indoff's eyebrows to rise.

"So other than at Burger Chef, you're saying that Mr. Polachek is the only person who saw you the entire day, and only when you and he spoke. Is that accurate?"

"No, I saw Gene twice after we spoke."

"Did he come back over to your garage to speak with you?"

"No, I saw Gene through his kitchen window on both occasions."

"How can you be certain he saw you?" Indoff asked, continuing to stare at John, seeking out any weakness.

"Because both times I saw him, we waved to each other."

"Explain."

"Well, the first time I saw Gene, I was waxing the driver's side door. Gene was washing dishes. We waved our rags at each other."

"At what time?"

"It had to be right around eight o'clock."

"And the next occasion you saw him?"

"Again through his kitchen window. I was sitting on the garage floor catching a breather."

"What time was it then?"

Instead of answering immediately as he had done with all of Indoff's prior questions, John paused before saying, "Detective, in all honesty, I can't be positive about the time. I do recall that it was completely dark at the time. I also remember that all I had to finish waxing was the trunk. I noticed when Gene's kitchen light came on, and he saw me sitting on the floor. Again we just waved at each other. As to the time, my best guess would be, nine, nine-ten at the latest."

As the detective kept writing, Butch entered the room. Indoff then said, "Chief, find anything interesting?"

"Only his computers, Sir. Nothing else you mentioned."

"Any kind of boots?"

"No, Sir. Just several pair of sneakers and dress shoes in the closet near the front door."

They viewed Neupaver approaching.

"Find anything, Tom?" Indoff said.

"Nothing," Neupaver said. "I went through every closet and all the dirty clothes. It would appear he hasn't washed clothes for a few days now. There's some dirty whites, two pair of jeans, a plum Polo shirt, a gray, long-sleeved shirt, and several wax-covered rags."

"Any of the clothing in his closet of interest to us?"

"No," said Neupaver. "Just casual clothing and a several expensive suits."

"How about in any of the other closets?"

Neupaver shook his head.

"Have you heard from Hughes yet?"

"He just called the cell. He should be here soon."

"Okay, let's just wait for him," said Indoff. "We'll let him decide what articles of clothing we should take. Mr. Valone's agreed to cooperate fully with us. When Hughes is finished, we'll drive Mr. Valone to Westland."

Indoff looked to John. "Do you still wish to cooperate, Mr. Valone?"

"Absolutely," he said. "Detective, I had nothing to do with those murders."

"We'll soon see. Chief Gill has told my partner and I what an outstanding individual you are. If all the testing comes back negative, and your story holds true, we can rule you out as the perpetrator. As for Mr. Polachek, Detective Neupaver and I would like to question him concerning Wednesday evening. Would you know if he's home now?"

"I think he works daylight this week. Check if you'd like."

"Any objections to us speaking with him, Mr. Valone?" queried Tom Neupaver, his cunning inflection sparking the room.

"None whatsoever, Detective,' said John. "Actually I'd like for you and your partner to talk with Gene. He'll tell you I'm not lying."

*****

"Mean Gene," John called from the deck of the house, viewing Gene as he stepped outside later that evening.

They met by the sliding doors leading into John's basement.

"Damn, I get home from work and the fuckin' cops are waiting in my driveway to beat me with a rubber-hose," Gene rambled, though seemingly amused by it.

"Ah, stop your griping," said John. "What'd you tell those guys?"

"Like we agreed," said Gene. "I told them we saw each other when I came over to see you at seven, and twice through the kitchen window at eight and nine."

"But you only did see me through the window at eight."

"Yeah, but you said that you were able to see me while I was in the kitchen at nine, so I told those smartass detectives I saw you sitting on the floor at nine."

"Gene, I'm not complaining," John said. "But if you don't remember seeing me sitting on the floor, you didn't have to lie for me."

"Nah, I wouldn't call it lying," he said, grinning. "Let's just say that I had a delayed recollection. Besides, it ain't your fault I didn't see your tired ass on the floor."

"Gene, you don't know what this means to me. The police suspect me for those murders. You're the only alibi I've got."

"Pal, it's been all over the news since they found those two stiffs. When I heard their names, I knew who they were. And I know how they pricked Mary. So I told those two clowns you were in your garage at nine, and I'd testify to it." He beamed a guileful smirk. "Fuck 'em."

*****

"Wake up, sleepyhead," Vicky chirped to John on Sunday morning. "Breakfast is ready."

"Yeah, yeah," he grumbled, pulling the sheet over his head.

Dressed only in a nightgown, she leaped onto the bed. "I'm so happy we're spending the weekend together. Last night was wonderful."

"That stupid opera we went to was lousy," said John, as he suddenly flipped the sheet atop her and wrestled her underneath. "Buncha fruitcakes singing."

"Oh, quit complaining," she replied. "Now come on, let me up before the sausage burns."

As she watched him pick at his eggs and sausage, Vicky's heart-shaped face cast an expression of concern. "I still can't believe the police thought you had anything to do with those murders."

"Take it easy, Vick, there's nothing to worry about. It's their job to question everyone even remotely connected to crime victims. Butch told me they have twenty other suspects, and their list keeps growing. Forget about it."

He glared in disbelief at the microwave clock. "It's almost noon. What time did we go to sleep?"

"Late."

"Let's go into town for a couple hours."

"Not before we discuss something," she said firmly.

"Oh jeez, one of those talks, huh?"

"Yes, one of those talks."

John eyed her attentively. "Alright, my love, go ahead."

"When are we going to get married?"

"I don't know, you tell me. You said you wanted a big wedding."

"The biggest Vernon Park's ever seen."

"Okay, it takes time to plan a big wedding. Invitations. Gowns and tuxedos. Reserving the church. The reception. All that fun stuff."

"Months."

"Then you pick the date. Just keep in mind that Mary's malpractice trial is scheduled for early April of next year. How about in May?" Softly John massaged the curving, bronzed skin of her thighs. "I'm hoping you'll have gained a few pounds by our wedding day."

"We'll see about that," she smiled.

"And what about the property I own out where Bob Cook lives? I keep telling you to go-over the blueprints. The contractor who drew them up said it would six months minimum to build the place. I've been waiting for you to tell me if you want any changes made?"

"No, it looks perfect the way it is."

"Then why didn't you say so earlier? I'll call the guy tomorrow morning and tell him to start. Let's say the house is done by next April. So get started on all the arrangements, we'll get married in May, then we can move right in."

Vicky sat quietly, her full lips narrowed with displeasure. "John, have them build our house," she finally said. "It's just that I was hoping we could move away from Vernon Park once we were married."

"You never mentioned that to me before," he said. "Why do you want to move? We both have family and friends here. Maybe when we get older we'll move, but why now?"

"I just like to move someplace where it's always sunny and warm. Someplace like San Diego or the Florida Keys."

"Sweetie, you've lived in Pennsylvania your entire life. You've never once griped to me about winter. Come on, tell me the truth. I've always been straight with you. Why do you really want to move?"

With her cobalt-blue eyes shining disenchantment, another long moment of silence ensued. "We can always make new friends, you know," she said.

"I'm sure we would, but what about our families?"

"We could visit them whenever we wanted to."

"Vicky, that might be okay with you," he said. "But I can't just pick-up and leave Mary alone. I'm the only family she has. Sure we'll live in our new house when we're married. That's fine with me, since I'll only be a couple miles from Mary. Then think about when we have kids. My mother will be more than happy to babysit her grandchildren."

"What if she gets sick again!" said Vicky in a hyper tone of voice–throwing her fork to her plate. "We're young, John. I want us to live our lives together. Us and our children. I'm not about to be her nursemaid."

In spite of his emotions beginning to churn, John drew a deep breath to retain poise. "Vicky, you're not going to be her nursemaid. Yes, my mother still has some health issues, but she's still able to function better than most women her age. She won't infringe on our lives. Regardless of her health, Mary tries to be as independent as she can. Believe me, she won't place any burdens upon either of us."

"She sure placed a burden on you for the two months you lived like a hermit while you gave Mary her antibiotics, didn't she?"

"Sweetie, you're wrong," he said. "Mary didn't ask me to stay home with her. I chose to do it. Mary's infection was the worst crisis of her life. She was in tremendous pain during most of those two months. I did my best to help see her through it."

An uncomfortable silence lasted between them as John viewed her with discerning eyes–unmistakably Vicky Gill was evaluating all her options.

"Alright, John, as usual you win," she said. "Call the builder and have them get started on our house. I'm going home to see my girlfriend who has planned weddings before. Maybe she'll give me some ideas."

"Call her from here."

"No, she's always on her cell."

"I thought you wanted to stay with me today?"

"I changed my mind."

CHAPTER TWENTY THREE

Only two weeks later, William Gill wasn't certain what to expect as he hustled into the offices of Westland County District Attorney Frank Dague. "They're waiting for you in the conference room, Chief Gill," a young woman said to him.

A compact, yet exceeding fit man in his early-fifties wearing a brown, three-pieced suit stood to greet him. "Come in, Chief Gill, we haven't had the pleasure. Frank Dague."

"Pleasure meeting you, Sir," said Butch, while they shook hands.

Dague turned to the table. "Let's see, you already know the detectives and Criminologist Ed Hughes. And of course you've met Captain Jack Arrigo of the state police."

"Yes, Sir, we met at the crime scene," Butch said.

"Hard to forget that grizzly sight, right, Chief Gill," Arrigo bid him from across the conference table, dressed in full police uniform.

"No doubt about it, Captain," said Butch, wincing.

"Please sit, Chief,' said Frank Dague. "Let's get started. Ed, why don't you begin by informing us of any conclusions you've reached concerning the evidence gathered and if anything correlates to either of the two prime suspects of our investigation to this point."

"We don't have much, but I'll review what there is," Hughes said. He blended in with the detectives, all sporting dark coats and loose ties. "The crime scene unit gathered some black rayon fibers located on the body of the male victim, along with a strand of hair that was on the bed where the female was laying. They were able to lift several sets of latent prints about the room and other fixtures. Lastly, they obtained a partial footprint from the carpet. The lab wasn't able to ascertain the exact type of boot, however they did calculate it to be a size twelve. As for the gun, I'm sorry to report we weren't able to raise the serial number. It appeared the serial number had been treated with some form of highly-corrosive acid, as well as having a grinder repeatedly applied to it. Whoever did it sure did a professional job. Gentlemen, that's the extent of our physical evidence. I believe you're all aware we printed and obtained hair and blood samples from Mr. Valone and the boyfriend—pardon me, his name slipped my mind."

"Bradley Sankavich," Tom Neupaver called out.

"Yes, thank you, Tom," Ed Hughes said. "Men, I realize at this stage of the investigation all indications point to one of them being the most-likely culprit. However absolutely nothing the lab or I have come across links either of them to the evidence. Their fingerprints don't match. DNA analysis was performed on their hair and blood samples. None were even remotely analogous to the specimens taken from the scene. I luminaled every sink and bathroom drain in their residences and found no residual blood. I luminaled and GSR-tested all four of the vehicles that the suspects had access to on the evening in question and didn't find anything. Finally, none of the dark garments seized for analysis were composed of the same type of fibers found at the scene, nor did any of the other items of clothing or shoes register even the slightest inkling of blood. Considering the amount of blood that must have been saturated into areas of the killer's clothing, our testing procedures still would have been able to detect some miniscule trace amount even if they'd been washed. Yet we were unable to find any traces of blood stain on any garment seized from their homes."

"Let's put the forensic evidence aside for now and assess the two main suspects, starting with Sankavich," said the district attorney.

"He had a strong motive," Lou Indoff said. "The woman he was living with was cheating on him with another man. That would account for the mutilation of DeTorrio's corpse."

"His alibi's solid," came Tom Neupaver's retort. "He was at a bowling alley in Mercer from six until nine-thirty that night. All the members of his bowling league vouched for him."

"According to the pathologist, the murders took place somewhere between eight and ten o'clock, Tom," said Indoff. "Yes, I tend to believe his innocence just as much as you do, yet theoretically it still would have been possible for him to have killed them."

"Come off it, Lou," snapped Neupaver. "You saw for yourself what a complete imbecile he is. If he'd try to mug an old woman, he'd run into a wall trying to escape. Sankavich. His name should be Stupidvich. How can someone like him be expected to plan, much less carry out such a crime that still has us baffled?"

"I agree on Stupidvich," said a smiling Frank Dague. "He certainly doesn't have the mentality to have pulled this off. Let's move to Valone."

"John Valone remains our only prime suspect," declared Neupaver. "He disliked both DeTorrio and Nichols, and his only alibi is a friend he's known and lived next door to since childhood."

"Chief Gill, what's your opinion on Valone?" asked Dague. "You grew up with him. Do you think Valone has what it takes inside him to commit such a vicious crime?"

"I don't believe so, Sir," Butch said. "In all the years I've known him, he's always been polite and respectful towards people. While it's true he disliked the victims, I assure you he was provoked by them at the incident at the hospital. I honestly don't think he's the type of individual who could carry out something as cold-blooded like this."

"I disagree with you, Chief," said Neupaver. "He still—"

"Detective Neupaver, if I may," Captain Jack Arrigo said, "Valone's not our man, either. When Detective Indoff interviewed Mr. Valone, the information he offered was noted. However, I personally interviewed Mr. Valone at the barracks the following week. Using the information he provided, I tried every trick in the book to mislead him into contradicting any of his previous statements. I tried to bait him by assuring him we had an eyewitness who could identify him. He volunteered to stand in a lineup. Despite our not having one, I demanded he take a lie-detector test. He agreed to it immediately.

While Mr. Dague instructed we not disclose the hair found at crime scene, I tried to rattle Valone into believing we had obtained DNA from another source in the room that was a perfect match to his DNA. I even insisted he was on videotape using DeTorrio's credit card at the gas station outside of Niagara Falls. Detective, he never even flinched. He remained calm as could be and insisted I had to be mistaken. I observed him very closely throughout the entire interview. Not one drop of sweat. Never fussed-about. Despite my insisting he contact a lawyer, he declined my offer. As Chief Gill stated, all Valone was towards me was polite and respectful. My opinion, the kid's a model citizen."

"What about Polachek, Valone's alibi?" Tom Neupaver could only counter. "Something about him rubs me the wrong way, Captain. His version as to when he saw Valone that evening was entirely too comparable to Valone's. It was as if they'd rehearsed their story in advance. Add to that, nobody can corroborate Polachek's attesting to his actually seeing Valone at the exact times they both claim to have seen each other."

"Nor can Polachek's version be refuted," said Lou Indoff. "Tom, remember when we spoke to Polachek's father? The man's an invalid pretty much confined to a wheelchair. True, Polachek was a bit abrasive towards us. But when you consider his situation, I can understand why. And we both looked through Polachek's kitchen window. You must admit that it's easy for Polachek to see into Valone's garages."

"How about the other neighbors you spoke with?" Dague asked of Indoff.

"There were several who saw Valone during the morning and afternoon hours," he said. "A Ms. Nancy Schriver claims she saw Valone shortly before seven o'clock when she was walking her dog. However, other than Polachek, nobody else saw Valone at home after that."

"What was Ms. Schriver's reaction towards your questions, Tom?" said Dague.

"Oh, brother," Indoff said, shaking his head. "Ms. Schriver certainly isn't shy about speaking her mind. She used several expletives towards us when I mentioned why we were seeking information on Valone."

"She called us 'assholes' more times than I can recall," said Neupaver. "I still think it was Valone."

"Alright, for the sake of argument, let's take Polachek at his word for the time being," Frank Dague said. "Simply by using the time-stamp on the Burger Chef receipt, and the phone-dump that verifies Valone was the telephone with Chief Gill's sister beginning at 10:14 P.M., we've established Valone was home at that time. Thus, if Polachek is telling the truth, that would leave Valone an approximate one hour and fifteen minute window-of-opportunity to have driven to the motel, committed the murders, and returned home. Comments?"

"Absolutely impossible," stated Jack Arrigo with conviction. "The killer had to be completely drenched in blood. That room had more blood spattered about than a slaughter house. Frank, you've seen the crime photos. It looked like something that would have made Charlie Manson cringe."

Arrigo turned to the criminologist and said, "Ed, assume Valone did use one of his vehicles. Also assume he had the seat covered so any blood on his clothing would not get onto the seat. Is it possible he could have hidden all evidence of blood?"

"Extremely doubtful," Hughes replied. "All three of the Valone cars have cloth interiors. Perhaps he could have concealed any evidence on the seat itself, although in all likelihood there still would have been trace amounts on the armrests, door, steering wheel, or the floor mat. I luminaled all those areas. The ultra-violet test was negative."

Arrigo's view returned to Neupaver. "As you were saying, Detective."

"Captain, I agree with you in that regard," Neupaver rushed to speak. "But there are other possibilities. The scenario I've been considering is Valone hired someone to kill them. You've seen Valone's financial profile. He's loaded. I say he's responsible. He had the strong motive, and he's wealthy enough to have paid somebody to do his dirty-work."

"If that's the case, why aren't there any unexplainable withdrawals shown on any of his bank accounts?" Arrigo shot back. "What'd Valone do, give the hitman an IOU? I got news for you, those guys only take cash, and lots of it. If you'll recall, the computer techie did a complete scan of Valone's PC's. There wasn't anything on either hard-drive that indicated he was surfing the web trying to find 'hitman-dot-com.'"

"He could have used another computer," said Neupaver.

"Hello!" shouted Arrigo. "Detective, professional shooters kill their targets and vanish. They don't use their victim's credit cards. They don't take any souvenirs of their crime. And they certainly don't take the time to chop the victim's dick off just for the hell of it."

"Okay, let's presume Valone didn't hire someone to pull the trigger," said Neupaver, his self-esteem bruised by Arrigo's colloquy. "Suppose Valone had an accomplice help him with transportation to and from the motel, and getting cleaned-up afterwards. It could have very easily gone down that way."

"Detective Neupaver, you're pissing in the wind," Jack Arrigo said. "We don't have one witness who can place Valone anywhere near the motel. His fingerprints weren't found at the scene. The footprint is from a size twelve. Valone wears size eleven. The root of the hair doesn't match his DNA. We don't have a single shred of physical or forensic evidence against him. Face it, we don't have a damn thing on Valone."

"Sorry, Tom, I'm forced to agree with Captain Arrigo," said Lou Indoff. "We still have to further investigate the potentials Ms. Silva provided to Mr. Dague. Relax, I've worked Homicide longer than you have. Something will break soon."

"Chief Gill, any final thoughts?" asked Frank Dague.

"Mr. Dague, while I don't have the experience these men possess, it seems obvious to me that John Valone wasn't involved," said Butch. "I agree it can be perceived he may have had a motive against the victims, yet he doesn't have any past history of violent behavior. As Captain Arrigo stated, none of the evidence can be connected to him. Sir, I'm certainly not a genetic engineer, but from what I understand about DNA testing, the results are indisputable. Therefore it seems to me that the only logical conclusion to be derived at this time is that he's innocent."

"Motive, means, and opportunity all sound weak to me," said Dague.

"I still say Valone's our man," Neupaver held firm. "I don't care what the DNA tests show or about any of the other arguments. My gut tells me he's responsible."

Jack Arrigo threw his arms up in disapproval. "Frank, your detective can believe whatever his gut tells him. It doesn't make any difference to me. As I've told you before, the murders had to be a result of a robbery gone bad. Some nut-job broke into their room, took their money, killed them for whatever twisted reason, then hightailed it to Niagara Falls. The perp's probably living in Canada now. That's how my official report to the Regional Commander is going to read."

Displaying a tight frown, Frank Dague stood to address them. "Gentlemen, I'm afraid we must continue exploring the possibilities. As of now, there isn't any tangible evidence against Mr. Valone. I feel we should proceed by concentrating upon the other potential suspects. It's quite apparent that Anthony DeTorrio had several enemies. In addition to the list of doctors Ms. Silva gave us, I subpoenaed Valleyview General Hospital for names of employees DeTorrio had terminated up until six months prior to his murder. He wasn't a very popular man to say the very least. As for Miss Nichols, well, she wasn't exactly a virgin princess herself. Sankavich told us she had sex with numerous other men besides DeTorrio both before and while they were living together. Too much time has already passed and the clock is ticking, hence we must move forward with the investigation. Keep Valone under consideration. However unless something incriminating surfaces against him, my office can't touch him. Right now, there isn't enough evidence of guilt for me to even seek an arraignment against him."

"One moment, Chief," Frank Dague called to Butch, as the other men were making their exits. "Chief, I sincerely appreciate all of your diligent efforts on behalf of my office's attempt to solve this case."

"I only did what I thought might be beneficial to the detectives and Captain Arrigo," he humbly replied. "Sir, if you would like for me to continue investigating this matter, I certainly wouldn't mind assisting in whatever capacity you see fit."

"Thanks, Butch, that won't be necessary anymore. Your job as Chief of Police must keep you busy enough. I did want you involved in the initial phases of the investigation since you were first to arrive at the crime scene. It came as a bonus when I learned you are well-acquainted with both Valone and Polachek. I had hoped your familiarity with them could better enable us to catch either of them in a lie that may have been overlooked by the detectives. Although when you happen upon Valone or Polachek again, keep alert for anything they may say or do that could prove advantageous to us."

"I'll keep an eye on them for you, Mr. Dague."

"That's all I can ask. Chief Gill, let me tell you something. In your career in law enforcement, you've built a solid reputation that you should be very proud of. All those I've contacted speak quite highly of you. Chief, there's a bright future awaiting you in law enforcement."

"Thank you, Sir," said Butch. "I appreciate the complement. I do my best."

CHAPTER TWENTY FOUR

John Valone's life had resumed course as the time passed. He had begun accepting consulting offers, his engagement to Vicky remained intact. Construction of his and Vicky's new home was underway. The police had stopped asking questions, the murders he had executed were now only fleeting slideshows of his mind–memories he was more than able to suppress. Yet, he remained concerned for Mary.

For while Mary Valone was seemingly happy as she adapted to her new lifestyle away from Valleyview General Hospital by continually being in contact with Janet Silva, taking up new hobbies, and by performing various works for charitable organizations in Vernon Park, she couldn't hide the fact from John that the pain she was coping with wasn't subsiding. During this time, Mary had sought after more neuro-specialists, only requesting they render an opinion–she was always denied. Word had spread like wildfire about her medical condition, along with her pending civil action. She was now persona non grata.

On an early October evening, John entered their home to find Mary seated on the couch, smiling while holding a paper. "John, I spoke with Dr. Mancini today!" she exclaimed. "Sam may have found a doctor who can help me."

"That's great, Ma."

"His name's Dr. Charles Tyler. He practices at Johns Hopkins Medical Center in Baltimore. Sam told me he read about Dr. Tyler in a medical journal. He's considered to be one of best neurosurgeons in the country."

"Make an appointment with him."

"I already did! Next Monday morning at his office at Johns Hopkins."

"Baltimore's about a four-hour ride. I'll drive you."

"I can ask Janet to take me."

"No, I'm driving you. I wanna meet this guy."

His brown eyes cast an aura of doubt. "Tyler, huh? Least he ain't no friggin' Arab."

*****

The densely-populated woodlands aligning Interstate 68 offered a tranquil backdrop for their drive through the panhandle of western Maryland. The many varieties of trees and assorted foliage were a montage of the colors of autumn, what leaves remained glistening in the lemony morning sunshine. Norman Rockwell himself would have marveled at the scenic magnificence of nature's pageantry.

With the Cadillac on cruise-control, John took a moment to stretch his leg from the pedals. Glancing at his sleeping mother, he pondered what her future held. Despite Dr. Mancini's optimism, his distress would not pass. Although Mary had kept persuading her level of discomfort was now manageable, he knew better. His once-vivacious mother was showing the effects of her pain. Dr. Mancini had initially prescribed ninety Vicodin per month–Mary's newest prescription was for one hundred and twenty.

Less than two hours later, as John walked from the parking garage after having dropped Mary at the main entrance, he observed the surrounding residential area. Johns Hopkins Medical Center was a combination of modern buildings, along with other connecting structures that appeared as archaic edifices, all linked by glass-covered walkways. "Hope this guy can do something to help her," John mumbled, as he made his way inside.

He found Mary seated in an enormous waiting area overflowing with people. "I'd say Dr. Tyler is slightly overbooked today," he said, squatting as a baseball catcher would.

"No, the woman at the front desk told me this is a shared waiting room. Dr. Tyler's right on schedule."

"Where are your films?"

"The woman at the front desk took them when I signed-in," said Mary.

Shortly thereafter, another woman emerged to lead Mary and John into an examination room. There stood a handsome, athletically-framed, meticulously attired African-American man clad in an olive-green suit. "Mrs. Valone, I'm Dr. Charles Tyler," he said, offering his hand.

"My pleasure, Dr. Tyler," she said–caught off guard, yet resolute upon not displaying any facial gestures that could be perceived as unfavorable. "Dr. Tyler, this is my son, John."

"Nice meeting you, Doctor," said John, gripping Tyler's hand.

"Please," said Dr. Tyler, gesturing for them to be seated.

"Dr. Tyler, if you would like for me to leave while you examine my mother, I'll be in the waiting room," John said.

"That won't be necessary," said the doctor. "Mrs. Valone, if you would, please lift your sweater up less than half-way."

"Dr. Tyler, please call me Mary," she said, then pulled her lavender sweater to her brassiere-line.

"Thank you, Mary," he said. "Now I'm going to gently probe the area around your incision. Please tell me the instant you feel pain."

"There," she said the first instance Dr. Tyler touched her.

"There," she said again.

Dr. Tyler placed his finger below Mary's incision. "How about here?"

"Yes."

Tyler eyed her with sympathy. "Thank you, Mary," he sighed. "That's enough."

Following his review of her MRI's and medical reports, Dr. Tyler said, "Mary, have you ever heard of a rhizotomy?"

"No, I haven't, Dr. Tyler."

Taking a replica of the human spine in hand, Tyler positioned himself where they could see. "Mary, I'm convinced a rhizotomy will diminish your level of pain to a large extent. Allow me to explain why you're having such severe pain. Nerve roots originate from the spine. Each cluster of nerves move through what are called facet-joints, a cartilage-like substance that shields each root juncture while enabling the nerves to pass through. They and the vertebrae constitute barriers of protection for the centralized nerve origination points. Naturally each nerve moves away from its point of origin along the spine and disperses to its designated location. I would approximate ninety to ninety-five percent of the lumbar nerve centers control all mid to lower body torso sensory locations, as well as govern many vital bodily functions." Dr. Tyler paused. "Any questions, please feel free to ask."

"I understand to some extent, Doctor," said Mary, her tone reverent.

"Go ahead, Dr. Tyler," said John. "I'll catch-up sooner or later."

Tyler smiled, then said, "Mary, as I'm sure you've been told, due to your infection, your lower lumbar region has formed scar tissue. I'm certain that your pain is emanating from the L4-L5 and L5-S1 facet-joints. The only conceivable methodology to help ease your pain would be to have a rhizotomy performed."

"Dr. Tyler, I'm a bit apprehensive about having another back surgery," she said. "No disrespect, but I was told any additional surgery could result in my losing bodily functions."

"No disrespect taken, Mary. Whoever advised you not to have further surgery of the spine was correct. However a rhizotomy is not an evasive surgical procedure. Please let me explain. A rhizotomy entails the insertion of trocars introduced into the targeted facet-joints under fluoroscopic guidance. I would not be making any incisions."

"Excuse me, Dr. Tyler," she said. "What's a trocar?"

"A trocar is just a thin, hollow metal tube."

"Thank you, Doctor. Sorry to have interrupted."

Tyler nodded politely and said, "Mary, once you're in the OR, you would lay flat on your stomach. You'll be given a local anesthetic that will numb your lower back. You'll also be given a Valium-drip to relax you. The lumbro-sacral area would be prepped in usual sterile fashion.

At that point, I would insert the trocars. Once they're in place, I would then introduce a probe with an attached laser. At each site, one by one, I'll stimulate each of the various nerves by grasping them with the probe's forceps. At that point, whenever simulation results in your experiencing a twinge of pain, I'll then activate the laser. The nerve will be severed, burned, at eighty degrees centigrade. Mary, I do not wish to frighten you, but you must remain conscious throughout the entire procedure that would last an hour at most. The reason being I will need for you to tell me what sensations you're feeling so I will know what nerves to laser."

Only a brief pause before Mary said, "It doesn't sound too bad, Doctor."

"It really isn't," said Dr. Tyler. "Mary, in all candor, it's your only realistic alternative. However, there is a serious detriment that pertains to your situation."

"I'm not surprised, Doctor," she said. "I've experience nothing but detriments ever since my surgery."

"Oh, that's quite apparent," said Tyler. "Your scar tissue is very austere, yet I'm certain the procedure will alleviate a great deal of your pain. Unfortunately what concerns me is the fact that much of the scarred region of tissue adjoins your intestines. Due to the tissue's proximity to your intestines, my past experiences dictate there are entangled nerves within that regulate and maintain bowel functions. Therefore when I rouse a nerve during the procedure, it is absolutely imperative that if you feel the slightest sensation in your bowels, the nerve must not be burned. Needless to say, it would only compound your problems."

"I understand, Dr. Tyler," said Mary. "I certainly don't want any additional complications like those. Can you estimate as to how this constraint will limit the total effectiveness of the procedure?"

"Honestly, there isn't any feasible mode to make such a determination. Your eventual level of pain reduction could range anywhere between thirty to eighty percent. We'll just have to see how you feel afterwards. Another drawback of the rhizotomy is the fact that while the laser completely severs the nerve, the disunited nerves remain in a state of propinquity. In other words, they will eventually regenerate. What I'm leading up to is the vast majority of patients undergoing a rhizotomy require more than one."

"About how many more, Doctor?" Mary asked of him.

Dr. Tyler frowned. "Depending upon your body's healing powers, it could take as many as four rhizotomys before the nerves finally lose their resiliency to regenerate and become completely inactive."

"How will I know when it's time to have another rhizotomy?"

"You'll know, Mary," said Dr. Tyler. "Unfortunately your pain will slowly reoccur. Just please don't wait until you're in agony again before you decide to return."

Without hesitation, her faith in him secure, Mary said, "Dr. Tyler, I'm willing to have it done. Is there anything else I should be aware of before we finalize everything?"

"There is one last concern on my mind. Normally I have my patient's begin taking oral antibiotics a week prior to admission and continue on them for a week thereafter. However, due to your past history, and due to the fact that I will need to perform some testing upon you, I would ask for you to be admitted five days prior to your rhizotomy, and stay at Hopkins at least three days following your procedure. I'd like to have you carefully monitored for infection. I realize this will pose an inconvenience upon both yourself and John, but it is in your best interest. I refuse to take chances with my patients' health."

"I don't have a problem staying," Mary said, looking to John.

"Neither do I," he added. "Doctor, after what happened before, I think it's for the best."

"It is, John." said Dr. Tyler. "Mary, even though the possibility of your contracting another infection is extremely remote, I'll sleep better knowing you're definitely not infected once you go home." A tenuous pause. "Because quite honestly, another serious infection could possibly prove fatal."

"I knew my infection was severe," she said.

"Without any question whatsoever," said Tyler. "I was totally abhorred when I reviewed your films and reports. You were terribly neglected post-op."

Mary snuck a peek at John. "Okay, Dr. Tyler," she said, her face brimming with confidence. "I'd ask for you to perform my rhizotomy as soon as you can."

Dr. Tyler studied his upcoming schedule and said, "The earliest I can take you would be two weeks from today, Monday, October 27th. I'll have my staff handle all the details."

"Thank you very much, Doctor," she said. "I'll make it until then."

"Mary, I'm sure you will," he said. "Heaven only knows how you've made it this far."

*****

"Well, what did you think of him?" John asked of her, the moment they were outside of the waiting area.

"John, he's a wonderful man. Extremely intelligent. Articulate. Courteous. Honest. Although what I liked the most is that Dr. Tyler has a deep sense of compassion for people in pain. Yes, I was a little surprised he's African-American, but I don't give a damn. I like the man and I trust him."

CHAPTER TWENTY FIVE

Robert Cook lounged with his feet propped atop his desk when Art McNally opened the office door. "Well, Mr. Cook, how would you evaluate your client's depositions?"

"They were excellent. I knew they'd do well, but Mrs. Valone was spectacular. Her recollection of the even the smallest detail astonished me." Robert Cook grinned in satisfaction. "And the kicker was she never let that suave Walt Tibeau get under her skin during the entire deposition. Have a seat, Art. Stay a while."

"I knew he was only blowing smoke up your ass when every time you contacted his offices, he'd have one of his errand-boys return your call."

"Good old Walt used that same gimmick when I was there. Try's to lull his opposition into thinking he may have handed-off the case to a junior partner. No, on a case of this magnitude, I was certain nobody except Walter J. Tibeau would occupy first-chair."

"Ever see Jimmy Stewart as a lawyer in an old movie? That's Walt Tibeau. So easygoing, he's almost downright passive. The jury can't help but like him. But give him one tiny opening, let him pinpoint one inconsistency in a witnesses' testimony, he'll reach down their throat and tear their heart out."

"No doubt about it," said Bob. "The few times I was privileged to see Tibeau in action, he sure impressed the hell out of me. I must admit that I'm an admirer of his talents."

McNally shook his head. "Don't let Tibeau see it. I've seen him in court a lot more than you have. Walt Tibeau is a very formidable opponent. The man plays nothing but hardball with anyone who dares cross him. And when Tibeau senses fear, he goes straight for the jugular."

"I said I admired him. I certainly don't fear him," was Bob's prideful reply. "Art, this case means more than a chance for a big payday. Not only do I want justice for Mary Valone, this is my shot to show Tibeau that I belonged at his firm. He always kept me prepped for significant cases, though he never entrusted me with anything except petty details."

"Robert, you're an intelligent, highly-precocious young lawyer, but you'd best remember one very important fact. When you worked for Tibeau, his clients were on the other side of the aisle. The side that usually prevails in malpractice cases."

"I know, Art. I've read many transcripts of Tibeau's cases."

McNally eyed him with an expression of reservation. "Transcripts may tell you what was said, but they don't tell the truth in malpractice cases. Bob, know this going in. Most doctors out there today think they're high priests of society. They'll take the stand, look you, the judge and jury straight in the eye and tell on lie after another. The Mafia's conspiracy of silence pales in comparison to a doctor accused of malpractice. They have their holy code of deference that must be maintained at all costs. You can have evidence up the ass against them, yet they and their henchmen will arrive at other plausible versions to create doubt among the jury."

"Slow down, Art," said a calm Bob Cook. "Damn, you're foaming at the mouth."

"Yes, Sir, that's what they've become, the medical Mafia where everyone turns deaf, dumb and blind to anything that could incriminate one of their sacred brotherhood. The Sicilian Code of Omerta in America, circa 2008. Even the Mafia doesn't attempt to guise wrongdoings to the depths physicians will sink to. When a member of the mob gets caught snuffing someone, they clam-up and do their time like a man. Put a doctor on the stand, they'll swear one lie on top of another just to preserve honor amongst themselves."

"Arthur, I am perfectly aware that doctors leave whatever moral values they may have outside the courtroom whenever they testify on behalf of one of their own."

"That's just it, Bob!" said the fiery Irishman. "When it comes to saving deference in a courtroom, none of them have any moral values. Don't ever forget something I was told a long time ago. The Mafia buries their enemies. Doctors bury their mistakes."

Cook remained impervious to say, "Even so, we've got plenty of hard evidence against them. There's Mrs. Valone's films. Her medical charts. Cameron's reports—"

"Meaningless," he scoffed. "You think a jury's going to even bother sorting through that scientific bullshit. You're fucked without expert witnesses who are willing to stand up to those bastards, look the jury in the eye and tell them the defendants are guilty as sin. For your sake, I hope that trip you took to New York pays off soon, or else you'd better hop another plane real quick."

"Well, Arthur me lad, take a good look at these," said Bob, gleaming in contentment. "They were delivered Federal Express late last week. I wanted to surprise you."

As McNally anxiously opened the first envelope he was tossed, Bob went on to say, "That's from Dr. Terrence Bates, a board-certified radiologist from New York City, whose opinion concludes that Mary's infection was readily discernable on both MRI's that Cameron took at his office, and Cameron misinterpreted it. The others from Dr. Ronald Worthington, a prominent neurosurgeon who lives in Oyster Bay, Long Island. His report definitively concludes Nasser ignored every possible contingency that Mary had become infected."

"What about Dr. Elliot?"

"Didn't I mention to you what I decided about Elliot?"

"Not since the last time we spoke."

"Art, I think it wise not to drag Dr. Elliot into this too far. He only saw Mary for maybe five minutes. He never gave her a complete examination—"

"His diagnosis was still an error, Bob."

"Yes, his diagnosis of mechanical back syndrome was in error," said Cook. "However when I deposed him, Dr. Elliot admitted that he was wrong. Obviously Elliot had to be named in the lawsuit, or else the other two sleazeballs would have concocted some story to funnel all the blame onto him. We've got expert testimony against Cameron and Nasser, while in essence Dr. Elliot is neutralized from accepting any of the culpability. Read his depo. Elliot wasn't about to take the fall for his business affiliate."

"Have you deposed Cameron or Nasser yet?"

"Not yet," said Bob. "Still waiting for Tibeau to contact me."

McNally finally nodded in concurrence. "Your rationale is sound, Bob. If you tore into Elliot just because he's in business with Cameron, it could look bad to the jury." Art shook the envelopes at Bob. "Just make sure those two guys are ready to testify by April."

"We've already come to terms," said Bob Cook. "Dr. Bates gets ten thousand to testify plus expenses. Dr. Worthington wanted fifteen thousand, plus. Arthur, they're as good as gold."

"You needed them," said Art. "You never would have gotten past the first pre-trial conference with only Dr. Mancini's affidavit to substantiate Mary's claims."

"No chance. Dr. Mancini isn't an expert in either field, although he'll still make a solid witness. He's been Mary's PCP for years, and he comes across as a very sincere man."

"Yeah, I like him. He's one of the few doctors I've met who doesn't think they can walk on water. Okay, how about Dr. Tyler? Did you get in contact with him yet?"

"Oh, yeah," Cook replied with a bright smile. "I spoke to him a couple days after Mary and John got home from Baltimore. They have nothing but the highest praises for Dr. Tyler. I plan on taking a ride to Baltimore myself to meet with him whenever he has time."

"How's Mary feeling now?"

"Much better. She's already weaned herself off her pain medicine."

"I'm glad to hear it. Mary's a very classy lady."

"Yes, she most certainly is," said Bob, his facial expression further amplifying his delight. "Art, I researched Dr. Tyler on the internet. His reputation at Johns Hopkins is impeccable. People from all over the country go to him."

"Did you ask Dr. Tyler?"

"He'll testify, though only as Mary's treating physician."

"Did you tell him you wouldn't be asking the magic question?"

"Sure did," Bob said. "I told Dr. Tyler that we only need his testimony to substantiate Mary's continuing medical issues. I made it clear that I wouldn't be asking him to affix guilt on any of the defendants."

"How'd he sound to you?"

"Absolutely perfect. Best part was when Dr. Tyler mentioned that he really enjoyed getting to know Mary and John."

"Any idea when you'll meet with him?"

"I'm not sure. Dr. Tyler asked me to notify his staff whenever Tibeau selects possible dates to record his testimony."

"Can't he come in person to testify?"

"He's willing to if he's able," said Bob. "Problem is we don't have an exact trial date yet, so Dr. Tyler suggested we videotape his testimony just in case he has a scheduling conflict. Just by speaking with him, I got the impression Dr. Tyler doesn't take much down-time."

"It would be better if he testifies in person," Art said.

"I agree, Art, although I certainly wasn't about to argue with the man. Dr. Tyler told me he'd be more than happy to testify if I could give him an exact date, but I can't. Obviously it's better to have his testimony on video than risk not having it at all."

"True. What about Dr. Yoder?"

"She's a maybe," Bob said. "She claims since she was only a physician brought in on a consult, it isn't appropriate for her to testify against the doctor who issued the consult. Dr. Yoder said she felt bad for Mary, but she kept hedging when I was at her office."

"She could help your case," said Art.

"Yeah, she may have helped to some extent," Bob said. "Although the truth is I know we have a top-flight neurosurgeon from Johns Hopkins on our side. Dr. Yoder, we can't be sure of. Art, I'm not about to play guessing-games with her. No, Sir, not at this trial."

"I suppose you can't blame her," Art said. "Cameron would have blacklisted her straight out of Pittsburgh."

"That's why she's hedging. Once Tibeau saw her on the witness list, Cameron would have warned her not to testify." Bob smiled as he said, "It's okay, Art. If I had to choose between them now, I'd still prefer having Dr. Tyler as another of Mary's treating physicians."

Casting a look of apprehension, Art McNally said, "So you've got two experts and two treating physicians. Right?"

"Right."

"Bob, that isn't enough medical testimony! Walt Tibeau believes in the concept of strength in numbers at malpractice cases. You should realize that."

Robert Cook could only grin before saying, "Let me guess. You didn't listen to any of the messages I left on your phone."

Hurriedly Art reached into his shirt pocket to toss his cell phone atop Bob's desk. "You figure out how to work the damn thing!"

"Judge Albert Watson."

"You drew Watson?"

"Uh-uh." Bob's eyes twinkled. "Tibeau nearly fainted when the clerk pulled Watson's name. I'm sure you're aware of Judge Watson's long-standing policy of keeping the expert testimony balanced in malpractice cases. He even limits the number of treating physicians and character witnesses on both sides."

"You are so lucky to have him on the bench," said Art, still shaking his head. "In civil cases he usually rules in favor of the plaintiff on decisions that could go either way, and he doesn't tolerate any shenanigans. Bob, I was in court a few years ago when he chastised a defense attorney right in front of the jury. Never before had I seen any judge become so irritated with the jury present."

"For sure he would've been Tibeau's last choice."

"Betcha he has some of his grunts searching for any possible slant he could use to have Watson disqualified."

"Nah, Judge Watson's record is beyond reproach. Tibeau isn't going to risk alienating Watson with some futile attempt to relieve him. No, Tibeau's too shrewd to pull a maneuver like that."

McNally smiled as he said, "Bob, sounds to me like you've got everything under control."

"Hope so."

"Any other potential witnesses you need me to interview?"

"Nope. I already have several character witnesses ready to go. We'll use as many of them as Judge Watson allows."

From his top drawer, Bob took a folder and slid it across his desk. "Read and sign."

"What's this?" said Art.

"Look at it."

"C'mon, Bob, I'm tired. Just tell me what it is."

"Arthur, not only are you the best legal investigator I've ever known, you're also my friend. You've stuck by me throughout this dry-spell I've been having. You're barely been charging me for your services. That's my reward to you for all of your loyalty. It's a contract that states you'll receive twenty percent of my net earnings from the Valone case."

McNally's jaw dropped. "Bob, I don't know what to say—except thank you."

"There's only one proviso attached," said Bob. "I'm buying you some quiet suits before April. All grays and navy-blues."

"What for!" said Art, as he stood to model his multi-colored, checkerboard blazer. "They don't make clothes like this anymore."

"We won't go there, Art," said a smiling Robert Cook. "Nevertheless we can't have the jury distracted, since you'll be sitting beside me at trial."

"Huh?!"

"Art, the Valone's don't want me taking on another attorney for trial. If Tibeau sees I don't have any help, he'd do everything he can to make me appear unprepared. So your job will be keeping all of the paperwork organized and at my fingertips. This case is going to be presented in a very professional manner. I can't be fumbling through papers while the jury's waiting. Well, you up to it, partner?"

"Definitely, partner," Art replied–shaking Cook's outstretched hand.

"Arthur, we're gonna win this case."

"Malpractice cases are the toughest," he said. "But I really think you've got a legitimate chance with this one. Hey, have there been any settlement rumblings yet?"

"Nah, Tibeau always waits until after discovery and the final pre-trial conference. Maybe when he sees our ammunition, he'll advise them to settle. But I'm not counting on it. To Walter J. Tibeau, recommending a settlement is the equivalent of defeat."

"He always used to be that way, Bob."

"And from what I've heard, he still is," said Cook. "Besides, it's my belief that Mary wouldn't accept a settlement, regardless of how substantial the offer. She's extremely insistent about having her day in court. And knowing John like I do, she'll have it. I'm sure you've noticed just how adamant they both are about this litigation."

*****

"Freeze! You're under arrest for WWD," yelled Butch from the Vernon Park police car to John Valone as he walked Broad Avenue.

"—the fuck's WWD?"

"Walking while drunk," said the chief. "C'mon, get your butt in here. I forget the last time I saw you."

Closing the door behind him, John said, "When you were out the house with them other sherlock's, that's when."

"Yeah, I guess it was. John, I'm sorry, they wanted me in on the investigation—"

"Forget it!" he said. "Butch, old buddy, old pal, ain't no hard feelin's."

Butch smiled at his intoxicated friend. "I'm glad you're not mad at me, John."

"Butch, I ain't mad at nobody. Man, life's been good to me. Me and Vick's getting' married. My mom's doin' great. I got the best bunch of pals in the world. I got a few bucks in the bank. Hell, what else can a guy want."

"I'm happy Mary's doing okay."

"Okay! Butch, she's doin' fantastic! Last summer she could barely get outta bed. Now all she does is clean the damn house or go runnin' around with Janet." He let out a burp. "Hey, where the fuck's Gene?"

"I saw his car parked—"

"Yeah—that's right, the little guy hadda go home."

"So everything's goin' good for you and Vicky?" Butch asked.

"Ahhhh, she gotta little pissed while I was in Baltimore, but she got over it."

"When's the wedding?"

"Hell, I don't know, sometime next May. She's takin' care of all that junk." An awkward pause. "Well, what's the latest?"

"About what?"

"You know what I'm talkin' about."

"You mean about the investigation?"

"Yes, about the investigation, ya big troll."

"John, you aren't even considered a suspect anymore," Butch said. "Last I heard, the DA's convinced it was a robbery-homicide, and there isn't any way possible you could have been involved."

"Gene said one of those dickheads was around when I was in Baltimore."

"Yeah, that was Neupaver. When the DA found out, he ordered Neupaver to stop wasting time on you and to keep looking into their other suspects. John, believe me, you're in the clear."

"Chief Gill, come in please," they heard a voice call from the police radio.

"Butch, that's a big weight off me," said John. "I'm just glad that hair turned-up."

"Give me a sec," Butch said, while reaching for the handset.

"Gill, here. What is it, Luzansk?"

"Chief, there's a 10-53 at the intersection of Belmont and Village Drive. Over."

"Any one injured? Over?"

"No, but the vehicles are blocking the intersection. We may need a tow truck. Over."

"10-4, Luzansk. I'm on my way. Over and out."

"Whatsa 10-53?" asked John.

"Minor car accident. John, I'd better get going. You okay to drive?"

"Hell, yeah."

As he neared the accident scene, Chief William Gill suddenly slammed on the brake. A surreal moment of revelation rocked his consciousness as if he'd been struck by lightning. *"How could he possibly know about the hair? Dague ordered everyone from the start not to reveal anything about any evidence. The detectives and Hughes never said anything. Captain Arrigo said he never mentioned it during his interrogation. It wasn't in the media. I didn't tell him."*

CHAPTER TWENTY SIX

The calendar having turned to February of 2009, the crowd at Mike's Pub finally departed into the wee-morning hours following The Pittsburgh Steelers' thrilling victory in Superbowl XLIII, Gene Polachek wobbled from the men's room. "We're drinkin' all damn night!" he announced in boisterous voice. "Mike don't like it, tough shit."

"I'll stay open all night," said Michael Perella. "Just so I lock the door by two-thirty."

"Ah, Butch got stuck workin'," said Gene. "He won't bother us."

Dave Bodette was next to say, "Just so I get home by Tuesday. That was the greatest fuckin' football game of all time." He elbowed Gary Rowland. "How 'bout it, Rol? Sharon won't care if I stay out all night. Karen won't bitch at you too much."

"Fucking 'ey!" said Rol, a charmingly drunken smile on his face. We're way ahead on John's house. Fuck it, we can take tomorrow off."

"Oh, Mr. Innkeeper!" Dave called to Mike. "I'm buying."

"About time," quipped Bob Cook.

"Watch out, the roof might cave in!" said Gene.

"Don't go pickin' on poor Davey," countered Rol. "He bought a round last year."

"Now don't go exaggerating," Mike said. "Dave bought a drink tonight. I saw when the moths flew out of his wallet."

"Damn tightwad, you only gave Dale a five-buck tip." Gene added.

"Ah, why don't younse guys go fuck yourselves," said Dave, causing them to howl in laughter.

Seated next to Bob, John Valone sipped his beer savoring the relaxed atmosphere of camaraderie he so enjoyed. He found himself appreciating why each of them meant so much to him–how they were all woven together into the fabric of his life.

While the others persisted in heckling Dave, Bob leaned near to John and said, "What's up with you? You were the quietest person in here tonight."

"Anything new on Mary's case?"

"John, it couldn't be going any better. I took Cameron's and Nasser's depositions this past Thursday. All they did was lie under oath. And you were right about Nasser. He doesn't have an ounce of humility in him. Believe me, I'll be able to use that against him at trial. I'll make the jury hate that sonofabitch."

"Sounds good, Bob," said John–yet the anxiety his body-language portrayed remained intact.

"C'mon, what else is bothering you?" asked the astute attorney.

"What makes you say that?"

"Why didn't Vicky come out with you?"

"She didn't want to. She told me to have a good time watching the Steelers."

"Maybe she's learned you need some space of your own."

"Maybe." A heavy sigh followed. "Just been alotta little things about her lately."

"Like what?" Bob said.

"I'm not sure."

From behind the bar as he re-stocked the coolers, Mike said, "Hey, guys, there's reuben sandwiches and gyros leftover in back. Help yourselves."

As their friends dashed into the kitchen, Bob said, "Okay, what's with Vicky?"

"Bob—I'm not sure."

Cook leaned closer to him. "C'mon, you can tell me."

"I don't know, Bob," he said. "When I stayed home with Mary last summer, Vicky didn't like it. Then I took Mary to Baltimore, and she got mad again."

"So she missed getting laid."

"Yeah, maybe that was part of it. The truth is Vicky's afraid she's going to end-up getting stuck taking care of Mary."

"John, granted your mom still has some health concerns," said Bob. "But Vicky's seen for herself that Mary's been feeling a lot better since her rhizotomy. Right?"

"Yeah, she has."

"And you explained to her that Mary's probably going to need a couple more rhizotomys in the future. Right?"

"Yeah."

"She agreed to have the house built. Right?"

"Yeah."

"And from what I saw, there weren't any problems between you and Vicky over the holidays."

"No, the holidays went great this year."

"So what's the problem?"

"Lately she's just been—distant."

"Like how?"

John looked to his cell phone atop the bar. "We used to call each other six, eight times a day and I'd talk for as long as she wanted," he said. "Then she just quit calling. Sometimes she answers my text messages. Sometimes she doesn't. When I call her, I usually get her voicemail. And if she does answer, she always tells me she's too busy to talk."

"You told me that Vicky said she's been busy at the real estate office. Maybe you've just been catching her at the wrong times?"

"Yeah—maybe."

"You gotta hunch Vicky's just trying to use you for money like the girl you were bangin' out east did? John, I never told you this before, but I was so glad when you dumped that tramp. You really dodged a bullet there."

"No, it's not about money, Bob," he said. "Vicky never mentions anything about money to me. She even wants to stay at the real estate office until we have kids."

"Mind my asking how things are going in the bedroom?"

"When she wants sex, I go to her place. Not that much anymore, though."

Bob Cook draped his forearm over John's shoulders and said, "Pal, take it from an old friend, women can be funny at times. All truly good women offer us love, fidelity, genuine companionship, loyalty, and the willingness to openly confide in them. Yet they all have their quirks to some extent, just as we do. Who knows, maybe Vicky's nervous that she'll have to adapt to a different lifestyle once she's married. Hell, it could be anything. Just always keep in mind that Vicky needs her space, too. Believe me, when you two get married, you'll find all this out for yourself."

"I hope you're right, Bob."

"Hey, she agreed to go to Wheeling this coming Friday, didn't she?"

"Yeah, she really sounded excited when I asked her."

"See, there's nothing to worry about." Bob grinned. "I can't wait to see her at Wheeling in one of those slinky outfits she wears. When Diane isn't watching, I'm going to undress her with my eyes."

Finally a smile. "That's okay with me, Bob," he said. "I've been doin' the same thing to Diane ever since we were in junior high."

Rol, Dave, and Gene emerged from the kitchen. Gene said, "Hey, Mike, what are they gabbin' about?"

"All I heard was somethin' about the Wheeling trip," said Mike.

"What about it, John?" said Gene. "You and Vicky still goin'?"

"We're all going," he said cheerfully. "I already reserved a table in the clubhouse for us. All you gotta do is pick us some winners."

"Ah, I can pick them hounds," Gene said.

John smiled at Gene, and said, "Mike, I remember your brother used to go to Wheeling with The Italian Club crew. I think I'll give him a call and invite him to come with us."

"He won't go," said Mike–without a second thought.

"Why not?"

Mike slid the cooler door shut and said. "Ask him. Not me."

"Did he do something to piss you off again?"

"No, actually Denny's been pretty nice to me lately. Everything seemed okay with him, although anymore it's like he doesn't give a damn."

"Any idea why?"

"My guess is that he's sick."

"With what?"

"John, you know how Denny is," said Mike. "Lately he's been stopping in here a couple afternoons a week. All he does is get stinko drunk and he keeps pressing at his stomach. I tried asking him, but he keeps saying nothing's wrong. So last week I called his son. Denny Junior told me he didn't know anything about it."

"Me and Dave saw him in here last week," said Gary Rowland. "Damn, was he in a nasty-ass mood."

"Denny practically drank a fifth of Jack Daniel's that afternoon," added Dave.

"How about Elaine?" said Bob. "Maybe Denny told her something."

"All he tells our mother is that it's due to the kidney he lost in Vietnam," Mike said. "But there's something else wrong with him. He's been losing alotta weight."

"I'll call him," John said. "Maybe he'll tell me what's going on."

"You can try," said Michael Perella. "But take my advice. Don't get him riled-up. Yeah, he always was bull-headed, but I've never seen him acting like this before."

*****

Gene Polachek's best bet of the night held to form as they rooted another greyhound across the finish line. Everyone was enjoying their night at the races; the atmosphere at the racetrack was exciting; the food excellent. Yet as Dennis Perella persevered in his attempt to cast the impression he was part of their revelry, they all had observed his morose look clouding his face–along with the excessive amount of liquor he'd been consuming.

After Denny had cashed his ticket, there was John blocking his path. "Den, let's take a quick walk around the joint."

"I need another drink."

Soon they stood at the clubhouse bar. "Hey, big tits, get over here," Denny growled. "Gimme three triple JD's on the rocks and a Miller Lite."

Infuriated by Denny's unruliness, a young man boldly swiveled-about. "Mister, you'd better watch your mouth when you're talking to my girlfriend, or I'll wipe the floor with you."

In the blink of an eye, the man defending honor was savagely bludgeoned from his chair, befallen by a vicious punch to his forehead.

"Who's wipin' the floor now, punk!" shouted Denny, as the youngster reeled to lift himself up.

"Don't come at me, punk!" Denny roared, demons spewing from his dark eyes. "Try it, you'll be in the fuckin' morgue."

Minutes later, they settled on seats in the top row of the grandstand.

"Well, Den, we sure didn't make any new pals in there," said John.

"These punk kids today are all the same," he muttered-already on his third drink. "They get a tattoo and an earring, and they think they can scare some sissy. Buncha fuckin' cunts. Ain't none of them got the balls for a good fight."

"You got that right, Den," said John, smiling in agreement. "Dennis, if it's okay, I'd like to discuss something with you."

"Yeah, yeah, I figured as much. Those detectives still pestering you?"

"No, that's not—"

"Any more interrogations?"

"No."

"Noticed any strangers parked around your neighborhood?"

"No."

"Then stop worrying about it, they ain't got nothin' on you," said Denny. "That half-wit Dague had to have his people investigate every angle on you because you hadda be one of their leading suspects. They couldn't make a case against you, so forget it. If it's your conscience, just try to disassociate the event from your mind. That's what the army shrinks in Nam would preach to us when we took heavy casualties."

"Denny, what I did doesn't bother me at all," said John. "I'd like to talk about you. I've heard you aren't feeling that well."

"Did Mike put you up to this?!" Denny snapped at him.

"Den, don't get mad at Mike," he said. "All Mike did was mention that you might be sick. Don't blame Mike. I wanted to ask you myself."

"Drop it, John."

"Denny, if you do have some kind of health problem and you're not sure what to do, we'll talk to my mother about it. She was a medical secretary. Maybe she can suggest a doctor for you to see."

"Yeah, doctors sure did her alotta fuckin' good," he snarled, then finished his drink. Immediately a frown indicated his regret. "Sorry, kid, that was over the line."

Dennis heaved a deep-felt sigh. "Ah, what the fuck, we ain't got any secrets between us. John, I'm beyond any kind of help. I got liver cancer."

"Oh, God," John faintly said, bowing his head.

"Yep, I'm done for. I've been to a couple oncologists. I won't make it through the year."

"Can't they operate?"

"Nah, the guy I was going to said I'd die on the operating table."

"What about chemotherapy or radiation?"

Denny shook his head. "My cancer is too widespread to even try radiation. All chemo would do is maybe give me another couple months. Fuck it, I don't want that toxic shit in me that'll make me puke my guts out while only delaying the inevitable. John, it ain't worth it to me. No, my friend, I'd rather die a man than like some coward clinging to life. I learned in Vietnam that a coward dies every day. Not me, pal, I'm only dyin' once. And besides, I shoulda been killed when the gook's ambushed my platoon. Tell you somethin' only my best friends know about me. When they told me all my buddies were dead, my attitude became that every day I lived from then was gravy since I shoulda died with them."

"What about your son?" John said, wiping tears from his cheeks.

"Hell, my kid's got it made. He's on full academic scholarship at Penn State including room-and-board, renewable every year just so his grades are good. As smart as he is, that won't be a problem. He'll have my property. I've got the money you gave me stashed-away for him, and I've got plenty of life insurance. He'll be okay."

"I haven't seen your son for years now so he might not remember me. Let him know that he can count on me if I can ever help him."

"That's kind of you, John. Thanks. Maybe if you run into him when he's home from college, you can slip him a couple bucks. But that's all. He has to learn how to make it on his own."

Dennis Perella patted his disheartened friend's knee and said, "John, listen to me. You're the only person I've told about my cancer. I expect you to keep it quiet."

"But—"

"No buts!" Denny charged. "Don't tell no one a fuckin' thing. I don't want my son or Mike makin' a big fuss, and I sure don't want my mother having a heart attack when she finds out. The less time she has to grieve, the easier it'll be on her. If anyone asks, tell them I gotta stomach ulcer and the doctor says I'll be okay. You can do it, no sweat. You fooled the cops, so you sure as hell can fool that bunch at the table."

Denny took hold of John's knee. "Promise me, John."

"Denny, you got my word," John said, his voice cracking, yet his profound facial expression confirming his allegiance. "You've kept my darkest secret. I promise I'll keep yours."

CHAPTER TWENTY SEVEN

Located in an ivory tower known as Kincade Plaza high above the Pittsburgh skyline, a defense briefing was scheduled in the offices of Tibeau & Associates. Doctors' Nasser and Cameron sat along one side of the lengthy boardroom table taking in the picturesque view. Across from them were three younger men reviewing piles of legal documents, as well as their own case notations as they awaited Walter Tibeau. The air was suffused with a pre-battle tension.

Shortly thereafter, Tibeau made his entrance. "Gentlemen," he said in greeting, all eyes trained upon him as he moved to the head of the table. Tailored immaculately in a dark blue suit, the fifty-eight year old man with graying hair of common frame and appearance surveyed his clients brooding faces. "Doctors, please be at ease. All they have is an accumulation of allegations. Not an accumulation of proof."

An appreciative chuckle carried around the table.

Having softened their atmosphere, Tibeau said, "In case you haven't already been introduced, these young men are, from left to right, Mr. Beaumont, Mr. Jordan and Mr. Lee. They're all talented attorneys whom will provide logistical support and backup during the entire tenure of the trial. Depending upon how smoothly the trial progresses, I may call upon them to question some of the nuisance witnesses."

Following their demure acknowledgments, Dr. Cameron took the lead. "Walt, how would you assess her lawyer?"

"Robert Cook, while a bit inexperienced, is an extremely intelligent and capable attorney. He was very thorough when we conducted the depositions. And although at this stage in his career he isn't entirely adroit in the courtroom, my opinion is he will make up for it with his tenacity."

"He's an idiot," a twitchy James Beaumont dared contradict, causing the two physicians to laugh.

"James, let's not forget that idiot was employed here," said Tibeau in calm fashion–though in discourse that stilled all. "An idiot whom I thought very highly of. Doctors, regardless of Mr. Beaumont's less than favorable opinion of opposing counsel or whatever you may personally think of Mr. Cook, do not ever underestimate him. Please remember that."

"Did Cook quit or was he fired?" persisted Dr. Nasser.

"Let's just say we had a falling-out," replied Tibeau, always the diplomat. "Alright, first order of business. As you know, Dr. Elliot was here last week. It is a certainty they will not pursue him with the same veracity as they will either of you. Mr. Cook may ask him questions that will necessitate Dr. Elliot affirm he wasn't involved in any aspect of Mrs. Valone's post-operative care. Nothing else. In all practically, Dr. Elliot stands a moot defendant."

"Just so his testimony doesn't hurt Dr. Cameron or I," said Dr. Nasser.

"He won't, Rasheem," said Dr. Cameron.

"Absolutely not," Tibeau said to confirm. "Other lines of questioning towards Dr. Elliot would only be ruled as hearsay. Doctors, understand that Mr. Cook's tactic of only placing your heads under the guillotine is superb. He realizes Dr. Elliot is totally irrelevant. Nor did he name Shadydell Heights Hospital in the litigation. Hence the jury will not perceive him as trying to indiscriminately impute guilt upon anyone he can. Robert Cook wants their attentions focused solely upon you, which is the exact stratagem I would utilize if I were him."

A timid knock on the door was followed by a woman poking her head into the room. "Mr. Tibeau, I'm sorry to disturb your meeting, but Mr. Harrison's on the phone."

"Thank you, Mrs. Reeves," said Tibeau–keeping his view upon his clients. "Tell him I'll be few moments. Doctors, as I'm sure you're aware, Barton Harrison is the CEO of Penn-Med Insurance. We've discussed your case quite extensively. When we last spoke, Mr. Harrison was of the belief that we should extend an offer to Mrs. Valone. Mr. Harrison is calling to inform me as to what determinations his people may have reached concerning a settlement amount. When he asks if either of you would be amiable to a settlement, how should I respond?"

"Tell him no," said Nasser. "I pay Penn-Med a hundred-sixty thousand a year as it is now. Even if I were to settle for chicken-feed, my insurance would still increase substantially."

"I agree," followed Cameron. "I already have two strikes against me. Another could put me into the high-risk bracket. I can't afford that."

"Doctors, I can appreciate your reservations," Tibeau said. "However, realize that we are dealing with a potential eight-figure jury award if we were to lose. In addition, by extending even a token sum, the judge would not perceive us as being totally disdainful towards Mrs. Valone."

"There's no way in hell I'll ever sign the release authorizing any settlement!" shouted Dr. Nassar. "No, Sir, not a red cent!"

"Walt, tell Harrison he's incorrect if he believes we're in trouble," said the self-confident Dr. Steven Cameron. "Neither Rasheem nor I did anything erroneous in our care of that woman. Assure him our case is defensible, with no risk his precious insurance company will have to pay any amount."

"Very well, I'll relay your sentiments to him," said Tibeau. "Doctors, why don't we take an hour. We'll put everything into perspective this afternoon."

*****

Walter Tibeau sat alone in the conference room, his serenity being tested due to his clients extended absence. Despite the image he exuded as a docile man blessed with ultimate composure, behind that placid facade was a technocrat in every sense. A steel-edged man who approached the law as a precision machine. He would not tolerate apathy when it came to legalities–especially from his own clients. Yet as anyone of proper character, he erased any aspect of indignation as the two physicians hastened into the room. "Welcome back," he bid.

"Sorry, Walt," said Cameron. "We had to wait for a table a LeCirc's. Three hundred damn dollars for lunch."

"Shut up, I paid," was Nassar's rebuke, his word's slightly slurred. "Hey, where are the associates? If I'd known they were going to be late, I could have had another martini."

"Their attendance is necessary," Tibeau dryly said. "What I'd like to do now is comprehensively review this case without any apprehensions about anything we discuss. Understood? Neither of you should hold back one single detail, regardless of how trivial it might seem. We've reviewed many of the key dynamics at our previous meetings which have given me consummate knowledge of every aspect of this case. However I'd like to assess the predominant issues again. I'm paid to win this case, and I want you gentlemen thoroughly prepared."

"That's why we're here, Walt," said Nasser. "Steve keeps telling me that you're the best damn defense attorney in town."

"Without rival," added Cameron.

"Thank you both. Now I'd like to get started."

"Before we do, what did Harrison have to say?" asked Dr. Nasser.

"I told him that Dr. Cameron and yourself strongly desire to bring this case to a verdict," said Tibeau. "Quite honestly, Mr. Harrison's a bit apprehensive about our taking such a hard-line stance. However since we're permitted to extend an offer whenever we choose, Mr. Harrison decided to go along for the time being."

Tibeau paused, then said, "Doctors, as your attorney, I'm obligated to inform you that I made a verbal agreement with Mr. Harrison to keep him apprised as to how the trial is progressing. Keep that in mind. Also remember the longer we hesitate, it will likely cost Penn-Med more when we do tender an offer to Mrs. Valone."

"Mr. Tibeau," said Nasser, "Dr. Cameron and I stand firm in our decision. We're going all the way with the case since neither of us are liable for her infection. We have the utmost faith that you'll be able to prove our complete innocence."

"Truthfully, I'm never pleased with a settlement," said Tibeau. "Yet two key factors must be weighed. One, there is a tremendous downside due to the overwhelming expenses Mrs. Valone's healthcare has brought about. Dr. Cameron, allow me to explain the numbers to Dr. Nasser since this is his first malpractice case in Pennsylvania."

"By all means do so," he said.

"Dr. Nasser, in Pennsylvania, when a jury finds for the plaintiff, they are compelled by law to award an amount equal to seven times the total of all medical expenses incurred as compensatory damages. Right there, that's a million and change. Add to those any additional costs Mr. Cook will argue she deserves due to any future surgeries at Johns Hopkins, and the total compensatory damages could approach somewhere in the vicinity of one and a half million. Then we have punitive damages. And in this case, Dr. Nasser, the sky's the limit. Mrs. Valone was in perfect health until the infection she contracted—"

"I shouldn't be held culpable for her infection!" Nasser exclaimed. "Infection is always a possibility in any surgical procedure."

"Yes, Doctor, I understand your position. Yet I'm saying that's it not unusual for juries to award up to twenty million dollars in punitive damages in malpractice cases. Even if the jury were to award Mrs. Valone only five million in punitive damages, that would still push the total award near the seven million dollar range. In my estimation, that's the minimum amount she would receive if we were to lose. Key factor number two. Mr. Harrison sent this case to four independent organizations who analyze malpractice lawsuits. After they evaluate the evidence, along with enacting the case in a mock-trail, they calculate the statistical probability of total acquittal. Doctor, in four separate scenarios, the highest percentage of probable victory was a mere sixteen percent. Now of course there isn't any way they can account for the many intangibles that will come into play in this or any other case. Although to be perfectly candid, Mr. Harrison doesn't like our chances."

"Mr. Tibeau, you really surprise me," Dr. Nasser said, in snobbish tone that unmistakably signified his disfavor. "Steve has done nothing but boast about your expertise to me ever since Mrs. Valone filed suit, yet it sounds as if you're trying to coax us into surrendering. Damn you, I won't do it! You and Harrison can both kiss my ass!"

"Dr. Nasser, please," said Tibeau, unruffled by his tirade. "I gave you Mr. Harrison's viewpoint, not mine. As far as I'm concerned, statistical probabilities are irrelevant in malpractice cases. While I believe yourself and Dr. Cameron have a good chance of winning this case, I must say this litigation isn't going to be easy. It will take substantial effort upon everyone's part."

"That's more like it," said the abrasive Dr. Nasser.

"Alright, continuing on," said Tibeau. "I've spoken with many of your colleagues whom are willing to take the stand in your defense. I'll use all I'm permitted, but for now we're going to concentrate on the short-list of our primary witnesses."

"Huh? The short-list of our primary witnesses?" said Nasser.

"Doctor, Mr. Cook has filed a motion that will in all likelihood limit our medical testimony as the judge deems necessary to contest Mrs. Valone's expert opinions. His brief to Judge Watson argues it would bestow an unfair impression upon the jury if we were permitted to call numerous experts to contradict his one expert for each of you. In addition, his motion states that a barrage of expert testimony would only lead to redundancies that would slow down the trail. I'm very familiar with Judge Watson's record. He customarily sides with the plaintiff in secular evidentiary matters such as these."

"That's absurd," said Nasser. "Never have I heard of anything as ridiculous. We should be allowed to call all the witnesses we want."

"Walt, at my last trail we were able to present four experts in my defense," said Cameron. "Why are we limited now?"

"First of all, Judge Watson didn't preside over your previous trial. Secondly, while you did have four physicians testify in various expert capacities during the Owens' trial, it was Judge Fontana's ruling that the case presented considerably more complex issues surrounding the woman's treatment and subsequent death, therefore requiring an expert to refute the opposition's diversified claims of malpractice. However, after Judge Watson scrutinized the discovery materials Mr. Cook and I submitted, it has become his contention there are only a few major fundamental medical issues that will be germane in this trial. Judge

Watson is of the opinion there will be a very narrow scope of scientific testimony required, since the crux of Mrs. Valone's case revolves around her post-surgical care up until her infection was discovered. Please don't get me wrong, having solid medical testimony is a vital component to our defense. Although in essence, your fates are contingent upon whom the jury believes, yourselves or Mrs. Valone. Understand, Dr. Cameron?"

Dr. Cameron looked to the ceiling and huffed. "Yes, Walt."

Tibeau opened a binder neatly partitioned by tabs and said, "Dr. Cameron, we must prove that while you do possess the necessary credentials to interpret the various types of medical imagery offered today, nevertheless you sent the February 18th MRI taken at your office to a board-certified radiologist at Shadydell Heights Hospital. We must also convince the jury that you did not overlook the possibility Mrs. Valone could have developed an infection, and you did everything within reason to persuade her into having a sed-rate conducted. Mrs. Valone claims you were negligent in these areas."

"All three times she came to my office following her operation, I believed she could have contracted a surgical infection and I told her so," argued Dr. Cameron. "Nevertheless, she refused the sed-rate. All she wanted was pain medication. As for her MRI's, Dr. Schmidt explained the circumstances."

"Yes, I've spoken with Dr. Schmidt at length," said Walt Tibeau. "His explanation will help negate their expert. With your testimony as to Mrs. Valone's unwillingness to have the sed-rate conducted, it should create some reasonable doubt amongst the jury."

While flipping through his case binder, Walter Tibeau peered above his reading glasses at his other client. "Dr. Nasser, your innocence hinges primarily upon your impressing the jury that you also encouraged Mrs. Valone to have the sedimentation-test since you did recognize her symptomology as probable infection. In addition, you must be perceived as having been altogether sympathetic to her plight. Mrs. Valone was quite emphatic during her deposition that you were totally opposed to the sed-rate, along with being, shall I say, offensive towards her at her visit to your office on February 26th, as well as when she was re-admitted to Shadydell Hospital. Mrs. Valone contends that you continually shunned her cries for help until her son resorted to bodily-force to coerce you into ordering the sed-rate. Since it's also your position that she wouldn't allow the blood test, I'm hoping to call three neurosurgeons, Dr. Jennson for sure, to offer their opinions that her noncompliance in this regard completely thwarted your efforts to conclusively diagnose her ailment. While the expert testimony will help, it remains absolutely indispensable that you convince the jury it was indeed your sincere intention to help this woman and did not disregard the possibility of infection."

"Mr. Tibeau, I pleaded with Mrs. Valone to go to the Shadydell lab for the sed-rate when she was in my office," he said. "As it was whenever she visited Dr. Cameron, all she wanted from me was more Percocet. I was placed in an impossible position due to her refusals. I was always courteous and empathic towards her. As for Mrs. Valone's son saying he had to force me to conduct the sed-rate, he's lying. I insisted she have it taken the first moment I saw her when she was re-admitted to Shadydell."

"Dr. Nasser, if you are able to persuade the jury that you made every sincere effort to help Mrs. Valone, along with all of the other witnesses whom I hope to call to attest to your steadfast character, I believe both yourself and Dr. Cameron will be vindicated of these malicious charges."

"Didn't I tell you Walt's the best?" Dr. Cameron said to Nasser.

"Please do not take anything for granted," cautioned Tibeau. "Alright, what I'd like to do now is update the status of Mrs. Valone's medical witnesses. First off, Mr. Cook has Dr. Yoder listed, albeit on a provisory basis."

"Strange, last I heard she turned down Mr. Cook," said Cameron in stoic tone.

"Dr. Yoder could be a troublesome witness."

"Walt, trust me," said Cameron. "Don't worry about Yoder. She won't testify."

Turning a deaf ear to bypass the reasoning behind Dr. Cameron's assurance, Tibeau went on to say, "Very well, how about Dr. Mancini? Other than his affidavit, is there anything else he could possibly attest to that I'm not aware of?"

"He doesn't know anything about the intricacies of neuro-medicine," said Cameron. "Mancini will only be a sympathy witness." *"I can't tell Walt that Mancini should have discovered Mary's infection," he thought. "Then he'll know I'm lying."*

"Next is Dr. Charles Tyler. We have his testimony on videotape. Did you gentlemen view the copies I had dubbed for you?"

"Yeah, I watched it," Nasser said with a grin. "Typical nigger."

"Doctor, I warn you not to take this man lightly," replied Tibeau, his tone of voice admonishing. "Dr. Tyler has extraordinary credentials. He's a foremost authority in his field at Johns Hopkins Medical Center. Quite frankly, I'm deeply concerned about him."

"Why?" said Cameron. "Tyler's testimony relates to his being a treating physician. He's not testifying as an expert."

"Did you watch the entire video?"

"No, I fell asleep during the last part."

Tibeau sighed. "Then you missed the most important part. At the end of his testimony, while Mr. Cook never formally asked him to accuse malpractice, Dr. Tyler volunteered his opinion that clearly insinuates negligence on both your parts. That's enough to overcome. Although what really disturbs me is the fact that Dr. Tyler's a highly-skilled, highly-polished African-American professional with a captivating ambiance about him. His presence alone will force me to expunge as many African-American's as I can from becoming jurors."

"Good!" crowed Dr. Nasser. "I hate those goddamned niggers."

Walt Tibeau's countenance portrayed his annoyance. "Dr. Nasser, do not ever let me hear you use that racial epithet again."

While scowling at Nasser, Tibeau went on to say, "The voir dire process starts with a pool of, on average, thirty prospective jurors. Usually ten will be disqualified as a result of a preemptory challenge. For example, a few might know yourselves, Dr. Elliot, Mrs. Valone, or anyone else involved in the litigation. Some of them will admit on their questionnaires they or a relative were involved in some type of dispute with a doctor or other medical province. Perhaps others will list fictitious reasons why they should not be placed on the jury, and so forth. Now we're down to approximately twenty people. If form holds true, Mr. Cook and I will be allowed to disqualify only four others using our challenges for cause. The remaining twelve will be your jury."

"We'll be okay," said Dr. Cameron. "You'll have enough chances to eliminate the blacks."

"Maybe so, but there are other classes of people that would best be removed as well," Tibeau said. "Our ideal juror profile is a male, preferably between the ages of twenty-one to forty, without formal education and a menial job. That general categorization happens to coincide with a relatively high percentage of African-American's registered in the county. However, due to Dr. Tyler, I haven't any choice but to eliminate as many of them as I can. The men will look upon him with hero-worship, and the women will admire his charisma and good-looks. Their votes will be set in concrete against us."

"Yeah, those people really do stick together," was another of Dr. Nasser's churlish comments. "Mr. Tibeau, explain the criteria you're planning to use for jury selection."

"Putting race and sex aside, my primary objective will be to rule-out any college graduates. We don't want individuals whom may better be able to comprehend the scientific facts. The grouping of potential jurors I want are those stuck in dead-end jobs earning minimum wage. They just aren't of the mindset to award money, especially large amounts of it, to anyone. Common sense, gentlemen. At the end of the trial, when the judge notifies them of the scale used to determine compensatory damages, that huge monetary figure alone will make them envious. And when the judge informs the jury there aren't any boundaries placed upon punitive awards, jealously can take over, especially if they haven't yet decided one way or the other. As for my preference to male jurors, men are usually inclined to be less sympathetic than women when it comes to civil venues. Men of any age group also tend to be more skeptical than women. If a man has a shadow of a doubt about any detail, chances are he'll vote for acquittal. Conversely, women listen to a plaintiff's sob story, true or false, and their minds are instantly made up in their favor. Since the plaintiff is a middle-aged woman, this factor especially comes into play."

Dr. Nasser flashed a haughty grin and said, "Sounds simple to me. No older black women school teachers."

"I suppose you could put it that way," said Tibeau. "Doctors, assuming we are encumbered with some jurors whom I've classified as negative, we still hold the advantage since it takes nine members of the jury to arrive at a verdict. The number one intangible in our favor is that any juror simply doesn't cherish the thought of finding against a physician. The average person has it embedded deep into their subconscious that doctors are incapable of mishap. Legal annals are replete with malpractice trials that show this factor to be a doctor's most overriding advantage. Ergo, unless the evidence is entirely overwhelming, I've always adhered to the premise that the opposition cannot win their case. We must lose it for them."

"Don't worry about us, Walt," said Dr. Cameron. "We won't let you down. This type of nonsensical lawsuit must be discouraged or else patients will be suing doctors for hemorrhoids."

"Positively," said Dr. Nasser.

Tibeau nodded slightly before saying, "Very well, next I'd like to briefly touch upon their experts. Steve, Dr. Terrence Bates is a board-certified radiologist whose report states that Mrs. Valone's infection should have been discovered when you took her first MRI at your office on February 18th. Dr. Schmidt's testimony should help neutralize Dr. Bates, but how are you planning to respond to Mr. Cook's accusations during cross-examination?"

"I'm simply going to stress the fact that Dr. Schmidt was away at the time, as well as the circumstances that occurred to Dr. Frazier. Obviously her rejection to the sed-rate was the sole reason why I did not conclusively discern infection within a reasonable amount of time."

"And on the March 3rd MRI?"

"Mary's infection presented itself more definitively. Both Dr. Schmidt and I were able to ascertain the infectious process."

"Dr. Schmidt reviews nearly all of your offices' films?"

"Yes, Sir."

"And why didn't you ever insist Mrs. Valone have her sed-rate taken?"

"Sir, I did my very best to convince Mary to have her sed-rate taken on all of her office visits. For some reason beyond me, she refused. All Mary wanted from me was more Percocet."

"And why did you give them to her?"

"It was my duty as her treating physician to help alleviate her pain."

"Very good, Steve," said Tibeau. "You excel at keeping your explanations in basic context. You've testified like a pro at previous trials, hence I haven't anything but supreme confidence in your abilities on the witness stand."

Cameron lounged in his seat, his ego bolstered by the attorneys' praises.

As Tibeau thumbed-through his notations, he said to Nasser, "Doctor, one of my staff must have the dossier of your past malpractice case. I recall you were sued in Michigan. Summarize the case for me."

"It wasn't anything consequential," he said in unapologetic tone. "The case revolved around the patients' failure to recover from back surgery. As a result of further complications, she eventually died. Despite my not being at fault, the neurologist and I decided to settle."

"Did the patient die from infection?"

"No, Mrs. Valone's the first infection I've ever had."

"You're absolutely positive of that fact?"

"Yes, I am."

"That's a huge plus," said Tibeau. "Mr. Cook won't be able to accuse you of having the propensity to infect your patients. Very well, with acceptable medical testimony that you weren't given sufficient opportunity to uncover Mrs. Valone's infection, it should refute Dr. Worthington's assertions of neglect. Now I'd like to review in general what you're going to say under direct examination. Please start at point when you operated on Mrs. Valone."

"She wasn't at serious risk. Mrs. Valone had—"

"Mrs. Valone is certainly proper," Tibeau stopped him. "Although I suggest you also refer to her as Mary. It will sound more compassionate to the jury."

"Mary had a partially-herniated lumbar disc, resulting in a fragment of disc-material becoming entrapped in proximity to her sciatic nerve. Therefore it necessitated extreme precaution while exploring the L4-L5 lumbro-sacral region. I was able to extract—"

"Excuse me, Doctor. You should keep the technical aspects of her surgery a bit more elementary, yet not deliberately attempting to insult the jury's intelligence. I realize it can be a tedious balance, but I'm certain you will be able to. You must always remain down-to-earth on the witness stand, without appearing or sounding condescending."

Nasser shifted uncomfortably in his chair. "Mrs. Valone had a partially-ruptured disc-body of her lower spine. I located and removed the disc fragment. I did not detect any other injury to the surrounding tissues. I then fused a small section of bone to lend stability to her spine. Mrs. Valone—Mary came through the surgery quite well."

"That was excellent, Dr. Nasser," said Tibeau. "Simple and straightforward while instilling in the jury that you're an accomplished neurosurgeon. Also, your voice wasn't of a patronizing nature. Please remember the proper voice enunciation is always one of awed familiarity towards your craft. Very well, subsequent to her surgery, Mrs. Valone went to your office. What type of solutions did you put forth to her being in pain?"

"I told Mary I thought it might be possible—"

"Not you thought it might be possible, Doctor!" Walt Tibeau interrupted, now in reprimanding mode. "A vague statement such as that will leave you extremely vulnerable on cross-examination. Mr. Cook will have the jury believing you were either guessing or incompetent. Answer all questions concerning Mrs. Valone with absolute conviction. Never sound evasive. Leave no margin for subjective analysis on the jury's part. Now please try again."

"Mary came to my office with back pain and spasms. I told her that based upon her symptoms, it was my belief that she had contracted an infection. I implored of her to have an innocuous—basic blood test to confirm my diagnosis. However she declined. As Mary did with Dr. Cameron, she demanded I give her more Percocet."

"Much better," said Tibeau. "Always emphasize she rejected the sed-rate. Alright, what happened when her son had Mrs. Valone re-admitted to the hospital?"

"I was in the OR most of the morning. I hadn't been informed that Mary was admitted until Dr. Cameron phoned me. Steve advised—"

"Dr. Cameron."

Nasser's nostrils flared. "Dr. Cameron advised me that Mary had been re-admitted and required my immediate attention."

"And what happened when you attended to Mary?"

"Knowing the pain she was in, I told the nurse to ready an injection of Demerol prior to my going into her room. Then I went into see Mary. It was at that time when she finally consented to the sed-rate. I left the room to inform the lab myself. Then her son assaulted me."

"Dr. Nasser, answer one very elementary question for me," said Tibeau with challenging design. "In both Mary and John Valone's depositions, they vehemently avow that you totally dispelled the possibility of infection. I asked them many times if it were possible they somehow misunderstood your intentions that morning. Yet every time I asked, their responses only grew more fervent that you completely ruled-out the possibility of infection. The Valone's stated that you shunned this contingency by saying, to quote them, 'I don't get infections.' Doctor, why do you suppose they would say something as derogatory like that about you?"

"They're fucking liars. That's why."

Walter Tibeau prefaced his next words with a sober facial expression. "Well, Dr. Nasser, for both of your sakes, you'd better be able to convince the jury that your version of all of the events following her operation is the truth. Because alike the judge, I believe the scientific and expert testimony will not have significant bearing upon the verdict. Hence the main thrust of our case is contingent upon yourself and Dr. Cameron persuading the jurors that you're being totally forthright with them in all respects, especially in that you made every conceivable effort to help Mrs. Valone."

"Now let me tell you something, Mr. Tibeau," Nasser fired in return. "Believe me, I'm elated our judicial system functions as it does. Though it amuses me to no end that a group of uneducated buffoons get to decide complex litigations such as this. Here I am at the pinnacle of my career, having achieved a towering stature in my chosen profession, yet I'm forced to justify my actions to people who can't even spell neurosurgeon."

"Just keep in mind this trial will not pose many of the usual intricacies of most malpractice cases," Tibeau said. "As I've already mentioned, we can't hope to overwhelm the jury with an abundance of scientific testimony."

All too familiar with his client's elitist persona, Walt Tibeau then said, "And by the way, Dr. Nasser, in malpractice litigations I've found that more times than not, even uneducated buffoons can decipher the truth."

With a thud, Tibeau closed his binder. "That's enough for today, I'm running behind schedule. We'll further refine your testimonies as the trial draws near. Allow me to review a few miscellaneous items. Trial is slated to begin on Monday, April 6th. I anticipate the case lasting the entire week, perhaps longer depending upon the judge, so I hope you've cleared your schedules according."

"I've cancelled everything until the middle of May," said Cameron.

"Yes," huffed Nasser. "My schedule is on hold. This trial is going to cost me plenty."

"I realize that, Dr. Nasser," said Tibeau. "I'm sorry, but your reputation is at stake."

Tibeau looked to Dr. Cameron and said, "Steve, the trial will be completed way before mid-May. You can resume seeing patients by the latter part of April at the very latest."

"I know, Walt," said Cameron. "There's a national medical symposium being held in Las Vegas during the first two weeks of May that I'm planning on attending."

Tibeau nodded his approval. "Very well then, some tactics to keep in mind. Select only three conservative business suits, preferably dark blues or grays, to wear throughout the trial. We don't want to impress the jury with your wardrobes. Next, don't ever arrive at the courthouse together. Always walk in separately. Once inside the courtroom, while you may sit near each other, do not sit side-by-side. Jurors tend to become suspicious when they observe defendants whispering to each other. There shall be no talking with Mrs. Valone or anyone else on her side. Never. Unless I'm with you, don't ever discuss the trial outside in the hallways, downstairs in the mezzanine, or during a recess anywhere in the courthouse. You might be overheard by a member of the jury or an acquaintance. Doctors, do not forget it could take only one minor uncomplimentary or flippant remark to destroy this case. Until the court day is over, maintain a humble face, remain calm in the courtroom and around the building, and keep your mouths shut."

There wasn't anything remarkable about his lecture–yet to Walter Tibeau, it irrevocably stamped him as being in command. As with all technocrats, even the obvious must be prepared for. "Dr. Nasser, I have a final observation I'd like to mention," he said. "Please do not take this as my being intrusive, but I can't help notice you have some sort of skin rash."

"I was in Europe a month ago, Walt. It must be a lingering allergic reaction to something I ate. I'll be seeing a dermatologist."

"Fine. Doctor, you're an extremely handsome man, and I want our side to benefit by it with the female jurors. If the rash hasn't healed before trial, please use something to conceal it. I want the ladies on the jury to swoon whenever they see you."

Tibeau checked his wristwatch to say, "Very well, I still have a few minutes remaining. Any questions or suggestions?"

"Walt, I'd like to ask something," Dr. Cameron said. "We're ready for trial and I presume Mr. Cook will say they are as well. Isn't today their final opportunity to request a delay?"

"Correct."

"If Cook doesn't want the trial delayed, would the judge be inclined to allow any last-minute postponements on their part?"

"It would depend upon the circumstances. Normally at this stage, both sides stipulate they're prepared for the scheduled court date and desire to go forward. Judge Watson is very obsessed with keeping to his docket. In addition to his own considerations, not only does the judge realize the income you men are forfeiting because of this, he also understands Mr. Cook must notify his experts with the projected timeframe he expects them prepared to testify. Therefore it would take something out of the ordinary for Judge Watson to declare a postponement."

"Okay, a hypothetical question. Suppose, just suppose that for whatever bizarre reason, either of Mrs. Valone's experts has a problem making it to court once the trial has begun. What would happen then?"

"That's a tough call, Doctor," said Tibeau. "I suppose Judge Watson's only viable option would be to have someone take the stand and read their depositions verbatim, since at that point it would be impossible for Mrs. Valone to hire a new expert without causing an excessive delay. However if Mr. Cook were to protest as I would, that solution might be ruled upon as unfair by an Appellate Court on appeal since the judge's action could be viewed as prejudicial against Mrs. Valone. Ergo, Mr. Cook would certainly petition for a mistrial and Watson would more than likely grant it. Judge Watson has always been overly-liberal to plaintiffs in civil litigations since he absolutely despises when a case he's presided at gets overturned on appeal."

"Another hypothetical," pressed Dr. Cameron. "We have about a month until the trial starts. Suppose one of their experts notified them within the next week or so that they've had a change of opinion, hence refuses to testify. What would the judge do then?"

"My assumption is Judge Watson would insist Mr. Cook at least make an effort to seek a suitable replacement before the trial begins."

"And just suppose he couldn't find a replacement? If you filed a Motion to Dismiss, any chance Watson would be inclined to grant it?"

Tibeau stretched his arms above his head in thought. "Possible," he said. "I can say without reservation that precedent would be in our favor. As to whether or not Judge Watson would follow them remains to be seen. Still, it's possible. Steve, why these questions? Have you some information you haven't told me about?"

"No, Walt," he said. "Rasheem and I were just wondering."

As it was ever since he'd begun analyzing their case, once again Walter Tibeau felt a knot of morality twisting deep within the pit of his stomach. In all his years as a defense attorney, never had any client posed such inquiries. "Well, even if one of their experts did refuse to testify and Mr. Cook were able to replace them in time, our chances could not get any worse. As I've mentioned, while I don't believe the expert testimony shall be extremely paramount in this case, it will still play a key role. And to be perfectly blunt, Bates' and Worthington's reports are devastating evidence. If their testimony is as damning as their reports, and you can rest assured Mr. Cook will make certain that it is, they will present extreme difficulties for us. Doctors, the fact of the matter is that we couldn't do any worse with another expert witness replacing either of them."

CHAPTER TWENTY EIGHT

With Art McNally's many cautions reverberating throughout his mind, Robert Cook walked with confidence into Judge Albert Watson's chambers once he and Walt Tibeau were summoned. Their expected courtesies exchanged beforehand, the crafty Tibeau had made a few genteel references to their upcoming showdown attempting to probe for weaknesses. While keeping within the boundaries of propriety, Cook remained careful to sidestep the wolf in sheep's clothing ploys–vigilant not to yield anything that could give Tibeau the slightest edge.

Judge Watson was reviewing his case outline when the two attorneys entered his chambers. As Walter Tibeau, the judge was nearing the crossroads of his sixtieth year. The sincerity of his mere personage engendered admiration. His distinguished features, graying hair, and the spider webs of time spread across his face marked him as an altruistic image of a man truly blessed with wisdom. His days spent as a prosecutor were only a distant fog of his youth. Serving on the bench had become his rightful vocation.

"Let's proceed, men," said the judge. "First, my decision on Mr. Cook's motion to limit the expert testimony. My objectives as they pertain to this litigation coincide with the arguments stated in the motion, hence I am ruling in Mr. Cook's favor. Robert, you'll ask your two experts for their professional medical opinion as to the negligence of Dr. Cameron and Dr. Nasser. Walt, I'll permit you only one line of expert testimony to contradict each of Mr. Cook's experts."

"Thank you, Your Honor," said Bob.

"Judge Watson, I accept your ruling," followed a gracious Tibeau. "However in Dr. Tyler's testimony, he makes certain inferences that my clients are at fault. Therefore I ask some latitude when I question some of the other physicians whom will testify for the defense."

"Very little, Counselor," said Watson. "I won't permit your stacking the deck against the plaintiff's experts. I'll extend you a narrow path of leeway. However the moment I sense you're beyond reasonable parameters, I'll ask you to move on. Are we understood on the issue?"

"Yes, Your Honor," said Tibeau.

"Next is Dr. Harold Elliot," Watson said. "As for the stipulation you both agreed to concerning Dr. Elliot, do we have any final issues in that regard?"

"No, Your Honor," Tibeau said.

"That's correct, Judge," Bob said. "Mr. Tibeau and I took his deposition. Dr. Elliot swore under oath he doesn't have any direct knowledge—"

Watson raised a hand signaling for Bob to cease. "Say no more, Counselor. I get the picture."

"Your Honor, if I may," said Tibeau. "While I will not seek to illicit direct testimony from Dr. Elliot as it would pertain to Mrs. Valone's case, I do plan on calling him to testify on his own behalf."

"Dr. Elliot's more than entitled to take the stand," replied Judge Watson, still eyeing his notations. "Very well, since we're all in agreement on the issue of expert testimony, let's move on Mrs. Valone's treating physicians. Mr. Cook, you have three treating physicians listed. Do you intend to seek testimony from all three?"

"No, Your Honor. Just Dr. Tyler and Dr. Mancini."

"You're not calling Dr. Lorraine Yoder?"

"No, Your Honor. She doesn't want to get involved."

Acquainted with the circumstances, Albert Watson could only nod in acknowledgment. "Well, I've reviewed the documentation that was subpoenaed from Shadydell Heights Hospital, Dr. Yoder's records amongst them. You'll be entitled to submit them into evidence."

The judge continued viewing his notes. "Mr. Tibeau, I count a total of twenty-six witnesses on your list." Watson lifted his head to say, "They're all doctors."

"Correct, Your Honor."

"No wives or family members? No office staff for character witnesses?"

"Doctors' Elliot and Cameron are divorced, and Dr. Nasser is single," Tibeau informed. "As for any office staff, it was my clients preference."

"No, I'm afraid that won't due," said Watson. "Gentlemen, I expect your case presentations to be streamlined. While I will not place any restrictions on other relevant witnesses, I emphasize the word relevant. I won't allow a parade of witnesses marching to the stand only to extol the virtues of the three defendants. Mr. Cook has his two treating physicians. Therefore, Mr. Tibeau, I will permit you to call two doctors to testify for each of the defendants for starters."

"Your Honor," said Tibeau, retaining his composure. "The defense requires more than six witnesses. Surely you realize that."

"Of course I do," said Watson. "Again, you may call upon as many relevant witnesses as the defense requires. Just keep in mind that I shall not look kindly upon any repetitious medical testimony. Now I'd like to reach an agreement in regards to the character witnesses. Mr. Cook, you have fifteen potential character witnesses listed. Would it be possible to pare your list down to some extent?"

"I can manage with five, Your Honor," Bob quickly replied.

"Well, Mr. Tibeau, how about it?" asked the judge in testing manner. "I'll even permit you to double Mr. Cook's count. If your former protégé here can manage with five character witnesses, I would think the old master can present his defense with a total of ten character witnesses."

Walter Tibeau was boxed into a corner. He knew the judge sought his consent to his proposal. Albert Watson's reputation as pro-plaintiff held him at a strategic disadvantage–a disadvantage he had no yearnings to add to. Finally he said, "Your Honor, I'll agree to your limiting the character witnesses, with the proviso that I may be permitted to question them about more than one particular client."

"Agreed," said Watson.

With Bob hiding his delight, the judge said, "Since this trial will be devoid of many tangential matters commonly involved in malpractice suits, this should not be an intricate case. While the expert testimony is mandated, I believe the underlying factor that will ultimately prove the linchpin is which accounting of the events the jury believes truthful before Mrs. Valone's infection was brought to light. Hence my rationale for asking you both to condense your presentations. I will not have the jury confused by a plethora of nonessential testimony. Both side's witnesses will state their opinions, and our jury will plainly detect the contradictions. Then we'll let them make up their own minds as to whom they believe."

"Fine by me, Judge," said Bob.

"Your Honor, "Tibeau said, an air of caution about him, "I do not wish to sound adversarial, but proving my clients innocence depends upon other variables that will require confirmation of certain medical facts. Naturally a few points of contention may be revisited during my direct. I hope you won't hold this against the defense."

"Come now, Walt. You know I'm not a biased judge. Certainly you may refer to any previously covered topic for foundational purposes. But I warn you, I'll be listening very carefully for any roundabout methods you might use in pursuit of further emphasizing testimony when it isn't called for."

"Your Honor, in theory that sort of approach might be applicable," said Tibeau. "Although as you're well aware, there are many intricacies involved in the extraction of testimony. I will do—"

"Counselor, perhaps it would be best if you'll permit me to clarify the issue as I see it," the judge cut in, venting only a trace of annoyance. "I've never presided over any case involving Dr. Steven Cameron, however Judge Fontana has. He and I go way back. Judge Fontana and I have a habit of talking shop. As you're aware, he presided over Dr. Cameron's previous malpractice trial. Well, Judge Fontana informed me that you used every maneuver in your repertoire to elicit redundant testimony on your client's behalf, despite his many admonitions that you were pushing the envelope. He also mentioned several occasions when he believed Dr. Cameron and his fellow doctors were, shall I dare say, greatly embellishing while on the witness stand."

"Judge Watson, I would never suborn perjury from any client."

"I'm not even suggesting the possibility," replied Watson. Nevertheless, it just so happens that I've overheard similar opinions from other judges whom were on the bench in which Dr. Cameron testified in an expert capacity. To put it mildly, Dr. Steven Cameron's reputation is severely besmirched among many Allegheny County judges. Now here's another interesting tidbit. I won't reveal the source, but I've learned that in the only case Dr. Nasser testified as an expert, a member of the opposition claimed his testimony was laced with countless perjuries."

"Judge Watson, are you insinuating that you'll not be able to maintain total neutrality towards Dr. Cameron and Dr. Nasser?" Tibeau countered in tone bolder than he preferred.

"Not by any means, Walt," said the judge. "You know me better than that. We've both been around the block too many times. I would never allow my judgment to be swayed by any personal sentiments. Although now you can appreciate why I want to truncate as much of the minutia as reasonably possible without prejudicing any of your clients or Mrs. Valone. And regardless of any personal sentiments, it's always been my philosophy that an unpretentious approach towards malpractice cases usually results in the best chance for the correct verdict to be reached. After all, justice is what we're all striving for here. Isn't it, Walt?"

With Tibeau silenced, the judge said, "Gentlemen, I'm obligated to state the following at the end of our meeting. However, since I sense friction, I'll say it now. If either of you have a problem with my presiding over this case, I suggest you file a motion across the street to recuse me from the bench, since tomorrow is the deadline."

Only a short pause before Judge Watson said, "Mr. Tibeau, shall we continue?"

"Of course, Your Honor," he quickly replied.

In the spirit of fairness, Watson looked to Bob. "Mr. Cook?"

"No problems, Judge."

"Next item," said Watson. "Have you gentlemen exchanged all pertinent documentation that you'll be presenting in your case?"

"I have fulfilled my discovery obligations to Mr. Cook," said Tibeau.

"I have as well, Your Honor," Bob said. "However, Mrs. Valone's health has been in decline recently."

"Are you asking for a postponement?" said Watson–taken by surprise.

"No, Your Honor," was Bob's reply. "I only wish to inform the Court and Mr. Tibeau of the fact that Mrs. Valone has been in contact with Dr. Tyler since our previous conference. Unfortunately she's beginning to feel some of the same type of pain she experienced prior to her rhizotomy."

"Will Mrs. Valone be healthy enough for trial?"

"Oh, she'll be here, Your Honor," Bob declared. "Mrs. Valone is scheduled to undergo another rhizotomy in July. Neither Mrs. Valone nor I want to jeopardize this case. My client has suffered too many hardships as it is now due to Dr. Nasser's and Dr. Cameron's neglect."

"Sorry to hear she needs another rhizotomy," said the judge.

"So am I," followed Tibeau. "Mary's such a splendid lady. It's a real tragedy that she developed a post-operative infection."

"The real tragedy is that it took seven weeks for Mary's infection to be diagnosed," said Bob in roused voice.

"Come now, men," said Watson, holding up a hand for quiet. "Save your arguments for court. Next on the agenda. Are there any points that were established at our previous sessions that either of you would like to review or contest?"

After the attorneys had declined his offer, Watson said, "There is a final issue that I'm curious about. Has there been any headway made towards a settlement?"

"Judge, I'll let Mr. Tibeau answer that," Bob said.

"I apologize, Your Honor," said Tibeau. "Settlement negotiations are not eminent at this time."

"What are you and your clients waiting for, Counselor?" said Watson. "I thought I made my feelings perfectly clear at our last conference that a settlement would be a logical avenue to pursue in this case. Perhaps if you submit an amount, all parties can work towards a mutually-satisfactory agreement."

"Judge Watson, at the moment we aren't planning to tender any offer."

His facial expression perplexed, Watson said, "Mr. Tibeau, let me get this straight. Penn-Med could get hit with an eight-figure judgment, yet even a base-offer hasn't been extended to Mrs. Valone? Has Mr. Harrison gone soft in the head?"

"Your Honor, my clients maintain their complete innocence. They believe this case is defensible, and wish for me to resolve it in court."

"Counselor, I suggest you contact Mr. Harrison. At least set a monetary starting point for future negotiations."

"Your Honor, I haven't any desire to sound quarrelsome," said Tibeau. "According to my clients, there shall be no future negotiations. It is their position they haven't committed any wrongdoings against Mrs. Valone, hence do not wish to be held as scapegoats in this matter."

With a shrug of his shoulders, Watson said, "Very well then, Mr. Tibeau. We all know how the game is played. Your camp can wait until we're nearing a verdict until they decide it prudent to extend an offer. Although at that point, will Mr. Cook advise his client to accept an offer? Or will Mrs. Valone be willing to take it? I suggest you have your clients and Bart Harrison consider that."

"Judge Watson, my clients are determined to see this case to a verdict."

"Okay, Walt," he said. "If your clients insist on an all-or-nothing battle, so be it. However I am very well-briefed on this case, ergo I'm forewarning you ahead of time about my policy whenever the defense takes such a hostile position in a matter such as this appears to be. For arguments sake, let's assume you lose. If the verdict does go against your clients, you'll most certainly appeal the award based upon the grounds that it's excessive. And in the majority of cases, I would first confer with the winning side and advise they accept a reduced settlement unless they want to go through the appeals process. As you know, if they decline my advice, then it's solely up to the Appellate Court's discretion whether or not to grant the appeal."

"Your Honor, I'm sorry," Tibeau said. "It isn't within my authority to force either my clients or Penn-Med into seeking reconciliation."

"I realize your position," said Judge Watson. "But I'm putting you on notice right here and now that if you do lose, since your clients are taking the all-or-nothing approach, that is the same attitude I'll have after the trial's concluded. I will not play the role of *King Solomon* for your clients. Then I'll personally speak with a few old friends of mine across the street and suggest they deny your appeal, regardless of how outlandish the award might be. Tell your clients and Bart Harrison that's the way it's going to be if the verdict does indeed come down against them."

His reprimand complete, Judge Albert Watson pushed away from his desk. "Gentlemen, we're done. I expect to see you in my courtroom at 9 A.M. on Monday, April the 6th."

CHAPTER TWENTY NINE

On a warm afternoon for mid-March, John Valone pushed a lawnmower up the banked terrace leading to his driveway. His chest and legs matted with perspiration, he was pleasantly surprised to see Vicky Gill's Kia Sportage descending towards him. The lawnmower off, he moved towards her. "Hi there, cutes," he said. "Long time no see."

"Can we talk?" she asked in soft-pitched voice.

"I would certainly hope so. If I weren't so grimy, I'd give you a big hug and kiss."

Stepping out of her Kia, Vicky noticed an emerald-green Lexus parked in the garage. "Did you get a new car?"

"It's Mary's birthday present," he said. "She always liked Janet's Lexus, so I figured I'd get her one. I'll get you one if you'd like."

"So Mary's home?"

"Nah, her and Janet volunteered to do something at the church."

Observing her blue eyes dart-about at everything but him, John said, "C'mon, Vick, loosen up a little. Let me grab a quick shower and we'll talk. Whatever's been bothering you, we'll work it out."

"John, I can't stay long," she said, her anxiety seemingly increased. "Let's just talk inside for a while."

After he'd wiped his muscular frame, John draped the towel around his neck. Seated across from her at the kitchen table, he was mindful of the grim aspect cast upon her face.

"Have you been out to see our house yet?" he asked.

"No."

"It's almost done. They're doing some stuff to the outside trim. Then all they need is to paint and lay the carpeting. You can pick whatever colors you want."

"John, I don't want to talk about the house."

"What about our wedding? Everyone keeps asking me where their invitation is."

A cryptic facial expression served as her answer.

"Vicky, look I know you're upset with me about something. My God, the last couple months we've barely talked. Every time I've been able to get a hold of you, you'd always say you were too busy. Well, you're not too busy now. Just please tell me what the problem is."

"I spoke with Butch last week."

"Yeah, so did I."

"He told me that Mary's going to have another operation."

"Yeah, in July at Johns Hopkins. Dr. Tyler thinks—"

"I know all about it!" she snapped. "Butch told me that's all you talked about the last time he saw you at the bar."

Overlooking her heated inflection, he said, "Vicky, it's no big deal. As I was trying to say, Dr. Tyler told Mary the first time that she'd probably need a couple more rhizotomys. Look, you already know Mary's trail starts pretty soon. Once that's over with, we'll be getting married. We'll go on a honeymoon anywhere in the world you'd like. After we get home, I'll probably take Mary to Baltimore again. She won't have to stay as long—"

"I didn't drive over here to discuss your mother," she said, her tone now an unsteady blend of temper and sorrow. She removed her diamond ring. "I came here to tell you that it's—over between us."

"Awl, come off it, Vicky. Don't get so dramatic because of—"

"John, I'm pregnant."

"That's fantastic!" he said, leaping from his seat. "But how—"

"Six weeks pregnant," she rushed to say. "The baby isn't yours."

His heart skipped a beat as he sank down, his face turned ashen. "Six weeks, huh?"

"John, I'm sorry, I didn't mean for this to happen."

"Then why did it happen?"

"I've been re-evaluating our relationship for months now. In all honesty, I think it's best we go our separate ways."

"—Why?"

"Every time we'd see each other, all you'd want to talk about was your mother's trial or her bad back. Never about us. Never about our future."

"So you decided to retaliate by letting some guy knock you up?"

"I didn't intend to get pregnant. It was an accident."

"And accident!" he said in raised voice, though vying to maintain his self-control. "Vicky, explain something to me. Every single time we had sex, you'd make me use a condom. Deep down, I wanted to get you pregnant, but I respected your desires to wait until we were married. So do you really expect me to believe you'd spread your legs for the first swinging dick that just happened by? Do I really look that stupid?"

"It doesn't matter anymore," she said, while gathering her belongings.

"Vicky, wait, let's be adults about this. Listen to me, I still love you and I still want to marry you, regardless of the baby. I'll treat the kid like it was my own."

"John, I'm sorry, you don't understand. I've already decided to marry my baby's father."

"Your what! Your gonna marry some sap you had a one-night-stand with? Some guy you've know for what, six, seven weeks now."

"I've known Chris since last year when you were stuck at home with your mother," she said. "I have very strong feelings for Chris."

His eyes glazed-over. "And you've been sleeping with him ever since?"

"No, I wasn't!" she shrieked. "I was tempted to, but I never did because I held out hope for us. I just finally accepted the fact that you're a lost cause."

"That's bullshit, Vicky! You fucked the guy outta sheer vindictiveness, didn't you?!"

"I did not! Chris invited me out one night and one thing led to another, that's all. Chris loves me. He pays attention to me. He's a respectable man who enjoys the same things I do. He and I are getting married and we're moving to Florida."

"So you're just going to throw me away like I never meant anything to you? Like I was yesterday's garbage!"

"John, what it all comes down to is that Chris and I have more in common than we did. He enjoys going to operas and other events with culture. Your idea of culture is a night out watching sports with your friends. That's it, end of story."

Fearful of another outburst, she kept a cautious vantage as she walked sideways towards the garage door.

John followed her into the garage. As he leaned against the Cadillac, he said, "Vicky, tell me the truth. You really don't love this Chris guy. Your infidelity was because you didn't want to deal with my mother's health problems. Right?"

"Believe whatever you want," she said, hurrying to tie her shoelaces. "It doesn't make any difference to me."

"What's the matter, too ashamed to admit it? C'mon, get it off your chest."

"Damn you! You want the truth, here it is. Yes, it is because of Mary. She's a great lady, but I can't cope with her health. Having a sick mother-in-law would place too much stress on me. I won't live my life having to worry about her needs every day."

Despite his inability to shake the sadness from his face, her ultimate betrayal forbade John from exhibiting any further sentiment. "Well then, I guess this is goodbye. Again. Like the French say, 'c'est la vie.' Goodbye, good luck, have a nice life."

"John, I wish you the same," she said softly, dabbing at her teardrops. "I truly do. But you know what. Something tells me you won't."

*****

Three hours later, John opened the front door to find Bob Cook displaying a beleaguered face comparable to his own. "Bob, what's wrong?"

"Everything. Your mom home?"

"Yeah, she's in the living room. Hey, chill out. It can't be that bad."

"Believe me, it is."

With Mary and John on the couch, Bob's eyes lifted from the floor. "I hate saying this, but we've lost both our expert witnesses."

"What!" John boomed.

"That son of a bitch Cameron got to them," said Mary.

"Someone sure got to them," Bob said. "Two priority-mails were delivered to my office this afternoon from Bates and Worthington, both worded almost identically that they've had a change of opinion about Cameron and Nasser's negligence. Therefore they refuse to testify. Whoever coordinated this, their timing was perfect."

"Why was their timing perfect?" asked John.

"Tibeau and I had our final pre-trial conference last week. At the time everything was in place, so the case is officially assigned to the docket. Without expert testimony, the judge will be compelled to dismiss the case."

"Did you tell the judge?" Mary asked of Bob. "Maybe he'd be willing to allow a continuation until we can replace them."

"Yes, I spoke with him. Judge Watson isn't very happy about the situation, but it's too late for him to grant a delay. Judge Watson realizes we have a valid case, and he'd be leaning to our side if we can overcome this. However, due to recent precedents, he pretty much indicated to me that he wouldn't have any other recourse other than to dismiss."

"Can't you at least try?" she urged in desperate voice.

"If I don't have any other alternative, sure I'll try," said Bob. "Let's say the judge did offer us a continuance. Tibeau would immediately file a Motion to Dismiss with the Court of Appeals. Judge Watson told me they'd most likely follow precedent and overturn him. That would be it. The case would be closed."

Mary gazed downwards and said, "Bob, it isn't your fault "Don't blame yourself for this. You've learned for yourself what bastards they really are."

"Screw Worthington and Bates," said John. "What can be done to rectify the situation in time for the trial?"

"John, it's going to be impossible for Bob to find new experts in time," Mary insisted. "Dr. Cameron is too influential around Pittsburgh for any physician to testify against him."

Following a prolonged sigh, John said, "Okay, we get new experts. Bob, any ideas?"

"At this point, there's only one possible solution. We can try using expert witnesses commonly referred by the legal profession as 'hired guns.' Usually they're retired physicians who occupy their time by evaluating medical cases and testifying at malpractice trials."

"I remember a doctor at the hospital mentioning them when he was being sued," Mary said. "Let's give them a try, Bob."

"Mary, they're our only alternative," Cook said. "When I left the office, Art was on the internet searching for possible candidates. He's going to make a list of our best potentials, five radiologists and five neurosurgeons. First thing tomorrow morning, I'll try to contact them. If they sound like their interested and can manage the time constraints, I'll review their curriculum vitae, what hospitals they've worked at while actively practicing medicine, and a summary of cases they've testified in."

"Do it," she said.

Bob Cook pulled his cell phone. "Let me give Art a call."

Only seconds passed before Bob said, "Art, I'm with them now. Hold on, I'm putting you on speaker. Okay, find any yet?"

"We may have lucked-out, Bob," they all heard Art McNally's voice. "I just got off the landline with a retired radiologist from Georgia, a Dr. Claude Lucas. Told me he'd be glad to meet with you to review Mary's medical history."

"Any possible connections to any of them?"

"I don't see how, his curriculum vitae is posted on the website. Dr. Lucas has lived in Atlanta his entire life. Cameron and Elliot went to med school in Pittsburgh, and they've been here ever since. Nasser went to med school in Illinois. He worked in Detroit until he moved to Pittsburgh."

"How'd Lucas sound to you?"

"Sharp as a tack."

"Great. Any other radiologists near Atlanta that you like?"

"Closest is a guy in Macon, Georgia."

"You talk with him?"

"No."

"Alright, how about a neurosurgeon?"

"There are two women I really like. One lives in Myrtle Beach, South Carolina. The other lives near Chapel Hill, North Carolina."

"You speak with either of them?"

"No. Though by their vitas, they've never worked anywhere near Pennsylvania."

"Neither did Bates and Worthington!" shouted Mary in frustrated tone.

"What was that?" said Art.

"Mrs. Valone's angry," Bob said.

"Can't say I—blame her."

Robert Cook remained silent, the gears of his mind spinning until he said, "Okay, Art, here's what I want you to do. Book me on the first flight to Atlanta tomorrow. Make it one-way. You got phone numbers for the radiologist in Macon and both neurosurgeons?"

"No. Only fax numbers."

"Okay, email everything you have to my house. I'll call Dr. Lucas and tell him I'd like to meet him at his earliest convenience. Then I'll fax the radiologist from Macon and the two neurosurgeons that I'm very interested in their services, and I'll be in contact with them soon."

"Sounds good to me. Anything else I can do?"

"No, I'll review everything when I get home. Okay, Art. Thanks."

Bob flipped his cell, then said, "Oh well, we'll just have to wing-it from here."

"Bob, I'm sure you're doing what you think is best," Mary said. "But even if you do find new experts, what's to stop Cameron or Nasser, maybe even Elliot, from getting to them?"

"Mary, I know for a fact from when I was at Tibeau's firm that these doctors could care less who they testify against. Believe me, Cameron's gang won't sabotage us again by influencing any of these physicians once they're on our side."

"I think you should talk to as many experts as possible," said John.

"I can't, John," Bob said. "Time's running out. The trial starts in less than three weeks. I can't be flying all over the country to interview doctors. It takes time for them to review all the documentation. We just have to hope that the experts Art found come through for us. If for whatever reason they don't, I'll still have a chance to contact other experts."

"You're gambling with my mother's lawsuit!" he growled at his lifelong friend.

"John, please calm down," said Mary.

A lengthy silence ensued until he said, "Sorry. Both of you."

"John, I think you have a few misconceptions about these doctors," said Bob. "Let me explain it all to you, then tell me what you think. Okay?"

"Yeah, Bob. Go 'head."

"John, you know every detail pertaining to your mom's case. You know all about the medical documentation, all the films, and all of the normal, expected post-operative care Cameron and Nasser failed to provide. Every last bit of objective evidence favors Mary. All they have going for them is the perjured testimony they and their pals will offer. You've read Bates' and Worthington's reports. Their opinions were absolutely scathing against Cameron and Nasser. I guarantee our new experts conclusions will be the same."

"How can you be so sure?"

"Number one, the facts are irrefutable. Number two, simply because these retired physicians do this all the time. They understand that a plaintiff needs definitive medical evidence to substantiate their allegations of malpractice. They also understand the difficulties plaintiffs incur while trying to secure expert testimony. Once they've evaluated Mary's case, the facts will speak for themselves and they'll be with us all the way."

"What assurances do we have that they'll show-up in court?"

"Because part of their contract is a legally-binding agreement to testify," said Bob. "Paid medical experts realize their reports aren't of any real significant value unless they're prepared to offer testimony in support of their conclusions. That's why their called hired guns. They aren't concerned about any retaliatory measures from anyone since most of them no longer actively practice medicine. That's why they're our only chance."

Running his fingers through his hair, John looked across the brass-and-glass coffee table. "Alright, Bob," he said. "Go for it. We've come too far to quit now. You need any more money?"

"No, I've got more than enough. I'll keep all the receipts—"

"I don't want the receipts, Bob," he said. "I trust you. If you need more money while you're away, give me a call. Just make sure you land us two expert witnesses. I refuse to let my mother's case go down the tubes."

"I intend to do my very best to see that it doesn't."

After Robert Cook had bid Mary farewell, he waved John towards the door. "Don't worry," he said. "I promise I'll find your mom the best expert witnesses I can."

"I know you will, Bob. Thanks."

Cook studied the mournful facial appearance John continued to impart. "You okay?"

"Yes."

"You sure—"

"Skip it, Bob. Just find the fuckin' witnesses."

CHAPTER THIRTY

An American court of law. Actual living theatre–where the cruelest axiom any lawyer must comprehend is having pure and absolute righteousness on their side doesn't guarantee a triumphant outcome. Nor does being painstakingly precise while submitting the facts they know in all certitude are accurate. It takes the mental acuity to remain immersed in the trial; always staying in the moment; guarding against complacency to evade the many attempts the opposition will use to blur the truth; control of all thought-processes and emotions. All must be accomplished in order to prevail.

The first phase of Mary Valone's trial was to select a jury–a precarious array of hunches and intuitions. Some guardian's of the law shine upon it, while others are apt to fail. To excel at the discipline, it takes an intrinsic sense to gaze inside the vast continuum of ideals and moral values that may subsist within any given person's mind and soul. Fortuitous insight at best. Or as with most, sheer luck.

The entire morning was spent reducing the thirty-one member panel to twelve. With the assistance of Art McNally and Michelle Campus, a psychologist who advises attorneys on jury selection, Robert Cook's goal was to retain individuals they viewed as undeniably impartial. People who would carefully listen to all the facts, dissect them accordingly, then reach an indifferent conclusion based solely upon the evidence.

His intent was to eliminate those whom they sensed either through polite inquiry or by reviewing their questionnaires suggested that for whatever their motivation might have some type of predisposition against Mary Valone, a pro-bias for the defendants or the medical profession in general.

Naturally Walter Tibeau and his team sought hold of any prospective jurors whom they believed possessed such sentiments. In addition, he endeavored to banish the college-educated women and those above median income. Yet his foremost objective was to purge the African-Americans.

As fate had it, the jury pool was comprised of only six African-Americans. While the law doesn't permit an attorney to disqualify any individual predicated upon the color of their skin or ethnic heritage, Tibeau stealthfully navigated around the guidelines. In quiet conference with Robert Cook and Judge Watson, he cited justifications for removal of the remaining African-Americans by claiming various perceived animosities he felt they may harbor against the defense. One such woman whom Cook desperately wanted to keep was dismissed solely because she had worked in a hospital some twenty-five years ago.

Judge Watson could plainly see Tibeau's strategy, yet knew it prudent not to take issue. Judges seldom contest an attorney's rationale during the selection process since refusing to accept even the most marginal argument for discharge could be used as grounds for appeal. Of greater significance, they were now on record. Watson wasn't about to give Tibeau any discernible excuse for claiming his presence would prove detrimental towards his clients. This was a case he had circled on his calendar.

Shortly before noon, the panel consisting of five men and seven women were finally seated. All things considered, Bob was pleased with the group. After they'd been reduced to twenty, Michelle had given Bob the names of whom she felt were the twelve optimum choices–ten of who had escaped Walter Tibeau's sharpened ax using his challenges for cause.

The jurors now in place, Watson looked to the attorneys. "Mr. Cook?"

"Your Honor, the plaintiff is very happy with our outstanding jury."

Across the aisle, Tibeau arose. "Your Honor, the defense is also quite pleased to have these excellent citizens serving as our jury."

"Very well, gentlemen," said the judge. "Thank you."

Watson turned to the jurors and said, "Ladies and gentlemen of the jury, it's been a long morning, so we'll be taking our recess for lunch now. Before we do, I would like to commend each of you on your willingness to perform your civic duty in this trial. I assure you the attorneys and I will do everything practicable to move things along as efficiently as we can. Please remember the following instructions until the trial is resolved. Please refrain at all times throughout the course of these proceedings from any contact with the litigants or their attorneys. They have been warned not to seek you out and I'm instructing you to do likewise. If any of the parties should deliberately approach you, regardless of how casual the encounter might seem, inform the bailiff. Don't pay any attention to any opinions other individuals may have. Your conclusions are all that matter. Not theirs. Again, you have my sincere thanks. Enjoy your lunch, and please return to the jury room before one o'clock."

*****

"Mr. Cook, you may proceed," announced Judge Watson, with everyone poised in their seats.

"Thank you, Your Honor."

Approaching the jury, Bob's eye contact exuded both friendliness and confidence. "Ladies and gentlemen of the jury, my name is Robert Cook. I represent the plaintiff in this case, Mrs. Mary Valone. What I am about to say is not meant to be taken as evidence. It's merely a broad overview of the events that have transpired that has resulted in my client being forced to seek justice in a court of law. Both defense counsel and I shall have the opportunity to address you so you will be better prepared to follow along with the actual evidence with greater readiness as it gradually evolves before you."

Jurors are always most attentive at the inception of a trial. In spite of their already having some knowledge as to the proceedings at hand, they're curious about the stature of the case and the quality of the attorneys. Casting an image of assembling his thoughts, Bob paced slowly in front the jury box–a seasoned ploy, forcing their focus onto him.

"For those of you whom may have sat on civil juries before, perhaps you've seen the litigants disputing whether or not the injured party may have a trivial claim against another individual. Well, I can promise you there isn't anything trivial about this case. No, this is a significant case that involves medical malpractice. Malpractice that could have, and should have been easily prevented."

Standing at the near side of the jury box, he directed their attentions towards Mary, who was seated alone at a table off to the side. "This lady is the plaintiff, Mrs. Mary Valone. As the evidence will conclusively prove, she is a victim of gross negligence on the part of the defendants."

His voice turned monotone. "Yes, Mary is a victim of gross negligence, plain and simple. If I may, I'd like to speak briefly about her personal background. Mary Valone was a hard-working career woman in excellent health who never had so much as a toothache before the many shameless events you will learn about came to pass. Mary is a widow. While raising her son as a single parent, she obtained a job as a medical secretary. She was a highly-dedicated employee with an impeccable work record. Also for your information, Mary's never been involved in any kind of legal trouble whatsoever, nor with any other type of litigation prior to this. To put it bluntly, Mary Valone has led an exemplary life."

Presenting one's case first is an enormous advantage. Walt Tibeau used to tell his junior associates that first impressions–if they were indeed poignant–could win the case before a single witness testified.

With all eyes locked upon he and Mary, Bob resumed. "Unfortunately Mary Valone developed a medical condition that could befall any of us at some point during our lives. She had what is known as a partially-herniated disc of her lower spine. This is a serious ailment and we'll delve into much greater detail concerning her plight as well as other relevant issues of Mary's medical history as the trial progresses."

With deliberate purpose he glared towards the opposite side of the courtroom where the defendants were seated. "Mary's herniated disc was initially diagnosed by the defendant, Dr. Steven Cameron. Dr. Cameron then referred Mary to the defendant, Dr. Rasheem Nasser, who eventually performed Mary's back surgery on January 17th, 2008. To their credit, the diagnosis was correct, and Mary's subsequent operation successfully alleviated her back problems."

Bob Cook stole a peek at the defense table. Walt Tibeau remained a statue of tranquility.

"Now I'm sure you've noticed there is a third defendant in this case, Dr. Harold Elliot. Ladies and gentlemen of the jury, Dr. Elliot is a named defendant simply due to a matter of the law. I'm certain Judge Watson can clarify Dr. Elliot's standing to you much better than I can. For now, please be aware that Dr. Elliot hasn't any true bearing in this entire litigation. He has done nothing to harm Mrs. Valone. Therefore she does not hold anything against him. As I said, I'm sure Judge Watson will explain Dr. Elliot's status to you with far greater wisdom than I."

His emotions racing, Robert Cook drew a deep breath and said, "Members of the jury, the events I'm about to outline for you occurred over a seven-week span after Mary Valone was discharged from Shadydell Heights Hospital on January 19th of 2008, until March 4th, 2008. This timeframe will be the primary focus of our case. After Mary had been home for approximately three weeks following her surgery, she began to experience severe back pain. A pain completely unlike any of her previous symptoms had brought about. A pain that grew progressively worse every day. The evidence will show that all throughout this time, Mrs. Valone was persistent in seeking help from Dr. Cameron and Dr. Nasser. What was causing her pain? Ladies and gentlemen of the jury, Mrs. Valone had developed a post-operative surgical infection of her spine."

Facing the defendants, Bob pointed at Cameron. "Mary first sought Dr. Cameron's help at his office on February 12th. During this visit, Dr. Cameron committed several errors of judgment. Instead of having Mary undergo a complete blood work-up in order to help him determine if Mary was infected, he chose not to. Instead, allow me to tell you what Dr. Cameron did."

"Your Honor, Mr. Cook—"

"Opening statement, Mr. Tibeau," said Watson. "Continue, Mr. Cook."

"Dr. Cameron gave Mrs. Valone pain medication and told her to go home and exercise!" said Bob, his voice scaled to an incredulous pitch.

"Mary returned to Dr. Cameron's office on February 18th," Bob said, reverting to his usual tone of voice. "It was during this visit when Dr. Cameron committed another series of heinous mistakes. Dr. Cameron had Mary undergo an MRI, a visual image of her lower spine. He told Mary there wasn't anything unusual about it. The testimony you shall hear will prove beyond any reasonable doubt that Mary Valone's infection was clearly visible on the MRI and Dr. Cameron misinterpreted it. Mary then asked Dr. Cameron to perform a blood test, specifically a sedimentation-rate. A test that conclusively measures the red blood cells of the body and detects the presence of infection. Keep in mind, members of the jury, Mary was a medical secretary. She has knowledge of such testing procedures. Instead of his ordering Mary's blood test has she requested, Dr. Cameron gave Mary more pain medication and assured her that everything was normal."

Silence abounded as the jury, along with the assemblage of courtroom mavens continued to gape at the defendants. Bob desired to hold the moment longer, though Judge Watson's clearing his throat suggested otherwise.

Robert Cook went on to say, "Once again Mrs. Valone returned to Dr. Cameron's office on March 3rd. Dr. Cameron performed yet another MRI on Mary. Again he told her there wasn't anything depicted on the film. Again Mary asked, no begged Dr. Cameron to conduct a blood analysis. Again Dr. Cameron declined. So what else did Dr. Cameron do for Mary on March 3rd? Nothing except prescribe more pain medicine. You'll learn through expert testimony what he should have done. So for all intents and purposes, Dr. Steven Cameron, who was primarily responsible for Mary's aftercare, one of the physicians to whom Mary Valone had entrusted her very life, washed his hands of Mary's lingering cries for help. In essence, he had all but abandon Mary Valone until her infection was finally determined when she was re-admitted to Shadydell Heights Hospital. After weeks of excruciating agony following her surgery. Members of the jury, Dr. Cameron certainly wouldn't get many votes for Humanitarian of the Year."

"Mr. Cook," Judge Watson interposed, "your last comment was inappropriate."

"My apologies, Your Honor, I retract it from the record."

Bob could readily see the anger burgeoning in many of the jurors faces. "Yes, ladies and gentlemen, it was a total of seven weeks after her operation before Mrs. Valone finally began receiving treatment for infection. By then, the infectious process raging throughout her body had caused massive damage. Damage that has resulted in Mary's suffering tremendous pain. Damage that will necessitate her needing future surgical procedures. Damage she must live with for the rest of her life. Damage that Dr. Cameron's negligence and ineptitudes could have easily prevented. That, members of the jury, is medical malpractice."

"Why aren't you objecting?" whispered Douglas Lee, serving as Tibeau's second-chair.

Remaining stationary, Walter Tibeau disregarded his advice.

"Now as to Dr. Rasheem Nasser's involvement in regards to Mary Valone's post-operative care," said Bob, cynicism in his tone. "He's the man sitting next to Dr. Cameron."

With all eyes now trained on Nasser, Bob Cook moved to his desk. Scrolling through a legal pad, he allowed their torrid stares to linger before saying, "Since Dr. Cameron was incapable of rendering any plausible solutions during this traumatic period of time, Mary drove to Dr. Nasser's office on February 26th in the hope of garnering his opinion as to what could possibly be causing her unbearable pain. Members of the jury, you may find this hard to believe, yet the evidence will support what I am about to say. On the only occasion he saw Mrs. Valone, Dr. Nasser did nothing for his ailing patient. You may be asking yourselves what he should have done. Well, let's talk about that for a moment. Dr. Nasser could have ordered additional films be taken. He didn't bother. Dr. Nasser could have consulted with other physicians if he wasn't certain what Mary's problem was. He didn't feel this course of action was necessary, either. As a matter of fact, Dr. Rasheem Nasser's only conclusions to Mary Valone during her office visit were there wasn't anything seriously wrong with her and that she was, and I quote Dr. Nasser, 'acting like a child.'"

"Objection, Your Honor," Tibeau said. "Counsel is supposed to be making an opening statement, not offering hearsay to belittle my client."

"Overruled."

"Now we come to Dr. Nasser's most regrettable mistake," proclaimed Bob Cook, his words bursting with scintillating contempt. "Ladies and gentlemen, as she did with Dr. Cameron, Mary Valone pleaded with Dr. Nasser to order the identical blood test Dr. Cameron should have ordered. Still, Dr. Nasser refused. Yes, you heard me correctly, he refused. Why you ask, did Dr. Nasser hold so resolute? Any competent surgeon, regardless of how simplistic the operation they may have performed, must always fear the threat of a patient developing some sort of infection. This is a cardinal rule for any surgeon. From the very first moment when he learned Mary Valone was experiencing discomfort anywhere near her surgical site, a siren should have sounded within Dr. Nasser's mind to test for the possibility of infection. All he needed do was call the laboratory at Shadydell Heights Hospital and have them draw a test-tube of blood from her arm. The sample would have been quickly analyzed and the results would have indicated beyond any doubt that there was in actually some sort of infectious process festering throughout her body. However, members of the jury, Dr. Nasser chose not to go along with Mary's desire he order the blood test. Permit me to tell you why he didn't feel it was necessary."

With burning disdain Bob pointed at Nasser. "That egomaniacal surgeon, who is supposed to hold his patients well-being above all else—"

"Your Honor, I object!" Tibeau adamantly called. "Counsel—"

Shunning courtroom etiquette, Cook's baritone voice topped his former boss, "had the gall to tell Mary Valone, 'I don't get infections!' Well, Doctor, you sure got one this time, didn't you!"

"Objection! Objection!" screamed Tibeau. "Your Honor, Mr. Cook's remarks are totally uncalled for. They are insulting, unprofessional and completely without regard to the proper framework of an opening statement. I ask his outburst be stricken from the record, and I also ask you admonish Mr. Cook for his ignoring my call of objection."

"Sustained," said a low-keyed Judge Watson. "Mr. Cook's last few sentences are expunged. Mr. Cook, your dialog is to immediately cease whenever an objection is made. Nor will I tolerate any further affronting remarks directed towards any of the defendants. Do I make myself clear?"

"Your Honor, I apologize to the Court and to the jury," he replied courteously–positioned so only the judge could see the glint of his eyes.

After a passing glance at his legal pad, Bob moved towards the jurors. "Ladies and gentlemen of the jury, I'd like to conclude by saying that I have unsurpassed faith in you. I know that once all the evidence has been presented, each of you will easily note the many failures and omissions made by the defendants in their post-operative care of Mary Valone that has resulted in their blatant negligence and will arrive at the correct verdict. I thank you for your attention."

Returning to his seat, Robert Cook had accomplished his objective. His plan was to infuriate the doctors. Walt Tibeau had schooled him that irate witnesses are more apt to stumble during cross-examination, especially if they had something to hide. As for Judge Watson striking his sordid criticisms of Dr. Nasser, nevertheless Bob had achieved his goal. His chastising words were already ingrained into the jurors' memory. The example law professors use is a church tower bell: one may be forced to stop pulling the rope, yet the chimes will continue to echo for a long time afterwards.

Walter Tibeau conducted his opening statement in his accustomed comely style, continually casting a meek image. Remaining serene while denying Cook's allegations directed at his clients, he strove to win the jurors trust through his unpretentious approach. He'd always felt the worst mistake any defense attorney could make was to project the impression of being in damage-control mode at such an early stage. If the jury even sensed him troubled about Bob's brash remarks, they might be subconsciously influenced into believing there must be some creditability to his opponent's case.

Perceiving he'd defused some of the jurors' animosities after the fireworks Bob had stirred, the refined defense attorney methodically noted the pivotal issues of contention involved in the case. He didn't attempt to belabor his assertions with the same rank fervor as his foe had applied. Tibeau's technique was to only plant the seeds of his defense and rely on his witnesses conveying the medical pretenses that would ultimately dismantle the plaintiff's case. His experience had taught Tibeau to avoid saying anything derogatory about the plaintiff in a snippy fashion. He dared not risk alienating a juror by displaying a lack of empathy for Mary Valone when they would invariably come to realize to some extent all she had endured. For even if they didn't believe malpractice had taken place, a resentful juror still might vote guilty out of spite and then be persuasive enough to coax his or her counterparts likewise. The sapient philosophy that made him a prosperous defense attorney was truly quite basal: Always extend a plaintiff unmatched sympathy while putting their significant witnesses through a meat-grinder.

"Members of the jury," he said, "all the defense asks of yourselves is to please keep an open mind until all of the evidence has been presented. Please do not draw any conclusions until every last fact has been prudently examined. Opposing counsel has portrayed my clients' attitudes towards Mrs. Valone as being arrogant and altogether uncaring. I assure each of you there could not be anything further from the truth. To the contrary, their testimony will clearly indicate just how saddened they are about Mary. How it was their utmost desire that her surgery and post-operative care would have gone flawlessly. My clients are deeply troubled about Mary's health as it exists today, and it is each doctor's most heartfelt yearning that Mary soon returns to the excellent health she enjoyed prior to her surgery. However, while I'm certain everyone in this courtroom hasn't anything but the deepest compassion for Mrs. Valone, you must not let your emotions sway your impartiality of the law as it applies to this case. For the testimony and evidence the defense shall present will clearly illustrate that any of my clients are not guilty of malpractice in the slightest degree."

Tibeau paused briefly, then said, "Ladies and gentlemen, I am not presumptuous enough to stand here and infer that I can tell you the exact reason or reasons why Mrs. Mary Valone did not heed her doctors' advice subsequent to her operation. It will be your duty to listen to the testimony as well as to review all of the evidence in order to arrive at Mrs. Valone's reasoning. I'd like all of you to know beforehand that you'll be hearing a great deal of conflicting testimony as this trial unfolds. Testimony you will all come to understand must be either mistaken or untruthful. Therefore each of you must be able to weed-out the inaccuracies. Hence when the time comes for you as a group to decide upon a verdict, I'm positive each of you shall possess the wisdom that will enable yourselves to arrive at the correct determination that my clients should be vindicated of the charges against them. You'll see for yourselves the defendants are not the crass villains Mr. Cook has represented them to be. No, not by any means. These are dedicated men of medicine. Men whose sole ambition in life is to use their vast intellect and abilities to see to the care and treatment of all their patients. Doctors who utilize their skills to subsidize virtue. These three devout physicians stand for everything that is good about mankind. Members of the jury, I thank you for your attention."

His head bowed, Tibeau retreated to his seat. The crafty pro took a moment to impassively study his audience. Some of the jurors' body-language, along with his finely-honed instincts suggested he had attained his intent of securing partial trust.

Judge Watson glanced to the clock above the jury-box. "We're going to make it an early day. When we resume tomorrow morning, counsel for the plaintiff shall call his first witness."

Except for the defense team, the courtroom had emptied. While Tibeau and Doug Lee gathered their extensive documentation, they heard the footsteps of a rather obese man dressed in a gray suit similar to Tibeau's approaching them.

"Bart," said Tibeau, "I thought you weren't coming today."

"Oh, I was in the area, so I decided to stop by," said Barton Harrison. "Hey, Walt, I thought Cook was pretty impressive."

"He was superb," Tibeau replied, almost envy in his tone. "Bob knows every nuance of her case. A fact I hope the doctors can now appreciate. Maybe now they'll realize what we're up against."

"Despite their unwillingness, should I arrange for settlement talks?"

"Not yet," said Tibeau. "Although be prepared to make her an offer. A substantial offer. Bart, I'm concerned. This case has a bad feel to it."

CHAPTER THIRTY ONE

Clad in a navy-blue dress that extended just below her kneecaps, the months of impatiently waiting for a public forum to air her declarations of malpractice were over as Mary Valone took the witness stand.

Since the burden of proof always rests with the plaintiff, judges are accustomed to allowing a great deal of latitude during their testimony by foregoing traditional question-and-answer exchanges upon direct examination. Usually the plaintiff is given opportunity to tell their version of the events, while being guided by their own attorney. This can tilt heavily in the plaintiff's favor. A believable plaintiff could result in an insurmountable barrier of the defense to conquer.

With Robert Cook only interposing to emphasize or expand upon an issue, Mary's specific recall of even the most diminutive particulars was phenomenal. In concise, chronological sequence she described the material facts of her case. For someone who had never been in a courtroom before, much less the witness stand, Mary Valone was exhibiting an inordinate amount of poise.

While the doctors and Barton Harrison squirmed in their seats, Walt Tibeau sat quietly alone at the defense table–Douglas Lee relegated to a small table behind him. Through the guise of staid countenance, Tibeau observed the distinct sincerity Mary was conveying upon the jury. He'd withheld several objections, wary of provoking the jury. Tibeau was caught between a rock and a hard place, since he understood Cook and his client were being granted an abundance of freedoms. Any objections on his part would be quelled by Bob simply asking the same question phrased in different context. The master tactician recognized that the sooner such a profound and knowledgeable witness such as Mary Valone had completed her direct testimony, the better.

It was nearing two-thirty when Mary had finished. Aware he still held the upper-hand, Bob Cook decided to follow through with an idea he and Art McNally had contemplated during their lunch hour and afternoon recess.

"Your Honor, I realize what I'm about to request may seem a bit irregular," said Bob, maintaining a calm authority. "Since Mrs. Valone's testimony has encompassed a great deal of facts, I would like the opportunity to highlight some of the most essential facts of her case for our jury."

"Mr. Tibeau, any arguments?" said Watson.

"Your Honor, may we approach?" he promptly replied.

"Please do," said the judge, beckoning them towards the side of the bench out of the jury's earshot.

"Your Honor, I think it unfair Mr. Cook wishes to have Mrs. Valone further bolster her already lengthy testimony," ventured Tibeau in hushed voice. "You made it perfectly clear that you wanted no redundancies in testimony. Quite frankly, that's all this ploy will bring about."

"Judge Watson, my sole objective is to have Mrs. Valone underscore only the pivotal issues," Bob countered. "Her testimony is the cornerstone of my case, and in the interest of justice our jury deserves to have a solid understanding of all notable points of contention. I give you my word I'll be brief and will stay within the scope of her previous testimony."

"It isn't appropriate, Your Honor," insisted Tibeau. "Her testimony would be redundant. I strongly object to your allowing this."

"Mr. Cook, I'm going to grant your request," said Watson, as he observed the scowl on Tibeau's face. "However I'll sustain any objections if you stray from testimony that's already been placed on record."

"Understood, Your Honor."

As soon as Tibeau was seated, Bob said, "Mrs. Valone, in reference to your first visit to Dr. Cameron subsequent to your surgery on February 12th, what did he say when you asked him to conduct a sed-rate?"

"He told me to trust him, that I wasn't infected," Mary said.

"And Dr. Cameron gave you a prescription for thirty Percocet, a pain-killing narcotic, and advised you to begin a moderate exercise program?"

"Yes."

"Alright, let's now focus on your second trip to see Dr. Cameron on February 18th. You've testified that he took an MRI. True?"

"True."

"What, if anything, did Dr. Cameron tell you that MRI depicted?"

"Dr. Cameron said there wasn't anything out of the ordinary depicted."

"Did Dr. Cameron review the MRI himself or did someone else render their opinion?"

"Dr. Cameron told me that was his own opinion."

"Did Dr. Cameron ever sáy that he was planning on having your films reviewed by another doctor, specifically a board-certified radiologist?"

"No. He never mentioned any board-certified radiologist to me."

"And did you again ask Dr. Cameron to conduct a sed-rate?"

"I did."

"And how did he respond?"

"He declined to do so."

"You've testified that Dr. Cameron gave you another prescription for Percocet. True?"

"True. He wrote me a script for sixty Percocet."

"Two prescriptions for Percocet in six days? Dr. Cameron must have realized that you were in terrible pain. True?"

"Calls for speculation," said Tibeau.

"Overruled. You may answer, Mrs. Valone."

"Thank you, Your Honor," Mary said.

As Bob had instructed, Mary resumed eye-contact with the jury and said, "He knew. I had made it abundantly clear to Dr. Cameron that the pain in my lower back was becoming intolerable. All he kept telling me was that my back needed more time to heal."

Robert Cook observed the frowns leveled by many of the jurors. "Dr. Cameron's prognosis was in error. Wasn't it, Mary?"

"It most certainly was in error."

"What did Dr. Cameron do next?"

"He asked Dr. Elliot to see me."

"And what did Dr. Elliot do for you?"

"He spent about five minutes with me," she said. "After only a cursory examination, Dr. Elliot surmised that I had what he referred to as, a 'mechanical back syndrome.'"

"Was Dr. Elliot's diagnosis correct?"

"No."

"Do you fault Dr. Elliot for his mistaken diagnosis?"

"No."

"Why not?"

"First of all, Dr. Elliot wasn't aware of all the facts of my condition since I wasn't his patient. And secondly, Dr. Elliot made it perfectly clear that he wasn't a radiologist, and he suggested I continue to follow Dr. Cameron's advice."

"And did you follow Dr. Cameron's advice by going to his office again?"

"Yes. On March 3rd of last year."

"What did Dr. Cameron do for you then?"

"He took another MRI of my lower spine, and gave me sixty more Percocet."

"And what did Dr. Cameron say in regards to the MRI?"

"He said it was normal."

"Did you again ask him to conduct a sedimentation-rate?"

"I did. Again he declined to do so."

"Very well, Mary," said Bob. "Let's move to Dr. Nasser. You went to his office without an appointment on February 26th of last year. Please refresh the jury's memory. What exactly did Dr. Nasser do for you?"

"Absolutely nothing."

"You've testified that you asked Dr. Nasser to conduct a sed-rate. True?"

"I did."

"And what did Dr. Nasser say to you then?"

"Dr. Nasser told me that he did not get surgical infections, and to stop acting like a child," Mary replied, her soft-spoken feminine voice taking on a sharp edge.

"Sounds as if Dr. Nasser took a very cavalier attitude—"

"Your Honor!" Tibeau vigorously interjected.

"Sustained," said Watson. "Move it along, Mr. Cook."

"Mrs. Valone, please explain to the jury exactly what a sedimentation-rate blood test entails."

"A laboratory extracts a small quantity of blood from a patient and a complete blood analysis is performed. The results of each specific category are assigned a numerical value that should fall between established parameters if they are normal. If any value is outside of a normal parameter, this will alert a physician that a problem could exist."

"And yet Dr. Nasser refused to send a specimen of your blood to the laboratory at Shadydell Heights Hospital for such a rudimentary test?"

"Yes, he refused."

"So approximately one week later you were re-admitted to the hospital. True?"

"True."

"And when Dr. Nasser saw you, did he then order the sed-rate?"

"At first, no. My son had to use bodily-force on Dr. Nasser to make him consent to having my sed-rate taken."

"And finally, your sed-rate confirmed to Dr. Nasser as well as to Dr. Cameron that you did indeed have a massive infection. True?"

"Yes."

His head lowered, Robert Cook huffed loudly as he moved towards the jurors. The many observers clustered in the rear of the courtroom looked to each other in stunned amazement. Walt Tibeau kept tight-lipped; Judge Watson remained serene with chin cupped in hand; Cook stood silent, observing the murals about the courtroom.

Having savored the moment, he said, "Mrs. Valone, I have one last question in reference to a subject you only touched upon earlier. Taking into consideration everything that's occurred due to the severity of your infection, is it your personal opinion that you would still be alive today if your infection had not been finally discovered at Shadydell Heights Hospital on March 4th, 2008?"

"Your Honor, I must object!" Tibeau blurted out, devoid of his usual charms. "Mrs. Valone is not qualified to answer. Her response would only be sheer conjecture."

"One moment, Counselor," said Judge Watson. "Members of the jury, while Mrs. Valone was employed at a hospital, she is not a doctor. It would require a medical degree for her answer to be accepted as scientific postulate. Our judicial system permits such inquiries provided it's explained beforehand that an unqualified witnesses' answer to such a question is simply their own belief, yet it carries no scientific basis in fact. Therefore you may give whatever weight you so choose to her response."

"Your Honor," said Tibeau. "Mrs. Valone's answer would only be speculation on her part. She isn't qualified to respond."

"My decision stands, Mr. Tibeau. Mr. Cook asked for her personal opinion, not a definitive scientific conclusion. We'll let the jury decide for themselves what credence they should apply to Mrs. Valone's opinion."

"Judge Watson, you're being completely unreasonable about the issue."

"Mr. Tibeau, overruled," declared the judge, his tone becoming a touch surly. "Please do not make me repeat myself. Now would the reporter kindly read back Mr. Cook's question."

"That won't be necessary, Your Honor," said Mary. "I remember the question."

"Then you may answer, Ma'am," said a kind-faced Judge Watson, smiling at her.

"Mr. Cook, it is my personal opinion that I would have been dead and buried today if I had not been placed on antibiotics when I was re-admitted to the hospital then or shortly thereafter. I'm very blessed to be alive today."

In measured strides, Robert Cook approached the witness stand. Both he and Mary were nearing tears. "Mary, I thank you for your patience in describing to the Court and to the jury all of the many unpleasant circumstances you've been forced to endure since your back surgery."

Bob looked to Judge Watson and said, "Your Honor, that concludes my direct examination of Mrs. Valone."

"Very well," he replied. "Mr. Tibeau, it's your choice. You may begin your cross-examination now or wait until tomorrow."

"Tomorrow will be fine," said a frustrated Walter Tibeau.

As Bob held Mary's hand as she stepped from the elevated platform, Judge Watson said, Ladies and gentlemen, we've all had a full day. We'll adjourn a bit early today. Court will reconvene at 9 A.M. tomorrow. Please remember all of my admonitions. Court adjourned."

Minutes later, Cook emerged from the courtroom to find John Valone standing in the emptying hallway. "Where's everybody at?"

"Art took them all downstairs," he said. "Bob, you were terrific in there."

"No, your mom was terrific."

Cook glanced about the hallways before saying, "C'mon, these walls have ears."

When they came to the elevator, Bob pressed the 'Up' arrow.

"You hit the wrong button," John said.

"No, I didn't. We need to talk."

"So tell me on the way down."

The elevator door slid open. "We're going to the eight floor," said Bob. "There's an office up there nobody uses."

Once their privacy was secured inside the vacated office, John said, "Alright, now what's your problem?"

"Just a few points I'd like to remind you of. After your mother's done tomorrow, the pace of the trial is going to speed-up, and you'll be next on the stand. Don't forget what I told you about answering my questions. You're not going to receive the same liberties as Mary was permitted, so respond truthfully to my questions while keeping your answers straightforward. Just be yourself and try to relax."

"Understood."

"Next I want to re-emphasize what you must keep in mind when Tibeau does his cross on you. Above all else, don't underestimate him.

Don't let his tranquil demeanor fool you while he's questioning Mary tomorrow because he doesn't have any other option but to be polite to her since the sympathy factor's in play. Sure he'll try to confuse her however he can to convince the jury his saintly clients are innocent, yet he'll be courteous about it. But if you give him an opening, he won't be as nice to you."

"Bob, we've already gone over this. I'm not scared of him."

"No, I want you to fear him! John, trust me, Walt Tibeau's a dangerous man in a courtroom. That's why it's imperative you don't give him any openings. He'll probably go easy on you at first, trying to lull you into a false sense of security. Then before you know it, he'll be all over you. Believe me, Tibeau realizes he's in big trouble considering the quality of Mary's testimony. Just be prepared in case he does come down hard on you."

"Fuck him," said John. "Tibeau's just another high-priced mouthpiece who defends the scum of the earth."

"Oh, that's just fuckin' marvelous," said a disgruntled Bob Cook. "Take the stand tomorrow with that kind of attitude. Say something stupid like that. Go 'head, make an ass outta yourself. You'll feel like you've been carved to pieces after Tibeau's done with you."

Bob arose from the wooden bench they were seated on to kick his briefcase.

"John, I'm starting to wonder if I should even call you tomorrow. One sudden burst of volatility outta you could cause Mary's case to go right up in smoke."

Valone leveled a cold stare at him. The fury that shadowed every contour of his face demanded Bob stop antagonizing him.

"I'm not on the fuckin' witness stand now," he said in contentious tone. "I'm talking in private to one of the best friends I have. I'll be a perfect gentleman when Tibeau questions me. When it's appropriate, I'll limit my answers to yes or no. If I'm not sure of his question, I'll ask him to please repeat it. I won't start any of my answers with 'I believe' or 'I would guess' because that would leave me wide-open. Tomorrow I'll wear this same blue suit, a white shirt, and another quiet tie. Okay, ya big prick, happy now?"

"Very much so," said Bob, as he sat. "John, I'm sorry if I offended you, but I had to be sure that you're primed to testify. I realize there's a lot of venom inside you because of all Mary's been through. It was better for you to vent your anger on me than on the witness stand. I need you on that witness stand tomorrow to help corroborate the facts."

"Damn straight I'm angry," he said. "You'd feel the same way if some doctors deliberately tried to kill Diane or someone else in your family, then insulated themselves with an expensive shyster and a buncha lying scumbags to escape being held culpable."

With a shrug of his broad shoulders, Bob said, "John, it's just the nature of the beast. Civil courts across America are inundated with malpractice cases simply because most doctors detest admitting they fucked-up. To them, it isn't about the money. It's about pride."

"Hypocrites. Fuckin' hypocrites."

Cook slapped his knee. "Hey, look at the flipside. Be thankful for Dr. Tyler."

"I am, Bob. Dr. Tyler's a great guy. Okay, let's get going. I promise I won't do anything to hurt our chances. This case means too much to all of us."

"Not yet," Bob said. "John, I'm only saying this because of our friendship. I'd like to talk about Vicky."

"I don't."

"John, I realize she hurt you, but you've got to get over her. You've got to do all you can to overcome the state of depression you're in. You're subconsciously distancing yourself from everyone."

"I don't need a Psych 101 lecture. I'm alright."

"That's just it, John, you're not alright!" Bob implored of him. "Listen to me, I'm saying this as your friend. You've got to move on. Put Vicky behind you. Get out of that shell you've been hiding in. When the trial's over, get on with your life. Find yourself another girl. Start working again. You can't just stay home like some recluse and sulk. Put your—"

"I get the message, Bob," he abruptly returned.

Valone stood to glare hard at him. "Tell Gene he's got a big fuckin' mouth. Now I'd like to get outta here before rush-hour."

CHAPTER THIRTY TWO

"Good morning, Mrs. Valone," said Walter Tibeau. "I hope you're feeling well today."

"Not especially," she said. "My back is sore."

"I'm sorry to hear that, Ma'am. I'll try to be brief. During your first office visit to Dr. Steven Cameron on February 12th of last year, you testified that Dr. Cameron suggested you start a mild exercise regiment, and he gave you a prescription for Percocet. Correct?"

"Yes."

"Do you believe Dr. Cameron gave you a proper examination that day?"

"Considering I did not have a scheduled appointment, yes."

"Under the circumstances, would you say that Dr. Cameron did all he could in order to discern what your ailment was?"

"No."

"What should he have done?"

"He should have ordered my sed-rate as I asked him to."

"Dr. Cameron stated in his deposition that he was willing to order your sed-rate, yet you declined."

"He's mistaken."

"We're you on any other pain medications during this time? "Yes. Darvocet."

"And those were obtained by Dr. Mancini, your Primary Care Physician?"

"Yes."

"Had Dr. Mancini given you a prescription for Darvocet?"

"No, he gave me one box of samples that physicians receive from pharmaceutical sales representatives."

"So you were medicated when you saw Dr. Cameron on February 12th?"

"Yes. I was in pain."

"And you remain certain that Dr. Cameron did not order your sed-rate that day as you previously stated?"

"Yes, I do."

"Very well, Mrs. Valone," said Tibeau. "So it is your testimony that all Dr. Cameron did for you on February 12th was suggest you try exercising, and he gave you a script for Percocet. Ma'am, is that an accurate summation of your abbreviated visit that day?"

After a flicker of hesitation, Mary answered, "Yes."

"Therefore is it safe to say that you still had faith in Dr. Cameron?"

"At that time, yes."

"Fine," Tibeau said, remaining in demure mode. "Mrs. Valone, I'd now like to shift our discussion to your scheduled appointment to Dr. Cameron on February 18th. Let us begin with the MRI Dr. Cameron conducted at that visit. You've testified Dr. Cameron told you he did not notice anything out of the ordinary on the MRI. True?"

"Yes."

"And you have also maintained the premise that Dr. Cameron overlooked the infection depicted on your MRI due to the fact that he is not a board-certified radiologist. True?"

"Mr. Tibeau, the massive infection I had was discovered at Shadydell Heights Hospital only fifteen days after Dr. Cameron's MRI," Mary replied. "It's not my premise. It is a fact. Dr. Cameron did not properly interpret my MRI."

Despite his not presenting any outward signs, Walter Tibeau stood impressed with her resolution. A peripheral glimpse of the jury told him they felt likewise. *"Not now. They'll understand when Schmidt explains it,"* he thought. Tibeau then said, Mrs. Valone, you also contend that Dr. Cameron was remiss for again failing to order your sed-rate. Correct?"

"Correct."

"And did Dr. Cameron give you any more pain medication?"

"Yes. He gave a script for sixty Percocet."

"Yes, the same amount he gave you on February 12th. Correct?"

"No, Sir," she said. "Dr. Cameron gave me thirty Percocet on February 12th."

"My mistake, Mrs. Valone," said Tibeau, patting his forehead. "Thirty Percocet on February 12th is accurate. And it was during your February 18th office visit when you briefly spoke with Dr. Elliot. Am I correct?"

"Yes. Dr. Elliot and I spoke on February 18th."

"Alright, Mrs. Valone," said Tibeau. "Now turning your attention to your March 3rd office visit with Dr. Cameron. During this visit, Dr. Cameron took another MRI of your lower spine. True?"

"True."

"Dr. Cameron also gave you a prescription for sixty Percocet. True?"

"True."

"And during this visit, Dr. Cameron again declined to order you sed-rate. True?"

"True."

Tibeau moved towards the jury-box, casting a suspicious face. "Yes, the jurors have heard your testimony along these lines. You remain persistent that for some unfathomable reason, Dr. Cameron always declined to order such an unostentatious test as a sed-rate. Ma'am, I do not want you to guess, although I—"

"Objection as to form," Bob called.

"Rephrase," said Watson.

"Mrs. Valone, please enlighten the jury by giving them one logical reason as to why Dr. Cameron would be so reluctant to have the lab draw a test-tube of your blood, perform the proper analysis, and report their findings to him?"

"Because Dr. Cameron told me he had spoken with Dr. Nasser about me," she replied. "Since there wasn't any swelling or inflammation near my incision, Dr. Cameron told me he believed the same as Dr. Nasser that I was not infected. And I'm not guessing, Mr. Tibeau."

"Ma'am, I certainly do not have any wish to antagonize you," he said. "However, doesn't the possibility exist that you may very well be mistaken about Dr. Cameron's unwillingness to order you blood tested?"

"I know what Dr. Cameron told me."

"Perhaps mistaken is a poor way to categorize what could have taken place. Mrs. Valone, maybe you somehow misconstrued the term sedimentation-rate to imply some other form of evasive testing procedure you were fearful of. Could that have been the reason?"

"No, Sir. I knew well before all of this started what a sedimentation-rate is and how it is taken. I misconstrued nothing."

To the surprise of everyone, Walter Tibeau actually smiled before saying, "Yes, Mary, I couldn't agree with you more. After listening to your recital yesterday on the subject on how the sed-rate is quantified, your statement is certainly logical. Unfortunately there is another significant variable that must be factored into this equation. When you were discharged from Shadydell Heights Hospital immediately following your surgery, you were not on any pain medications. True?"

"True. I didn't need any."

"However in the weeks subsequent to your operation, by your own testimony you've admitted to taking dosages of narcotics in what I presume were in the hopes of stymieing your pain. Now I'll ask you again. Isn't it conceivable that you may be wrong about these allegations?"

"Sir, if you're implying that I wasn't cognizant of my behavior during the time I was on pain medication, you're the one who's mistaken."

"Mrs. Valone, I certainly don't question your integrity," stated Tibeau, somberly beginning the confrontation he knew was his only opportunity to cast suspicion. "Although it is a well-known medical fact that whenever any person takes excessive amounts of an opiate-derived narcotic, some of the many possible side effects can include lethargy, induced stupor, sluggish and erratic behavior patterns, lack of concentration, and loss of memory. Is that fair to say?"

"If one overmedicates, yes."

"Now if you'll remember from your own direct testimony, when Mr. Cook asked a question pertaining to when Dr. Cameron first gave you Percocet, you told Dr. Cameron that you knew Percocet is a strong painkiller. Do you recall saying that to Dr. Cameron?"

"Yes, I do. Mr. Tibeau, while it's true I was taking Percocet during this time, I was never in such an incoherent state of mind such as you're implying."

"Mrs. Valone, you received three prescriptions from Dr. Cameron. True?"

"True."

"The first was for a quantity of thirty, the other two for a quantity of sixty. True?"

"True."

"And approximately how many Percocet did you consume between your initial office visit to Dr. Cameron on February 12th until you returned to Shadydell Heights on March 4th?"

Mary took a moment before she said, "I would estimate ninety-five."

"You took ninety-five Percocet over a twenty-one day period? Mrs. Valone, presuming your estimate is within reason, that would equate to your taking almost five Percocet per day."

"Sir, I was in terrible pain."

"Be that as it may, Mrs. Valone, that's a tremendous amount of narcotics for you to have taken, yet remain so unremitting that you were entirely cognizant about every word that was spoken between yourself and my clients. Ma'am, to make such a claim under oath is a very fine distinction on your part."

"That, Sir, is your opinion."

The viper deliberated the moment. Her responses remained unyielding. Tibeau felt it time to challenge.

"Percocet is a very powerful narcotic, Mrs. Valone!" he said in bold tone of voice. "You were taking nearly five pills per day. Add to those any of the Darvocet you may have been taking in addition to Percocet. Any competent doctor whom might testify in this court of law would agree that your judgment was at least somewhat blurred from your overmedicating yourself, thereby resulting in the possibility that your recollections towards the issue may very well be askew. Yet you remain obtuse to acknowledge the fact that Dr. Cameron did insist you have a blood test and you rejected his advice due to your misinterpretation of his intent."

Proud of his client, Robert Cook stood to say, "Your Honor, maybe I'm the one who's obtuse. Was that a question or a dissertation on Mr. Tibeau's part?"

With the courtroom audience chuckling before Judge Watson could respond, Mary said, "Your Honor, I'm more than willing to answer Mr. Tibeau."

Albert Watson could only grin at her. "Then you go right ahead, Ma'am."

Undaunted by Tibeau's condemnations, Mary turned back towards the jury and said, "I remember what Dr. Cameron kept telling me. They can put all the doctors they want up here to claim I wasn't in control of my mental faculties and they would all be wrong. The honest to God truth is that every time I asked Dr. Cameron to take my sed-rate, he rejected my idea, either based upon his beliefs or those of Dr. Nasser's. I'm positive what Dr. Cameron's answer always was. It was always no."

"But how can you be so sure if you were always incognizant whenever you spoke with Dr. Cameron?" said Tibeau.

Mary Valone's green eyes burst aflame. "I never said I was incognizant whenever I spoke with Dr. Cameron! Don't be putting words in my mouth, Sir."

"Mr. Tibeau, I think we've reached an impasse along these lines," said Judge Watson. "I suggest you move on."

"Yes, Your Honor," Tibeau said, as he made his way towards the defense table. Hurriedly he shuffled through his legal pad and said, "Mrs. Valone, let's discuss the role Dr. Nasser played in your post-operative care. As with Dr. Cameron, it remains your assertion that Dr. Nasser disapproved of your having the sedimentation-rate performed. Isn't that so?"

"It was disapproval, Sir," Mary said, pushing back the auburn hair that flashed over her forehead. "He outright refused until my son threatened him."

"Yes, I'll discuss that with your son later. Tell me, Mrs. Valone, why is it that you believe Dr. Nasser had some sort of secret agenda for not ordering your sed-rate?"

"There wasn't anything secret about it," she said in fervent tone. "Dr. Nasser told me that his patients, quote, 'don't get infections.' Therefore due to his unswerving reliance of his surgical talents, along with the fact that he feared a sed-rate even being conducted on one of his patients would somehow denigrate his superlative reputation in the Pittsburgh medical community, he refused to acknowledge the possibility and damned my being tested."

"I suppose it would be a waste of time to repeat my same thesis that you were so heavily medicated during—"

"Your Honor," called Bob. "Not only do I object to the form of Mr. Tibeau's question, he's also badgering Mrs. Valone."

"Rephrase, Mr. Tibeau," said the judge, his eyebrows raised. "And watch yourself."

Walt Tibeau paused to gather his thoughts. Finally he said, "Mrs. Valone isn't it true that Dr. Nasser was not your first choice to perform your operation?"

"Yes, that's true. I wanted Dr. Duncan Campbell."

"Is this the real reason why you so despise Dr. Nasser?"

"Sir, during my initial stay at Shadydell Heights, I never bore any ill-will against Dr. Nasser. I'd never even heard of Dr. Nasser until Dr. Cameron recommended him to me. It was simply my own personal preference to have Dr. Duncan Campbell perform my operation since he has an unsurpassed reputation for excellence."

"So it's your testimony that you didn't harbor any resentment towards Dr. Nasser prior to your surgery?"

"Yes. I never would have approved Dr. Nasser for my operation if I had."

"Very well, Mrs. Valone," said Tibeau.

To his acute instincts–as it had been since they'd first met at her deposition, Mary remained without ambiguity. *"She continues to impress the jury with the courage of her convictions,"* he kept saying to himself.

As Tibeau sorted through his written notes, Judge Watson noticed the bailiff flagging him. A few jurors were signaling they need a break.

"Ladies and gentlemen, we'll take a brief recess," said Watson. "Remember my admonitions. Please return in ten minutes."

"Mrs. Valone is one tough lady," said Barton Harrison, when he, Douglas Lee, Walter Tibeau, and clients were gathered in the outer corridor.

"Walt's going to make her crack," Dr. Nasser said.

"Don't be too sure about that, doctor," said Tibeau in blunt contradiction. "I've already taken my best shots at her. I only have a final issue to pursue. After that, our only refuge is to get Mrs. Valone off the stand before she damages us any further."

Douglas Lee braved to speak. "Sir, I don't wish to sound presumptuous, but shouldn't you ask her—"

"Mr. Lee, I was trying cases while you were in diapers," fumed Tibeau. "Your duties are to have ready any documentation I require. Now return to your desk and make certain our materials are properly arranged."

Once Lee had departed, Dr. Cameron said, "Easy, Walt. The boy's only trying to help."

"I know, Doctor," he said. "I'm just growing more and more irritated at how Mrs. Valone is handling herself, not to mention how Watson forces me to my knees every chance he gets."

The quiet Dr. Elliot took the opportunity to say, "Mr. Tibeau, I think it would be wise to get her off the stand. Perhaps you'll be able to catch her son in a lie."

"I doubt it," said Tibeau. "His deposition was just as unyielding as hers. He never once vacillated in any of his responses."

"He's a real hothead," said Cameron.

"He never communicated any such tendencies to me," Tibeau said. "As you and Dr. Nasser suggested, I did everything possible to annoy him at his deposition. The more I tried, the more affable he became."

"Then try harder," insisted Dr. Nasser. "Believe me, it won't take much to get him to blow his stack."

"Maybe," said Tibeau. "We'll see how his direct goes." A hard sigh. "Although if he's as superior a witness as his mother, I'll hardly even bother with him. He's a highly-impressive young man who comes off as altogether believable. We can't have him further buttressing her testimony while adding additional empathy for his mother. Gentlemen, that's a classic no-win scenario if there ever was one."

"Look at them," said Nasser, while eyeing their opposition gathered at the opposite end of the hallway. "That Cook really thinks he's something."

"Can you blame him?" said Tibeau, glumly. "Right now, Bob knows he can win."

"Men, are we ready to talk settlement?" asked Harrison.

"No!" said the tandem of Nasser and Cameron–Elliot abstaining.

Again Walt Tibeau sighed. "We'd better get in there. Last thing I need is Watson berating me in front of the jury for being late."

"Hold up a minute, Walt," said Cameron. "Didn't she say yesterday that she never took any kind of pain-pills at any time in her life until this?"

"Yes."

"Then I want you to get her to testify that she's never asked any doctors besides Mancini and I for pain-pills."

Tibeau shook his head. "It wouldn't accomplish anything, Steve. The jury would come away with the impression that were grabbing at straws. Her pharmacy records are already in evidence. There's nothing improper about them."

"Make her testify that she never asked anyone else for any kind of pain medications," said Cameron. "Trust me, I know she's lying."

"Steve, what's this in reference to?"

"I'll have to tell you later," he said, pointing to the doorway where Douglas Lee stood furiously waving to them. "I'd say the judge's on his way."

Once everyone had resumed their places, Walter Tibeau approached the witness stand. "Mrs. Valone, I've only a few loose-ends remaining. To begin, I'd like for you to explain something to the jury. You've testified that despite your constant prodding, both Dr. Cameron and Dr. Nasser refused to conduct your sed-rate. However what I'm unable to grasp, if that's the truth, then why didn't you ask your own doctor, Dr. Samuel Mancini, to order the sed-rate for you?"

"He wanted to, but I felt it best if I could somehow persuade Dr. Cameron into changing his mind."

"That doesn't answer the question I put forth, Mrs. Valone," said Tibeau. "I asked you why you did not have Dr. Mancini order your sed-rate?"

Mary softly nodded in regret. "Because Dr. Mancini had referred—"

"Motion to strike as non-responsive!" Tibeau called.

"Granted," followed a meek Judge Watson. "Mrs. Valone, would you like the court reporter to repeat Mr. Tibeau's question?"

"No, thank you, Your Honor," said Mary. "I understand his question. May I be permitted to explain, Mr. Tibeau?"

"Please do, Mrs. Valone," said Tibeau. "We're all quite anxious to learn the truth."

Mary faced the jurors and said, "Dr. Mancini had referred me to Dr. Cameron since I needed a neurologist. So following my operation, it was understood that Dr. Cameron was to be in charge of my aftercare. Not Dr. Mancini. I was worried that if Dr. Mancini overstepped Dr. Cameron's authority, it would cause problems between them. At the time, Dr. Cameron was the only neurologist on staff at Valleyview General Hospital. I feared that if I did have Dr. Mancini ask the laboratory at Valleyview to conduct my sed-rate, Dr. Cameron would find out. Then, if Dr. Mancini had need to refer another patient to Dr. Cameron, Dr. Cameron would not accept the consult. To be perfectly honest, I was concerned about Dr. Mancini's medical practice."

"So all you've just said really boils down to is you were afraid of hurting Dr. Cameron's feelings, and that's why you didn't want your family physician to supersede on your behalf," said Tibeau in patronizing whimsy. "Ma'am, my response is that your explanation doesn't comport with your many pretenses that you were in such dire pain during this time."

"Mr. Tibeau, in retrospect, all I can say is that if I had it to do all over again, I would have listened to Dr. Mancini's advice and had my sed-rate taken without any reservations whatsoever as to how Dr. Cameron would have reacted."

"Mrs. Valone, I ask you to look at your jury. Do you honestly think these twelve people that foolish to believe such a preposterous story?"

"It's the truth."

"Is it really?"

"He's badgering, Your Honor!" rumbled Robert Cook.

"Sustained," said Watson. "Counselor, Mrs. Valone has answered your question. Move on."

The echoes of her words complete, Walter Tibeau could hear a murmur of admiration originating from the jurors. Their gesture of applause informed that his calculated maneuver to incite had only strengthened the jury's affections for Mary Valone. As he walked towards the defense table, Tibeau sensed twelve sets of eyes blowtorching the skin from his body.

"Mrs. Valone, I like to touch upon what has transpired after your infection was successfully eliminated," said Tibeau, his intonation now docile. "Immediately subsequent to your antibiotic therapy, to whom did you entrust your aftercare?"

"Dr. Samuel Mancini."

"Could you specify what Dr. Mancini was able to do on your behalf?"

"There wasn't much he could do," she said. "Basically he just monitored my health in general."

"Yes, that's certainly understandable," said Tibeau. "While I'm sure Dr. Mancini is an excellent physician, he doesn't specialize in neurology. Does Dr. Mancini still provide your pain medication?"

"When I need pain medication, yes."

"If memory serves, you now take Vicodin, a far-less addicting drug as opposed to Percocet. Am I correct, Ma'am?"

"Yes."

"Mrs. Valone, just so it's clear for the jury, during the entire tenure subsequent to your operation, you've only been prescribed pain medication by Dr. Cameron and Dr. Mancini. Have I omitted anyone?"

"No."

"Please take your time, Mrs. Valone," said Tibeau in a tone accentuated with kindness. "How about Dr. Charles Tyler from Maryland? Has he ever offered to give you any type of pain medication?"

"No. When I left Johns Hopkins, I didn't need any."

"My mistake, Mary," Tibeau said. "Of course I should have recalled that fact from your direct testimony. Naturally since the procedure Dr. Tyler performed upon you did help eliminate your back pain for a length of time, there wasn't any necessity for you to ask Dr. Tyler for any type of pain medications. True?"

"True."

"And prior to your operation, other than Darvocet samples Dr. Mancini had provided for you, did you ever cause to ask any doctor for pain medication?"

"No."

"Ma'am, I realize that you've been through a tremendous amount of strife, so please take another moment to make certain you haven't forgotten anyone."

"Mr. Tibeau, prior to my operation, all I've ever taken for headaches and such were Advil or Tylenol. I never took anything prescription-strength."

"Mrs. Valone, you're positive that in all the years you've been going to Dr. Mancini prior to your operation that you never asked him for any type of pain medication?"

"Yes, I'm positive."

"How about dentists? Did you ever ask a dentist for pain medication?"

"No."

"Any other doctors you may have asked for pain medicine?"

"No."

"So it's your sworn testimony that until your back problems began in January of 2008, you've never in your life asked any physician for any kind of prescription-strength pain medicine?"

"That's correct, Sir. I'd always been blessed with good health until my herniated disc and subsequent infection."

"Mary, thank you very much for your patience," said a humble Walter Tibeau. "Ma'am, I wish you Godspeed."

"Mr. Cook, redirect?" said Judge Watson.

"Mrs. Valone, now I'd like for everyone to be clear on something," Bob commenced, while pacing towards the jurors. "In spite of how Mr. Tibeau chose to make light as to why Dr. Mancini didn't conduct your sed-rate, isn't it true that you felt having Dr. Cameron order the blood tested was the wisest possible resort, since at the time both yourself and Dr. Mancini believed that you would be continuing to treat with Dr. Cameron?"

"Unfortunately, true," she sighed.

"Mary, you knew hospital protocol. You knew that you would encounter great difficulties finding another neurologist who'd be willing to take you on as their patient if and when Dr. Cameron possibly had, I say possibly had, signed-off as your treating physician. True?"

"True."

"And you found this to be most definitely true once you relieved Dr. Cameron of his duties?"

"Absolutely true."

"To put it mildly, you were stuck with Dr. Cameron. Weren't you?"

"Yes, I was."

Casting a spiteful expression, Bob said, "Yes, you most certainly were stuck with Dr. Cameron."

"Objection," said Tibeau.

"Sustained."

"Withdrawn," said Bob–eyeing the jury to reinforce his point. "Mary, Dr. Cameron and Dr. Nasser have their offices in the Shadydell Heights Hospital Professional Building adjacent to the hospital. You drove yourself to their offices a total of four times. Please describe the traffic conditions you would generally encounter on your way to and from their offices."

"It isn't too difficult a trip," she said. "Although traffic on Route 55 can become heavy near the hospital due to the shopping mall being close by."

"Can traffic become stop-and-go at times?"

"Yes."

"And as I'm sure the jury knows, there are several red lights along the stretch of Route 55 between Vernon Park and Shadydell Heights Hospital."

"Yes, there are," she replied, nodding in concert with many of the jurors.

"Mary, during any of these trips, were you ever involved in any sort of an automobile accident?"

"No."

"Were you ever cited by the police for any kind of moving violation such as speeding or reckless driving?"

"No."

"My, it would seem to me that a person able to drive along such a road in traffic without having a single traffic mishap certainly must have been cognizant enough—"

"Objection as to form," said Tibeau.

"Rephrase, Mr. Cook," Judge Watson said.

"Mrs. Valone, since you were never involved in any sort of traffic altercation while driving to either doctor's office during the time of your infection, isn't it fair to say that you must have been cognizant when driving through such traffic conditions on Route 55?"

"Yes, I was always able to drive safely."

"And despite the many inaccurate innuendos made by Mr. Tibeau in regards to the issue, if you were cognizant enough to navigate through traffic on Route 55, isn't it fair to say that you were equally cognizant while in the company of the defendants?"

"Yes, I was always cognizant when I was at their offices."

"Mary, one last question. If through the efforts of Dr. Charles Tyler, if he is again able to alleviate most, if not all of your back pain, what would you do with any remaining pain medication you might have?"

"I'd flush every damn pill down the toilet."

Cook nodded to the jurors. "Thank you, Mary. Nothing further."

"Mr. Tibeau, re-cross?"

Walt Tibeau peered above his reading glasses. "Nothing else, Your Honor."

Judge Watson nodded his approval. "Mrs. Valone, this Court thanks you for your testimony. You may step down, Ma'am."

The judge then said, "Members of the jury, let's call it a morning. When we return from lunch, counsel for the plaintiff will present his next witness."

CHAPTER THIRTY THREE

John Valone took the witness stand that afternoon. As Robert Cook had hoped, his testimony went without a hitch. Well-mannored, unambiguous and straight to the point for the entire duration. Despite the emotional distress he was under, John responded by displaying an articulate style–a style that came across has highly poignant to the jury.

While Bob Cook's design didn't require him to recount every aspect of negligence that had transpired following Mary's surgery, the attorney selected several befitting instances where John's testimony would best intertwine with hers. By referring to only specific events that John had either witnessed or possessed first-hand knowledge of, thereby adding verification to Mary's testimony, Bob Cook was able to further accentuate many facets of her case the jury was already aware of, while preventing Walt Tibeau opportunity to denounce John's testimony as merely prepossessed embellishment.

John was most inspiring while fastidiously describing the events of March 3rd, when upon his arrival home he had found Mary crawling on the floor. The jury appeared to place his actions in high esteem as he testified how he'd telephoned Sam Mancini to inform him of Mary; drove her to the hospital; insisted she be admitted; then spent the night at her bedside. They never stopped beaming at him as he'd described how he had given Mary her antibiotics. And three of the young women on the jury continued eyeing him with enthrallment.

As his testimony neared its end, Cook had intentionally waited until asking him to relate the chain of events that led up to his physical confrontation with Dr. Nasser. Bob was pleased while discretely studying the jurors' facial expression as John soft-spokenly related the malice behind his forcing the neurosurgeon to order Mary's blood tested. Bob easily discerned the jury didn't hold John's actions against him. Conversely, Bob Cook felt many of the jurors' faces hinted they approved of John's actions towards the unsympathetic Dr. Nasser.

After Bob had concluded, Judge Watson looked to the clock. "Mr. Tibeau, its two-forty-five. Would you prefer to start now or wait until tomorrow?"

"My cross will only take a few minutes, Your Honor," he replied promptly–astonishing the entire courtroom.

"Very well then," said Watson. "You may proceed."

Tibeau arose from his chair and said, "Mr. Valone, did you ever accompany your mother on any of her office visits to either Dr. Cameron or Dr. Nasser?"

"No, Sir."

"Why not?" Tibeau snapped in brusque tone. "Wasn't it obvious to you that she was in pain?"

"Yes, it was very obvious to me that my mother was suffering," he said. "I offered to drive my mother to her scheduled appointments, but she didn't want me to miss work."

"Weren't you concerned about her ability to drive?"

"No, Sir. I wasn't concerned about her ability to drive. I was concerned about her pain."

"Did you ever see—no, strike that."

Tibeau remained hushed, trying to solve the dilemma he was facing.

Judge Watson then said, "Mr. Tibeau, please continue."

Walter Tibeau put forward a casehardened glare. "Mr. Valone, do you enjoy threatening people's lives as you did Dr. Nasser's?"

"Objection," said Bob. "The question's argumentative."

"Withdrawn," Tibeau said, before the judge could rule. "Nothing else."

"Mr. Cook, redirect?"

"Nothing further, Your Honor," said a calm–relieved Robert Cook.

And then court was adjourned for the day.

*****

Wednesday morning passed quickly as Janet Silva first took the witness stand. Janet attested to Mary's exceptional repute, along with the high standards she had upheld throughout the years of her employment at Carbondale-Mercer and Valleyview General Hospital. While Janet praised her friend and former co-worker with accolades, Walt Tibeau held silent–never objecting to a question posed. Bob Cook noticed how Tibeau seemed oblivious as to what was being placed into the record, his mind preoccupied upon the consequential issues yet to unfold. He knew Tibeau was of the mentality that plaintiff character witnesses were of no real import to the jury's deciding the eventual outcome. Bob's reliance was complete when Tibeau declined to cross-examine Janet.

Following Janet to the witness stand was Emil Polachek. Mr. Polachek confirmed to the jury that he had lived next door to Mary for over thirty years, and he felt fortunate to have her as his neighbor. For whenever Mr. Polachek needed assistance, he could always count on Mary's help.

During the afternoon session, Bob called the Valone's Pinewood Lane neighbors, Kim Huber and Nancy Schriver. They offered affirmation that Mary Valone, a once-vibrant woman who'd always seemed to be bursting with energy whenever they had seen her at various neighborhood gatherings or outdoors in her garden the spring and summer previous, had become housebound, a prisoner of her own health. As before, Walt Tibeau didn't raise any questions.

As Ms. Schriver walked towards the rear of the courtroom, Judge Watson studied Bob's conditional outline that detailed the plaintiff's remaining witnesses, and the order in which he was prepared to call them.

"Counselors, please approach," said Watson.

With both attorneys now at his side, the judge said, "Mr. Cook, I see you intend to introduce Dr. Lucas' testimony next. However, you've noted that Dr. Lucas' testimony will last slightly over two hours. Do you have another witness available?"

"Sorry, Your Honor," said Bob. "I do not. I've kept my character witnesses to the minimum as you directed."

"Well then, considering the length of Dr. Lucas' testimony, I think we should wait until tomorrow to begin the presentation."

"I agree, Your Honor," Bob said. "Dr. Lucas' testimony is an integral component of Mrs. Valone's case. By presenting it to the jury split into two stages would only serve to disrupt the continuity of Dr. Lucas' testimony."

"No argument," said Tibeau.

"Tomorrow it shall be," said Watson.

As Tibeau and Cook moved away from the bench, Judge Albert Watson turned to the jury. "Ladies and gentlemen, both attorneys and I have agreed to adjourn a bit early today, the sole reason being the upcoming witnesses' testimony will last beyond three o'clock. But have no fears, we have made considerable progress and we're ahead of the schedule I had estimated. Besides, you've all deserve a break. Please do not forget my admonitions. We'll see all of you here tomorrow morning."

CHAPTER THIRTY FOUR

There was a quiet buzz teeming from the jury box as Judge Watson made his entrance. After engaging in his usual amenities with the more vocal of the lot, the man wearing the black robe of justice stood by a large flat-screen television stationed in front of the jurors. "Sorry, ladies and gentlemen," he said. "We won't be watching Regis and Kelly this morning."

His remark brought a skittish chuckle throughout the courtroom.

"Today's proceedings shall be somewhat different than you've grown accustomed to," said Watson. "The testimony that will be offered is to be presented on videotape. What you'll be seeing are the videotaped depositions of three doctors which will serve as actual testimony in this trial. All were placed under oath, were then questioned by Mr. Cook and Mr. Tibeau using the standard format, the only exception being that I wasn't present. However, I've since conducted a comprehensive review of the testimony in chambers with both attorneys and a video technician. So you'll notice a few edited portions on the tapes when a momentary gap appears on the screen. These voids resulted when one of the attorneys objected to the others question. If I overruled their objection, there won't be any interruption in the playing of the tape, and you are to disregard any grievances stated. However, if I felt the objection was appropriate, I instructed the technician to erase that portion of tape. You'll also hear when one of the parties asks to go off the record. This resulted in a stoppage of filming, which is perfectly acceptable."

Not observing any bewildered facial expressions, Watson went on to say, "Please pay very close attention to the testimony of these doctors. As you would expect, the subject-matter deals with various medical concepts, which in turn involves some scientific testimony. Therefore it can be somewhat complex at times. I suggest you take notes. If there's something you do not comprehend, write it down. I'm sure one of your fellow jurors will be able to provide some insight while you're deliberating a verdict in this case."

Watson took another moment to peruse them–this was the portion he wanted to emphasize. "Members of the jury, please keep in mind that the testimony you shall see today is to be given the same equal validity and consideration as you would give to any other witness who already has or will testify during the course of this trial. Just because testimony has been provided on videotape is not reason for you to assume any sort of unfavorable inferences against the doctors, nor to what they will be attesting to. I assure you this is not the case by any means. Scheduling conflicts or other logistical constraints have led to their testimonies being videotaped. I ask all of you to please watch closely and carefully evaluate what each doctor has to say, while giving their testimony the identical amount of authenticity as you would if they were sitting here before you today."

Judge Watson paused prior to saying, "Are there any questions before we begin?"

Robert Cook gazed in appreciation as the judge signaled the bailiff to dim the lights. The jury trusted Albert Watson–better still, they liked him. Yet in spite of Watson's favorable pledge, Bob wished it hadn't come to this. He wanted Mary Valone's experts on the witness stand, not just images on a television screen.

The first video contained the testimony of Dr. Claude Lucas, a retired board-certified radiologist. Although time's depredations had fallen upon him, his voice gruff, his face wrinkled and droopy, the retired physician from Georgia retained a sublime personality. His catalogue of credentials and achievements were impressive, as Dr. Lucas had practiced medicine for forty-two years as a neuro-radiologist–a specialist in interpreting film studies of the brain and spine.

Seen referring to his report while Cook questioned him off-camera, Dr. Lucas stated that upon reviewing Mary Valone's MRI taken on February 18th, he'd immediately noticed the infection.

While Dr. Lucas was shown pointing to the film best depicting where infection was most apparent, Bob was heard to say, "Dr. Lucas, have you reviewed both sets of MRI's that were provided to you?"

"I have."

"The MRI that you are currently directing our attention to was taken when?"

"February 18th, of 2008."

"Dr. Lucas, have you formulated an opinion with a reasonable degree of medical certainty as to the performance in this case of Dr. Steven Cameron, the neurologist who claims infection wasn't visible on Mrs. Valone's MRI that was conducted on February 18th?"

"Yes. In my professional opinion, Dr. Cameron misinterpreted Mrs. Valone's MRI. The infection delineated is very discernable. Hence he failed to draw the appropriate conclusion that the lady was infected, the source of origin being the abscessed pocket in the soft tissue masses contiguous to the L4-L5 disc-space."

"And in reference to Mrs. Valone's MRI conducted on March 3rd, of 2008, please tell the jury in your professional medical opinion as to how you would categorize Mrs. Valone's infection at that point."

"Mrs. Valone's infection on the March 3rd MRI was undeniable."

"Dr. Lucas, in your expert medical opinion, did Dr. Cameron's many oversights fall below the accepted normal standards of professional medical competency in regards to his to his care and treatment of Mrs. Mary Valone?"

"They most certainly did."

Walt Tibeau had begun his cross-examination by attempting to cast doubt on Dr. Lucas' present-day capabilities due to the fact he was now retired. While he didn't ask the doctor's age, Tibeau posed several questions pertaining to Lucas' career–making it easy for the jury to approximate.

His next onslaught revolved around the idea that Dr. Lucas was, as Tibeau's had phrased it, a 'professional and available witness.' He did so by inquiring about the fees Lucas was being paid to render his opinion. Tibeau then attacked Dr. Lucas' previous appearances in numerous trials across America by forcing the doctor to admit that since his retirement, he'd never once testified for a defendant in a malpractice lawsuit–thereby insinuating his viewpoint must be biased in favor of the plaintiff.

After taking the better part of an hour, Walter Tibeau was satisfied that he had established sufficient inroads for skepticism that the elderly physician's opinions were slanted solely for monetary gain. "Dr. Lucas, allow me to pose a hypothetical question," he was heard saying in a voice that exuded a high degree of confidence. "I ask you to presume that another physician besides Dr. Steven Cameron had evaluated Mrs. Valone's films. Are you taking the position that you're more qualified in the field of neuro-radiology than they might be?"

"I am."

"Alright. Now presume that the doctor who reviewed Mrs. Valone's films is a board-certified neuro-radiologist such as you are. However this doctor is presently in the prime of his career. Therefore his training and continuous learning experiences in the field of neuro-radiology would certainly place his level of expertise to be, at the very least, equivalent to your own. Bearing this scenario in mind, do you still take the position that your opinion must be superior?"

"Yes, I do."

"May I ask why?"

"Sir, any competent radiologist would not have overlooked the infection present in Mrs. Valone. That is, not unless they were as inept as Dr. Cameron."

With the camera remaining trained upon Dr. Lucas, there was a fleeting period of silence. Tibeau had longed to vigorously contest the doctor's response, yet chose against it. Lucas was a crafty old bird, unyielding in his beliefs. To dispute the issue further would have done more harm. Tibeau then said, "Dr. Lucas, is it a fair assessment to make that in any field of specialization involved with radiology, all forms of visual imaging are subject to interpretation?"

"They are, thought to limited extent."

"And during your long career, haven't you either seen examples yourself or read about them in the literature where, let's say, five perfectly competent radiologist may have reached an identical diagnosis about a patient. However, a sixth radiologist then arrived at a contradictory conclusion upon examining the same films as the others had, and that lone radiologist's diagnosis was eventually proven correct. Situations such as this do occur from time to time, don't they, Dr. Lucas?"

"On exceptionally rare occasions, yes."

"And despite all of the marvelous technological advancements made in recent years, isn't there always some margin of error in any of the specific disciplines of medicine?"

"Unfortunately true."

"Therefore wouldn't it be fair to say there's always some degree of doubt when it comes to the final conclusions of any radiologist, regardless of how proficient his or her qualifications and expertise might be?"

"Not in this case there isn't."

"Your answer is solely based upon the premise that you believe Dr. Cameron misinterpreted the images that you say conclusively denoted infection. Isn't that correct, Dr. Lucas?"

"Oh, they were misinterpreted. There's absolutely no question about it."

"Perhaps another radiologist viewed these same images as being something else other than infection. Isn't that possible, Dr. Lucas?"

"Certainly is, Sir," said the doctor. "I would not be testifying on behalf of Mrs. Valone if the infection had been correctly identified. Although for the life of me, I couldn't even begin to speculate on what they thought was depicted on the MRI's."

Dr. Lucas' eyes shifted downward. "However, my professional judgment of Dr. Cameron's gross negligence is not restricted to my inspection of the lady's MRI's. My judgment is also founded upon the fact that not one mention was made anywhere in Dr. Cameron's February 18th report of anything abnormal being visible on the MRI. Regardless of what Dr. Cameron may have attributed any abnormality to, he still should have noted it on his report. It is standard medical procedure to list anything out of the ordinary in the report summary. Yet Dr. Cameron's comments in the report state that everything appeared normal. In my professional opinion, this was a significant omission on Dr. Cameron's part. An omission so erroneous that it strongly suggests that Dr. Cameron's abilities to properly evaluate any type of medical images aren't anywhere near the level of professional competency."

"In your opinion," Tibeau sparred, in tone reeking of sarcasm.

"Yes, in my professional medical opinion."

"Nothing further, Doctor."

Next was the testimony of Dr. Judith Rathway, a semi-retired neurosurgeon who still practiced in South Carolina. An attractive woman, she cast an appearance youthful than her sixty-three years of life should have beset upon her. Tastefully attired in a blue dress adorned only by a modest strand of pearls, her onscreen image suggested both professionalism and charisma. The fact that she was a woman who achieved great success in medicine had made Dr. Rathway an easy choice for Robert Cook. In addition to her intelligence and pleasant aura, Bob knew she would impress the female jurors by being the only woman physician who would be testifying in a trail dominated by all the male doctors on Tibeau's finalized witness list.

After they'd discussed her curriculum vitae, Dr. Rathway placed a small skeletal model of the human spine upon her desk. She proceeded to provide the jury with a basal understanding as to how the many intricacies of the human spine functioned, while correlating Bob's questions as they related to Mary Valone. While Dr. Rathway offered concise explanations, her responses contained mostly fundamental terminologies. As Bob had asked of her, Dr. Rathway wanted the jury to be able to grasp the concepts, yet she wasn't coming across as a sacrosanct of the medical community talking down to peons.

The lesson in human anatomy completed, Bob began his questioning in earnest. "Dr. Rathway, have you reviewed all of the pertinent materials of this case, including the deposition of Dr. Rasheem Nasser?"

"Indeed I have, Mr. Cook," she replied, her voice remaining a sweet harmony of gentle assertiveness and southern charm.

"Dr. Rathway, were you able to arrive at an opinion based upon a reasonable degree of medical certainty as to whether Dr. Nasser was negligent in his care rendered to Mrs. Valone at any time subsequent to his performing surgery upon Mrs. Valone on January 17th, 2008?"

"Yes, I have."

"What is your professional medical opinion, Dr. Rathway?"

"His actions were extremely negligent. The basis of my opinion is that he operated upon a patient whose recovery progressed exceptionally well for the immediate two weeks subsequent to her surgery. But shortly thereafter, Mrs. Valone began experiencing intense pain that devastated her. And Mrs. Valone continued to have persistent, intense pain for the next three to four weeks, displaying the typical symptoms and behavior patterns of a patient suffering from a disc-space infection. Obviously this was something Dr. Nasser failed to consider."

"Doctor, isn't there an unsophisticated blood test indicated whenever a physician does suspect any type of bodily infection?"

"Yes. The sedimentation-rate is always taken."

"Dr. Rathway, I'd ask you to state with a reasonable degree of medical certainty, whether or not the actions of Dr. Nasser with respect to his treatment of Mary Valone constituted a deviation from normal, accepted standards of medical care during this same timeframe?"

"Yes. Most definitely."

"Please explain why you're so strongly inclined to believe so."

"The simple truth is that Dr. Nasser failed miserably in his communications with Mrs. Valone. Apparently he must have felt she was a complaining or unstable patient. However, regardless of how he perceived her, as Mrs. Valone's surgeon it was his responsibility to make certain of all the facts. Dr. Nasser should have ordered Mrs. Valone's sed-rate taken immediately upon hearing she was experiencing even the slightest amount of pain. Or he should have instructed Dr. Cameron to take it. Either would have been acceptable. However since Dr. Nasser evidently had assumed Mrs. Valone only being a nuisance, he instead chose to ignore her. That was a very serious breach of medical ethics on his part."

"Dr. Rathway, did Dr. Nasser's actions, again with a reasonable degree of medical certainty, substantially contribute to Mrs. Valone's requiring any additional surgical procedures?"

"Yes."

"Why, Dr. Rathway?"

"Nothing was done to control the acute infection and its spread, thereby resulting in inflammation to the disc-space as well as the surrounding nerves and tissues. This has caused some permanent and irreparable damage. Ultimately when some healing did occur, it left the area scarred, of greater consequence the nerves that radiate through the facet joints at the L4-L5 spinal locality. So unfortunately, due to Dr. Nasser's neglect, Mrs. Valone will have pathological scar tissue contributing to some level of chronic pain for the remainder of her life."

"Could all of this damage have been avoided if Dr. Nasser had simply followed through with Mrs. Valone's sed-rate when advised she was experiencing pain?"

"Yes, without any doubt. The vast majority of damage done to Mrs. Valone's body would have been prevented."

Although Walt Tibeau wasn't nearly as belligerent with Dr. Rathway as he'd been with Dr. Lucas, he followed a similar tact by asking questions that implied Dr. Rathway was shading her opinion because she was being paid to testify. Yet he never made mention of the fact that she was semi-retired. He didn't dare infuriate the female jurors by insinuating she was too old, thus must be out of the loop of modern medicine. Tibeau's philosophy was that most women tend to take unsurpassed umbrage when any man makes such a brazen inference by suggesting one of their own is outdated. To Tibeau, going against such a maxim would have been comparable to playing Russian Roulette with six bullets.

Upon entering the core of his defense, Tibeau had said, "Dr. Rathway, you've based your opinions with respect to Dr. Nasser solely on the information provided to you by Mr. Cook. Isn't that correct?"

"Correct."

"Did you ever examine Mrs. Valone?"

"No."

"Have you even met Mrs. Valone?"

"I have not."

"Doctor, the reality of the situation is that the stack of documents on your desk does not give you any plausible method of ascertaining what truly was said, or any other events that might have occurred between Dr. Nasser and Mrs. Valone subsequent to her operation. Wouldn't you agree?"

"Not necessarily, Sir."

"Why do you say that, Dr. Rathway?"

"Because while I was reviewing this case, I took the time to reconstruct the events as they were chronicled in the documentation as well as reading Mrs. Valone's, Dr. Cameron's, and Dr. Nasser's depositions. Hence it is my professional opinion that I'm very familiar with all of the pertinent issues of this lawsuit."

"That may be, Dr. Rathway. However you've maintained that one of your reasons for assuming Dr. Nasser was negligent is due to your allegation that he failed to properly communicate with Mrs. Valone. I ask you, how can you be absolutely certain this was the actuality of the situation?"

"Mrs. Valone specified in her deposition that she tried to speak with Dr. Nasser at his office and on the telephone, yet he basically all but ignored her. Mr. Tibeau, that is failure to communicate. There just isn't any other way to define it."

"Doctor, suppose I told you that Dr. Nasser was keenly aware of Mrs. Valone's health and he was very concerned about how she was progressing. However, due to his very demanding schedule as a neurosurgeon, he felt it wiser for Mrs. Valone to be seen by Dr. Cameron in order to his better obtaining a comprehensive status of Mrs. Valone's health. Would that fact change your opinion on the issue?"

"Not at all, Sir. In my opinion, that's an extraneous point. It was Dr. Nasser's responsibility to .learn for himself what Mrs. Valone's condition actually was. Something he never bothered doing until the woman was re-admitted to the hospital with a raging infection."

"You're mistaken in that regard, Dr. Rathway. Dr. Nasser did try to help Mrs. Valone at his office subsequent to her surgery."

Even on video, the jury was able to discern how Dr. Rathway's facial expression spewed her displeasure before she'd said, "Yes, and it's my understanding that he treated Mrs. Valone as if she were some complaining neurotic instead of heeding her pleas for help. That alone tells me what a dreadfully callous individual Dr. Nasser must be."

At that moment, Tibeau had felt it best to yield. Dr. Rathway's fervor was escalating to a dangerous crest. "Very well, Dr. Rathway," he'd politely said. "You're entitled to your opinion. Now in reference to your assumption that my clients must be negligent because neither Dr. Nasser nor Dr. Cameron failed to order Mrs. Valone's sed-rate, isn't it a fact that you really haven't any way of knowing with absolute certitude whether or not either physician did attempt to convince Mrs. Valone to have her blood tested for infection?"

"Mr. Tibeau, allow me to clarify my opinion on this matter. While I do fault Dr. Cameron, it's my contention that Dr. Nasser was equally, if not more to blame for this obvious oversight."

"May I ask why you hold such a viewpoint?"

"For God's sake, Dr. Nasser was her surgeon. Mrs. Valone had bestowed her trust in him. Since it was by his own hand that she could have become infected, Dr. Nasser should have taken the lead when Mrs. Valone began experiencing pain, especially when you take into account that she was discharged from Shadydell Hospital in excellent health. The moment Dr. Nasser learned that Mrs. Valone was undergoing even the slightest discomfort, he should have been alerted to check for infection. Yet he chose to disregard the possibility as if Mrs. Valone's pain were a figment of her imagination."

"Yes, but as her neurologist, Dr. Cameron was in charge of Mrs. Valone's post-operative aftercare. Shouldn't this alleged blame be placed upon him?"

"Sir, I can't answer your question as to the legalities of the issue, but morally and ethically, I strongly disagree. It's my position that Dr. Nasser should be held more accountable than Dr. Cameron. It was Dr. Nasser's moral obligation to supervene on Mrs. Valone's behalf, regardless of what Dr. Cameron may have believed. Yet after reviewing this case, I'm of the opinion that Dr. Nasser operated on Mrs. Valone, then to put it bluntly, totally disregarded his fiduciary responsibilities by abandoning Mrs. Valone when she needed him the most."

"Dr. Rathway, to be perfectly candid with you, I would concur with your hypothesis if I wasn't aware of all the facts. However your assumptions are based entirely upon the premise that Dr. Nasser deliberately chose a path of indifference as it applied to Mrs. Valone's post-surgical care. Wouldn't you agree that neither Dr. Nasser nor Dr. Cameron should be held liable for Mrs. Valone's hardships if they did indeed try to convince her to have her sed-rate taken, and then Mrs. Valone, for whatever reason, declined their advice?"

"Mr. Tibeau," said Dr. Rathway with a huff. "Why on God's green earth would Mrs. Valone, whom I understand possesses a greater knowledge of medicine than the average person might, why would this woman who was in such acute pain during this time decline to have an ounce of blood drawn from her arm? Why would she, when it would have conclusively proven infection was the true source of her pain. Sir, you're the one making assumptions. And they make positively no sense to me whatsoever."

"It may seem that way to you, Dr. Rathway," Tibeau was heard. "But with all due respects, you can't swear under oath this truly was the case with Mrs. Valone. Yes or no?"

"No, I cannot."

"Thank you, Dr. Rathway. I've nothing further."

The final video played was that of Dr. Charles Tyler. As did the previous witnesses, every aspect of his personage suggested an unbounded professional. It had taken Bob Cook nearly twenty minutes to detail Dr. Tyler's sterling credentials since the neurosurgeon from Baltimore held a lengthy list of achievements and awards to his credit. Yet all the while they reviewed his accomplishments, Tyler remained humble–almost to the point of shyness about discussing his illustrious career. Off camera, Bob had to signal Dr. Tyler to keep his voice up.

Using a chart that displayed the posterior view of the human spine, Dr. Tyler explained some of the complexities that were involved in a rhizotomy. As Dr. Rathway had, he'd kept his dialog to a level easy to comprehend. Dr. Tyler looked to the camera when he was finished.

"Dr. Tyler, please describe the size of the metallic instruments, I believe you referred to them as trocars, that you used while performing Mary Valone's rhizotomy."

"The trocars I used on Mary were eleven inches long. Their circumference measures five-eighths of an inch."

"Similar in size to a common drinking straw?"

"Yes."

"Dr. Tyler, how many trocars did you place into Mary Valone's body during her rhizotomy?"

"Four."

"And approximately how deeply were they inserted?"

"The maximum depth was almost three and one-quarter inches."

"Would their placement have resulted in Mrs. Valone being forced to tolerate some amount of additional pain?"

"Absolutely. Even though her lower back had been anesthetized prior to the insertion of the trocars, a fairly substantial level of discomfort ensues while they are in place, as well as a day or so afterwards."

"And why is it that you can't give Mrs. Valone or any of your other patients a general anesthetic while they are undergoing a rhizotomy?"

"It's imperative they remain awake in order to describe what sensations they're feeling once I've stimulated a nerve root. Otherwise I would be burning nerves without knowing if they were an actual source of pain."

"Dr. Tyler, a rhizotomy sounds pretty intimidating. Let me ask you, did you ever have a patient who had consented to the procedure and then changed their mind at the last minute?"

"Yes. Several."

"To the best of your knowledge, why would you surmise the majority of them did so?"

"Calls for speculation," Tibeau was heard.

"You can answer, Doctor," Bob had followed. "Our judge will deal with it."

"Based upon their reactions, I would say most of them were frightened by the size of the trocars."

"Now in reference to Mrs. Valone, did she ever display the slightest bit of fear or apprehension at any time when you first explained how a rhizotomy is performed?"

"None."

"Not even when she saw the trocars?"

"No."

"How about during her rhizotomy? Was Mary ever frightened then?"

"No."

"Dr. Tyler, suppose I were to tell you there may be testimony offered in Mrs. Valone's trial that will claim she refused to have a sedimentation-rate of her blood taken because she may have been afraid of having her arm pierced by a needle of ordinary size. What would your response be?"

"I would consider it ludicrous."

"Suppose I were to tell you there may be testimony offered in Mrs. Valone's trial that will claim she was abusing her pain medications to the point of being disoriented much of the time. How would you respond to that?"

"Once again I would consider it ludicrous."

"Why, Dr. Tyler?"

"Never once have I seen Mary in such a state. In addition, during the time she was in Johns Hopkins after her rhizotomy, Mrs. Valone continually declined the nurses when they asked her if she needed the pain medications I had approved for her."

"Dr. Tyler, how would you appraise Mrs. Valone's overall character?"

"That's somewhat irrelevant," a kind-voiced Tibeau was overheard."

"You can answer, Doctor," Bob had said.

"Mrs. Valone is a very gallant woman," followed Dr. Tyler. "I haven't anything but the utmost admiration for her. Despite all the anguish she's been forced to endure, Mary has not given up hope. It is my sincere desire that someday I'll finally put a halt to the suffering Mary's been forced to live with due to the flagrant and inexcusable actions of Dr. Nasser and Dr. Cameron."

"Off the record, please," Tibeau had said.

There was a momentary gap in the video. When Dr. Tyler reappeared on screen, Bob Cook had said, "Dr. Tyler is it your opinion that the post-operative care that Mary received was not up to normal and expected medical standards?"

"Yes. Without any doubt."

"Dr. Tyler, thank you for your testimony. Mr. Tibeau, your witness."

"Thank you for your time, Dr. Tyler," Walt Tibeau had said. "I haven't any questions."

CHAPTER THIRTY FIVE

Before trial resumed the following morning, Dr. Samuel Mancini, Janet Silva, and the Valone's were gathered in the hallway near Courtroom 410, as Art McNally stepped towards them at a relaxed gait.

"Where's Bob?" John asked of him. "It's almost time to start."

"Relax, John," said Art, smiling at everyone. "Bob's here. He and Tibeau are in the judge's chambers talking right now."

Art looked to Dr. Mancini and said, "Doctor, Bob told me to tell you that you'll be going on the stand. One way or the other."

"Bob called me early this morning," said Dr. Mancini. "I understand."

While Sam Mancini was explaining what Bob had informed him of, Art McNally–the designated sentry–abruptly cleared his throat, gaining their attention that Dr. Nasser was approaching them.

"Morning, nice people," Dr. Nasser said. "You, too, Valone."

"Fuck you," immediately came John's reply. "Get away from us or you'll be spittin' teeth."

With a wry smirk, Dr. Nasser continued on his way.

*****

"Your Honor!" Walter Tibeau cried out in, the confines of Judge Watson's chambers. "It isn't fair. As Mrs. Valone's current treating physician, I should be entitled to cross-examine him as I see fit based upon what he testifies to as well as his deposition."

"He said it himself, Your Honor," Bob responded, pointing to yesterday's court transcript. "He can't have it both ways."

A protracted silence resulted until Judge Watson said, "Mr. Tibeau, allow me to read the question that you asked of Dr. Rathway. Quote, "Yes, but as her neurologist, Dr. Cameron was in charge of Mrs. Valone's post-operative aftercare. Shouldn't this alleged blame be placed upon him?" Unquote. You put it on the record, Mr. Tibeau."

"Judge Watson, I recall what I asked Dr. Rathway," said Tibeau, maintaining a non-confrontational tone of voice. "You're taking my question to Dr. Rathway completely out of context."

"Mr. Tibeau, please," Watson said, "I've already made my ruling on Mr. Cook's motion. Mrs. Valone explained the circumstances behind her not adhering to Dr. Mancini's advice in regards to the sed-rate when you cross-examined her. Mr. Cook has stipulated in his motion that he will not ask Dr. Mancini to attest to anything derogatory about your clients' post-operative care of Mrs. Valone. Ergo, anything you would ask Dr. Mancini along those lines would go beyond the scope of Dr. Mancini's direct. In my opinion, I feel it an equitable arrangement for both the plaintiff and your clients."

"Your Honor, it isn't justice that Mr. Cook be allowed to dictate—"

"Walt, old boy, face the facts," the judge cut in. "Mr. Cook isn't dictating anything. We all agree on what you asked Dr. Rathway. Also as I recall from Dr. Mancini's deposition, his testimony in regards to Mrs. Valone's post-operative care is entirely comparable to hers. I know you like a book, Walt. You'll do anything you can to make it sound as if Dr. Mancini should be held entirely liable for Mrs. Valone. We all realize that isn't the truth. Ergo, in the interest of justice, my decision stands."

"Your Honor, I'm considering asking for a mistrial," said Tibeau.

Watson cast a stern glare at Tibeau.

"I won't grant a mistrial. In my opinion, you don't have sufficient grounds."

Walter Tibeau pondered the moment before saying, "Judge Watson, your ruling could give me grounds for appeal."

"It's your constitutional right to pursue any appeals process you may deem necessary for your clients," said Watson. "The Court of Appeals is a block across the street. Do as you may."

Yet another quandary for Walt Tibeau. Judge Watson had stymied his intent to belittle Dr. Mancini in front of the jury. Unable to tarnish any of the previous witnesses, Tibeau saw Mancini as his final opportunity. Adding to his dilemma, to risk further provoking the judge would only prove detrimental to his case. Tibeau opted for the conservative path.

"Fine, Your Honor," he said, "I'll abide by your ruling, with one caveat. If Mr. Cook makes so much as the slightest inference to Dr. Mancini as to how my clients allegedly neglected Mrs. Valone, he's then opened the door."

With his hand cradling his chin, Watson said, "If Mr. Cook opens the door, then I will permit you to cross-examine Dr. Mancini along those same lines. Fair, Mr. Tibeau?"

"Yes, Your Honor."

"Fair, Mr. Cook?"

"By all means, Your Honor."

Albert Watson began buttoning his black robe. "Alright, Counselors, let's get out there. We have a lot of anxious people waiting for us."

*****

"Dr. Mancini, how are you today?" said Bob.

"I'm okay, Mr. Cook," returned the humble physician.

Bob moved to his favored spot by the jury and said, "Dr. Mancini, you are Mary Valone's family doctor. True?"

"True."

"Where did you attend medical school, Dr. Mancini?"

"Penn University."

"Excellent university," said Bob. "Doctor, are you a married man?"

"I am. I have my wife Anita and four adult children."

"Dr. Mancini, not only are you Mrs. Valone's physician, was there ever a time when you worked in close proximity with Mrs. Valone?"

"Yes."

"Please elaborate, Doctor,"

"Mary was the Medical Staff Secretary at Valleyview General Hospital until she went on long-term disability last year. I served as the President of the Medical Staff in 2005 and 2007. During those terms, I spent some of my time working in Mrs. Valone's office."

"We've heard testimony that Mary was an extremely efficient secretary. Is that true?"

"Mary excelled at her job," Mancini said, smiling. "Ever since she's been away from the hospital, the office has had as many as three secretaries performing the same job functions Mary used to complete by herself."

"And how do you know this to be fact?"

"I was again voted Staff President for this year."

"Does your position as the Staff President require much effort on your behalf?"

"No," he said candidly. "Just minor data-entry and some paper-pushing. The secretaries do all the work."

"Prior to her long-term disability, how would you, just in general, classify Mrs. Valone's health?"

"Mary never had any health issues prior to her herniated disc."

"How long have you been acquainted with Mrs. Valone?"

"Oh, thirty, thirty-one years now."

"Are you also acquainted with her son, John?"

"I am. I delivered him at birth."

"And you're his doctor as well?"

"Yes."

Robert Cook strolled towards his desk. Glancing at Tibeau, he envisioned him a lion waiting to pounce. His questions to Mancini had been safe. Although Bob had initially planned to discuss the role Dr. Mancini had played in her antibiotic therapy along with her current health, he dared not give Tibeau any opportunities.

"Thank you for your testimony, Dr. Mancini," he said. "I've nothing further."

"Mr. Tibeau," called the judge. "Your witness."

"And how many thousands of dollars are you being paid to testify here today, Dr. Mancini," prodded Walt Tibeau.

"I'm not being paid, Sir."

"Really! May I be so bold as to ask why not?"

"My testimony is a courtesy to Mrs. Valone."

"Your Honor, what is opposing counsel leading up to?" said Bob.

"Move it along, Mr. Tibeau," required Judge Watson.

"Nothing else," mumbled Tibeau in despair.

*****

Having reclaimed there space out in the hallway during the morning recess, Bob Cook said, "Okay, does everyone understand? As much as wanted Dr. Mancini to testify in greater detail, Tibeau would have the legal right to cross-examine him. Then Tibeau would have portrayed Sam as an inferior doctor who failed his patient, and would have insisted Sam be held to blame. After all the expert testimony, we couldn't risk it."

With Mary, John, and Janet all appearing in accord, Mary said, "Bob, I think you did the best thing. It wasn't Sam's fault that I didn't listen to him. Sam's a damn good doctor with morals."

"He sure is, Mary," said Bob, clutching her hand. "Don't worry, once the jury starts their deliberations, they'll realize why I didn't question Sam more than I did. The sed-rate issue is the key element to your case."

"Bob, that Lee kid's heading inside," said Art McNally.

Putting on a serious face, Bob squarely eyed Mary and John Valone. "Alright, I'm warning you. Prepare yourselves. Now it's their turn. Now you'll be listening to doctors without morals."

CHAPTER THIRTY SIX

"Mr. Cook, you may proceed," Judge Watson announced to his courtroom, as the gallery was settling into place.

Bob stood to say, "Your Honor, on behalf of Mrs. Valone, the plaintiff rests."

"Very well, Counselor. Mr. Tibeau is the defense ready to begin its presentation?"

"We are, Your Honor. I call Dr. Steven Cameron."

To the surprise of many, it took only to the lunch recess to complete Dr. Cameron's direct examination. The abridged duration of his testimony paled in comparison to the term Mary Valone had spent on the witness stand. Yet Walt Tibeau's design to secure his clients acquittals was one he'd used successfully for years. His fundamentally-sound objectives were to portray Dr. Cameron a paragon of virtue, while emphasizing his being an integral member of the Pittsburgh medical community. And most paramount, have the doctor well-mannerly disavow the wrongdoings contended by Mary Valone.

Robert Cook had surmised Tibeau's strategy. His nerves taut while his former employer performed his courtroom wizardry with Dr. Cameron, Bob anxiously awaited his chance. He recalled Tibeau's lectures that in any malpractice lawsuit, keep the defendants testimony as uncomplicated as practical. Allow the opposition to bombard the jury with as much labyrinthine documentation at their disposal. Tibeau's viewpoint was simply to have medical testimony prepared to countermand the evidence; thereby leading to confusion; bringing upon uncertainty; consequently resulting in a not guilty verdict.

When court resumed at 1 P.M., Robert Cook prepared to embark upon his long-awaited castigation of Dr. Cameron. Appearing composed as he walked the aisle to retake the stand, Dr. Cameron retained his morning aplomb, his blue suit crisp, his dark red hair coiffed to perfection.

Moving to his accustomed position near the jury-box, Bob dispensed with courtroom formality and charged forward. "Dr. Cameron, you are a board-certified neurologist. True?"

"Yes."

"Neurology being your chosen field of expertise?"

"Yes."

"Your formal schooling and training lasted a total of how many years?"

"Counting my internship, ten years."

"How long did you study radiology while in medical school?"

"Three years. Radiology was my sub-specialty."

"And while you are permitted to render your opinion on all forms of medical imagery, isn't it true that you are not a board-certified radiologist?"

"Yes."

"Approximately how long does it normally take for a physician to obtain the formal education and training needed to become a full-fledged, board-certified radiologist once they've entered into medical school?"

"Including an internship, generally five to six years. Provided of course they pass the board examinations."

"Yet with only three years being the total extent of your education in the field of radiology, you evaluated Mrs. Valone's—"

"Objection!" Tibeau sharply broke in. "Mr. Cook is misrepresenting the facts as they apply in this case. Dr. Cameron testified as to his arrangement with the Shadydell Heights Hospital Radiology

Department. They were responsible for having Mrs. Valone's films evaluated. Not Dr. Cameron."

Before Watson could rule, Bob said, "Your Honor, may we approach?"

Taking their stations away from the jury, Bob went on to say, "Your Honor, the summary reports of both Mrs. Valone's MRI's taken at Dr. Cameron's office were included inside the packets with the MRI's. I'm not contesting the MRI report taken on March 3rd. However on the February 18th report, there isn't any mention of anyone from Shadydell Radiology ever reviewing it. Only Dr. Cameron's conclusions and signature are listed on February 18th report."

"Is this true, Mr. Tibeau?" the judge posed of him.

"Your Honor, Dr. Cameron has since amended the February 18th report," said Tibeau. "Dr. Bernard Schmidt did eventually review Mrs. Valone's MRI."

"Has the initial report already been introduced into evidence?" asked Watson.

"Yes, Your Honor," said Bob. "The initial report is Plaintiff's-14. The amended report is Plaintiff's-15."

"Then your objection's overruled, Mr. Tibeau," said the judge.

"Your Honor, Dr. Cameron testified that he sent the MRI to the Radiology Department at Shadydell Heights Hospital," Tibeau said. "Certainly a clerical error can't be held against him."

"Overruled, Counselor. Now step back."

Seizing the moment, Bob said, "Dr. Cameron, in reference to Dr. Schmidt, he is a radiologist at Shadydell Heights Hospital. True?"

"Yes. For over twenty-five years now."

"Do you ever consult with any other radiologists concerning any film studies taken at your office?"

"Occasionally I may seek other members on staff," said a calm Dr. Cameron. "Although I prefer Dr. Schmidt's opinion. He has a wealth of expertise to draw from."

"Very thorough, is he?"

"Yes. Very thorough."

"You've testified that Dr. Schmidt interpreted Mrs. Valone's February 18th MRI. True?"

"I did."

Instantly Cook stalked towards Art McNally, who handed Bob a paper.

"Your Honor, this is a copy of Mrs. Valone's February 18th MRI report," Bob said. "Plaintiff's-14. May I give it to the witness for his inspection?"

"You may," Watson said.

After Cameron had glanced at the page, Bob said, "Dr. Cameron, do you recognize this document?"

"Yes. It's the incomplete summary report that was automatically generated on Mrs. Valone's February 18th MRI."

"As you may recall, when Mrs. Valone's son retrieved both of the MRI's conducted at your office, this report was included inside the packet with the February 18th MRI. Is that true?"

"Yes. We keep them together all the time."

"Doctor, look at the bottom of the page," said Bob, his voice climbing. "The findings on the report are yours. Yours, Dr. Cameron. There isn't one solitary item listed on the report that mentions Dr. Schmidt or anyone else from the Shadydell Heights Hospital Radiology Department ever reviewed the February 18th MRI. Explain this discrepancy, Dr. Cameron."

"It was due to a clerical oversight."

"A clerical oversight! Isn't that a coincidence?"

"May I explain what truly occurred?" an unruffled Dr. Cameron asked.

"Go right ahead, Doctor."

"Mr. Cook, you must understand that Dr. Schmidt reviews nearly all of my patients' films. Mrs. Valone's first MRI was conducted on February 18th. Dr. Schmidt was away from the hospital from February 17th through March 2nd on family business. As a result, Dr. Schmidt did not review Mrs. Valone's MRI until he returned to Shadydell Heights on March 3rd. Most importantly, since Dr. Schmidt knew he was going to be away, his duties in the Radiology Department were placed upon Dr. Carl Frazer. A member of Dr. Frazier's clerical staff apparently did not see the posted note I had attached to Mrs. Valone's

MRI ordering it be given top priority, and mistakenly filed it in the Radiology Department."

"Why didn't you personally check with Dr. Frazier's clerical people to see the status of Mrs. Valone's MRI?"

"I did," said Cameron. "I was informed that Dr. Frazier had reviewed Mrs. Valone's MRI and all appeared normal."

"When did you contact Dr. Frazier's office?"

"I don't recall for certain."

"With whom did you speak with at Dr. Frazier's office?"

"I have no idea. Perhaps Dr. Frazier can answer that for you."

"Dr. Cameron, regardless of your explanation, the fact remains that yours are the only findings on Mrs. Valone's initial report. True?"

"On the initial report, yes, that's true," he said. "However, please keep in mind that I knew Mrs. Valone had an appointment with me on Monday, March the 3rd. It was later that same evening when Dr. Schmidt and I reviewed both sets of Mary's MRI's. It was then that both Dr. Schmidt and I clearly noted the presence of infection. Hence at the time, my primary obligation was to help Mrs. Valone. Not to worry about paperwork."

Despite Cameron's passing blame onto Dr. Frazier's clerical staff, Bob remained resolute. Though it was evident Dr. Cameron was graceful under fire, Bob intended to continue altering the ferocity of his voice in the hope of provoking Cameron into a fit of temperament. "Dr. Cameron, regardless of Dr. Frazier's clerical people, the fact remains that the only notations made on Mrs. Valone's February 18th MRI report are those made by yourself. True?"

"On the initial report, true."

"Therefore you reviewed Mrs. Valone's February 18th MRI prior to submitting it to the Shadydell Heights Radiology Department for Dr. Frazier's opinion. Yes or no?"

"While it's true that I did review the MRI to a limited extent, I was waiting for—"

"Your Honor, the witnesses' answer is non-responsive," Cook loudly interrupted. "I did not ask what Dr. Cameron was waiting for. I asked if he did review Mrs. Valone's February 18th MRI prior to submitting it for Dr. Frazier's opinion."

"Dr. Cameron, answer Mr. Cook's question," instructed Judge Watson.

"Did you review Mrs. Valone's February 18th MRI, yes or no?" said Bob.

"I tried—"

"Yes or no, Dr. Cameron!"

"Yes," he said begrudgingly, his inflection rude.

"Dr. Cameron, it is Dr. Claude Lucas' expert medical opinion that you are guilty of malpractice due to the fact that Mrs. Valone's infection was clearly visible on the February 18th MRI, and you misinterpreted the findings. Your response?"

"That isn't true. I've stated what occurred with the February 18th MRI."

"Dr. Lucas also contends that you are negligent due to the fact that upon the same MRI report summary, you failed to list any physiological changes to Mrs. Valone's spine. True?"

"No, Mr. Cook," said Cameron. "As I stated in my direct testimony, the report summary was automatically generated before I could amend it. My secretary should not have placed it with the February 18th MRI."

Determined to maintain an up-tempo pace, Bob said, "Dr. Cameron, it's been established that Mary Valone came to your office three times subsequent to her surgery. During your direct testimony you prefaced some of your answers by alleging on all of these visits you advised Mrs. Valone to have her sed-rate conducted, and yet she always declined. True?"

"Definitely true."

"Also when asked why Mrs. Valone had refused to allow you to take her sed-rate, you inferred that Mary must have been, to use your own term, 'confused,' due to her overmedicating herself. True?"

"Yes, I believed that the most logical deduction," said Cameron. "Mrs. Valone admitted herself that she was taking Darvocet supplied her by Dr. Mancini prior to my giving her the first prescription for Percocet."

"Oh, I see," Bob snapped. "So you're blaming Dr. Mancini for Mrs. Valone's post-operative care."

"No, not at all," Cameron said in a tone of voice meant to curry favor.

"When Mrs. Valone was discharged from the hospital, who knew they were primarily responsible for her post-operative aftercare?"

"I was."

"The fact is written on her discharge papers. Isn't it?"

"Yes."

"Dr. Cameron, do you really believe Mrs. Valone was frightened of such a harmless procedure as a blood test?"

"Probably not."

"Therefore in your mind as we speak today, the reason Mrs. Valone refused to have her sed-rate conducted was most likely due to the fact that she was confused because of the excessive amounts of pain medication she was taking. True?"

"Yes. As I've stated, it's the only rational conclusion that I've been able to arrive at."

"Is it fair to say that when Mrs. Valone's problems first surfaced following her surgery, you made every conceivable effort to help her?"

"Sir, I did everything possible to learn exactly what was troubling Mary. Despite our differences here, I still consider Mary a friend. Nevertheless my hands were tied because she wouldn't take my advice concerning her sed-rate."

"Doctor, Mrs. Valone came to your office at approximately four, five and seven weeks subsequent to her surgery. True?"

"True."

"On each occasion, you wrote her a prescription for Percocet. True?"

"True."

"Why did you do so?"

"She appeared to be in pain."

"Doctor, you've testified that you were aware of the fact Mrs. Valone had seen Dr. Nasser on February 26th. True?"

"True. Dr. Nasser and I spoke many times about Mary. We were very concerned for her."

"So all throughout the time following Mrs. Valone's surgery, you had a patient in severe pain whom you had been giving Percocet. Now if you'll recall, Mr. Tibeau totaled the—"

"Your Honor, does opposing counsel wish to ask a question of Dr. Cameron?" harped Walt Tibeau.

"He most certainly does," an unflappable Robert Cook fired back. "Your Honor, Mr. Tibeau goes to great lengths to lay foundations for his questions. Why does he become so irritable when I attempt to do likewise?"

"Proceed, Counselor," said Watson, his knowledge of trial stratagems alerting him a commotion was soon at hand.

"Dr. Cameron, if you were so worried about Mrs. Valone, why didn't you do something for her other than prescribe her Percocet?"

"Simply due to the fact that I wasn't certain what was causing Mary's pain."

"Regardless of your uncertainties, you did know she was in pain. True?"

"To some extent, true."

"Fortunately for Mrs. Valone, her son took her to Shadydell Hospital where the sed-rate was finally performed."

"Very fortunate indeed."

A twinkle in his eyes, Robert Cook stepped around the side wall of the witness stand to position himself directly in front of the doctor. "Gee, Dr. Cameron, now I'm the one who's confused. There's something I just can't seem to fathom about your post-operative care of Mrs. Valone. According to your own testimony, you knew Mary personally. You knew she was in pain. You knew it was in Mary's best interests to submit herself to the blood test. Then why didn't you insist Mary have the sed-rate performed?"

"Despite the untruths that have already been attested to in this courtroom, I did insist to Mrs. Valone that she have her sed-rate taken."

"Dr. Cameron, do you know what perjury is?!" stormed an emotionally-charged Robert Cook."

"I am not lying, Sir!" said Cameron, the level of his voice elevated near Bob's.

"Your Honor, I object," Tibeau hurriedly interceded. "Mr. Cook doesn't have any right to make such a defamatory accusation against Dr. Cameron."

"Sustained," held Judge Watson. "Mr. Cook, control yourself."

Robert Cook's disrespect for Dr. Cameron effused throughout the courtroom. "Know what I think, Doctor? I think you and your pal Dr. Nasser over there just didn't care about Mary Valone."

"Your Honor!" Tibeau shouted.

Yet before Tibeau could chose his next words, Bob Cook thundered, "You and Nasser didn't want her infection found! You both wanted her to die!"

"Ignorant bastard, how dare you!" bellowed Dr. Cameron–his pious façade now a crumbling illusion.

"Order! Order!" yelled Judge Watson, slamming his gavel several times. "Mr. Cook, you know better than to make such a statement. One more outburst like that and I'll find you in contempt. And Dr. Cameron, you'll kindly refrain from any further use of profanity."

"Your Honor, Mr. Cook should be sanctioned for such deplorable conduct," followed Tibeau, attempting to place the moment's strain upon his boisterous opponent.

"Mr. Tibeau, when you're elected to the bench you may sanction whomever you see fit," said the judge. "Until then, permit me to run my own courtroom. The reporter will redact the record accordingly."

"He can't redact that church bell," Bob thought.

Judge Watson waited until the murmurings around the court had quieted. "Now, Mr. Cook, do you have any additional questions for Dr. Cameron?"

"No, Your Honor," said Bob, his hot glare remaining fixated on Cameron. "I'd say we're all tired of listening to him."

Desperate to restore luster, Walt Tibeau began his efforts to rehabilitate his client. While Dr. Cameron's demeanor immediately reverted to proper, Tibeau observed many of the jurors again casting circumspect eyes–their looks so sour, so unsettling, he barely skimmed the areas he was prepared to revisit. It was now imperative to get Dr. Cameron off the stand, thereby not giving Robert Cook any opportunity to goad him further.

Tibeau's plan was to put Dr. Schmidt on next, though decided it preferable to complete the day with five physicians who were availing as character witnesses. The defense's case had suffered a major setback as Bob Cook had effectively drubbed Dr. Cameron. The evils implied now seemed plausible to the jury. Walt Tibeau desperately needed these renowned Pittsburgh doctors to resurrect the jurors' mentality about the embattled defendant before the day was over.

*****

Dr. Bernard Schmidt led off for the defense Friday morning. His testimony would prove gilt-edged, as the polished physician helped add credence to Dr. Cameron's testimony. Schmidt's urbane appearance, in conjunction with his extended curriculum vitae as a neuro-radiologist supported a powerful mnemonic–something the jurors could not overlook.

Now at the quintessence of his testimony, Tibeau said, "Dr. Schmidt, just so it perfectly clear for our jury, is it a fact that you and Dr. Cameron reviewed Mrs. Valone's MRI taken at Dr. Cameron's office on March 3rd?"

"We did."

"When did this review take place?"

"That same evening on March 3rd."

"At approximately what time, Dr. Schmidt?"

"My best guess would be 8 P.M."

"And what was your and Dr. Cameron's diagnosis?"

"Mrs. Valone was indeed infected," he said. "There was a significant finding of an abscessed pocket of infection lineal to her L4-L5 vertebrae."

"Now as to Mrs. Valone's MRI taken on February 18th at Dr. Cameron's office, please tell the jury exactly occurred with this set of MRI's."

"Dr. Cameron did submit them to the Radiology Department at Shadydell Heights Hospital," said Dr. Schmidt. "However I was away due to a family matter. Therefore all of my responsibilities were placed upon Dr. Carl Frazier. Regrettably an inexperienced member of Dr.

Frazier's staff put Mrs. Valone's MRI's in storage. As a result, Dr. Frazier never had the opportunity to review them."

"Yes, that is regrettable," said Tibeau. "Dr. Frazier testified yesterday as to what did occur in your absence. Dr. Schmidt, upon your return to the Radiology Department on March 3rd, did Dr. Cameron contact you?"

"Yes. I spoke with him that same evening."

"Why did he contact you?"

"To inquire about Mrs. Valone's February 18th and March 3rd MRI's."

"So Dr. Cameron was indeed concerned about Mrs. Valone's wellbeing?"

"Absolutely he was."

"Dr. Schmidt, in your deposition, you stated that after you located Mrs. Valone's February 18th MRI, you then reviewed it. True?"

"True."

"Dr. Schmidt, despite your knowledge of Mrs. Valone's condition, please inform the jury what your conclusions were on this MRI."

"Before I begin, I'd like to point out that I never took into account the possibility that Mrs. Valone was infected," said Schmidt, continuing in his unceremonious manner. "I interpreted the February 18th MRI with absolute and total objectivity. As if Mrs. Valone were a healthy patient without any complications being filmed post-operative."

"Perfectly understandable, Doctor," Tibeau said. "Please continue."

After looking to his report, Dr. Schmidt said, "Upon my study of Mrs. Valone's February 18th films, I did observe a shadow in close proximity to her L4-L5 vertebrae. However, I believed the shadowed area was consistent to the bone-graft performed upon Mrs. Valone by Dr. Nassar."

"Therefore your conclusions as a board-certified neuro-radiologist would have been the same as Dr. Cameron's preliminary conclusions listed on the initial report generated at Dr. Cameron's office," declared Tibeau in animated manner.

Schmidt nodded as he continued eyeing the jury. "Yes, my opinion would have been identical to Dr. Cameron's. I would have believed the shadow entirely consistent with the bone-graft as well."

"Dr. Schmidt, at anytime subsequent to Mrs. Valone's surgery, did you ever talk with Dr. Cameron in regards to Mrs. Valone?"

"Several times."

"Generally speaking, what was your opinion as to how Dr. Cameron felt Mrs. Valone's post-operative care was progressing?"

"Sir, I was under the distinct impression that Dr. Cameron was at his wits-end trying to convince the woman he needed more information to conclusively determine what really was causing her pain."

"Therefore, if Mrs. Valone had gone through with the sed-rate when she first began experiencing post-operative pain and the results had indicated the existence of bodily infection, would this have helped Dr. Cameron arrive at the best course of action to take for Mrs. Valone?"

"Without any doubt."

Walt Tibeau held out a hand towards the jury and said, "Dr. Schmidt, one final point. In your professional judgment as a board-certified neuro-radiologist, have you an opinion based upon a reasonable degree of medical certainty whether or not Dr. Steven Cameron should be held negligent in any aspect whatsoever with respect to his post-operative treatment of Mrs. Mary Valone?"

"I do."

"Please tell the jury your expert medical opinion."

Schmidt reinforced eye contact with the jurors. "In my professional medical opinion, I honestly believe Dr. Cameron did nothing wrong. Dr. Cameron's aftercare of Mrs. Valone was entirely contingent upon his ability to gather any and all information on Mrs. Valone, and then formulate the correct diagnosis. I honestly believe those were his true intentions. However, one must consider the constraints Mrs. Valone placed upon Dr. Cameron by refusing to have her sed-rate conducted."

Sensing the pendulum beginning to swing his direction, Tibeau said, "Thank you for taking time from your busy schedule to testify today, Dr. Schmidt. Nothing further."

Slowly approaching the jury-box, Robert Cook gauged Dr. Schmidt an extremely dangerous proposition. Though it was necessary to dispel his testimony, Schmidt had already fallen hard on his own sword to protect Dr. Cameron.

Bob began by saying, "Dr. Schmidt, regardless of your opinion, were you ever present when Mrs. Valone was at Dr. Cameron's office?"

"Objection as to form," said Tibeau.

"Overruled," Watson said. "Witness will answer."

"No, I was not," followed Dr. Schmidt.

"Consequently you haven't any actual knowledge as to what Mrs. Valone may or may not have asked of Dr. Cameron. True?"

"True."

"Perhaps Dr. Cameron just assumed Mrs. Valone wasn't infected."

"No, Sir," Dr. Schmidt held firm. "I've known Dr. Cameron for many a year now. He is an extremely conscientious neurologist, completely dedicated to the medical profession. I'm certain Dr. Cameron did all he could to convince Mrs. Valone to have her sed-rate conducted."

Bob elected not to push the issue. Clearly Dr. Schmidt wasn't about to say anything that could be construed even remotely detrimental towards Cameron. He, alike the defendants, were members of the same fraternity. "Dr. Schmidt, only in reference to Dr. Cameron, after you study his patient's films, how do you normally communicate your findings to him?"

"It depends."

"Would you please expand upon your answer, Dr. Schmidt," said Bob.

"If Dr. Cameron asks me to expedite a particular case, I'll inform him of my opinion as soon as I'm able. If there isn't any pressing urgency, I'll record my observations on the report and give them to Dr. Cameron or one of his staff whenever I see them."

"As to Dr. Cameron's business affiliate, Dr. Harold Elliot. Do you review his patients' films as well?"

"For the most part, yes."

"In pretty much the same capacity as you review Dr. Cameron's films?"

"For the most part, yes."

"Yet Dr. Cameron and Dr. Elliot have their own practice. True?"

"True."

"Dr. Schmidt, I would think that your own duties in the Radiology Department at Shadydell Heights Hospital must keep very busy. May I ask why you burden yourself even further by voluntarily reviewing the bulk of Dr. Cameron's and Dr. Elliot's film studies?"

"Our hospital administrator approves of any staff radiologist to review any doctors' medical images," said Dr. Schmidt. "Provided they are located in the Professional Building next to Shadydell."

"And why is that, Dr. Schmidt?"

"Simple economics, young man. Our doctors bring considerable revenue streams to Shadydell Heights Hospital. Revenues our facility must maintain in order for us to continue providing our patients with the highest quality of medical care they deserve."

"Such as the quality of medical care that Mrs. Valone received?"

"Objection," said Tibeau.

"Sustained," Judge Watson said. "Next question, Mr. Cook."

"Dr. Schmidt, in regards to Mrs. Valone's February 18th MRI. Under the conditions you previously outlined, you've testified that your expert findings would have been exactly those of Dr. Cameron's. True?"

"True."

"Yet your expert findings were proven incorrect by Mrs. Valone's March 3rd MRI taken at Dr. Cameron's office. True?"

"True."

Bob looked to the jurors, his facial expression one of bewilderment as he said, "Doctor, only fourteen days separated those MRI's. True?"

"True."

"Dr. Schmidt, there has already been testimony offered in this trial that substantiates any competent radiologist should have, or at the very least, considered infection a possibility on the February 18th MRI. Your response?"

"Under the conditions I've stated, Mrs. Valone's infection wasn't discernable to me," said Dr. Schmidt, keeping his benign nature intact.

"Yet on the March 3rd MRI, her infection was very discernable. True?"

"True."

"Explain to the jury how that was possible, Dr. Schmidt?"

"Could be any number of reasons."

"Doctor, there is only one particular reason germane in this case," said Robert Cook. "We have all heard testimony that Mrs. Valone was suffering from a massive infection. True?"

"Massive is a subjective term."

"Alright, let's try it this way, Dr. Schmidt. Regardless of how you choose to categorize Mrs. Valone's infection, it was certainly prevalent on the March 3rd MRI. Yes or no?"

"Yes."

"And yet by your own admission, the area of infection was not discernable only fourteen days prior. Yes or no?"

"Yes."

"Then Dr. Schmidt, please explain how on one day any designated area of human tissue could be visualized as healthy, yet only fourteen days later infection is readily discernable."

"Mr. Cook, you must realize there are many variables that must be taken under consideration," said Dr. Schmidt. "Yes, I freely admit that after I had compared both of Mrs. Valone's MRI's, I was astonished as to how rapid the infectious process had spread. I can only surmise it correlated to the specific strain of infectious disease."

"Have you encountered other such instances similar to Mrs. Valone's during your career?"

"Yes."

"Approximately how many?"

"Honestly, I haven't the slightest idea."

"Is it fair to say that situations comparable to Mrs. Valone's occur with some frequency?"

"Vague," Tibeau called.

"Rephrase, Mr. Cook," said the judge.

"Okay, Dr. Schmidt, is it fair to say that in most cases of bodily infection discovered within any patient, the infectious process depicted on an MRI would present itself with more clarity than Mrs. Valone's did?"

"Young man, to answer your question would only be a generalization on my part," replied Schmidt. "Doctors deal in scientific fact. Not generalizations. Established, proven scientific facts. However the concept you seem unable to grasp is that there can be exceptions to even the most quantified scientific fact."

Facing the jury, Bob conspicuously rolled his eyes demonstrating his opinion of Dr. Schmidt's trite response.

"Yes, Doctor, I suppose exceptions can occur," he said. "Dr. Cameron's overall behavior concerning Mrs. Valone's post-operative care has included numerous exceptions—"

"Objection," growled Tibeau.

"Sustained."

"Nothing further," said Bob, refraining from another tumultuous exchange.

It took only ten minutes for Walt Tibeau to questions Dr. Harold Elliot. While it was common knowledge Elliot had not been involved with Mary Valone's aftercare, Tibeau's questions were solely designed to portray him an unaware business associate caught in the crosshairs of an unjust litigation. Since Dr. Elliot hadn't even hinted any of the plaintiff's testimony had been fallacious, a short cross-examination was all that was required–Robert Cook aspired to keep the jury's attentions primed for Dr. Nasser.

"Good morning, Dr. Elliot," said Bob.

"Good morning, Sir," Elliot replied.

"Dr. Elliot, you've testified that you only briefly saw Mrs. Valone on February 18th. Is that true?"

"Yes."

"And following your brief examination of Mrs. Valone, it was your possible diagnosis that Mrs. Valone could have had as you termed, 'mechanical back syndrome.' True?"

"True."

"This diagnosis was incorrect. Wasn't it, Dr. Elliot?"

"It was."

"Thank you, Dr. Elliot," said Bob. "Nothing further."

After the judge had excused Dr. Elliot, Walt Tibeau arose to say, "Your Honor, may we approach the bench?"

With both attorneys standing in their accustomed positions away from the jury, Judge Watson said, "What's on your mind, Mr. Tibeau?"

"Your Honor, I'd like to inform you that I intend to call Dr. Nasser next. I request we take our morning recess a bit early so I won't be forced to stop during my direct."

"Fine by me," said Watson. "Mr. Cook?"

"No complaints, Your Honor."

"Granted, Mr. Tibeau."

*****

As Walt Tibeau had timed it, Dr. Rasheem Nasser's direct testimony was completed only moments before noon. His intention was for the jury to reflect over the neurosurgeon's testimony during their lunch hour. Tibeau had reverted to the technique he'd used with Dr. Cameron–his questions systematically proficient; emphasizing Dr. Nasser's sterling career achievements; while maintaining simplicity for the jurors.

Wearing a custom-tailored gray suit, Nasser was clad in his usual sartorial splendor, his personage on the witness stand manifesting into a genteel aura for the jury to behold. To those unfamiliar, the doctor emerged as genuine. And though he'd remained soft-spoken and courteous, Rasheem Nasser's inability to sequester his trait of a pretentious aristocrat did surface at times–in spite of all Tibeau's coaching.

Yet throughout the week, Mary and John Valone had viewed a trenchant decay in the doctor's once-glorious regal appearance. The magnetizing panache they'd first seen at Shadydell Heights had faded. What had been a captivating face now shown wither. The skin blemishes that plagued Dr. Nasser persisted, the flesh-tone makeup applied about his neck and face unable to sufficiently mask them.

As the courtroom emptied for lunch, Bob Cook remained at his table.

"Robert, want me to bring you a sandwich from the deli?" asked Art McNally, while standing near the exit with Diane Cook, Janet Silva, and the Valone's.

"No, thanks, Art," said Bob. "I want to go over Nasser's stuff again."

"Can I help you with anything, Bob?" Mary asked of him.

Turning towards them, Bob shook his head. “No, Mary, I’m fine. Go ahead and get some lunch. If I’m not sure about anything, I’ll be down.”

While the others waited in the hallway, John hurried to Cook’s side.

“You’re doing great, Bob,” he said. “Now get this fuckin’ guy. Get him good.”

His determination exposed, Bob Cook said, “John, he’ll need a proctologist after I’m done with him. So help me, I’m gonna chew that lying Arab scumbag a new asshole.”

CHAPTER THIRTY SEVEN

"Dr. Nasser, I remind you that you're still under oath," said Judge Watson, the pitch of his words a shade more expressive than they had been with those whom previously had retaken the witness stand.

"Yes, Your Honor," said Dr. Nasser. "Thank you."

With his resolve set to test Nasser's fortitude, Robert Cook glanced at the jury as he moved to his preferred location. A scorching tension permeating the air, Bob noticed the jurors appeared to be bracing themselves for the verbal slugfest they sensed at hand.

Ignoring the customary greeting of the witness, Bob said, "Dr. Nasser, let's start with why you didn't administer antibiotics to Mrs. Valone both before and after her surgery."

"Unless there is a previous history denoting susceptibility to infection, I don't place any of my surgical patients on antibiotics."

"And why is that?" Bob asked, his range of voice openly taunting. "Isn't it considered a practical approach for a surgeon to order a broad-spectrum antibiotic for a patient set to undergo any type of evasive surgical procedure?"

"I would not consider antibiotics a practical approach. I'd say more of a precautionary measure."

"A precautionary measure that's beyond you?"

"Objection," called Tibeau, equally attuned to the pending strife. "Your Honor, counsel is being facetious."

"Sustained," said Watson. "Mr. Cook, next question."

Robert Cook observed the half-smile Nasser tried to conceal by dabbing at his cheek. Even at this early juncture, Bob readily distinguished the metamorphosis of the doctors' personality as compared to the morning session.

"Let's not quarrel over semantics, Doctor. Tell the jury why you didn't order any antibiotics for Mary Valone."

"I believe it an unwise policy to order antibiotics for any patient prior to surgery. I'm from the old-school of medicine that ordains a patients' system will be stronger during their operation and more resilient afterwards if they're not given antibiotics."

"That's all well and good, Dr. Nasser," said Bob. "However wouldn't you agree that infection is always a possibility for anyone undergoing an operation?"

"Infection occurs only in an irreducible minimum of surgical cases."

"Dr. Charles Tyler from Johns Hopkins used a less-evasive surgical procedure than you did, yet he gave Mrs. Valone antibiotics both prior and subsequent to her rhizotomy. Your response?"

"That was his prerogative."

"Yes, that most certainly was his prerogative, Dr. Nasser," snarled Bob Cook, mimicking the doctor's testy inflection. "And based upon the fact that Dr. Tyler did not infect Mrs. Valone such as you did, his prerogative must be wiser than yours."

"Argumentative," called Tibeau, remaining on the edge of his chair.

"Sustained."

"Well, Doctor, rather than further debate the point, let's just say your old-school logic and irreducible minimum theory about infections didn't hold true in Mary Valone's operation. Yes or no?"

"Unfortunately not."

Robert Cook had drawn his first drops of blood–he thirsted for more.

"Dr. Nasser, I'd ask you to describe some of the technical aspects of Mrs. Valone's surgery that you only touched upon earlier. If you have any specific recollections pertaining to Mrs. Valone's operation, would you be so kind as to share them with the jury?"

"Mary had a prototypical partial-herniation of her L4-L5 lumbar disc, with a diminutive fragment encroaching upon her sciatic nerve," he declared proudly, his smile pure reflex when discussing his expertise. "She was fortunate that I was able to extricate the detached segment of disc-material from her spinal canal before it caused irreparable damage."

"Would you classify this type of back ailment as ordinary?"

"Absolutely. Statistical studies show the L4-L5 disc is one of the most common for a person to injure."

"Did Mrs. Valone's surgery pose any sort of special or unusual difficulties for you?"

"None whatsoever. Mary's was a textbook case."

"Was Mary's infection a textbook case as well?"

"Objection!" Tibeau shouted emphatically. "Your Honor, that question is preposterous, even for Mr. Cook's standards."

"Sustained."

Able to hear the church bell chiming, Bob cast a discrete eye upon Walt Tibeau. From the trial's onset, his vaunted adversary hadn't been himself. Even now, deep into the litigation, Tibeau still wasn't the sophisticated montage of poise Bob had heard so many kudos praising his talents. It only elevated Bob's confidence knowing the seasoned attorney realized the scales of justice remained in Mary's favor.

"Dr. Nasser, from what has already been attested to, your post-operative prognosis of Mrs. Valone was nothing short of remarkable. Do you concur?"

"Yes. Mary came through the operation extremely well. Dr. Cameron and I agreed to discharge Mary a day early."

"Maybe you didn't hear me," said Bob, deliberately offensive. "Dr. Nasser, I didn't ask what Dr. Cameron and yourself agreed to. You were Mrs. Valone's surgeon, not Dr. Cameron. I want to know what your own thoughts were on Mrs. Valone upon her release from Shadydell Heights Hospital. What was your own prognosis, Doctor?"

Nasser's facial countenance reverted to surly as he said, "I was very optimistic as to how Mary's recuperation was progressing, and I believed she would make a complete recovery."

"Therefore you did not foresee any problems whatsoever?"

"No."

"If those were your true feelings, why did you choose to ignore Mrs. Valone when you learned she was having back pain some three to four weeks after she had been sent home from the hospital?"

"Sir, I never ignored Mary," he said. "Not in the least. Dr. Cameron always kept me apprised of her situation."

"Is that so, Dr. Nasser?" Bob continued to prod, his baritone voice measured to antagonize. "What about when you learned that Mrs. Valone had gone to Dr. Cameron's office on February 12th, 2008? Were you concerned then?"

"Yes."

"Mary returned to Dr. Cameron on February 18th and Dr. Cameron performed an MRI. Were you concerned then?"

"Yes, I was very concerned."

Bob was building momentum–and the self-centered neurosurgeon was playing right into his hands. "Dr. Nasser, let's discuss when Mrs. Valone saw you at your office on February 26th of 2008. Exactly what did you do for Mary that particular day?"

"I gave Mrs. Valone a thorough examination."

"Really? A thorough examination?"

"Yes, I did," said Nasser. "I suggest you check my office records. They indicate what my observations were that day."

"I've seen your office records, Doctor. They prove nothing."

"Objection," said Tibeau. "Dr. Nasser's office records have been introduced into evidence."

"And will allow the jury to decide what merit should be placed upon them," declared the judge. "Proceed, Mr. Cook."

"Dr. Nasser, according to your direct testimony, you have a clear recollection of Mrs. Valone's entire visit to your office on February 26th of last year. True?"

"True."

"Are you quite sure?"

"I am."

"Absolute, complete, total recollection?"

"Yes."

Bob Cook presented a docile appearance as he said, "Okay, Dr. Nasser, the floor is yours. Please tell the jury in your own words what you were able to ascertain about Mrs. Valone's deteriorating health during your examination."

"I was very troubled when I examined Mary. While there wasn't any swelling or discoloration near her incision, I was concerned about the heightened level of pain Mary seemed to be experiencing. I then told Mary to go to the laboratory at the hospital and have them draw blood for a sed-rate analysis due to the fact I feared infection had set in. Naturally if she had complied, I would have re-admitted her immediately."

"According to your direct testimony, along with the innumerable declarations made in your deposition, Mary spurned your advice that day. True?"

"True."

"And what course of action did you take after Mrs. Valone went home?"

"I got in touch with Dr. Cameron, who told me he was also cognizant that Mary's behavior was becoming somewhat erratic. I again informed him that I was fearful of infection."

"And what did Dr. Cameron tell you?"

"Dr. Cameron advised me that he would be seeing Mary again at his office within a week and he would make another attempt to persuade Mary to have her sed-rate taken."

"Dr. Nasser, if everything would have gone as you intended on February 26th, is it your testimony Mrs. Valone would have been re-admitted that day?"

"Yes. Time definitely was of the essence."

Bob Cook turned to the jury while casually adjusting his tie clasp. "Doctor, there's one tiny detail that you failed to mention that greatly interests me. During this alleged thorough examination, how was Mrs. Valone dressed?"

"She only had her blouse off."

"So if you were actually concerned that Mrs. Valone had developed an infection, and she was so unwilling to go to laboratory next door, why didn't you call the lab yourself and have someone come to draw Mrs. Valone's blood right then and there?"

A pause of indecisiveness before Nasser said, "That was my intent. However, when Mrs. Valone asked me for more Percocet and I declined to give her a prescription, she put her blouse on and bolted from my office."

"She just took off, huh?" Bob snapped his fingers. "Just like that."

"Yes, she did."

"What a crock," said Bob.

"Objection," said Tibeau.

"Ask a question, Mr. Cook."

"Dr. Nasser, during this so-called thorough examination, didn't you tell Mrs. Valone to stop acting like a child?"

"Objection!" shrieked Tibeau. "He's intentionally badgering Dr. Nasser while trying to distort the facts as they apply towards the issue."

"Next question, Mr. Cook," said Judge Watson, keeping in serene veneer.

"Dr. Nasser, do recall Dr. Judith Rathway's testimony?"

"Yes."

"Would this be such an occasion where you failed to communicate with Mrs. Valone?"

"Argumentative," Tibeau claimed.

"I'll allow it," Judge Watson said. "The witness will answer."

"That's her opinion," said Nasser. "I maintain I was always aware as to the status of Mrs. Valone's health."

"Really? Mrs. Valone's telephone records indicate she attempted to contact you twice prior to her returning to Dr. Cameron's office on March 3rd, yet neither call was returned. True, Doctor?"

Nasser squirmed noticeably before saying, "I don't recall ever being informed that Mrs. Valone ever tried to telephone me."

"Failure to commutate," announced a glib Robert Cook.

"Objection," said Tibeau.

"You've made your point, Counselor," said Judge Watson. "Next question."

"Doctor, when was the next time you encountered Mrs. Valone?"

"At Shadydell Hospital on March 4th, 2008."

"When her infection was finally found. True?"

"True."

"Dr. Nasser, do you recall telling Mrs. Valone that your patients', to quote you, 'don't get infections?'"

"I never said anything of the kind. Never."

"So Mrs. Valone is a liar?"

"Yes, she is. Maybe not deliberately since it's been proven that she may have been disoriented because of her drug abuse."

"How about John Valone? Why did he threaten you if you were so willing to order his mother's sed-rate that morning at the hospital?"

"Apparently he misunderstood my intentions."

"Was he disoriented on drugs, too?"

"Objection!"

"Rephrase, Mr. Cook," said the judge, sitting with his chin cupped, seemingly enjoying their clash.

"Dr. Nasser, John Valone testified under oath that he heard you tell his mother that you weren't going to order her sed-rate because it was completely out of the realm of possibility she had become infected. Mr. Valone also heard you say, once again I'm quoting you, 'I don't get infections.' That's why he became so irate! That's why he was ready to toss you from a ninth-story window!"

"He's lying."

A ripple went through the courtroom. Bob Cook allowed it to linger before he said, "Hypothetically speaking, Dr. Nasser, is it an appropriate premise that any surgeon who would make such a statement as 'I don't get infections' would being making said statement out of either sheer arrogance or sheer ignorance?"

Nasser sighed. "Yes, I suppose."

"You suppose!"

Walt Tibeau vaulted to his feet. "Your Honor, I'd ask for a brief recess. This entire line of questioning is unfair towards Dr. Nasser and has—"

"Denied!" Judge Watson forcefully exclaimed. "Sit down, Counselor."

His arms folded against his chest, Robert Cook pivoted towards the witness stand. "Dr. Nasser, you're under oath. You can be sent to jail for perjury in Pennsylvania. Why don't you just admit that your conceited pride would not permit you to believe Mrs. Valone was infected."

"You're dead wrong," replied Nasser, now in contentious tone to match Bob's. "As God is my witness, I did everything possible to help Mrs. Valone."

"Dead wrong, huh. That brings us to my next question. It's more than obvious that you didn't want Mrs. Valone's blood tested due to the fact you knew the results would clearly indicate your negligence. Therefore, who suggested the conspiracy that sought to silence Mary Valone until her infection would have eaten through her aorta and killed her? Yourself or Dr. Cameron?"

"Boy, are you full of it!"

Cook grinned broadly. "Let me tell you something, Doctor. I could say far worse about you. Far, far worse. To think that you're a duly-licensed—"

"He's badgering the witness!" Walt Tibeau cried out.

A slam of the gavel. "Next question, Mr. Cook."

With his facial expression mocking the doctor, Bob Cook returned to his spot next to the jury-box. "Dr. Nasser, if it isn't too much trouble, answer the following questions either yes or no. Prior to Mrs. Valone, didn't you consider yourself infallible to the possibility that one of your patients could ever contract a surgical infection?"

"No."

"Didn't you originally believe Mrs. Valone was just some complaining or neurotic woman who was hypersensitive to pain?"

"No."

"Didn't you criticize Mrs. Valone's behavior when she attempted to explain to you just how badly she was hurting?"

"No."

"Didn't you tell Mrs. Valone to stop pestering you with her petty complaints?"

"No."

"Didn't you even go as far as to call Mrs. Valone a, quote, 'child,' at your office?"

"No."

"Dr. Nasser, it was Dr. Judith Rathway's expert medical opinion that you are guilty of malpractice mainly due to the fact that you ignored the fiduciary trust Mrs. Valone had placed in you. Your response?"

"She's wrong. I never ignored Mrs. Valone."

"Dr. Rathway also claims it was your moral obligation as Mrs. Valone's surgeon to have taken the initiative to uncover what was causing her pain. Your response?"

"What was I to do?" said Dr. Nasser, while shaking his head to the jury. "Mrs. Valone always refused the sed-rate for myself and Dr. Cameron."

"So it's your position that everyone that testified on behalf of Mrs. Valone in this trial is either lying, completely mistaken, or at the very least greatly misrepresenting all of the relevant facts as they apply in this case. Does that about size up your stance, Dr. Nasser?"

"Yes, it does."

The neurosurgeon was startled by the ferocity of Robert Cook's striding towards him. Forcefully slapping his hands atop the wooden railing between them, Bob's handsome face projected a menacing gloss as he readied to pull the bell-rope again. "Dr. Nasser, you disgust me. You, Sir, are a total disgrace to the medical profession."

"Objection," called Tibeau, though his tone almost in vain.

"Sustained," followed Judge Watson. "Mr. Cook, do you have anything else material for the witness?"

"No, Your Honor," said Bob. "I'm through with him."

"Redirect, Mr. Tibeau."

With a sense of urgency, Walt Tibeau sprang from his chair. "Dr. Nasser, since Mr. Cook was so graciously permitted an attempt at reconstructing what occurred the day Mrs. Valone was at your office, I'd like to pose a different scenario. Now at the time you were dealing with a patient who was delirious—"

"Objection!" roared Cook. "Your Honor, despite Mrs. Valone being on pain medication during the time, there has been no evidence presented that in any way proves Mrs. Valone was ever delirious. I ask his wittingly errant term be stricken from the record."

"Granted," said Watson, shaking a bony finger at Tibeau. "You may make your hypothetical, Mr. Tibeau. However you will word it properly."

"Yes, Your Honor," he sighed. "Dr. Nasser, hypothetically you were dealing with a patient who could have possibly been overmedicated due to the strong narcotics they had been taking. Now presume you had just completed your examination. The patient then demands you give them Percocet. They won't listen to your reasoning. Isn't it possible that's why Mrs. Valone hurried from your office before you were able to telephone the hospital laboratory?"

"Yes. In my opinion, it is the reason why she refused to be tested. Mrs. Valone was furious with me when I told her that she would not be receiving any more Percocet from either Dr. Cameron or I until she had the sed-rate conducted." Nasser pointed to Bob, not hiding any ambivalence. "But as I told him, I never got the chance."

"You wanted Mrs. Valone re-admitted that day. Didn't you, Dr. Nasser?"

"Very much so. Mary appeared to be in desperate need of treatment."

"Dr. Nasser, one final item. Despite opposing counsel's brash and totally unfounded criticisms, have you testified truthfully during this civil proceeding where you stand wrongfully accused?"

"Mr. Tibeau, before God, I've spoken the entire truth."

"Thank you, Dr. Nasser. Nothing further."

"Mr. Cook, re-cross?" said Watson.

"That seems to be the reoccurring theme of your entire testimony that you stand wrongfully accused by everyone?" said Bob, his eyes riveted upon Dr. Nasser. "Doesn't it, Doctor?"

"Objection as to form."

"I'll allow it," said the judge. "Dr. Nasser, answer the question."

"Sir, since I haven't committed any disservices on Mary's behalf, I had no need whatsoever to fabricate any of my testimony at this trial."

Cook remained silent as he stepped towards the jurors. At the near side of the jury-box, he said, "Dr. Nasser, these twelve citizens will determine for themselves if you have fabricated any portion of your testimony."

"That's all I can ask," said Nasser, finally in modest tone. "Sir, my testimony has been entirely truthful."

A steely glare from Robert Cook. "Nothing else."

The judge exhaled loudly. "Mr. Tibeau, anything further?"

"No, Your Honor," said Tibeau.

"You may step down, Doctor," uttered the judge, staying within courtroom etiquette.

"Give the jury some extra time to talk about that liar," Watson thought to himself before saying, "Ladies and gentlemen, let's take our afternoon recess early today."

*****

When they returned, testimony was given by four prestigious Pittsburgh neurosurgeons. Well-prepared to come to the rescue of their fallen fellow, the knights in shining armor relayed where their paths had crossed with Dr. Nasser. Surprising none of the sizable audience that had filled the courtroom to capacity since the trial's inception, the essence of their testimony was all too predictable: they all believed Dr. Rasheem Nasser an unsurpassed neurosurgeon whose character was beyond reproach–nor had they ever been so privileged to encounter such a warm and caring individual as Dr. Nasser had demonstrated on a consistent basis.

The next witness, Dr. Wayne Jennson, had been purposely saved to complete the day. Tall, fit, resplendent, with glistening blonde hair, the youngest of the neurosurgeons was an impressive sight to behold. Walter Tibeau recognized what a superlative trump card Dr. Jennson would make–his youth and good-looks alone could help sway some of the female jurors. Dr. Jennson had also spent part of his surgical internship under the tutelage of Dr. Nasser. Tibeau had considered a bevy of experienced neurosurgeons to provide expert testimony, yet selected Jennson with the expectation he would be able to represent dimensions of Dr. Nasser's habitual mores better than any of the four previous neurosurgeons.

In tempo near tedium, Walt Tibeau leisurely reviewed the case with his marquee witness in the limelight. Asking questions carefully phrased to avoid Judge Watson's wrath, he enabled the young doctor to articulate many of the same exaltations as his colleagues-in-arms had before him.

Dr. Jennson was then asked to render his expert opinion to countermand Dr. Rathway's. With an almost melodramatic prose, Dr. Jennson declared Dr. Nasser's abilities in the operating theatre best exemplified the many profound masteries of modern-day surgical techniques. Jennson then substantiated his expert opinion that Dr. Nasser could not be held the least bit answerable for Mary Valone. Although she merited sympathy, Mary was at fault for the adversity that had come to pass. According to Dr. Jennson, the world of medicine would plummet into a state of anarchy if patients such as Mary Valone were permitted to disregard their doctor's advice, thus empowering them to pursue litigation with the allurement of huge financial gain. Considering the current downturn of the economy, Tibeau placed as much emphasis on the subject until the judge compelled him to move on.

Upon Bob Cook's concluding his cross-examination, Judge Watson summoned the attorneys to a sidebar conference. "Mr. Tibeau, I see that Dr. Jennson completes your list. I take it you're going to rest."

"Not yet, Judge," said Tibeau. "I may have a final witness on Monday. A doctor who may be able to rebut specific testimonies offered in the plaintiff's case-in-chief."

"And whom might this be?" queried a stunned Robert Cook.

"Your Honor, by no means do I wish to sound evasive," Tibeau replied. "I'm sorry, I honestly do not know his or her name yet."

"Elaborate further on what you do know," Watson demanded of him.

"Your Honor, since we are not permitted to have our cell phones on while in court, I quit carrying mine," Tibeau said. "However, Mr. Lee does carry his. During our last recess, Mr. Lee checked his cell phone and saw a text message stating that a doctor had called my office, and mentioned they have information germane to this case. Information that would contradict some of the plaintiff's witnesses."

"Where's Mr. Lee now?" said Watson, noting the empty table behind Tibeau's.

"Before Dr. Jennson took the stand, I sent Mr. Lee back to my offices to speak with my associate who sent the text message," said Tibeau. "Mr. Lee has instructions to contact the doctor immediately. Apparently he hasn't been able to speak with the doctor yet."

"Your Honor, this is trial by ambush," rumbled Bob, his voice raised to a level where Watson had signaled him. "Whoever this mystery witness is, Mr. Tibeau planned to use him from the beginning. He went about it in this manner so he wouldn't need to fulfill his discovery obligations. He's used this same motus operandi many times before."

Tibeau remained unshakable as he said, "Not true, Your Honor. Based solely upon what little information I have, I shall only be using their testimony to impeach some of Mrs. Valone's witnesses."

"Very well, Mr. Tibeau," said Watson with a huff. "Just as long as the testimony stays within the scope of what's already been placed into the record."

"I give you my word, Your Honor," Tibeau said. "They will only be a rebuttal witness."

"Does the defense intend to rest after the witness testifies?"

"It does."

Somberly the judge eyed Bob. "Mr. Cook, the law mandates Mr. Tibeau's rebuttal witness can testify," he said. "Provided they do possess information relevant to the litigation."

"Your Honor," said Cook, "I'd request Mr. Tibeau make an Offer of Proof before the witness is allowed to testify."

"Perfectly acceptable, Your Honor," Tibeau said.

Albert Watson's forehead crinkled as he weighed his options. "Alright, Mr. Tibeau, I expect your witness in chambers by Monday at the latest. Mr. Cook, I'll give you until Wednesday to find a witness for sur-rebuttal. If you can't find one, we shall begin closing arguments on Thursday."

CHAPTER THIRTY EIGHT

An aging man clad in a dark pinstriped suit took the witness stand late Monday morning.

"Do you solemnly swear the testimony you shall give will be the truth, the whole truth, and nothing but the truth, so help you God?" asked Clerk of Court Donna Kurtz.

"I do."

"Please state your name, occupation, and place of residence."

"Dr. Donald R. Burke. Doctor of Medicine. Former President of the Medical Staff at Valleyview General Hospital. Vernon Park, Pennsylvania."

"Please be seated."

Walt Tibeau approached the witness. "Dr. Burke, you have a job title similar to that of a previous witness who testified in this trial."

"Yes. Dr. Samuel Mancini. Since 2005, he and I have held the presidency of our medical staff on a bi-yearly basis."

"Would you please explain to the jury as to how this arrangement exists?"

"As of late 2004, our medical staff started electing their president to serve only a one-year term, with each succeeding term beginning on January 1st. Since Dr. Mancini and I are willing to accept the processes of maintaining organization, it has resulted in our taking responsibility for the office every other year."

"So the presidency of the medical staff at Valleyview General Hospital has rotated between yourself and Dr. Mancini for about five years now?"

"Yes."

"Dr. Mancini is currently the Medical Staff President. True?"

"True."

"Dr. Burke, prior to you and Dr. Mancini alternating terms as the Medical Staff President, were there any other doctors who ever held the presidency?"

"No. I was named Staff President when Valleyview General Hospital was founded in June of 2000."

"And you held the office for about five consecutive years before Dr. Mancini and yourself began rotating the presidency in 2005?"

"Yes."

"And Mrs. Mary Valone's job was to be the secretary to the staff president of Valleyview General Hospital. True?"

"True."

"Do you recall when Mrs. Valone was first employed in her former capacity as the Medical Staff Secretary?"

"At the inception of Valleyview General Hospital in June of 2000."

"So you're certainly acquainted with Mrs. Valone?"

"Yes, I am.

"Did you only see Mrs. Valone during your terms as staff president?"

"No. Even when I wasn't staff president, I would see Mrs. Valone at the various departmental meetings. Also, I would drop by the Medical Staff Office quite frequently in order to keep apprised of any ongoing situations and offer Dr. Mancini any assistance he might need. If he wasn't available, I'd discuss things with Mrs. Valone."

"Therefore, Dr. Burke, is it fair to say that you have worked within a reasonable proximity to Mrs., Valone from June, 2000, until she went on long-term disability last year?"

"Yes."

"Be it in the office or at different meetings regarding hospital business?"

"Yes."

"Did you and Mrs. Valone enjoy an amiable working relationship?"

"We had our share of differences," he replied, keeping a strict facial narrative.

"By your answer, Dr. Burke, it sounds as if you weren't on the same friendly terms with Mrs. Valone as Dr. Mancini is?"

"No. Most definitely not."

Walt Tibeau held his audience captive as he readied his stiletto. "Dr. Burke, can you cite a specific instance or set of circumstances that may have caused some animosity between yourself and Mrs. Valone?"

"Something especially comes to mind. I never appreciated it when Mrs. Valone would ask me to give her pain-pills."

Tibeau hesitated, attentive to the assorted groans emanating from some of the jurors.

"Dr. Burke, I don't seem to understand. We heard sworn testimony from Mrs. Valone and her son, John. Each stated under oath that Mrs. Valone had never taken any kind of prescription-strength pain medication prior to the onset of her herniated disc."

"Sir, I dislike saying this, but that is a complete falsehood."

"So is it your sworn testimony that Mrs. Valone had indeed used narcotics for some time prior to her herniated disc, and that she and her son have misled this Court of Law to believe otherwise?"

Dr. Burke turned to face the jury. "Yes."

Another momentary pause before Tibeau said, "Doctor, during the course of this trial, Mrs. Valone's pharmacy records beginning in the year 2008 were entered into evidence. Now in all fairness to the plaintiff, I must admit that not only did I review those records, but I also subpoenaed Mrs. Valone's pharmacy records for the years 2000 through 2007, just in case they might provide any pertinent data relevant to these proceedings. Dr. Burke, the only prescription they indicate Mrs. Valone ever obtained during this entire timeframe was a mineral supplement Dr. Mancini prescribed Mrs. Valone for a vitamin deficiency. If she was using other controlled substances as you say, how would you account for this discrepancy?"

"The pain medications she was taking would not show up on any pharmacy report," he declared, impervious to the heated glares he'd been receiving ever since his entrance.

Casually Tibeau moved to Bob's favored position near the jury-box. "Dr. Burke, would you please expand upon your previous answer."

"The Medical Staff Office is constantly inundated with pharmaceutical sales representatives. It's their job to convince our doctors to use their products instead of a competitor's. When a salesperson arrives, they usually bring complementary samples of their products and set up a display area. The various samples are meant for any doctor on staff to take and dispense them among their needy patients, mostly to their elderly patients on limited incomes. Many of the samples are various kinds of pain medication."

"Dr. Burke, did there ever come a time when you noticed some type of problem with this arrangement?"

"Yes."

"Please elaborate, Doctor."

"I first noticed a problem in August of 2004 when I was Staff President. Back then, we would just leave the displays as they'd been arranged. However I soon began to observe that on many occasions, large quantities of pain medicine were disappearing. So one day after Mrs. Valone had gone home, I counted how many boxes we had remaining. The following afternoon when I arrived at the office, there were twenty boxes missing. When I asked Mrs. Valone if any physicians had taken any samples earlier during the day, her answer was no."

"Do you recall what specific brands of pain medication were missing?"

"I do. Missing were eleven boxes of Lorocet, a drug somewhat equivalent to Percocet in strength, along with nine boxes of Vicodin."

"And as we've already learned, these are relatively potent narcotics, especially Percocet. Wouldn't you agree, Doctor?"

"Absolutely true."

"Dr. Burke, to the best of your knowledge, approximately how many pain-pills in total were contained in those twenty missing boxes?"

"Somewhere in the range of three hundred, give or take."

"And at the time, wasn't Mrs. Valone the only secretary working in the Medical Staff Office?"

"Yes."

"Dr. Burke, regardless of what was missing, it doesn't prove Mrs. Valone must have stolen them. I'm sure there had to be other possibilities."

"Maybe so, Sir," replied Burke, continuing in reserved tone as not to exude any favoritism. "However I then instituted new guidelines where all narcotics were to be locked in a filing cabinet that only the Medical Staff President was allowed to have access to."

"And what, if any, was Mrs. Valone's reaction to this change of policy?"

"Initially she didn't say anything. Then after a few months, every time I opened the cabinet to either store or retrieve pharmaceuticals, Mrs. Valone began complaining about some minor ache that was bothering her. She would then ask me if I could give her a box of samples."

"Did you ever give her any?"

"No, Sir," Burke said. "Those pills were meant to be used only as professional samples for our doctors to give their patients as they saw fit. Yet of far greater consequence, it's against federal law for any doctor to dispense a controlled substance without first ascertaining if they truly need it."

"What did you do next, Dr. Burke?"

"I suggested to Mrs. Valone that she speak to Dr. Mancini about any pain she was encountering."

"And what happened subsequent to that?"

"It put a stop to her requests. However, when January of 2005 rolled around and Dr. Mancini had been elected president, he discontinued locking up the narcotics. Hence Mrs. Valone again had access to the samples. And again, from what I was able to gather—"

"Excuse me, Doctor," Watson cut in. "From what you were able to gather is only sheer conjecture on your part. Limit your testimony to what direct knowledge you swear under oath to be the truth. Not what you assume to be fact."

"You filthy liar!" screamed Janet Silva from the gallery. "Tell them about the girl you were screwing in the doctors' lounge!"

"Order!" yelled Judge Watson, standing as he gaveled the room quiet. "Order! Ma'am, any further interruptions on your part and I'll have the bailiff remove you from the building."

With the crowd hushed by Janet's outburst, silence fell like a curtain. Tension filled the air as Watson continued to stare towards the rear of the courtroom.

"Proceed, Mr. Tibeau," said Watson.

"Dr. Burke, did you ever inform Dr. Mancini about Mrs. Valone?"

"Yes."

"And what, if anything, did he say in reference to Mrs. Valone?"

"He told me not to be concerned, that he would handle the problem."

Tibeau looked to the jury. "So Dr. Mancini was aware of Mrs. Valone's problem?!"

"Objection!" shouted Bob Cook, calling upon every bit of self-discipline to retain his composure. "He's asking for a conclusion."

"Sustained," said Watson. "Move it along, Mr. Tibeau."

"Dr. Burke, you again became Medical Staff President in January of 2006. True?"

"True."

"With respect to Mrs. Valone's situation, what, if anything, happened then?"

"Things reverted back to just as they had been my previous term. I kept the narcotics locked in the filing cabinet, and Mrs. Valone again began asking me for samples. Only by then, her requests were becoming more frequent."

"Since Mrs. Valone was Dr. Mancini's patient, did you again mention her behavior to him?"

"I did. Several times."

"To the best of your knowledge, what, if any, corrective measures did Dr. Mancini take on her behalf?"

"I don't believe he did anything."

"Why do you believe this to be the truth, Dr. Burke?"

"Because Mrs. Valone persisted in asking me for samples of narcotics, despite my telling her time and again that I wasn't about to give her any."

In unhurried foot, Walt Tibeau moved towards the opposite side of the jurors–fixing their field of vision upon himself and Mary.

"Dr. Burke, there's one final area I'd like to inquire about. Dr. Mancini, along with Mrs. Valone's boisterous former co-worker, Janet Silva, testified that Mrs. Valone was an efficient secretary. Would you concur with their testimony?"

"For the most part, yes. However I saw Mary many times throughout the years when it was quite apparent to me that she was in a totally incoherent state of mind."

Another collective wave of murmurs were heard among the courtroom.

Tibeau kept on. "As if Mrs. Valone had taken too many pain-pills?"

"Objection," said Bob. "Calls for both speculation and a conclusion."

"Sustained," ruled the judge, his disfavor unguised. "Mr. Tibeau, I think you've reached your limit with the witness. His testimony for 2007 would only be speculative. As for 2008, Mrs. Valone has already informed the jury that Dr. Mancini had provided her a milder pain medication both prior and subsequent to her operation."

"Very well, Your Honor," said Tibeau.

Walt Tibeau panned the jury, sensing a glimmer of hope. "Dr. Burke, thank you for your testimony. I've no further questions."

"Mr. Cook, your witness," said Judge Watson.

Bob rocketed towards the aging physician. "Dr. Burke, are you familiar with Mrs. Valone's work record?"

"Somewhat."

"Somewhat! You've just testified that you worked in the same office with Mrs. Valone for roughly seven years, and yet you're only somewhat familiar with her work record?"

"Objection," said Tibeau. "Your Honor, the doctor answered Mr. Cook's question as best he could. Dr. Burke is a man of medicine. He doesn't work in the hospital's Human Resources Department."

"Rephrase, Mr. Cook."

The fury on Bob's face was overwhelming. "Dr. Burke, prior to her back problems, do you have any idea of how many days Mrs. Valone ever reported off sick?"

"I wouldn't have any way of knowing."

"Then permit me to afford you with that information," said Bob, as he grabbed a paper from Art. "Your Honor, Plaintiff's-1."

"Proceed, Counselor."

"Dr. Burke, Mrs. Valone reported off her job a grand total of four days after she had been promoted to Medical Staff Secretary in 2000. That's approximately one day's unscheduled absence every two years. Does that sound like the work record of a drug abuser to you, Doctor?"

"Calls for a conclusion, Your Honor," Tibeau said.

"I'll allow it," ruled Watson–against the grain of the law.

"Do you remember my question?" Cook exacted of him, growing more abrasive.

"Yes, I do," followed a calm Dr. Burke. "Sir, since I'm not accustomed to associating with drug abusers on a regular basis, I honestly can't offer an educated opinion on the subject."

His nerves affray, Bob sought to remain oblivious to the expressions being exchanged among the jurors. "Dr. Burke, are you aware of Valleyview's drug policies as they pertain to their employees?"

"My knowledge of the drug policy is nominal at best."

"Do you know that hospital employees are subjected to a random blood and urinalysis whenever hospital administration sees fit to test them?"

"No."

"But you did know there is some sort of drug program in place?"

"Yes. Although I'm not familiar with any of the particulars."

"Are you telling this jury that in all the years you've worked in the upper-reaches of Valleyview General Hospital that you haven't been privy to important policy implementations as they pertain to hospital employees?"

"No, that isn't true. I try to stay abreast of all hospital directives. However my primary concentration has always been for our medical staff."

"So, Dr. Burke, regardless of how knowledgeable you may or may not have been about the hospital's drug policies and how they're enforced, if you knew there was an existing employee drug program in place, why didn't you report Mrs. Valone to the proper authorities on any of those occasions when you described her as being totally incoherent?"

"I didn't want to see her get into trouble."

"Really, Dr. Burke!" he thundered, edging towards the railing that separated them. "You didn't want to see her get into trouble. How very magnanimous of you. But instead you're willing to testify in this Court of Law and commit perjury with your shabby attempt to slander Mrs. Valone's integrity! What rock did you crawl out from under?!"

"Your Honor," said a placid Walter Tibeau.

"Counselor, you know better than that," said Watson. "Next question."

Robert Cook nodded slightly to the judge. "My apologies, Your Honor, members of the jury, and to you, Dr. Burke" he said. "I'm sorry for making such an inappropriate comment. Doctor, please refresh my memory. I believe you mentioned that there were thirty boxes of pain medication unaccounted for when you first realized there may be an issue in regards to the pharmaceutical samples. True?"

"No. Twenty in total."

"That's right," said Bob. "There were eleven boxes of Percocet and nine boxes of Vicodin missing. True?"

"Eleven boxes of Lorocet, a narcotic similar to Percocet," Burke said. "But congratulations, Sir. Nine boxes of Vicodin is correct."

As if he were on the edge of an abyss, Robert Cook stood frozen. In spite of his longing to bring about additional upheaval, he recognized the potential of causing additional damage. Dr. Burke's disingenuous nature added to his crusty veneer marked him dug in for battle, not about to give an inch–Burke's own reputation was now on the line.

"Mr. Cook, anything further?" asked Watson.

Bob turned away. "No, Your Honor. Nothing else."

"Mr. Tibeau," said the judge.

"Doctor, was your testimony today entirely truthful?"

"Yes."

"Didn't you tell me earlier this morning that you wished you didn't have to testify against Mrs. Valone, however you knew it befitting in order to see justice served?"

"Yes."

"Didn't you also tell me that you feel very badly about everything that has happened to Mrs. Valone?"

"Yes."

"Thank you again for coming here today, Dr. Burke. I've nothing further."

"You're excused, Doctor," Judge Watson decreed in cold fashion.

The moment after Burke had made his departure, Tibeau said, "Your Honor, the defense rests."

"Chambers, Your Honor," said Bob.

Judge Watson nodded his concurrence. "Members of the jury, please return to the jury-room. You will be kept posted as to when trial will resume."

CHAPTER THIRTY NINE

Dr. Samuel Mancini was on the witness stand Tuesday morning.

"Dr. Mancini, I'm sorry that I had to ask you to testify again," began Robert Cook.

"Not a problem," said Mancini, his soft eyes already trained upon the jurors.

"Doctor, we have nothing to hide here today. Please tell the jurors we spoke as to what was attested to in this very same courtroom by Dr. Donald Burke."

"Yes, we spoke about Dr. Burke."

"And I specifically informed you as to the insinuations made by Dr. Burke that Mrs. Valone was stealing pain medications from her office. True?"

"Yes, you did."

"Dr. Mancini, how would you respond to Dr. Burke's insinuations?"

"He is incorrect. Mrs. Valone never stole any—"

"Objection," called Tibeau. "Dr. Mancini may only have direct knowledge of Mrs. Valone's office pharmaceuticals during the calendar years 2005 and 2007."

"Rephrase your question, Mr. Cook," said Judge Watson.

"Dr. Mancini, did you ever even suspect Mrs. Valone of stealing any pharmaceuticals from her office during the calendar years 2005 and 2007?"

"No."

"Regardless of any timeframe, has Mrs. Valone ever asked you to give her any pharmaceutical samples from Valleyview General Hospital?"

"Never. The only time I chose to provide Mary with samples, they came from my own office. Not from the Staff Office at Valleyview."

"It was Dr. Burke's contention that Mrs. Valone either stole or constantly harassed him to give her pharmaceutical samples during the latter half of 2004 and all of 2006. How would you respond, Doctor?"

"I don't believe him," said Mancini, shaking his head to the jury.

Bob Cook continued to use his peripheral vision to view Tibeau, whose facial expression was growing more disenchanted with each question.

"Dr. Mancini, Dr. Burke also swore under oath that he told you on several occasions that he suspected Mary Valone may have been hooked on pain medications during the latter half of 2004 and all of 2006. Dr. Mancini, did Dr. Burke ever mention anything of the kind to you?"

"Never."

"Dr. Mancini, you've been Mary Valone's primary doctor for almost thirty-one years now. True?"

"True."

"Doctor, prior to Mrs. Valone's operation in January of 2008, other than your giving her Darvocet, a mild, non-opiate pain medication, did you ever have reason to prescribe any other types of pain medicines for Mary?"

"Never."

"Dr. Mancini, isn't it true that prior to Mrs. Valone's operation performed by Dr. Nasser, you kept Mary off her job for a period of time because you knew she was in pain?"

"That's true."

"And during this same time, wasn't it your intention to prescribe a stronger pain medication for Mrs. Valone?"

"True."

"Yet she declined your offer?"

"True."

"If Mary was as addicted to pain-pills as Dr. Burke has misled this jury to believe, would Mary have declined a more potent pain medication?"

"Not in my experience."

"Dr. Mancini, please refresh the jury's memory. How long have you been a licensed medical doctor?"

"Over thirty-one years now."

"And during those entire thirty-one years, have you ever encountered any patient, any patient at all, who has become addicted to pain medications?"

"Sadly, yes."

"Dr. Mancini, please explain to the jury what physiological changes can occur to a patient who has become addicted to pain medications."

"When a patient does become addicted to any opiate-based medication, they build up a tolerance for the medication. As a result, they crave more of the medication than is prescribed. Eventually if any doctor is unable to gradually wean their patient off the medication, well, from that point, the patient is headed for misery."

"Such as being placed in a rehabilitation clinic in order to detoxify themselves. True?"

"True."

"Dr. Mancini, following Mrs. Valone's rhizotomy at Johns Hopkins Medical Center, you were responsible for prescribing Mary's pain medications. True?"

"True."

"And immediately upon Mary's return from Johns Hopkins, did Mary ask you to give her any pain medication?"

"No. Mary insisted she felt much better."

"Just so the issue is clear, Dr. Mancini, please tell the jury when you did give Mrs. Valone valid prescriptions for pain medications."

"I gave Mary three prescriptions for Vicodin following her antibiotic therapy last year," said Mancini. "And since the discomfort in her lower back is returning, I wrote Mary another prescription for Vicodin two months ago."

Robert Cook waved Plaintiff's-33 for the jury. "Dr. Mancini, your testimony matches exactly what is listed on Mrs. Valone's pharmacy records. Has Mary asked you for any more pain medication since her last prescription?"

"No, she has not."

"Dr. Mancini, if Mrs. Valone were a habitual drug abuser, wouldn't sound medical logic dictate Mary would have asked you for a stronger pain medicine than Vicodin?"

"Yes, it would."

"Doctor, you mentioned that if any patient is indeed abusing a narcotic, the best course of action for them is to be gradually weaned from the medication, else they could end up in a rehabilitation center. True?"

"True."

"Therefore if we are to believe Dr. Burke—"

"Objection as to form," said Tibeau.

"Rephrase," Watson said.

"Dr. Mancini, regardless of the period of time, if Mary Valone was abusing pain medications to the point where she was in an incoherent state of mind such as Dr. Burke testified, in your opinion how would it have been possible for Mary to completely discontinue using pain medicines as your testimony and the evidence indicates?"

"Impossible," he declared. "Mary would have experienced withdrawal symptoms such as fluctuations of her blood pressure, volatile mood-swings, rampant depression, cold-sweats, possible cardiac arrhythmia, perhaps even cardiac arrest."

"Hence weaning any patient off such medications is an absolute must."

"Yes."

"And in all the years you've been Mary's physician as well as your working with her at Valleyview General Hospital, did you ever once notice any of these symptoms?"

"Never."

"Thank you, Dr. Mancini," said Bob. "No further questions."

"And why should we believe you, Doctor?" fumed Walt Tibeau. "Why? Is it because you're so honorable?"

Supremely confident in Dr. Mancini, Robert Cook remained stoic. While perusing the jury, it was now Tibeau's turn to sense his case headed in a downward spiral.

"Sir, I've told the entire truth," said Dr. Mancini.

"So you're comfortable with your position that Mary Valone never abused pain medications in all the years you've known her?"

"Yes, I am."

"Dr. Mancini, regardless of your testimony, it remains fact that you can't say with one hundred percent certitude that Mrs. Valone never stole pharmaceuticals from her office. True?"

"Sir, I wasn't with Mary—"

"Motion to strike as non-responsive!" Tibeau cried out.

"Mr. Tibeau, if I may, I'd like to simplify the issue," said Judge Watson, turning to face the jurors. "Ladies and gentlemen of the jury, we all understand that Dr. Mancini wasn't with Mrs. Valone every single minute of every single day while she was at her office. Is that a fair assertion on my part?"

"Yes, Your Honor," most replied in unity, while others acknowledged in their own way.

"See how easy it can be, Mr. Tibeau," said Watson with a smile. "Now the jury has heard from Dr. Burke and Dr. Mancini. I'm certain they are more than able to ascertain the differences in their testimonies. We'll allow them to decide whom they believe. Any additional questions?"

Tibeau stalked towards the defense table. "I suppose not, Judge."

*****

During the recess called after Dr. Mancini's testimony, the attorneys readied to offer closing arguments. Judge Watson was imposing his standard ten-minute time limit on their last endeavors to convince the jury their side was in right. Although Tibeau and Cook had petitioned the judge to consider waiving his restrictions on final summations, each had come to the realization that ten minutes was more than sufficient. Both men understood they sing the praises of their respective clients until they were blue-in-the-face. In all actuality, it wouldn't count for much. Whomever the jurors believed concerning the sed-rate controversy, along with the rebuttal witnesses were the pivotal issues that would resolve the case.

Walt Tibeau went first. The battle-hardened attorney didn't apply his usual impassioned style that was his trademark. Nor was he about to attempt any smoke-and-mirrors gambits that might turn an undecided juror against the defendants. Instead his approach was to stick to the basics as he revisited many of the issues while pledging his clients' innocence.

When he'd finished spinning the facts as he wanted them perceived, the remainder of his allotted time was spent emphasizing to the jury just how truly moral, principled, and devoted these men they now sat in judgment over really were. How these three doctors had dedicated their lives to such a resplendent pursuit as the vast, challenging domain of medicine. They were restorers of health; compassionate healers; saviors of life. Being a physician wasn't just an occupation to this hallowed trio. It was their calling in life–their sacrosanct vocation. Their careers stood a testament for all that was good for mankind.

Since the burden of proof rested with the plaintiff, Cook held the advantage of going last. Albeit how ethical and heroic Tibeau had cast his clients, Bob set out to topple the fortified barricades that shielded their inviolability. As had Tibeau, he abstained from any grandstanding. For as Tibeau had always preached, if one's case afforded them enough legal firepower to present in a calm, unambiguous format during summation–then by all means do so. Save the cheap showmanship for those desperately scrambling for any last-ditch ploy to avoid defeat.

As Bob made his way through each meaningful juncture of Mary Valone's post-operative care, he in turn emphasized how many valid opportunities Doctors' Cameron and Nasser had to uncover the provenance behind the agony Mary's pain had brought. How tragic and needless all her sufferings were and could possibly continue for the remainder of her life unless Dr. Tyler was able to put a halt to her pain. All due to unmitigated negligence. Robert Cook was magnificent as he so eloquently summarized his case, all the while toning down his vociferous vocal cords. His time waning, he prepared to conclude.

"Members of the jury, despite much of the dubious testimony offered by the defense during this trial, ask yourselves two very important questions while you're deliberating a verdict. Ask yourselves what you would have done if you were suffering from the same intense pain that Mary Valone was forced to endure following her surgery. Then ask yourselves, does it make any sense whatsoever that someone who had just undergone such an operation would then become so mysteriously afraid, reluctant, or unwilling to provide their doctors any opportunity to utilize any and all means at their disposal in order to uncover what the actual source of their pain was for such an extended period of time? Think about it, ladies and gentlemen. This is the asinine rationale the defendants would have you believe. This is the reasoning they want you to accept as it relates to the debacle that was Mary Valone's post-operative aftercare. This is the scant thread that their entire defense hangs by. Think about it. It just doesn't make sense. On behalf of Mrs. Valone, my deepest thanks to all of you."

Judge Watson charged the jury shortly before 11 A.M. He'd made arrangements for lunch and supper to be served in the jury-room so their deliberations wouldn't be interrupted. He also issued them the freedom to determine just how long they would stay before calling it a day if their efforts to reach a verdict needed additional time. He didn't want them rushing to any incorrect conclusions.

After Dr. Elliot had bowed-out, the remaining two doctors and Walt Tibeau returned to his offices in the Kincade Building. Douglas Lee now manned the defense table, ready to call Tibeau the moment word came down.

Having retuned to Pittsburgh last Friday, Barton Harrison roamed the hallways, dismayed he hadn't listened to Tibeau's recommendations about a settlement.

Using his gray suit coat as a pillow, Art McNally lounged on a bench in the hallway, keeping a silent vigil with thoughts of retirement dancing through his head. He would contact Bob when it was time.

Cook, Janet Silva, and the Valone's had gone downstairs to the delicatessen at first. Their stress weighing heavily, they were becoming agitated with the crowd on the mezzanine level just going about their business. Then there were the many loyal supporters of Mary's case who kept insisting she had a winner. With Bob reaffirming that the longer they waited, the better their chances, the decision to get a hotel room was made easy.

One o'clock came and went. Two o'clock. Still no news. Three o'clock passed. Harrison kept popping into the courtroom to chat with Lee. Four o'clock. All those who'd waited this long didn't venture to leave, since they would not be permitted to re-enter the City-County Building unless escorted by either of the lawyers. Time was dragging. With the strain mounting with each passing minute, all understood it didn't bode well for the defense. Six o'clock. All was quiet.

Eight o'clock. The vending machine that sold snacks was empty.

The phone rang at nine o'clock.

Word spread like wildfire throughout the courthouse. "A verdict on a Valone case!" was the excited clamor on the mezzanine. "They reached a verdict! No hung-jury!"

Harrison soon walked into the courtroom. "How long were they out?" he asked of Lee.

"Almost ten hours," said Douglas Lee, not desiring to offer anything else.

"Looks like Penn-Med is up the creek without a paddle," one of the legal cognoscenti who'd been a daily spectator snickered from behind.

"You got that right, mack," another faithful observer commented. "The jury had plenty of time to find them guilty. What really took them so long was they had to agree how much money they should award Mrs. Valone."

The same African-American woman who was dismissed from the jury pool because she had worked in a hospital spoke out. "Hey, Mr. Harrison. I hope they give Mrs. Valone a million dollars for every lie those doctors told."

"Awl, c'mon lady, they can't give her that much," replied the second man, mustering all the sarcasm he could. "If they did, poor Harrison there would have to buy a new calculator. His doesn't count that high."

"Thirty million guaranteed," said another woman. "I know, I've worked as a paralegal. I've never heard so many obvious lies in my life."

"Tact on another ten million for that old goat Burke!" exclaimed the most serene lady among them.

The judge now on the bench after everyone had entered, he motioned for the bailiff to summon the jury. As they marched in, the jurors all wore grim faces, their eyes downcast. A suffocating pressure filled the courtroom as they settled into their seats.

Robert Cook tried to hide his excitement.

Art McNally envisioned a trip for he and his wife to Ireland.

At the defense table, Walt Tibeau sat numb, experiencing a feeling of queasiness. Tibeau could see the vultures circling, now certain his glossy reputation for excellence was about to take a hit.

"Mr. Foreman, I understand you've reached a verdict," Judge Watson said.

"We have, Your Honor," responded Alex Quinn, a stocky postal-employee who had been selected to head the jury.

"Please hand it to the bailiff."

Quinn gave the folded piece of paper to the bailiff, who passed to the judge. Watson looked at it, stared hard with raised bushy eyebrows, then handed it to Donna Kurtz, Clerk of Courts.

"The clerk will please read the verdict," said Watson.

"We, the jury, in the above entitled action, find in favor of the defendants, Dr. Steven D. Cameron, Dr. Rasheem M. Nasser, and Dr. Harold S. Elliot."

"Unbelievable!" someone shouted, as Cameron and Nasser sought to congratulate Tibeau. People leaped from their seats. An incessant buzz rippled throughout the courtroom as if it were one voice.

"Damn fools on that jury!" came chastisement from the crowd of onlookers assembled near the doorway.

"Twelve assholes is more like it!" declared the lady paralegal.

"Order! I'll have order!" yelled Judge Watson.

It was evident to all that Judge Watson was unsettled by the verdict.

After those who remained had quieted, Watson looked to the jurors. "Ladies and gentlemen of the jury, the Allegheny Court of Common Pleas thanks you for fulfilling your civic duty by serving as jurors in this trial. I know it's rather late, but Mr. Cook and Mr. Tibeau would appreciate if you could stay just a bit longer. It's traditional for the attorneys to question jurors after a case has been adjudicated. Those willing to stay shall remain in your seats. However you aren't under any obligation to stay and may leave at any time."

A final rap of the gavel. "We stand in adjournment."

Along with Art and Janet Silva, Cook moved across the aisle to console his client. Mary Valone was a proud woman. Her face remained inexpressive while she gazed at some of the jurors making hurried exits. She held her head high, withstanding her urge to weep.

John Valone remained seated in the gallery, the shocking ending to his mother's trial held him a prisoner of the moment–stark realism of the verdict having knocked the wind from him.

Soon thereafter, Dr. Nasser and a heavily-muscled younger man in a casual shirt swaggered his way. "Better luck next time, Valone," heckled the doctor. "Oh, and by the way, fuck you. Want to try punching me now, go ahead."

Seeing the possible confrontation, Bob Cook rushed to John's side. Dr. Nasser sneered at them, seemingly ready to throw a punch until finally stepping out of reach. He and the body-builder broke into a sadistic laugh as they made their way towards the exit.

"You okay?" asked Bob.

"Yeah," said John, barely audible.

"What'd that piece of garbage say to you?"

"Nothing."

"John, I'm sorry, I just don't know what else I could have done. Despite all their lies, Art and I still thought we were going to win."

"It isn't your fault, Bob."

"Yeah," he mumbled, struggling to recoup his own emotions. "John, I want to talk with the jurors. Then tomorrow I'm going to request a meeting with the judge. I'll stop by the house and let you know what I find out. Take care of Mary. Please tell her how sorry I am."

"Thanks, Bob."

After bidding farewell to Bob, Art, and Janet, Mary and John Valone despondently walked to the parking garage across the street. Still in a state of shock, neither said a word. They were in anguish. Psychological anguish. Anguish that can tear at one's heart forever.

As John closed the window after paying the parking attendant, Mary finally broke their silence. "I still don't believe it."

"Me either."

"How could they not have seen through all of their lies?"

"I don't know, Ma."

"Remember when Dr. Yoder said my infection could have killed me?"

"Yeah."

"Maybe we'd both been better off if it had."

CHAPTER FORTY

The Valone's were inundated with guests Saturday morning. Mary's friends from the hospital. Neighbors. John's friends. What was intended to be a small gathering turned into an open-house. And though everybody meant well, a stifling aura of duress imbued the air. They all realized the miscarriage of justice. Everyone also understood the bitterness that remained deeply entrenched within their hosts.

Bob Cook arrived shortly after noon to find Mary, Janet, and Dr. Mancini in the living room already on their second bottle of wine. Seated around the kitchen table with John were Gene Polachek, Dave Bodette, and Mike Perella.

"Let's hear it, Robert," Janet demanded of him.

Bob Cook sat on the chair across from the couch. He let out a huff before saying, "Six of them stayed, including the three who voted guilty. Every juror there told me they not only respected and felt great sympathy for Mary, they also believed she testified honestly. The three on our side were convinced Nasser and Cameron were completely at fault and refused to believe otherwise."

Cook shook his head when Mike offered to toss him a beer. "But the three who voted to acquit said while they felt Cameron and Nasser did neglect Mary to some degree, they weren't positive if it constituted malpractice."

Bob hesitated, leery of saying, "Mary, the truth is we held the upper-hand throughout the entire trial. Eight jurors voted guilty on the first ballot. But after talking with them, I'm sure Dr. Burke's the main reason why we lost. The three who voted in our favor made it obvious they completely disregarded his testimony. And the impression I got from the opposing faction was they and most of the other jurors were leaning our way when deliberations began because Dr. Mancini's testimony negated Burke's. But in the end, after seven more ballets, it was Burke's testimony that swung the majority's vote against us."

"What about all of Mary's witnesses who testified those sonsabitches were negligent?" flamed Janet, keeping her role as spokesperson. "What was their testimony, chopped liver?"

Cook sighed. "I don't know, Janet. All I can say is that not one of the jurors expressed anything negative about any of our witnesses, including our experts. All those against said they considered the expert testimony a toss-up."

"How in the fuck could they have been impressed with that pack of lies their expert's told!" shouted Janet with peak ire.

Bob wasn't caught off guard by the buxom blonde spirit. "Janet, I wish I knew. All I heard was they believed Dr. Lucas, and they admired Dr. Rathway. And they all respected Dr. Tyler and Dr. Mancini. Still, they made it sound like it all came down to Burke. In spite of their knowing Burke's loyalties were with Cameron, the group who believed there might be some truth to his testimony won-out. Using Burke's testimony as a platform, they were able to persuade the majority there was too much reasonable doubt to find the doctors guilty of malpractice. Truth is, all of the dissenters told me that if there'd been some sort of middle-ground they could have used to decide the verdict, that's the way they would have voted."

"What does that mean! They only wanted to find them half-guilty! Was Mary only half-neglected!"

"So where do we go from here?" Mary spoke out.

"I'm afraid it's hopeless," said Bob in baneful tone. "Judge Watson and I went through the entire transcript yesterday looking for possible grounds for appeal. There aren't any."

"But they were all lying!" said Mary. "Couldn't you use that a grounds for appeal?"

"I wish I could," Bob said. "No, we'd have to prove beyond any doubt that they knowingly and willingly lied while under oath before I could even present a brief to an appellate judge so they could consider a motion requesting a retrial. Mary, I'm sorry. Unless one of the doctors actually confessed to committing perjury, we don't have a chance."

The room remained silent until Janet said, "Sam, tell Bob what went on at the hospital the other day."

"Ryan Orselak came into office this past Thursday," Mancini said, disgust plainly etched upon his face.

"For those of you here who might not know, Ryan Orselak was appointed Administrator after poor, poor, Tony DeTorrio met with such an untimely demise," said Janet.

"He's a decent guy, too," said Dr. Mancini. "Anyway, I told Orselak he'd better inform Burke to keep out of the office when I'm there. As far as I'm concerned, I don't want anything to do with him from now on."

"Damn it, Sam, tell Bob what else Orselak said about Burke!" Janet demanded.

"Yeah, what's the old coot up to now?" asked Bob.

"Burke won't be around for quite a while," the doctor submitted. "He'll be too busy at his own office seeing his own patients, since he'll be attending a medical symposium that's being held in Las Vegas early next month."

"What a joke," uttered Cook. "Frigin' Burke should be arrested for impersonating a doctor. What are you saying, Sam? Just that he's going out there on a vacation he can use as a tax write-off?"

"This is the part that'll blow your mind," said Janet. "Hurry up, Sam, tell him."

Sam Mancini set his glass down. "No, Robert. According to Mr. Orselak, Dr. Burke and his mistress will be the guests of three Pittsburgh-area physicians. Care to guess who they might be?"

Cook's jaw dropped. "Get outta here."

"Yes, Sir. The three defendants."

"Bobby, that proves there was collusion between those fuckers!" Janet blurted out. "Couldn't you get proof of their trip and show it to the judge?"

"It wouldn't do a damn bit of good," Bob said. "Just because Burke testified on their behalf doesn't mean he isn't allowed to associate with them. At most, it would only be regarded as tangential evidence. No, we'd need definitive proof of perjury for an appellate judge to even consider a motion for a retrial."

"Damn it! Get some!"

"Janet, I've been through every last document. There's nothing we can do."

Together the group in the living room looked towards the kitchen table.

"Everyone, we've been talking about this appeal idea all morning," said John. "We all know it's impractical. As much as it hurts, I think the best thing to do is let it drop. Bob did a super job, but we came up one vote short. Sure I wanted them found guilty, but according to Bob's viewpoint on our being granted an appeal, it's useless. We know none of them will ever admit they lied, so why drive ourselves crazy about it. So my mind's made up. The best thing we can do is to forget about any further legal action. Hopefully it'll bring a sense of closure, and my mother can get on with her life."

*****

The afternoon having turned into evening, only Janet remained. She and Mary were on the couch nipping at another bottle of wine when John came bounding up the stairs.

"Ma, I've been thinking," he said, taking a seat between them. "You've been under too much stress for too long now. A nice trip to a warm place before your next rhizotomy would do you a world of good. And Janet, to show my appreciation for all your support during the trial, I'd like for you to go along. A nice vacation is just what both of you need to forget about all of this."

"How about it, Jan?" said Mary, all the wine she'd consumed fueling her spontaneity.

"Oh, I'd sure love to go lay on a beach again," Janet said.

"That's what I want to hear," he said. "It just so happens that while I was online, I looked on Travelocity. They have tour packages available right now for Aruba and The Bahamas."

"Jan, let's go back to that same hotel we stayed at last year," Mary said. "The Ocean Palms Hotel and Casino. I loved it there. The hotel was clean. The beach was beautiful. We even won a few dollars gambling."

"That's one of the hotel's they're offering in the package," John said.

A frown crossed Janet's lips. "Aruba's fine with me," she said. "It's just that I'm a little short on money right now."

"Don't worry about the cost of the trip," said John, as he wrapped his arms around their shoulders. "It's my treat. I'll even give both of you twenty thousand gambling money. Just go have fun. You both deserve it."

"John, why don't you come with us?" asked Mary. "You certainly could use a vacation. And your birthday's pretty soon, too.

"Ah, I don't feel like the beach," he said. "I'd just drink all day like when me and the guys went to Atlantic City. See, Jan, that's another reason why I'd like for you to go along. You'd be doing me a big favor by keeping Mary company. Knowing you, if any beach bums try to put the make on my little mother, you'll tell them to get lost."

Janet hugged him as she said, "Well, if you put it like that, I guess I'll have to keep Mary safe from the rift-raft."

"Great. Then we're all set. Alright, the package they're advertising to Aruba is for eleven days that leaves on Monday, the 27th. I get online and confirm two first-class tickets and a suite at The Ocean Palms Hotel and Casino."

"John, please come with us," said Mary. "You need a vacation, too."

"Ma, don't worry about me," he said, smiling. "I'm okay. I just want you and Janet to enjoy yourselves. You two girls can get suntanned during the day, and hang out in the casino at night."

"What are you going to do while we're gone?"

"Oh, I've got plenty to keep me busy. I need to get my life back on the right track. I'm going to contact some of my connections at the corporations I used to work for and asked if they might need me again.

I have a backlog of work to do on my own computers. Then there's lots of stuff that needs done around the house and yard. The cars need waxed. Heck, I'll even try washing clothes again."

*****

Early Monday morning, Janet drove to their house. John loaded their suitcases into Janet's Lexus, kissed them goodbye, and cheerfully waved as they departed for Pittsburgh International Airport. The garage door that sheltered the Cadillac was opening the instant they turned off Pinewood Lane.

He pulled into Denny Perella's driveway a short time later. Unseasonably cool for late April, the morning breeze brought about a chill as he knocked at Denny's door. No response. John started towards the garage, walking across the cobblestone path.

"Whoever you are, get the fuck outta here!" he heard Dennis yell.

"Hey, Den, wake up. It's John Valone."

Dressed in a dirty tee-shirt and khaki shorts, Denny opened the door. "You picked a great fuckin' day to come visiting," he said with a yawn. "I was up late last night."

"Sorry, Den. Guess I shoulda called first."

"Yeah, yeah, get in here. I'm freezing my nuts off."

While Denny reheated a pot of coffee, John sat at the cluttered kitchen table, pretending not to notice how debilitated Denny's powerfully-built body had become. It was a woeful sight how his muscularity had all but conceded to his cancer. The thickness about his entire person was gone, his body in the process of shriveling to a skeleton. Denny's eyes, though they'd always been dark and foreboding, now shown as if the light of life had already been drained from them. He had the look of a man waiting for the Grim Reaper to stick him into the ground and pat him with a shovel.

"So how's your son doing?" John asked, straining for conversation.

"Good. He likes it a Penn State."

"What's his major?"

"He wants to be some kind of an engineer."

"He's a smart kid, Den. He'll make it."

Already he'd grown tired of the chit-chat. "John, I'm glad you stopped by, but is this a social call or you got something else on your mind?"

"I guess a little of both."

"I figured as much."

After he'd placed their coffee on the table, Denny said, "I heard what went on at your mom's trial. Sorry she lost, but I hope you're not thinking-up something stupid."

"Let's talk about it later."

"No, John. Right now. What are you planning?"

"Dennis, I'm going to kill those fucking doctors," he snarled, his words ringing like cold death.

"Oh, that's real fuckin' smart. What are you expecting to do, just walk into the hospital, shoot the three scumbags, and turn bulletproof when the security guards start shooting at you?"

"All five of them."

"Huh?! I thought your mom only sued three doctors."

"She did. There's two more I want dead."

"John, you're outta your fucking mind! You'll never whack five guys before hospital security shoots you!"

"It's not going to happen at any hospital," he replied in malicious voice. "I'm positive they'll all be in Las Vegas next week for some medical symposium. With a little luck, I'll be able to grab a couple of them in their room, and wait for the rest of them to show. Then they're all history."

"You're crazy! You won't have any way of knowing where they'll be or what they'll be doing. And the second one of them sees you, they'll call Security."

"I'll have to chance it."

"I can't fuckin' believe this! You're actually serious?"

"Damn straight I am."

"Oh, fuck. Okay, I got nothin' better to do. Tell me everything you know about their trip."

"I know for a fact they're all staying at some gigantic hotel that just opened early this year. Ever hear of The Olympus?"

"Yeah, I saw the TV show they did on the opening. But how you so sure they'll all be staying there?"

"Easy. I called Dr. Cameron's office. He has a woman named Agnes working for him. Gullible as can be. I told Agnes that I was a med-school pal of her boss who wanted to surprise him. Agnes was more than happy to give me all the details. Cameron's going to be with four other doctors. They're all flying together, and she booked three suites at The Olympus for two weeks. They leave Friday."

"John, you'll never get away with it. DeTorrio was a turkey-shoot compared to this."

"I don't care."

"Listen to me, stupid! All the Vegas hotels got security cameras up the ass. If you think you're just gonna walk into one of their rooms and start blastin', forget it. You'd need to learn a little about their daily movements first. Your only shot is to watch them for a few days until you see some kind of pattern. Then maybe, just maybe, you can get them when they're away from the hotel."

As John sipped his coffee, Dennis reached for a bottle of Jack Daniel's. Filling his cup, he said, "You're gonna get caught this time, kid. Take my advice. Forget it."

"Maybe. Although I really don't give a fuck anymore. Those cocksuckers aren't going to get away with what they did to my mother. They're not going to get away with all the lies they told in court. No, pal, I'd be miserable for the rest of my life if I didn't try."

Passively Dennis shook his head, knowing John to be endowed with the same obdurate temperament as his own. "You know you can't fly out there."

"No way," he said. "Security at airports is too tight because of nine-eleven."

"You realize how far it is to Vegas?"

"About twenty-four hundred miles. As long as I just stop for gas, I figure it'll take around forty hours. I could make it quicker, but cops love to stop out-of-state drivers for speeding."

"What about sleep?"

"I'll just take a quick nap in the car when I get tired."

"That means you'll be gone for at least five days. How about your mother? What are you gonna tell her?"

"She and her pal Janet just went on vacation. She'll never even know I was gone."

Dennis managed a grin. "Just like the last time, huh. Okay, what about your biggest problem? Let's just say you did kill them and got out of Vegas alive. The minute the Nevada cops get word about the stiffs, eventually they'll make inquiries back here. Then someone who knew the dickheads tells them that the victims were just involved in a nasty lawsuit with your mother. Guess who immediately becomes numero uno on their suspect list?"

"I do."

"That's right, John, you do. Then the state police, the county mounties, probably even the F.B.I. will be pounding at your door. What are you gonna tell them?"

"I talk with Gene. We'll figure something out."

"You can't, John. Then he'll know all about it. I remember your telling me that Gene only suspected you killed DeTorrio. This time, he'll know for sure."

"It's a calculated risk I have to take. I trust Gene. He kept quiet the last time they pressed him."

Placing the bottle of Jack Daniel's behind him, Denny's sunken face displayed no emotion. Suddenly an outstretched arm whisked both their cups to the floor.

"John, you really are a dumb fuck!" he shouted with deliberate insult. "Your plan won't work! They'll catch you! You'll get the electric-chair!"

"I don't care."

"Fuckin' maniac! You aren't gonna take no for an answer, are you?!"

"Would you!"

"Oh, fuck. Welp, it's obvious that everything I just told you went in one ear and out the other. Whatta you want from me?"

"A gun they can't trace, some ammo, and a phony driver's license just in case I'm forced to show ID. Can you handle it?"

"Maybe. What else?"

"That's all."

"So let me get this straight," Dennis said. "You're gonna drive practically two days nonstop, knock on one of their doors when you think the time's right, and if you get them all together, that's when you'll start shooting. Then you'll leave The Olympus and drive another two days home with little or no sleep. That about how you got it figured?"

"Just about."

"John, you're a fucking simpleton! You ain't got a snowball's chance in hell of getting away with it! Any way it goes, you're done for. Can't you fuckin' understand?!"

Valone smiled before saying, "Well, Den, to be perfectly honest with you, I was kinda hoping you'd be in the mood for a road trip. Trouble is, I can't ask. You've got your health and your son's future to consider. No, I'll just have to go by myself."

In spite of Denny's continued piercing glare, the scowl fell from his face. "You know, this probably is the best shot you'll ever get at them. And from what Mike told me, they sure got it coming. Adding insult to injury is some bad shit. Tell you what, pal. I think your chances would be a lot better if I came along for the ride."

"Damn straight they would," said John. "But what about your son if we get caught?"

"Ah, he'd survive. Nothing bothers that boy. It wouldn't affect him financially because I've already put everything in his name. Besides, even if we did get caught, he wouldn't have to worry about me standing trial. I'll be dead by then anyway. So what's it gonna be? You want me in on this or not?"

"Hell, yes!"

"Only on one condition," said Denny.

"Name it."

"Unless I think we got a decent chance of pulling it off, we just hang out for a week and come home. I'm not gonna let you commit suicide."

"Good with me," John said, grabbing Denny's outstretched hand.

Displaying a wide grin, Perella eyed him with whimsy before saying, "Two fucking simpletons. That's what we are, two fucking simpletons. Ah, what the fuck. I always wanted to see Las Vegas."

CHAPTER FORTY ONE

They departed Vernon Park shortly after midnight Tuesday.

Westbound on Interstate 70, they passed through the panhandle of West Virginia and entered Ohio. While John was tense about what awaited them, he kept his uneasiness sequestered. Denny remained overly talkative, almost to the point of being hyper as he entertained one potential contingency after the next–all the while guzzling Jack Daniel's at a rapid rate.

Dawn hadn't arrived as they crossed into Indiana. In his drunken languor Denny had fallen asleep, finally allowing John the solitude he desired. Three hours later, they traveled through southern Illinois. After navigating the maze of congested thoroughfares that weaved through metropolitan St. Louis, the sprawling views provided by the open Missouri plains came as a welcome relief to John. Predominately accustomed to small-town settings, he marveled at tracts of unoccupied land so expansive that spanned the horizon.

Two hundred and fifty miles later at a truck-stop nearing Kansas City, Denny teetered out of the car to find John pumping gas. "Where are we?" he asked with a cotton-mouth.

"Almost at the Kansas border. You feelin' okay?"

"I need to go to the crapper. Go grab a sandwich."

"Nah, there's plenty of lunchmeat in the cooler. Go ahead and get yourself something to eat if you want."

Under normal weather conditions, the flatlands of Kansas would not have posed any difficulties. Yet they bore a rigorous assignment this afternoon. Soon after leaving the truck-stop a pelting rainstorm had begun, only letting up sporadically the entire four hundred-twenty miles across the state. With John focused on piloting through the torrential downpour, Denny continued to discuss the many hurdles they would encounter while swilling his whiskey. John was beginning to grow weary, yet Denny wasn't in any condition to drive.

With the Cadillac low on gasoline, they approached Colorado. Finally they spotted another truck-stop. While Denny pumped the gas, John went about removing the trash they'd accumulated–included were two empty fifths of Jack Daniel's.

They reached Denver after another hundred and sixty miles. Directly beyond the city limits began the arduous climb up the leeward slopes of the Rocky Mountains. The eighteen-wheeler's crawled up the steep, lengthy inclines. What other traffic there was moved at speeds slower than the posted speed limit of seventy-five, the altitude hindering their engine's efficiency. But the Cadillac's engine purred as they soared steadily upward, ascending Interstate 70's mountainous terrain. By full moon's glory they admired the splendor of majestic mountain vistas, their crests kissing the sky remained frosted in snow.

Nearing the ski resort of Vail, John coasted off the road. He was bleary-eyed, the rest- area too inviting to bypass. Making his way behind rows of trucks, he parked at the far corner of the lot. With Denny under a blanket asleep in the back seat, he vied to make himself comfortable. Unable to slow his mind, he tossed about before dozing to sleep.

It was a combination of the mountain cold and the trucker's headlights that induced John to awaken. After he'd started the engine, he headed for the service pavilion. Afterwards, stretching the stiffness from his legs while looking at a map on display, John determined he'd slept less than an hour. Yet he felt totally reinvigorated. His adrenalin was again coursing.

Obsessed by his mission, he resumed the drive. The remaining miles through panoramic western Colorado whizzed by quickly. Already on his third can of Pepsi, he heard Denny stirring as they rounded a hairpin exit ramp, as he prepared to stop for fuel soon after entering Utah.

"You awake, kid?" mumbled Denny.

"Wide awake."

"We still in Colorado?"

"Nope. Just hit Utah."

"How we doin' on time?"

"Close to what we figured."

"Good. I need more sleep."

The cruise-control was set at seventy-five upon resuming their journey. As John admired the expanse of the west, they reached the junction where Interstate 70 came to an end near the town of Cove Fort, Utah, the highway splitting to funnel travelers onto Interstate 15.

Now southbound on I-15, Denny managed to sit up. His system had finally purged the alcohol. "Kid, I need a pit-stop," he said. "I gotta piss like a horse."

"There's another truck-stop a few miles down the road," he replied. "Can you hold it, or you want me to pull over now?"
"I'll wait. I don't want some Mormon cop arresting me for dicky-waving."

The warmth of the dry desert heat took them by surprise as they stepped from the car. The night before it had been in the low-thirties in the Rockies. Here in the late morning of southern Utah, the temperature was already into the eighties. When John went inside to pay for the gas, he was happy to see Denny buying a large hoagie and a quart of milk. Although it was more than obvious Dennis Perella's cancer had turned him into a pathetic alcoholic, his mind remained astute. He realized they were getting close to their destination–it was time to slow down on the whiskey. Once they were in the car, Denny said, "John, remember this place. There's a couple dumpsters out back. We'll put all our stuff in them on the way home."

After passing through a mountainous sweep in the northwest corner of Arizona, a short distance from the southern rim of the Grand

Canyon, they saw a sign suspended above the roadway that read: Welcome to Nevada. The Silver State.

"Next rest-stop you see, pull over," said Denny. "We gotta switch license plates."

It was almost 2 P.M. Pacific Daylight Time on Thursday afternoon when they came upon the outskirts of Las Vegas. Accounting for the time differential due to crossing three time-zones, they'd been on the road for forty-one hours. Scores of billboards advertising the many opulent hotels informed them they remained some ten miles away from the heart of Las Vegas. Close enough. They'd agreed it foolish for John to stay at another hotel nearby The Olympus–why risk being arrested later if he'd been caught on film by a surveillance camera as a mere hotel guest.

Exiting the highway, they pulled into a tacky motel named Cactus Flower. The grubby motel owner didn't inspect the forged Oregon driver's license John had placed on the counter. He could care less who the unshaven man wearing a trucker's ball-cap was. All that interested him were the two Benjamin Franklin's underneath.

With room key in hand, John hopped into the car where Denny lay stretched across the back seat. Only seeing one other car as he swung through the dusty parking lot, he pulled to the curb. While unloading the trunk, he motioned Denny inside.

John sat on the bed flipping through television channels, fighting fatigue while Denny showered and shaved. Soon emerging from the bathroom, Denny wore a white shirt and tie. Next he slid into his pants. Without a belt, they would have fallen from his thinned waist. But his chocolate-brown, double-breasted suit coat fit to perfection, dramatically improving his appearance. Denny hadn't been to button the coat when he was a barrel-chested bull.

"I hope they let me into The Olympus lookin' like this."

"You look okay, Den. Alotta suits come with baggy-ass pants. Just keep your coat buttoned when you're walking around."

"Yeah, it's good enough," said Denny as he twisted to observe himself in the mirror. "You sure I gotta be all duded-up to meet these guys?"

"Denny, they're doctors," John said. "They won't give you a second thought if you look like some average tourist. You gotta make a good first impression on whatever one of them you talk to, or else we're just here on vacation, too."

Perella threw his arms upward and said, "How in the fuck's a guy supposed to have any fun wearing a damn suit and tie."

John began snickering. "Ah, stop acting like a child," he said. "That's exactly what the surgeon told my mother. Just remember why we're here."

He tossed Denny a stack of money held together by a gum-band. "There's twenty-five grand. I got more out in the car for you if you need it."

"I don't need this much. All I'm doin' tonight is going downtown and getting me a hooker. It's strictly business after that."

"Flash money, Den," John said. "If you do get close to one of them, you gotta have lots of cash. That'll impress them. Get some twenties for tips. All you got there are hundreds."

"How much you say the room costs?"

"The rack-rate is a thousand per night for a suite."

"A thousand bucks a night!" Denny roared. "Damn, for a thousand a night, that should include a suck and a fuck."

Fifteen minutes later, the Cadillac was rolling down the famed Las Vegas Strip. The grandeur of the hotels enthralled them. Multi-colored glass-and-granite cathedrals of decadence that sprang from the desert sand, each transcending all demarcations of spectacle while glistening outrageously in the afternoon sunshine. They passed Circus Circus. The Venetian. The Mirage. Caesar's Palace. The Bellagio. Paris. The MGM. The Luxor. Each a tribute to 21st Century architecture. All fabulous in their sheer magnificence.

At the west-end of Las Vegas Boulevard towered the spectacular Olympus Hotel and Casino. Named for the mythical abode of the Greek Gods, it was massive, gaudy, seemingly more extravagant than any of the others. A tantalizing sight for even the most seasoned traveler. Highlighted by an array of colors, the giant marble columns and assorted monoliths, colossal golden statues, botanical gardens, and the enormous water fountains surrounding the planetary structure were all spellbinding.

As he prepared to turn into The Olymus' parking garage, John suddenly tapped the brake and continued straight.

"You saw the camera, huh?" said Denny.

"Sure did, Den."

"Remember, they're everywhere in this town."

Minutes later, they were parked on a service road leading to McCarron International Airport.

"Okay, let's go over this again," said John, his tone assertive. "Their plane lands tomorrow afternoon at twelve-fifty, so you got alotta time to scout the place. Then go enjoy yourself. Buy the biggest steak you can eat, go get laid, have a few drinks, whatever you want. Don't forget though, keep a low profile. If you feel like gambling, go someplace else. The less chances people in The Olympus have to recognize you, the better. Just make damn sure you're somewhere inconspicuous close to the front desk tomorrow when they check-in."

"Don't sweat it, I won't miss them," Denny said. "I saw Cameron's picture in the paper when him and Elliot opened their office. I remember thinking to myself that Cameron looked like Captain Kangaroo."

"Captain who?"

"Never mind, kid," Denny smiled. "He was way before your time. Relax, as much as you've described them to me, I'll recognize them."

"They should be all together since Cameron's supposedly picking up the tab for all their suites."

"I'll see them, John. Don't worry, I plan on staying sober until we're long-gone for this town. Listen, I still think I should try to pick us up a couple of those throwaway cell phones. The one I got only has about an hour left."

"We can't, Denny," he said. "Remember my telling you that I looked at a couple malls near Pittsburgh before we can out here? Even with the throwaway cells they make you show ID, and they go on a computer to verify your information. Then what?"

"Then how are we supposed to talk?" he grumbled. "That roach-infested dump you're staying at doesn't even have a damn telephone."

"Just like we planned from the beginning, I have to use a pay phone. Once I drop you near The Olympus, I'm gonna look for a pay phone close to my room. There's a bunch of nice places between the Cactus and here. When I find one with a pay phone, I'll give you a call on your cell. Maybe by then you'll at least have some ideas if it's possible or not."

*****

Secluded in a corner of a hideaway lounge the following afternoon at The Santa Rosa Hotel and Casino, John played the poker machine that was built into the bar. Except for a group of young men along the side, along with those periodically stopping to watch a score-ticker for updated baseball and basketball scores, the crowd was sparse.

"You ready for another beer, handsome?" a ravishing bartender called to him.

"Not yet, thanks," he replied in a friendly way.

"I'm Rachel. Let me know when you're ready."

Just beginning her shift, Rachel approached for the first time–a seductive countenance about her. "You're kinda cute. Are you out here in Fun City all by your lonesome?"

"No, I brought my girlfriend," he said.

"Where is she?"

John looked towards the casino. "Out there playing slots."

"She's crazy leaving a gorgeous stud-muffin like you alone."

"Ah, I'm the faithful type," he shyly replied.

Rachel was lovely, though she had to be discouraged. For whatever her intent, he had to remain just another face in the crowd. Although her outgoing nature was the norm in this mecca of gaming. Las Vegas is a fabulous vacation locale to see the many sights it has to offer. Yet those who envisioned beating the house at their own game where living a fantasy.

While walking the periphery of the casino before entering the bar, John surmised what awaited the majority of people he'd seen squandering their hard-earned money at the gaming tables, as well as those impulsively inserting dollar after dollar into slot machines. Most would be boarding their homeward-bound planes broke. Although their most-likely predestinations weren't nearly as bleak when compared to a certain assemblage from Pennsylvania whom had arrived at The Olympus. The prospect of their making the return flight home in the storage compartment loomed large.

It was nearing seven o'clock when Denny arrived, squinting into the dark, now crowded bar. He motioned John outside.

"What's with that outfit?" John said.

"Buddy, I bought these for you," Denny said. "There's a big poker tournament that just started today at The Olympus. The whole joint's swarming with guys wearing this same black coat, hat, and sunglasses. You'll blend right in with them."

"That'll work," he said. "Tell me more about them."

Denny glanced at the smoked-glass bubbles shielding the surveillance cameras. "Not here. You hungry?"

"I could eat."

"C'mon, I saw a pizza shop on the cab ride. I'm starving."

*****

A half-hour later, they were on a park bench with a pizza box between them. Palm trees behind them, they sat alone beyond centerfield of the baseball field.

"Kid, if I only had a few more years, I'd move out here," said Denny. "This town's like one big party."

"Yeah, well, the party's gonna be over real soon for those bastards," John said, his tone spiteful. "Tell me again who all checked-in."

Denny huffed as he reached for another slice of pizza. "Cameron and Elliot led the pack."

"Who else?"

"The old fart with some good-lookin' babe clinging to his arm.

"Burke and his girlfriend, Lisa Graham. Who else?"

"Hey, John, she looked hot."

"Fuck her, she's a scum-sucking pig. Who else?"

"The blonde pretty-boy."

"That's Jennson. Who else?"

"One other guy. The way you described him, he hadda be the surgeon."

"Average build, white hair, bad complexion?"

"Uh-uh. Fucker looks worse than me. What's with him?"

"Who cares. How many other women were with them?"

"None," said Denny while inhaling his pizza.

"Den, are you sure?"

"Yes, I'm sure. I was sittin' in a bar where I could see the limo's dropped-off at the main entrance. My eyes still work, and I wasn't drunk."

Feeling the whiskers about his cheeks, John said, "I know Nasser and Cameron aren't married, but I'm not sure about Elliot and Jennson. Maybe their wives went into the casino instead of waiting in line. Sure you didn't miss them?"

"John, I spotted all of them as soon as they walked into the main lobby. I'm telling you, there was only the one girl."

Valone gave him an excited slap on his leg. "Denny, our chances only improve without having to worry about any wives getting in our way."

"No shit," he remarked, reaching for another slice. "Eat."

Nodding in approval, John took his first slice of pepperoni pizza. What doubts he had in Denny's mental capacities were gone. Now he was prepared to risk his life for the vengeance he so dearly coveted.

"Well, you have fun last night?"

A momentary grin before Denny said, "Yeah, that little gal sure was nice to me. Amazing what greasing a bartender twenty bucks a drink can do in this town."

"What, the bartender help fix you up?"

"He tried to," said Dennis. "But I wasn't about to go calling one of his girls. Nah, way to chancy. Late last night I went downtown to Freemont Street to see the lightshow. That's where I found my own hooker."

"I don't understand," John said. "So how'd the bartender help you?"

"He gave me a list of the best lookin' showgirls in town who turned tricks on the side."

"Okay, but how'd the list help you?"

Denny gulped his Pepsi to wash-down the pizza and said, "The list helped me land Elliot."

"Huh?"

"Yeah. We had a couple drinks together."

John's pizza fell from his hand. "Get the fuck outta here."

Denny chuckled, yet his facial expression remained staid. "John, I'm not joking. Hell, he even bought."

"How did you ever manage to drink with Elliot?"

"Simple," Denny said, grabbing another slice. "I told him they were my showgirls. Elliot went for it."

"Whoa, slow down a sec," said a confused John Valone. "Den, I'm just a small-town guy living in a fleabag of a motel room out in the middle of the Mohave Desert right now. All I've been doing since we got here is sleeping and messin' with my laptop. Start at when they first came into The Olympus."

"Whatta dummy," he said, forcing a belch. "Okay, I was sitting at the bar while they were in the VIP line. After they'd registered, Captain Kangaroo went to the elevators with Burke and his bimbo. The Egyptian and goldilocks ran for the casino, and Elliot came into the bar. He only sat a few seats away from me. I didn't want to come right out and start talking with him, so I just kept to myself. A little while later I heard him ask the bartender if there were any classy hooker's around that he could recommend."

"Okay. And what'd the bartender say?"

"Since Elliot only had a five dollar bill to pay for his drink, the bartender told Elliot hookers weren't permitted in The Olympus. But as the bartender was walkin' away, Elliot saw him wink at me."

"Okay, then what'd Elliot do?"

"Nothin' at first," said Denny. "Hey, you want this last slice?"

"No, go ahead," John said. "What happened next?"

"Couple minutes later, the bartender went on break, so I told Elliot I might be interested in getting him some action. John, you were right about having flash money. When Elliot saw the wad of cash I was carrying, I had him by the balls. I gave Elliot a quick peek at the list, and I told him they were my showgirls."

"And he bought it?!"

"Hook, line, and sinker," said Denny, chewing at his pizza. "All he kept telling me was how his wife had moved-in with some loser named Ray. We started bullshiting and before long, me and him were best buddies. Poor guy was practically crying on my shoulder while we had another drink. And when we left the bar, I rode the same elevator with him. Their entire group is all on the 47th floor."

John cast a pensive facial expression while viewing the grove of palm trees spread behind. Shaking his head, he said, "It's a damn shame."

"What?"

"Dr. Elliot. The man never did anything to hurt my mother. Never said anything bad against her in court. Seemed like a nice guy." A prolonged sigh. "Damn shame."

"We ain't leavin' any witnesses!" said a forceful Dennis Perella.

"I know, Den, we can't. Alright, what's next?"

Denny glanced at his watch. "Next is I gotta get back to The Olympus and put my dumb suit on. I'm meeting Elliot at ten."

"What are you going to say if he wants laid tonight?"

"Bridgette and Jacquelyn are on stage tonight," he laughed. "I promised Elliot they're the cream-of-the-crop, and he gets his pick tomorrow. That's when we whack them all."

John eye's opened wide. He was stunned that the methodical, ever-plotting Vietnam veteran believed they were fully-prepared to carry out their intentions. "You sure we're ready, Den?"

"Tomorrow's our only real shot, kid. Once Elliot sees I can't deliver the goods, we're the ones fucked. Plus with the poker tournament, the joint will be wall-to-wall people again. Everything looks okay, so we're gonna have to chance it tomorrow. Be ready to go in the morning. The maids finish the suites before noon. Like we said all the way out here, that's the best possible time to whack them."

Digging into his blue jeans, Denny said, "Here's my extra card-key. Don't lose it, Security makes you show it before they'll let you on the elevators. When do you want me to call you again?"

"How about midnight? The pay phone's in The Santa Rosa's Race and Sports Book. They're open all night."

"Yeah, that's good," Denny said, his face inexpressive. "I'll let you know how it went with Elliot. Then we'll see if you still want to go through with this tomorrow."

"Denny, if you say it's a go, then it's a go."

Dennis Perella stood to say, "Alright, let's get moving. I don't want Elliot waiting for me. We'll talk about some more of the details on the way back to The Olympus."

CHAPTER FORTY TWO

On alert for anything out of the ordinary, John relaxed in the back-row of The Santa Rosa Race and Sports Book. Trying to appear unruffled by thoughts of impending danger, he flipped through the pages of *The Daily Racing Form,* yet his restless gaze kept shifting to the telephone behind him. His mind churned knowing the day of reckoning may only momentary phone call away from reality.

"Excuse me there, young fella, you like anything at Arlington Park?" asked a cigar-chomping man seated a few rows in front.

"Nah," came a non-descript response.

"Take a look at Spizzerinktum in the third. She went a big race her last start."

"Tough race, Sir."

"Yeah, but look how she closed her last race. This mare can outsprint all of them—"

Horse racing whiz paused in mid-sentence, his audience having dashed to the telephone ringing behind them. The cigar kept John in view as he began striding towards the exit.

"Hey, buddy boy, somebody give you a hot tip?"

His inquiry went unanswered.

*****

After scrutinizing his appearance in the Cadillac's mirror, John paced towards the crosswalk suspended over Las Vegas Boulevard that led to the main entranceway of The Olympus.

Soon jammed into a sea of humanity inside the hotel, he patiently moved with the flow through the crush of people not drawing any attention, disregarding the excited chatter all the infatuated tourists were making. The only images whirling about his consciousness were of the encounter soon to take place in Suite 4761.

Once he'd fended his way around a bottleneck of sightseers clustered in the lobby, there was a bounce to his step as he moved towards the bank of elevators only those wealthy enough to afford the hotel's expensive rooms were privileged to use. The gold-plated walls and the glittering crystal chandeliers were a dazzling vision. Up ahead stood a team of security guards obstructing the aisle-way leading to the elevators. They presented a formidable gauntlet for anyone not at liberty to pass. Able to see the guards inspecting the patron's key-cards, John held his in plain sight as he nonchalantly approached the blockade.

"Thank you, Sir," a guard standing behind a podium voiced. "Enjoy your stay at The Olympus."

He nodded in polite acknowledgement, then boarded an awaiting elevator. Immediately he pressed hold of the door-close button before any unwelcomed company could join him.

Now on the 47th floor, John scanned a quiet hallway. Nobody in his field of vision, he pulled his leather gloves tight as he neared the suite. If a hotel patron did emerge from another room, he would continue past Suite 4761. His heart pounding, he drew a deep breath after a final glance about the corridor. The door opened after one tap.

With Frank Sinatra belting out the second verse of *Strangers in the Night* on the hotel's sound-system, Denny whisked him inside.

"Now ain't that a beautiful sight?" he said pridefully, gesturing to the four doctors who sat motionless on the floor, all propped against a light beige couch handcuffed, their mouths wrapped with duct-tape.

Already paralyzed with fear, the panic in their eyes intensified once they recognized the unshaven face of the man wearing the black poker jacket and cap. This wasn't just a robbery as Denny had led them to believe after he'd captured them and looted their wallets.

As he moved directly in front of them, John smiled in astringent fashion at the four men–who stared back with unmitigated terror. It wasn't his intention to bluff. His icy facial expression relayed exactly was intended. He basked in the moment, seeing in their eyes they all realized they were about to meet eternity. So enjoying the fright his presence brought, a deliciously refreshing chilliness enwrapped body and soul.

"Not too shabby, Den," he said, while tightening the silencer of the .32 caliber pistol he'd been handed. "Where's Nasser and Lisa?"

"Sweet Lisa screamed," Denny said, indifferently. "She's in the bedroom sleeping for good. As for Nasser, he flew back home early this morning."

"The fuck you mean he flew home!" he growled, ignoring Denny's signal he lower his voice. "Why would the motherfucker have even bothered coming out here for one day? No way, Den, Nasser's gotta be around the hotel somewhere. We got time. We'll wait. I want him dead."

"Easy, kid," said Denny. "I'm positive Nasser's gone because Elliot and Jennson talked about him while we were having breakfast. Jennson wanted to get laid, too. They had no reason to lie then. Just be glad we got these dickheads. Now do what we came for and let's get the fuck outta here."

Denny's rational didn't appease. The one doctor John had sought vengeance against more so than any of the others had seemingly been spared by a quirk of fate. There was a sinking feeling in the pit of his stomach, yet the adrenalin rush he'd been experiencing intensified.

"Den, turn up the volume," said John. Glaring at the profusely sweating men benumbed on the carpet, his face transformed into a mask of rage. He ripped the tape from Wayne Jennson's mouth.

"Where's fuckin' Nasser?" he hissed, while forcefully mashing the gun barrel against the temple of the young physician's head.

The terrified doctor cringed, and began hyper-ventilating. "Dr. Elliot told me—he went home."

"Don't lie to me, scumbag! I'll kill you right now and decorate this room with your brains."

Barely able to catch his breath, Dr. Jennson continued to gasp. "Mr. Valone, I swear—that's what—what Dr. Elliot told me."

"Why'd he leave?"

"He was ill."

"You're lying! He slid the hammer ready. "Kiss your ass goodbye."

"I swear to God I'm—not lying," he panted, his eyes closed.

John stepped backwards. Disheartened, he slouched onto the edge of a chair facing the four men held in bondage. Pragmatism had hit had–Dr. Nasser had escaped him.

"Denny, take the tape off the rest of them," he said in a furious whisper. "If any of them have the balls to raise their voice or talks outta turn, blow their fuckin' head off and punt it across the room."

Denny complied, yet lingered behind the doctors while randomly placing the barrel of his .32 against the base of their necks. He feared his emotionally-charged friend would suddenly lose composure and begin shooting–John was too close to his targets.

"Yeah, Mr. Expert Witness, you swear to God," said John with resounding cynicism. "Just like you and all those other motherfuckers swore to God in that courtroom. You put your hand on The Holy Bible and took a sacred oath before Lord God Almighty that you'd tell nothing but the truth. But instead of the truth, all I heard come out of your mouth was one lie after another. Well, you got something to say, spit it out. Try to holler. I dare you. Me and my pal will use your head for a football."

"Nah, a soccer ball," Denny said. "I ain't catchin' his head."

Dr. Jennson was in tears. "I admit I lied for Dr. Nasser. If I could—"

"If! If! Hey, smart guy, if is the biggest word in the English language," John said. "If you had a shred of decency in you, you'd have told Tibeau to piss-off when he asked you to testify. But instead, you got up on the witness stand and made Nasser sound like some saint. Bad news, Doc. It's going to cost you your life."

"I'll sign a sworn avadavat that I lied. You mother will be granted a new trial."

"Yeah, right," said John. "Then we'll all go on our merry way and live happily ever after. No, Doc, you had your chance not to get involved with the trial, just like you didn't want to get involved when you cancelled my mother's appointment. It's too late now, so stop your sniveling and shut the fuck up. Denny, tape this piece of shit."

Other than Sinatra now singing *Summer Wind,* the room fell silent.

"Here's another liar, Den," said John. "Right, Dr. Burke. You know something, Doc, I gotta hand it to you. You're a shrewd old geezer. A man your age dicking such a young twat like Lisa. I heard from Janet how you even had the balls to bang her in the doctors' lounge. But your crowning achievement came when you got on the witness stand and concocted that story about my mother stealing pills. Made her sound like a real dope-fiend with all that incoherent bullshit. I gotta tell you, Doc, you were smooth up there. Smooth as fuckin' silk. If I didn't know any better, I mighta even believed you. Yes, Sir, Dr. Burke, you're quite a man. Somebody should write a book about your many exploits. Guaranteed it'd be a bestseller."

"May I speak?" asked Burke in trembling voice.

"Why not. Men facing firing squads are always granted a last request." John waved his .32 at the doctor. "Just remember, though. Soccer ball."

"Mr. Valone, I hated testifying against your mother. Truly I did. Mary's been a very dear friend of mine for many, many years. I just didn't have any other alternative due to the fact that I was under subpoena."

"Sure, Doc," he said tritely. "A little bird landed on Tibeau's shoulder and told him my mother was always stoned on pain-pills, so that enabled Tibeau to coerce you into testifying. Absolutely. I suppose your next lie will be how Cameron kidnapped you and poor Lisa into coming here. C'mon, Doc, cut the bullshit. You've probably been a no-good sonofabitch your whole miserable life. At least try dying like a man."

"May God strike me dead if I'm lying about being subpoenaed."

John pointed his weapon at Burke's face. "Tape him, Den."

With Burke's mouth re-taped, John squatted near the doctor's face, their noses only inches apart. "No, Dr. Burke. God isn't going to strike you dead. I am."

John stood to address Elliot. "Doctor, I'm sorry, I got no choice. You're just in the wrong place at the wrong time. You may be a jerk when it comes to deciding who to go into business with, but I know you didn't want my mother to die like your partner and Nasser did. Maybe in the next life you'll pick your friends a little more carefully."

After taping Elliot, Denny pointed to his watch to prompt him–his pistol against the back of Cameron's head.

John nodded while continuing to scowl at Cameron. "Last but not least, we come to that wonderful physician who deserves a lot of the credit for this entire fucking fiasco. That scholar and omnipresent humanitarian, the great Dr. Steve Cameron himself. Well, Doc, speak up. Got any lies you wanna share with us before your lights go out for good?"

"Valone, you'll never get out of this hotel alive," muttered Cameron, determined not to cower at the specter of death as his colleagues before him. "There are security cameras on all the floors."

"Still lying," said John. "My pal checked the layout. Yeah, there are tons of cameras downstairs, but not on the floors." He cast a vicious smirk. "How's it feel knowing your about to die, and you can't do a damn thing about it?"

"Fuck you, Valone. You don't have the balls for it," he fought to say, as Denny began taping his mouth.

"Hey, Doc, remember your pal DeTorrio and that ugly bitch he was screwing? Guess what, asshole, it was me who punched their tickets to hell. And you'll be joining them real soon, because there wasn't any way you and Nasser were going to get away with what you did to my mother. Yeah, maybe I'll get caught. I promise you I'll die happy since I'll always have the satisfaction of knowing that I put you in your grave."

His profound hatred ablaze, John didn't realize until that exact moment that Denny had guided him around the chair. With primal outrage, he lifted his semiautomatic. He aimed for Cameron's forehead and squeezed the trigger.

The first muffled discharge seemingly stopped time. Multiple shots later, four men lay dead. The air above a tinted pink hue. The couch behind them splashed with gouts of blood and skull fragments. Blood spewed from their gaping wounds forming stains of crimson in the plush beige carpeting.

"You okay, kid," asked Dennis, steadying him as he inspected John for any obvious blood-spatter.

"Yeah, I'm good," he said, softly.

"You ain't gonna puke, are you?"

"No—I'm okay."

Denny pried the gun from his hand. "John, what's done is done. Our next objective is to make it outta here. Understand?"

"Yes."

"Listen up now. Let me handle this. Go to my room like we said. Where's my key-card?"

"In my pocket."

"Remember my room number?"

"3437."

"Okay," said Denny. "When you walk out of here, take the stairs up to forty-eight. Make sure you take off your gloves in the stairwell. Don't chance leaving any stray hairs from your hands or wrists on this floor. Then the elevator down to my room. No shower, no shave. Change into your fresh clothes, but keep the cap and sunglasses until you get to the car. Then take the elevator to the lobby, and walk out of this ritzy cathouse nice and easy. Got it?"

"Got it."

"Don't wait for me in the room," Denny said. "And don't carry anything out to the car. Surveillance sees you carrying a bag without first stopping at checkout, they might get curious and zoom-in on you."

"I remember, Den."

"The Caddy parked on that side road where I showed you?"

"Yeah."

"Wait for me there. Okay, sure you know what to do?"

"Denny, I'm alright," said John in assuring tone.

A final look at the carnage they had brought to fruition. "Buncha scumbags. Fuck 'em, I'm glad they're dead."

As Denny clutched John's bicep, he said, "Check the hallway. If it's clear, get moving."

With Valone on his way, Denny neared the bodies for a closer inspection. The .32 caliber hollow-points had caused grotesque wounds, as all four doctor's gray-matter oozed from their shattered craniums. Despite not detecting the slightest ebb of life, he emptied what bullets that remained in his clip into their chests.

After he'd lowered Ol' Blue Eye's rendition of *Luck be a Lady,* Denny pulled a steak knife he'd taken from a room-service cart. Nimbly avoiding the stained areas of carpet, he stepped to a dry location near Dr. Jennson's body and squatted-down. He placed the handle onto Jennson's right hand, then wrapped the doctor's palm around it. Gently lifting it away, he threw it near the door.

Quick to maneuver away from the corpses, Denny took a vial of blood from his coat and crossed into the adjacent suite. Upon entering the bedroom where Lisa Graham's body lay, he sprinkled some about, causing red dots to appear on the carpet already saturated in her blood. Returning to Dr. Elliot's suite, Dennis scattered an irregular path of blood droplets behind him as he neared the bodies. After a lap around the couch, he stood in the same position where he and John had fired the fatal shots. There he drained what remained in the vial onto the carpeting, resulting in the blood forming an appreciable blot. He sought to create the illusion that a wounded assailant had been dripping blood while committing the unmerciful slayings. Once he'd secured the murder weapons and twenty-four spent shell-casings, he moved to the door. As John had done, he peeked into the hallway before making his way out.

*****

The dawn of Monday coming upon, an exhausted John Valone pulled onto the cobblestones. "We're home, Den," he said, poking at his arm.

"I'm awake," he muttered from the back seat.

"You always snore when you're awake?"

"Fuckin' wiseguy."

His forearms atop the headrest, Denny said, "Okay, wiseguy, when you called Gene, didn't he say the only time he noticed any police snooping around your neighborhood was when he saw Butch last night?"

"Yep."

"That's a good sign, John," he said. "The reports on the radio mentioned the bodies weren't found until Sunday morning. So allowing a few hours for the Vegas police to get the crime scene under control as well as the time difference, the earliest Butch coulda heard was late Sunday afternoon. There ain't gonna be no mystery when then died. So when you're questioned, stick the story that you never left home until Saturday. Alright, where were you beginning on Saturday morning at about ten until now?"

"I've been out here with you. We've been boozing since Saturday morning."

"What were we drinking?"

"Jack Daniel's and Coors."

"What'd we eat?"

"The stuff that's leftover in your cooler."

"What were we doing most of the time?"

"Saturday we were drinking and bullshitting until I passed out. Sunday we were drinking and watching the news on television until we passed out."

"Where'd you sleep?"

"On your recliner."

"Very good," Denny said. "Pop the trunk."

Both men now standing outside, Denny pulled his suitcase and cooler from the truck. "Run the car through that automatic carwash out by the club. When you get home, wipe the inside for fingerprints. Then start cutting grass. Your neighbors gotta see you."

Prior to yawning, John said, "I'm gonna try staying awake."

"Force yourself to!" demanded the ex-marine. "Use the same discipline you've had since Vegas. Now pay attention to me. Whenever you see Butch, don't start talking about the murders right away. Let him bring it up. Don't forget, he's still a cop, so don't be too gabby with him. When the higher-ups come, just stay calm while you're being interviewed, keep your story consistent, and pray those desert rats can't identify you on video. Don't let them con you like that Captain Arrigo tried. If they got you on video, they won't play games. They'll arrest you. Okay, you sure Gene knows what to say?"

"I just told him we were hanging out here since Saturday morning."

"Make sure he tells that to the police. Nothing else."

"He will. Figure any ideas how I can get Nasser?"

Sporting a vehement frown, Dennis slammed the truck shut. "Damn it! Forget him!"

"Sorry, Den, I can't. If I hadn't found out about this trip, he would have been the first one I went after."

"John, we talked about him the whole ride home," he said in disgust. "I'll make one more attempt to get it through your thick head just how rough things are going to be, provided the cops don't already have enough to arrest you. You listening?"

"Yes."

"It's guaranteed you'll be a prime suspect in a quintuple homicide," Denny assured him. "And since it occurred across state-lines, everybody will be involved. The county and state police from Pennsylvania and Nevada. Maybe even the F.B.I. Once their investigations starts, even if they can't prove anything right away, they'll keep digging. The DeTorrio investigation was a piece of cake compared to this, so forget Nasser."

"How long would you say they'll be keeping close-tabs on me?"

"Who knows! Could be months. Years. There's no Statute of Limitations on murder. If the F.B.I. doesn't take charge, Dague will be calling the shots on you. It all depends on what they uncover. Then you gotta think how Nasser will react. The fucker probably shit his pants when he heard the news. I'd bet all the cash I got in my bag he's already hired more security to help that big goon you told me about."

Perella wrapped an arm around his shoulders. "John, trust me on this. It's suicide to go after him. Please take the advice I've been giving you since Vegas. Don't go chasing after Nasser. You'll only end-up on death-row."

"Got any more untraceable guns?"

"No!"

"What about the alternative we discussed?"

Dennis Perella let out a deep sigh of frustration. "Kid, you really are a stubborn fuck."

"Just like you, pal."

"What's the use," huffed Denny, as he lifted his bag. "Alright, get the fuck outta here. I'll see what I can do. But even if I can scrounge everything I'd need, your chances are lousy."

CHAPTER FORTY THREE

"Butch, you big troll!" John shouted to Chief William Gill later that evening, as Butch descended the stairs.

"Hope you don't mind my letting myself in," he said. "Your garage doors are open."

"Nah," said John, while pointing his pool cue at Gene. "The little guy woulda tried something shifty if I'd gone to answer the doorbell. He's already stuck a hundred. Butch, I'm sorry about not calling you until this afternoon."

"It's not like you to ignore my calls, John," he said. "I've been trying to get in touch with you since last Friday. Your landline was always busy, and I kept getting your voicemail on your cell phone."

"Butch, I'm sorry, I wasn't ignoring you. The landline was busy because it was off the hook in Mary's room, and I was just so damn busy working on my laptop, I forgot I turned the cell off. I didn't even return Mary's calls until this morning."

"You were with Denny Perella from Saturday morning until this morning, right?"

"Yeah, I went out to spend a couple hours with him, but it turned into a two-day binge."

"Drunken bum," remarked Gene, as he studied the pool table. "You shoulda seen him this morning, Butch. He looked like he was ready to fall over pushing his lawnmower."

Gill's continued staid demeanor made it evident he was uneasy. "Well, what do you guys think about what happened in Las Vegas?"

"Someone did the world a big favor by killing those scumbags," John spitefully replied.

"John, no one can blame you for hating them," said Butch. "Still, that's a helluva thing to say."

"Why's that?" he said curtly, his eyes steady and defiant. "After all the grief they caused my mother, what'd you expect me to say. Butch, you know I'm not a hypocrite. With the exception of Dr. Elliot, I don't feel the slightest bit of sorrow for any of them. And I don't care who knows it."

"I watched CNN last night," said Gene. "They didn't show any actual pictures, but the reporters made it sound like a real bloodbath."

"Be glad you didn't see the Clark County Coroners' photos Frank Dague faxed me," Butch said. "Those things are gruesome. The national media is having a field-day with this. The way the doctors were lined up and executed, they're comparing what happened in Las Vegas to the Saint Valentine's Day Massacre."

John laughed while stepping to the pool table. "Ah, no way that's a fair analogy. Those Chicago gangsters were only bootleggers for Bugs Moran. They were just trying to make a living when they got machine-gunned by Capone's boys. The way I figure, they weren't even close to being in the same league for ruthlessness as the doctors were. Gene, deuce in the side."

Instantly, Butch stormed the pool table. "Forget the damn game! This is serious!"

Butch commanded their attention as they moved to sit, yet there remained a distinct sense of awkwardness about him. "Guys, here's the way it is," began the Vernon Park Chief of Police. "The Westland County detectives will be paying both of you a visit tomorrow. John, they'll be questioning you as to your whereabouts for the past several days. Gene, since you told me that you can verify seeing John leaving here Saturday morning, they'll be questioning you as well. Oh, they'll also be questioning Denny."

"What the hell is this?!" John shouted. "Some thief breaks into their room and kills them, and the police automatically think I was involved! Butch, this is crazy. I was with Denny. All we did was bullshit and drink."

"He's telling the truth about leaving Saturday morning, Butch," avowed Gene. "And just by the way he looked while mowing the lawn this morning, I'd say he had a nasty hangover."

"Tell it all to the detectives tomorrow," replied Butch, in inflection exuding his skepticism.

Boldly, Gene leaped from his chair. "Bet your ass I will! This sounds like the same old shit as before. I told you when I saw him leave on Saturday, and again you think I'm lying."

"Uh-uh, through your kitchen window," said Butch.

"Fuck off, Butch," Gene said.

Following a momentary stare-down, he turned to John. "Fuck him, I'm going home. You wanna shoot pool after this mope leaves, gimme a call."

John waited until Gene had exited through the sliding doors and said, "Butch, the news reports mentioned they died Saturday afternoon. Have the detectives check with all the airlines. They're strict since nine-eleven. Believe me, they won't find any record of me flying anywhere since my dad was killed. And after they talk with Gene and Denny, they'll know the only plausible way I could have been in Las Vegas Saturday afternoon was if I had Scotty from *Star Trek* beam me out there and back. That's it, pal. That's the only way imaginable I could have been there."

"John, the fact remains you had a strong motive. With all the national publicity the murders are generating, every possible angle has to be investigated. Now before we go any further, I need you to explain a few things."

Butch paused, his glare becoming even more pensive. "And you'd better be honest with me, because they'll be asking you the same questions tomorrow."

"Ask me anything you want," he said in unpretentious tone, although keenly alert of Gill's intensified mannerisms.

"Your mom and Janet went on vacation to Aruba when?"

"Last Monday."

"Isn't amazing how every time Mary goes to Aruba, different people who've crossed her in one way or another get found murdered in hotel rooms like DeTorrio was?"

"Hey, you're right. Sheer coincidence, Butch."

"Sheer coincidence, huh? I suppose it's also sheer coincidence that none of your neighbors except for Gene saw you this past week."

"What have you been doing, Butch, questioning my neighbors?"

"Damn straight I have. It's funny how everyone I asked said they couldn't recall seeing you until this morning. Mrs. Huber told me she thought you may have gone with your mother and Janet because the house was so quiet. She wasn't sure since some of the lights were on at night, but you could have just let them on."

"I never left this house until Saturday morning."

"How about Ms. Schriver? She walks her dog every day on Pinewood. She told me you usually go up to the street to talk with her and play with her dog."

"Last week I didn't."

"Ms. Schriver never even saw drive past one time."

"Hold on a sec," said John. "I never said I was driving up and down Pinewood. Other than going to Denny's, I never drove anywhere. As I told you, I spent most of my time down here on my laptop."

"So you were pretty much working on your computer until the weekend, when you just happened to go to Denny's house? That gives you another made-to-order alibi for the murders. Incredible. Yet another sheer coincidence."

"The fuck's wrong with you? Denny's dying. I feel bad that I haven't been out to see him more often."

"Sounds like you already got all the answers down pat, John," said Butch in surly voice. "Except you forgot one tiny little thing."

"What are you talking about?"

Butch sighed before saying, "Try explaining this. When I came through the garage, I checked your cars. Know those transparent stickers Rick puts on the windshield whenever he changes the oil?"

"He doesn't put them on my cars. I don't need a sticker on my windshield to remind me when it's time to change the oil."

"Yeah, I saw none of the cars have them," Butch said. "But what about the other stickers?"

"What other stickers?"

"The stickers Rick puts on the driver's door-jabs. Both the Cadillac and your Taurus have them."

A hard swallow. "So?"

Presenting a morose expression, Gill dug into his shirt pocket to show John the stickers he'd peeled off both vehicles. "Rick's a fussy guy. He fixes the newest sticker right on top of the old ones. Makes one neat pile."

"Big fucking deal," John's replied, in an intonation more indifferent than Butch ever dreamed he'd hear.

"Says here that the Cadillac's oil was changed on March 23rd. At the time, the odometer reading was 17,645."

"So what."

"So now the odometer reads 23,649, that's so what!" Butch yelled. "You've put over six thousand miles on the Cadillac since you had its oil changed six weeks ago! How could you possibly have managed all that mileage in six weeks?"

"Mary's trial in Pittsburgh."

"Okay, let's be generous," he said. "Maybe a thousand miles for the trial and other miscellaneous driving around. What about the other five thousand miles?"

"That's my business."

"Hey, John, wake the fuck up!" he growled. "This ain't some DeNiro movie. That answer won't cut it tomorrow. You'd better have a believable explanation where all those miles came from. But you know what, I don't think you'll be able to."

Stymied, Valone gave off a heated glare and said, "Butch, I don't care how many miles I put on my car. That still doesn't prove I drove to Las Vegas and murdered five people. You know, I think you actually believe I did kill them."

"My friend, I don't want to believe it," he replied. "But I'm telling you straight. The circumstantial evidence is beginning to stack-up against you."

"Say it to my face, Butch. You think I did murder them. Go ahead, say it!"

"Yes, I do!" he decisively shouted. "Too many things just have a funny smell. Mary's in Aruba again. Those doctors dying less than three weeks after Mary's trial ended. None of your neighbors seeing you for a week. The all-too convenient alibis Gene and Denny will provide you. And all that extra mileage on the Cadillac that's impossible to account for clinches it for me. I don't know if you were the actual shooter or if you hired somebody, but I'm positive you were out there. All I gotta say is that you, Gene, and Denny had better be able to sell your stories to the big-boys tomorrow, or else when Mary comes home, you'll be in county lockup with Gene and Denny as cellmates."

"Chief Gill, I think you've lost your fucking mind."

"No, John, you're the one who finally snapped, not me. You always were wired different than the rest of us. You couldn't settle for your normal method of retaliation by just beating the shit outta the guy who made you mad. No, this time your quest for revenge graduated you all the way to murder. Fucking murder. I hope you're proud of yourself."

Not exhibiting any outward signs of fear, Valone stepped to the pool table with cue stick in hand. Gill followed, his gait bordering on slow. Their constrained silence persisted while John chalked his cue ever so deliberately.

"If you're waiting for me to confess, you can forget it," he said. "I'll only confess certain sins to God. I'll only accept His damnations for my sins. Not yours. Not any judge's. Only God's."

"John, I've always loved you as a brother," Butch said, his voice subdued. "I don't want to see you fry for this. Just make me understand how such a great guy, a guy so courteous and full of respect for everyone, make me understand how you do something as cold-blooded as murdering five people?"

Remaining serene, John softly pocketed a ball. He stood straight, the expression on his face passionless.

"Old friend, I'll put it to you in very simple terms. I take The Bible literally. I believe in an eye for an eye."

"They didn't kill your mother."

"They wanted her dead!" he screamed. "That's the same fucking thing to me! They betrayed her!"

"That's insane."

"Is it?! When the Roman's crucified Christ, you or anyone else remember the names of the guys who nailed Jesus to the cross? No. Try asking anyone who Judas was."

"Alright, yes, they betrayed your mother. That still doesn't justify your killing them."

"Cameron and Nasser cost me your sister!"

"John, I can't even begin to tell you how sorry I am about Vicky," said Butch. "I know how badly she hurt you. Still, you know just as well as I do that people get shafted everyday in this dog-eat-dog world, yet they're all not out there gunning for revenge."

"Yeah, well, you have your beliefs and I have mine. Quite honestly, ever since you became a cop, you've become too noble. Too pro-establishment. Maybe that's why you can't appreciate where I'm coming from anymore."

"You're wrong, John!" he cried out. "I know it was you who killed DeTorrio and the girl. I had a feeling you were involved from day-one of the investigation. You never realized it, but I tried to convince the DA of your innocence while that Detective Neupaver wanted to keep pursuing you. But I still had my doubts until you let it slip about the hair they discovered in that bloody slaughterhouse. There wasn't any way possible you could have known about that hair unless you or somebody else you knew was there and planted it. If I was as noble as you think, I would have given you up then."

With a virulent look spraying his anger, John Valone raised his cue stick above his head and slammed it atop the oak table's side rail, shattering it. The sheer combustible fury his face displayed was galvanizing. "So to you, I'm just a homicidal psychopath who kills people for revenge. Well, Butch, let me tell you how it really is when people you trusted end up shitting all over someone you love."

Together they moved towards the leather couch. William Gill could readily discern a sense of anxiety.

"John, everybody knows what Cameron and Nassar did to your mom," said Butch, his tone turned soothing. "And we're all pissed about her trial. Yes, their behavior was deplorable in every conceivable way possible. Nevertheless, you went way too far this time."

"Did I?" he returned in stark contradiction. "Butch, let me put all of this into a different perspective for you, then tell me what you think. Okay?"

Gill's jaw tightened. "I'm listening, John."

"Say Amy needed an operation. You take her to a doctor, and he makes such a terrible mistake that he actually hopes she'll die, only because he's afraid his reputation will suffer. But Amy survives, and later you and she learn what really happened. So Amy sues. Her lawyer hauls the doctor into court, confident all the facts are in Amy's favor. But, what happens is the doctor and all of his country club golfing buddies tell nothing but lies to circumvent the facts. Then to top it all off, he even brings in another doctor who knows Amy, and has him fabricate some story to defame her character. As a result, the jury is deceived and finds him not guilty. Then instead of walking away humbly, quietly ashamed of himself, he has the balls to come right up to you, look you straight in the eye and gloat about it. Like he's rubbing your nose in shit. Tell me the truth, Butch. Don't you think you'd be tempted to pull your gun and blow him away right on the spot?"

"Sure I'd be tempted, but I wouldn't. As much as I'd hate it, I'd just have to live with the hope that the son of a bitch would get his just-due somewhere down the line."

Tears began trickling down John's cheeks. "I couldn't live on hope, Butch. Not with how they mistreated my mother gnawing away at me day and night. Never allowing me a single minute's peace. Every time I'd see Mary in pain, it tortured me. Every time I even think about Vicky, it reminds me just how badly they'd stuck it to Mary. It constantly reminds me how their neglect damaged Mary's life, and ruined mine."

Butch leaned forward to say, "John, I can only sympathize with everything you and your mom have been through. But if everyone just disregarded society's laws and took justice into their own hands, it'd be complete pandemonium out there. My God, the world's twisted enough as it is. I'm sorry, I still think you were wrong."

Following a prolonged period of silence, John lifted his sullen eyes to say, "Butch, do you believe in destiny?"

"A little."

"Maybe all of this was meant to happen just as it did. Maybe it's my true destiny to end- up on death-row."

"Maybe," Butch replied in hushed, mellow tone.

A broad smile instantly brightened his face. "Then again, maybe not."

Despite the conspicuous softening of Chief Gill's attitude, his next actions left John dumbfounded. His jaw plunged as Butch crumpled the stickers into a wad, and then tossed them at him.

"The reason I tried calling you last week was to wish you a happy thirtieth birthday, ya fuck. So consider those a belated birthday present. Now let's see if we can bail your ass outta this mess."

Valone remained speechless–yet the gratitude stamped upon his face was undeniable.

Butch slapped his leg in acknowledgment. "Just tell me a few things. From what I've heard, the Nevada authorities are working under the assumption that there were two shooters. Their preliminary report Frank Dague faxed me states they believe one of the perpetrators was stabbed. I sure hope you don't have any knife wounds."

"No," said John, his voice raspy. "None."

"So the blood they're perceiving to be one of the assailants won't match yours?"

"It won't."

"You're sure Denny knows what to say? Once they find out about his criminal record, they'll do everything possible to catch him in a lie."

"I'm not worried about Denny," said John, since having cleared his throat. "He promised me he'd slow down on the whiskey, and you know they'll never be able to intimidate him."

Contingency after contingency kept crossing his mind before Butch said, "Has Rick ever done any other servicing to the Cadillac?"

"No. It hasn't needed anything yet."

"All Rick's done to the Cadillac has been to change the oil?"

"Yes."

"What about the Ford?"

"Just oil changes and a set of tires."

"Mary's Lexus?"

"Rick's never even seen it."

"Gene still change his own oil?"

"Ever since that first clunker he had in high school."

Butch nodded in acceptance. "Alright, here's what to do. Take my car to the auto parts store. Buy a couple oil filters for the Caddy and the Ford. Get a few cases of oil, one of those gadgets they use to loosen the filter, and a pan to drain oil in. While you're gone, I'll wax the sticky marks off the door-jabs. And when you get home, have that little grouch next door get his ass over here. We've got plenty to talk about before tomorrow."

"Butch, you realize that you're risking an awful lot to help me," John said. "Last thing I'd ever want is having you as a cellmate."

"Fuck it. I owe you my life. We'll get our stories straight with mean Gene and get everything ready around here. Then we hope for the best."

CHAPTER FORTY FOUR

Months after the Las Vegas homicides, William Gill remained tentative while awaiting the meeting he'd been summoned to by Westland County District Attorney Frank Dague. Despite his knowing the subject-matter they would be discussing, Dague hadn't mentioned any of the specifics when he'd phoned the Vernon Park Police Station earlier that same morning.

As before, Butch had been asked to assist the Westland County detectives during the early days into their investigation of John and Mary Valone. After his abbreviated role had been completed, Dague's detectives kept working in conjunction with the Pennsylvania State Police and the F.B.I. What was so important now for him to be called on the carpet? Dague was aware of his friendships with John, Gene, and Denny. Had one of his indiscretions finally been exposed?

Dague's office door soon opened. "Come on in, Chief Gill," he said. "Nice seeing you again."

"Pleasure seeing you again, Sir."

Once they'd shaken hands, Dague bid him to sit. "Chief, I'm sorry that I had to ask you here on such short notice, but I need to bring you up to speed on the Valone investigation. Now I realize that except for the initial stages you didn't play an integral part of the investigation, yet I assure you that I appreciated your many efforts. You saved my people some valuable time and legwork. Rest assured, I would have asked you to do more had circumstances warranted it."

"Sir, I was glad to help in any way I could," he said, relieved. "I just hope some headway's been made on the case."

Frank Dague sighed in disgust. "Butch, this entire investigation has become a complete farce. Nobody's been able to come up with a single lead. Las Vegas Metro still doesn't have any suspects, and that hick from the Clark County Sheriff's Office is driving me nuts. He calls practically every day suggesting I make various inquiries into the Valone's that have already been checked and rechecked. All I keep hearing is, 'Pardner, try this. Pardner, do that.' Damn cowboy. He must be related to the sheriff."

"How about the F.B.I.?" asked Butch, venturing only a slight smile after Dague's commentary. "What's their take on how the investigation is progressing?"

"I haven't spoken with anyone from the bureau recently. Agent what's his name jumped the first plane to Washington when the DNA analysis on Valone came back negative. I presume they'll keep monitoring for any new developments with LVMP. However, unless somebody can prove the homicides weren't the result of just another Las Vegas robbery, the F.B.I.'s off the case."

"The F.B.I.'s convinced it was a robbery-homicide?"

"Without any question," said Dague. "Four very wealthy men in Las Vegas without a dollar or credit card amongst them. Add to that, ever since the economy took a nosedive, the crime-rate in Las Vegas has been climbing steadily."

"So at this point there still isn't anything to implicate John Valone?"

"Nothing," said Dague, while leafing through his case file. "As far as I'm concerned, he's clean. Captain Arrigo, Neupaver, and Indoff questioned him for hours. Your pal's a rock, Butch. He never fidgeted, never gave one ambiguous answer, never let out one bead of sweat while being interrogated. His DNA profile isn't even remotely close to the blood samples taken from the crime scene. He doesn't have a scratch on him. None of the airlines can confirm he took a flight. Nobody in Vegas can identify him. And even if I were to discount the Polachek and Perella claims about Valone, in my opinion his alibi is airtight since you saw him in Vernon Park the day before the crime."

"Mr. Dague, I'm positive it was him," Butch said. "As I mentioned to you, I was riding on Broad Avenue when I saw John driving his Cadillac. He even tooted the horn at me. I'm not certain of the exact time, although I'm positive it was on the Friday morning before the murders took place."

"Chief, you needn't defend yourself to me," replied Dague. "I know you're a trustworthy officer of the law. You proved that to me during the DeTorrio investigation. Regardless of your long friendship with Valone, I'm certain your obligations towards the law would take precedence over your personal sentiments. So here's where we are. The Clark County Pathologist determined the victims died somewhere between noon and 4 P.M. on Saturday, May 2nd. Obviously there isn't any way Valone could have drove to Las Vegas, committed the homicides, and then driven home in three days. So as far as I'm concerned, everyone can talk about motive from now to doomsday, but he didn't have opportunity."

"What about the theory that he contracted someone to kill them?"

"Indoff and Neupaver are still looking into the possibility, but chances are it'll only be another dead-end. As in the DeTorrio case, there isn't one iota of evidence that points to his hiring professionals There's no money-trail. Within the past year, the only three significant withdrawals from any of his bank accounts have been accounted for. Neupaver remains insistent Valone somehow arranged for the crimes." Dague shook his head slowly. "But as Captain Arrigo keeps telling him, professional hit-men don't kill on credit."

"And I know for a fact that John didn't work for an extended time prior to the homicides, therefore it isn't reasonable to presume he'd been saving money from his paychecks."

"I agree," said Dague. "We did a complete forensic audit of all of his banking transactions. Other than moneys from various portfolio dividends and interest that are directly deposited into separate accounts, he hasn't had any other income. We also audited Mrs. Valone. The woman uses her debit card for everything."

"Sir, the last time we spoke, you mentioned that The Olympus Hotel supposedly has a tremendous security system. I'd think they would have come up with something by now."

Frank Dague smirked. "I was misinformed about that, Butch. I've since learned that The Olympus has one of the worst Security Departments in Las Vegas. According to the Clark County Sheriff's Office, The Olympus' video library contains mostly DVD's of high-rollers gambling which they continue to accumulate. As for the plethora of other cameras spread throughout The Olympus, they only keep a limited backlog of video tapes. If nothing of consequence is filmed at any particular location during the six-hour span of the tape, they simply rewind it and use it again. Fools. They have a multi-billion dollar business to protect, yet they're pinching pennies when it comes to security."

"Sir, I've never been to Las Vegas," said Butch. "Although I was under the impression all the modern hotels have security cameras on every floor to safeguard their guests."

"Most of them do," Dague replied. "However The Olympus' director of security operations informed me that since the hotel is so large, the corporation who owns The Olympus chose not to install surveillance cameras on the floors. But since the murders, guess what the corporation decided?"

"To install surveillance cameras on every floor," Butch said.

"Exactly," said Dague. "In Vegas, they fire people for whatever frivolous reason they want. Whoever the empty-suit was who suggested the corporation could save money by not having surveillance cameras on the floors, guaranteed he's looking for another job."

Continuing to look puzzled, Butch said, "So there's nothing whatsoever on DVD or video tape that could even give the Nevada authorities a starting-point?"

"Not a damn thing, Chief."

"How about an employee whom may have come into contact with the perpetrator?"

"We faxed LVMP Valone's mug-shots," Dague said. "Nothing. Not one of their eleven thousand employees recognized him. Oh, they're still checking, although judging from what Las Vegas Metro told me, the entire process won't amount to much. According to LVMP, most casino employees have very short memories except for when it comes to big tippers. It's extremely doubtful that the perps were in The Olympus throwing money around like confetti before they committed the murders."

"Aren't there any other potential witnesses, Mr. Dague?"

"Not really," said Dague. "Las Vegas Metro assigned a taskforce to contact the hotels' guests for the entire week prior to the homicides. It's already been disbanded. They didn't have anything except a few counterfeit claims of seeing Valone in the hope of receiving a reward. Putting it bluntly, LVMP and the Clark County Sheriff's Department are fucked. And they know it."

Chief Gill wore a pseudo-frown while shaking his head. "What happens next, Mr. Dague?"

"Here's where my office stands at present. In spite of the case's overwhelming notoriety, it's been decided from up-above that we should phase-out our involvement. As you know, we've maintained round-the-clock surveillance on John and Mary Valone, as well as monitoring their telephone conversations. However, the Court Order to tap their phones expired in August. As for the surveillance detail, the state police and my detectives have been sharing the responsibility of shadowing them. Well, the State Police Regional Commander has orders to discontinue surveillance as of today. And due to the fact that the county won't authorize any more overtime, our county commissioners have instructed me to remove my men from the stakeout as well. How's that hit you, Chief Gill?"

"Maybe it's for the best, Sir," replied Butch, in unassuming voice. "From all you've said, it sounds as if it would only be a waste of manpower. And regardless of any animosities the Valone's may have held against the victims, I just can't fathom either of them masterminding something as unconscionable as what happened out in Las Vegas."

"Again I agree with you, Chief," he said. "I watched from the viewing room while they were being questioned. He hardly seems the criminal type, and Mrs. Valone is as pleasant as they come. Yet due to the national media scrutiny, along with Dr. Nasser's whining that he's in fear for his life, our county commissioners are nervous. Therefore, they've decided the safest approach is to have a safety-net ready just in case Nasser does catch a bullet, and word gets out that we had the Valone's under surveillance all this time and discontinued it for budgetary reasons. What they did was to approve an eight thousand dollar stopgap fund in order to maintain a part-time surveillance. It won't do a damn bit of good, however I'm prepared to offer you the assignment of taking over the job until the end of the year. Interested?"

"Yes, Sir."

"You'll be paid forty dollars per hour," said Dague. "That will give us two hundred hours of surveillance. Money sound fair to you?"

"Yes, Sir, the money's more than generous. Sir, I'll gladly take the assignment, but you know as well as I how ineffective it will be."

"Oh, I agree, Butch. In essence, it's only a half-baked political ploy. Nevertheless, that's how politics works. So let's make an arrangement that will satisfy the commissioners."

"Thank you for your confidence, Mr. Dague. What do you suggest?"

"Well, even though the commissioners have only approved this fund to protect their political futures, it's imperative that you stretch-out our surveillance until the end of the year, regardless of how futile it will prove," said the district attorney, again browsing his notes. "I'd say your best course would be to solely concentrate on John Valone. Keep an eye on him at times between say, 6 P.M. and midnight. However, in order for you to stay on Valone throughout December, change the durations of your watch. Maybe one night just ride past his house a few times and go home. Then the following evening make one pass down Pinewood Lane and stay hidden for a few hours. Stop in and say hello. Hell, have dinner with them if you want. Butch, I don't care what your methods are. Just so Valone knows he's still under surveillance. If you don't fall into any set-patterns, he'll realize it conceivable you may still be lurking somewhere in the neighborhood."

Frank Dague sat back in his chair, his hands cupped behind his head. "Putting all this political nonsense aside, according to the information Dr. Nasser gave me, I've come to the conclusion that we need only be realistically concerned about John Valone's constant whereabouts on three nights until the end of 2009. This will require your staying on him continuously. Butch, you may need some help on those three nights."

"It won't pose a problem, Mr. Dague," Butch said. "Even though I'm always on call, I have a good man in Sergeant Luzanski whom I can always depend on. I'll be able to maintain continued surveillance on whatever nights you see fit. What three specific nights are you referring to?"

"Dr. Nasser has medical committee meetings scheduled at Shadydell Heights Hospital that start at 7 P.M. on the second Wednesday of every month. The corresponding dates would be October 14th, November 11th, and December 9th.

"No problem, Sir," said Butch, while writing on his notepad. "Mr. Dague, couldn't Dr. Nasser just not go to any of his meetings?"

"No, Dr. Nasser has used all of his allotted absences. Therefore he must attend every meeting, or else he'll lose his surgical privileges for the remainder of 2009. After taking everything into consideration, I know if I were Valone and was planning on taking a shot at him, I'd try for one of those nights. Escape would be relatively easy from Shadydell as opposed to Nasser's condominium, and it will be dark by then."

"Don't worry, Mr. Dague, I'll be on him."

"I'm sure you will, Butch," said Dague, grinning at the chief's zeal. "But believe me, nothing's going to happen. Valone's too intelligent. Too sapient. If he really was behind the Vegas murders, he knows we'll never be able to arrest him unless Nevada pulls a rabbit out of their hat or unless he does something stupid. No, I just can't foresee him or any hitman ever trying to shoot Dr. Nasser."

Shortly thereafter, Chief William Gill was on his way home. "Absolutely unreal," he said aloud. "If that guy only knew." He chuckled to himself. "John must be the luckiest guy ever born."

*****

October and November rolled by without incident. The Valone household was always peaceful whenever Butch would drop by during his evening stints as John's personal watchdog. At first he'd felt embarrassed about his task, regardless of Mary and John's persuasions there wasn't any need to be. Both remained insistent that whenever

Butch was on-duty, he was always welcome in their home. Regardless of his being responsible that for making certain John didn't sneak away on a stealth errand of murder, that didn't imply he had to stay in his car. As it had been for the previous months while the unmarked patrol cars lay in wait, there wasn't anything covert when Butch was out and about Pinewood Lane. And with Mary constantly informing him that the neighborhood gossip as to John's possible involvement with the Las Vegas homicides still hadn't fallen-off, it made for better appearance if Butch came inside as opposed to prowling the street. The neighborhood wouldn't be as edgy.

Their willingness to accept the situation made his awkward chore more bearable. As each day passed, Butch grew more at ease. In spite all he knew of the transgressions John had brought to be, Butch's overall view of him hadn't changed. He couldn't help but hold John in high-esteem. And Mary remained the same affable lady he'd always known. They were good, God-fearing people, still trying to recover from the unimaginable burdens, stress, heartbreaks, and immured hostilities Mary's health concerns and malpractice trial had impacted upon their lives.

Yet notwithstanding all their many sincere congenialities, William Gill couldn't shake the surreal vibes he continued to sense. It was as if he were now firmly rooted within their clutches. As if both mother and son were toying with him–as a cat's-paw.

CHAPTER FORTY FIVE

With the snow pelting down on a blustery evening in December, Chief Gill skidded down the Valone's driveway. Twin spotlights illuminated the area about the garages, while every light inside the yellow brick house appeared to be on. As he trudged through the snow, he noticed Gene peaking from his front door.

"They ain't home, Butch," he heard Gene yell.

Butch waved to him. After looking through the garage windows, he made his way between the driveways. Stepping onto Gene's porch, he stomped the snow from his boots.

"They took Mary's car," he said to Gene, who kept the door opened slightly to avoid the bite of the howling wind.

"Damn, it's nasty out there," Gene said, once they were inside. "Yeah, I talked with John just before they went out. I figured if you were going to be on guard-duty tonight, I'd come over. But John told me that Mary wanted to go to the mall."

"What time they leave?"

"About two-thirty."

Butch gazed about the kitchen and living room, then said, "Where's your dad?"

"Upstairs watching TV."

Purposely Butch moved forward, his imposing physique wedgıng the smaller man into a corner. "Listen, Gene," he said in exacting fashion, "tonight's really important, so don't get cute with me. I want the truth. What else do you know?"

Gene Polachek, his wild, curly hair pointing all directions, looked to him with puppy-dog eyes. "Nothing, Butch. Honest. All John told me was that Mary wanted to go shopping at the mall."

"Did he say what mall they were going to?"

"No."

"Is he taking Mary to the mall close to Shadydell Hospital?"

"Butch, he didn't say."

"Don't lie to me, Gene," he mumbled, edging even closer. "What's he up to?"

"Butch, all he said was that he didn't want Mary driving in this weather, so he was taking her."

He grabbed hold of Gene's flannel shirt. "Where are they?"

"Butch, I don't know," said Gene. "I'm being honest with you. Hey, I know all you've done to help him. If I knew something, I'd tell you."

The chief's potent glare remained transfixed upon his friend while contemplating his words. It stood to reason that Polachek was being truthful with him–this time.

"Okay, I believe you," said Butch, stepping back. "I just don't know why they'd be out on a night like this. They've been saying all day that the weather was gonna get bad tonight."

"What's up, Butch? I thought all of that was over and done with."

"The doctor who got away from him in Las Vegas could be vulnerable tonight. I don't want John doing anything crazy."

"C'mon, Butch, his mother's with him," Gene said. "Even if he were planning to shoot the prick, he'd never do it with Mary around." A sly grin. "Now if she were in Aruba, I'd be on the first plane I could catch if I was that scumbag."

"Yeah, guess you're right," he said with a huff, though spoken trying to pacify his own fearfulness. "He say what time they'd be home?"

"Nope."

"Damn."

Butch reached into his hooded parka for his cell phone. After pressing one button, he placed the phone to his ear. The top of the phone soon flipped shut.

"Voicemail," he growled to Gene. "Why isn't he answering?"

"I don't know."

Chief Gill stared through the infamous kitchen window. The snowstorm was evolving into a whiteout blizzard. Regardless of Polachek's assurances, his instincts demanded he make the trip to Shadydell Heights.

"Gene, I gotta go," he said. "Gimme a call if they come home."

"Butch, you can't drive in all that snow with your Sonata," Gene said. "Go back to the station and get the police car."

"I have to chance it."

The snowplows were beginning to scrape pavement along Route 55 as he neared the hospital. The storm's intensity had eased during the latter part of his drive, as puffy snowflakes now floated atop those that were being furiously whipped about by the travailing winds. Traffic nonexistent, Butch coasted through the last stretch of red lights prior to turning up the steep gradient leading to the hospital. Enhanced by the shimmering glow of the moonlight, the snow and icicles draping the barren trees lining the rolling hillsides cast an eerie silhouette of incandescence.

His Hyundai Sonata slipping as he neared to top of the rise, Butch observed a dense mist hovering above the hospital caused by a combination of humidity and halogen floodlights that abounded throughout the entire complex. To most, it would have been fancied as a picturesque winter setting. On this particular night, Chief William Gill beheld it ominous.

At the crest of the hill, Butch pulled off to the side, unsure which of the gaited parking lots that surrounded the outer perimeter he should enter. He hadn't been there in years. The hospital seemed larger than he remembered, and he'd never even seen the adjoining professional building. Unresolved of his next move, he stepped from his car to survey the layout of the facility.

"Where would he be parked," Gill said aloud, while continuing to scan the many frosted automobiles. Except for the snow flurries, all stood motionless. Several minutes passed before he observed a group of people off in the distance making their way towards their cars.

His thoughts were suddenly interrupted by a thunderous roar that burst forth from the parking lot nearest the professional building. Instinctively diving to the ground, the sounds emitted by screeching distortions of metal and the shattering of glass had been unmistakable. Butch gawked in amazement at an immense orangish-red fireball blazing into the charcoal night sky. The many automobile security-alarms triggered by the explosion's concussion and flying debris were blaring their sirens. Aghast while picking himself out of the snow, he saw smoke billowing from what had been a car now engulfed in flames.

The blast kept those outside hypnotized, engrossed in fear and the incredulity of the charred wreckage. Butch readied to move closer, though held his ground upon seeing an automobile swing around the opposite side of the hospital. Steadily it approached his position. Even with its headlights off, Butch viewed a Lexus insignia with two occupants inside. With Butch standing alongside the road, the Lexus came to a stop. The driver's window powered down.

"How's it goin', you big troll," said John. "Hey, pretty nice bonfire over there."

Gill crouched down to place his forearms along the window-ledge. He knew it had to be, yet he still felt a shiver tingling about his spine the instant his eyes locked onto Mary Valone in the passenger's seat. He scowled at John. "You weren't ever going to quit until you got him. Were you?"

"Butch, this was my doing," declared Mary, opening her purse to display a small black box, a green strobe-light blinking on top. "Don't blame John. It was me who wouldn't quit until Nasser got what he deserved. Me, Butchie. I'm responsible for the explosion, not John. Arrest me if you want. My son knew nothing about what I intended to do tonight."

"Oh, jeez," Butch moaned softly, momentarily placing his forehead atop his wrists.

Lifting his head, Gill peered cautiously about the vicinity. Fortunately they weren't drawing any attention. Other vehicles hadn't passed their location, and all available witnesses to their presence remained clustered at the far side of the parking lot, agape at the smoldering vestiges of Dr. Nasser's Mercedes Benz.

"No, Mrs. Valone, the last thing I'd ever do would be to arrest you," Butch said. "I'm not condoning what you've done here, but I understand why you did it." He sniffled-away his tears. "And I respect both of you too much."

Butch sighed deeply to say, "I just hope Nasser was the last one. My nerves can't take much more of this."

"Nasser was the last one," said John. "I give you my word as your friend."

"God forgive me, I'm glad the bastard's dead," Mary followed with emotional fervor. "May he burn in hell forever."

Chief Gill extended a grimace. "Let's get outta here before someone sees us."

Epilogue

"You're right, Butch," John said, as he pulled his cell phone from his black suit pocket. "Mind checking the door while I call the little guy."

"I already told Gene that I'd take you home."

Valone pushed the curtains aside. "Yeah, he took off."

The chief returned to his Victorian chair. "Quiet out there."

"Good."

Butch saw his eyes moistening. "C'mon, John, the poor guy had terminal cancer. Last few weeks Mike said he was suffering more every day. You gotta look at this way. At least now he's at peace."

"Yeah, I guess," he replied, his voice hushed. "It's just tough for me to accept that he's gone. He meant a lot to me."

Butch nodded ever so slightly and said, "Alright, you ready to talk about today?"

"Let's see, the F.B.I.'s gonna bug the house," said John, his tone not as distraught.

"No. As of now, you're not a suspect. As I told you, Bernie Ferguson, the Allegheny County DA, questioned me at length today. Like we agreed, I was at your house from exactly six o'clock until a little after ten that night. Frank Dague made it perfectly clear to Ferguson that I didn't violate any of his orders by coming inside with you and your mom."

"Mary waved for you to come in for dinner," said John. "We had roast beef, mashed potatoes, corn, and a salad for dinner. After we ate, we watched *Goodfellas* when it started at six-thirty on Encore."

"You got it," Butch said, smiling in approval. "With me vouching for you, and since the demolition team was able to determine that the bomb didn't have an intricate timing mechanism, Ferguson rejected any notions of pursuing you further based upon the assumption that you could drove to the hospital before I got to the house, fastened it under Nasser's Mercedes, and got lucky he happened to get inside right before it blew at eight-fifteen. No, those demolition guys are sharp. They knew it had to be detonated at close-range. Also since they found the bomb contained C-4, they're certain that it wasn't the type that are made with fertilizer and ammonia. So since they're sure there isn't any way you could have obtained or even had knowledge how to use C-4, there's no way you could have constructed the bomb."

"Sounds logical to me, Butch. How about Vegas? They come up with anything yet?"

"Nope. They don't have any clues except for the planted blood."

"Are they going to keep after me?"

"I'm sure they're still searching for leads in Las Vegas," said Butch. "But not here. And when Dague heard about Dr. Nasser today, he was ready to go through the roof. Even before Ferguson ruled you were no longer a suspect for the bombing, Dague kept saying his office would be dropping everything connected to the Vegas homicides."

Exhibiting a quizzical face, John said, "I'm not sure I understand, Butch. What do you mean, when Dague heard about Nasser today?"

Gill's expression became one of wary. "Let's just say that as far as everybody who was at the meeting is concerned, both Las Vegas and Nasser are cases destined to go unsolved."

"I'm glad to hear it. But why?"

"John, I honestly think it'd be better if I told you another time," he answered in stilled tone. A momentary hesitation. "You're not going to like the news about Dr. Nasser."

"Get outta here, ya troll. When it comes to that scumbag, I'd believe anything. C'mon, I won't lose my head in here."

Precariously Butch eyed the entranceway to assure their isolation. Once he'd taken a deep breath, he said, "They had a young reporter named Al Marsh at the meeting today. He told us that right after the Vegas thing, he kept trying to interview Dr. Nasser. As you might expect, he always refused. Marsh went back to see him in October, and was again told to get lost. But the guy was persistent. He showed-up again at Nasser's office the week before the explosion. That time Nasser had Marsh bounced out on his ear. Okay, remember that steroid-freak you told me was with Nasser in court?"

"Sure. I think he was the same guy with Nasser in the car."

"He was the same guy. Name of Ahmad Suryakant. Supposedly he was Dr. Nasser's bodyguard."

"Fuckin' camel-jockey didn't do too good a job," John said, grinning. "What's the big deal about him?"

"Marsh saw him at Nasser's office. It was Suryakant who roughed-up Marsh. Suryakant was a well-known male prostitute in Pittsburgh. He been arrested a few times trying to pimp himself off in downtown Pittsburgh. Men or women, it didn't matter. He'd screw anybody who'd pay. So after the way Suryakant treated Marsh that day at Nasser's office, it really inspired him to dig into Nasser's background. After he'd done some research, Marsh found Suryakant had done thirty days in the county jail last year. And since he needed medications while he was in lockup, the name of the doctor who'd prescribed his medications was listed in his file. With me?"

"Uh-uh. Nasser was his doctor."

"No. Suryakant was a patient of a Dr. Kahlid Abdulaz. They referred to him as a specialist in—infectious diseases."

"Another damn towel-head," John said.

"Yeah."

"So what's your point, Butch?"

"Marsh went to Dr. Abdulaz's office the day after the explosion, and asked the receptionist if he could speak with the doctor," he said, apprehension in his tone. "When she asked what is was about, Marsh came right out and asked about Dr. Nasser. Naturally Dr. Abdulaz refused to talk with him, but Marsh noticed how flustered the lady was the whole time he was there. Even though Nasser and Suryakant were blasted to smithereens the night before, Marsh knew there had to be more behind her being so nervous. So Marsh waited until she got off work. That's when the receptionist told him the truth."

Chief Gill took tight hold of Valone's arm. "John, there isn't any easy way for me to say this, so I'm just gonna come right out with it. The receptionist told Marsh that Dr. Abdulaz had been treating both Nasser and Suryakant—for AID's."

Seemingly in a trance, John sat with his mouth wide opened.

Butch had verged upon the same thoughts as John was now contemplating. "Hear me out, John. According to the pathologist, the odds are infinitesimal that Nasser passed-on the virus to any patient by performing surgery on them. The only realistic possibility of Nasser's spreading AID's to a patient would have been if he'd cut himself during an operation and bled into the patient. Now again, according to the pathologist, his people pulled every surgical case Nasser conducted for the past couple years, and there's no mention that he'd ever cut himself."

Gill let out a heavy sigh. "Still, you'd better take Mary for a blood test just to be sure."

Awaiting a response, the chief kept still. To his surprise, he watched as John rubbed at the palm of his hand, appearing unphased by what he'd just been told.

"Well?" he dared ask.

"So that's the bad news you've been tap-dancing around all this time. Is that all of it?"

"Yes."

"You're sure there's nothing else?"

"Yes, damn it, I'm sure. I'm concerned about your mother."

Instantly John's electric smile showed his exhilaration. "Butch, she's had so many blood tests since her operation. Dr. Mancini's done more blood tests than I can count, and I was with Mary in Baltimore when Dr. Tyler did a complete blood-analysis last July. No way could they both keep missing something as drastic as AID's. And if Mary did have it, she'd be showing some symptoms by now. Hell, Nasser operated on her almost two years ago, and I saw for myself just how fast he went downhill. Yeah, I'll tell Mary and Dr. Mancini, but I know she doesn't have it."

"John, I'm so glad to hear that," Butch replied, smiling widely. "But regardless of the possibilities, I was still scared stiff."

"Nah, there isn't any way Dr. Mancini and Dr. Tyler could have missed it," he confidently followed. "Okay, anything else I should know?"

"Couple more things Alan Marsh mentioned today. From what I gathered, he wanted to break the story a few days after the explosion, but the brass called his editor and asked the paper to wait until they'd seized all of Abdulaz's files, along with interviewing people who worked for him."

"They find a file on Nasser?"

"It was hidden on Abdulaz's computer, but they found it," Butch said, his tone considerably more relaxed. "Nasser had been taking AZT and some other new drugs since May of 2007. Ferguson's staff couldn't get anything outta Abdulaz, but his receptionist gave a full statement. The story they discussed today that shocked me was when the lady overheard Dr. Abdulaz tell Nasser that he was intentionally spreading the virus by having unprotected sex. Supposedly Nasser just laughed at Abdulaz and said something like, 'Hey, I'm dying, so I might as well take as many of them as I can with me.'"

"Sick sonofabitch."

Gill nodded. "The receptionist also mentioned that Nasser had seen Abdulaz the same afternoon he'd flown home from Las Vegas. She said Nasser really looked bad that day."

"Sounds like his AID's was pretty far advanced."

"Probably, although there isn't any way they can be sure. Dr. Abdulaz is claiming medical privilege, so he ain't talking. The theory is that Nasser had begun to deteriorate at a faster rate, but without any definitive proof, it's anyone's guess as to how far advanced he was. All they have at this point is the receptionist's statement, and what they took from Abdulaz's PC. Oh, they found a PC file on Suryakant, too. His file indicated he'd been taking AID's medications since 2006."

"Was Nasser gay?"

"Nobody's sure."

"Can't they put a timeline on how advanced he was?"

"No. The pathologist said its all dependent upon an individual's immune system, and how they're able to fend-off the disease. He also mentioned that it might have been possible to determine just how bad they were with an autopsy. But since you pretty much vaporized the two scumbags, there wasn't any way to tell."

Once again John Valone seemed lost in the clouds. Refocusing, it was he who checked their solitude by glancing at the door. "Now you understand what a dickhead Nasser really was. Now you understand why I wasn't going to stop until he was dead."

Chief Gill could only nod his head in agreement. In his mind swirled the many ordeals Mary Valone had been forced to endure. Finally he said, "John, it's so sad, it's almost funny."

"What?"

"All my life, I've always perceived that all doctors had morality. Man, don't I realize now how wrong I was."

"Yeah, for the most part, so did I," he said. "Although with Cameron and Nasser's bunch, all they did were cast perceptions of morality."

"That's for damn sure," Butch said.

"Tell you what's really ironic about Nasser. He always claimed his patients never got infected. Yet he had the ultimate infection. How perfectly apropos. Once he realized Mary had developed an infection, he wanted her to die." John sighed to say, "You know, now I kinda wish I hadn't torched him. It sure would have been nice to see him die a slow, agonizing death."

"Ah, be glad he's dead," said Butch. "All the guys in Pittsburgh are. You did alotta people a favor by blasting those two back to kingdom-come, or else they both would've kept passing on the virus. Tell you what I think is perfectly apropos."

"What's that?"

"Remember on nine-eleven seeing or reading about some of the Arabs all over America cheering when the Twin Towers were burning? Nasser and Suryakant got toasted just like those innocent people who died in New York City that day."

"Good point, Butch."

"Here's another one for you. Think about all the shit that's gonna hit the fan once Marsh's story is released. All of Nasser's patient's will flip-out when they learn they were operated on by a doctor with AID's. They'll probably start a riot at the hospital. Then how 'bout all the people he slept with? They're going to be scared to beat all hell when they hear the news."

"Now I understand why they think the case will go unsolved," said John. "Who's to say somebody Nasser was screwing didn't reason it out. Maybe it was one of them who arranged the explosion."

"Possibly."

"Could have been anybody who had a grudge against Nasser, even Suryakant."

Butch smiled. "Yep."

Sporting a wide grin, John sat back in the Victorian chair. "Poor Ferguson's list of potential suspects will be overflowing before long."

"After hearing him today, I'd doubt it," Butch remarked. "Sure his people will look into the fanatical types, but he knows it won't amount to anything. Believe me, if you were there today, you'd know that Ferguson can wait to shelf this case. Then just wait until Marsh's story is released. The lawyer's will be knocking each other over to file suit against Nasser's estate. This whole mess will be in civil courts for years."

"And the name of the great Dr. Rasheem Nasser will be dragged through the mud where it belongs," said John, his brown eyes sparkling. "Mary and I will both take great solace out of that."

Following another peek to the entranceway, Butch edged closer. "John, even though I told you that I didn't want to know anymore than I had to, mind satisfying my curiosity about a few things?"

"Ask away, pal."

"Was Mary in on all of them?"

"Mary knew absolutely nothing about DeTorrio or the Las Vegas trip," he replied. "Despite all the scrutiny I received, she never suspected me. The truth is that I didn't intend for her to find out what I had planned for Nasser, but I messed-up. When I came home with the bomb, she was over Janet's. So instead of just leaving it in the trunk, I took it to the basement and hid it in a closet she never uses. Well, I shoulda known Mrs. Clean ran the sweeper in there. So she found it, and I told her everything. As for the night we blasted Nasser, I didn't want her coming along. Truth is, she wouldn't let me go without her. Butch, in my entire life I never saw her act like she did that whole day.

Mary actually insisted on pressing the switch herself. That's how much she hated that no-good bastard."

"And the bomb?" he said musingly. "After the demolition team examined the wreckage, they concluded it was an incinerary device most likely built by someone with extensive munitions training. Denny made it for you. Right?"

"Uh-uh."

"Did he help you with DeTorrio?"

"Yep. He planned it perfectly for me. He even drove to Niagara Falls to use DeTorrio's credit card just so I'd have a chance at some reasonable doubt."

"Denny's the one who stayed at The Olympus and captured them."

"Yep."

Their conversation carried on a few more minutes until they heard a knock at the door. Michael Perella peeked into the room and said, "Guys, sorry to interrupt, but we're about ready to call it a night."

Upon making their way back into the viewing room, Butch and John observed the Perella's talking with Mr. Cicero. Not wishing to intrude, they moved to the adjoining foyer by the front entrance to await a more timely opportunity to speak with the family.

"Butch, needless to say, I'll never forget all you've done for me. Like my friend in there once told me, I owe you."

"Ah, baloney," said Butch. "No big deal. John, I may not be the smartest guy around, but let me tell you what being in law enforcement has taught me. The general public really doesn't care anymore. With the exception of family, the necessities of life, and the price of gas, most people just don't give a damn anymore. They may pretend they care, although the plain truth is most of them don't. So that causes cracks in the system. Even in this crazy, high-tech world, there are plenty of cracks in the system. Good God, look at the healthcare your mom received. That was a gigantic crack in the system. Then the justice she should have received at trial fell through another crack. That scum DeTorrio was a crack all to himself. So when it's all said and done, everybody will merely chalk-up three more cases of unsolved homicides to three more cracks in the system, and forget about them."

As John pondered his response, they noticed Denny's son slowly ambling towards them. After shaking hands with the strapping young man, Butch said, "You hang in there, Den. Your dad would have wanted it that way."

"I will, Chief Gill," said Dennis Perella, Junior. "Thank you."

"Just call him Butch for now," said John. "When you're old enough to drink at your uncle's bar with us, then you can call him the big troll like the rest of us do."

"How 'bout this guy, Denny?" Butch remarked, bringing a much-needed grin from the young man. "No respect for authority."

"My pal, the chief of police," John said, as he placed an arm atop Butch's broad shoulders. "Nice to have friends in high places."

"So how's it going at college?" Butch asked.

"I really like it so far."

"Just remember what I told you," said John. "If you ever need any money, please don't hesitate to call me. I promised your father that I'd help you out until you graduate and get a job. I don't care what it is, if you want anything, let me know. Now you're sure you won't need any money until the house sells?"

"I'm okay, John, thanks. My dad had more than enough life insurance, and all my school expenses are covered under my scholarship."

"I'll bring you a check tomorrow for some spending money. I won't have you walking around Penn State with only lint in your pockets. Can't impress the chicks like that."

"John, really, I've got more than enough," insisted the somewhat bashful youth–a trait definitely not inherited from his father. "My dad had money tucked-away that I never even knew about until recently. To be honest with you guys, I couldn't believe he had so much saved."

John gave Butch a guileful wink. His partner-in-crime's son didn't know where the money came from.

"Alright, kid, don't forget. You ever need anything, give me a call and you got it."

"Thanks a lot, John," said Dennis in shy voice. "I hate to ask, but I may need some financial help down the road. My scholarship's limited to four years. After I get my Bachelor's, I may ask you to loan me some money. But I promise it would only be a loan."

"Young fella, if you want to go for your Master's or a PHD in engineering, I'll pay the whole freight. The way it is out in the job-market today, you'll need all the education you can get."

"I guess my dad didn't get a chance to tell you. I'm changing my major next term. I'd like to try to become a doctor."

"A wha—?" said John. "What kinda doctor?"

"I'm not sure yet," Denny said. "I'm leaning towards becoming a surgeon."

Without a flicker of emotion crossing his face, John looked to Butch–only to see him rolling his blue eyes upward. His forearms folded against his chest, John stared intently at his late friend's offspring. "So you wanna be a doctor, huh?"

"Yes, Sir."

"Why?"

"I want to help sick people."

"C'mon, kid, we're your pals," John replied. "You can level with us. What really appeals to you about being a doctor? What, making the big bucks or playing grab-ass with the cute nurses?"

"Honest, I just feel that I should devote my life to helping sick people."

Although John Valone sought to retain an uncompromising personage, he felt himself slipping. "Denny, if becoming a doctor is what you really want to do with your life, then I'll do whatever I can to help you make it. Provided you promise me one thing."

"Name it, John."

"Promise me you'll be a good one."

Mary, 1985